STAR WARS
THE HIGH REPUBLIC

The galaxy celebrates. With the dark days
of the hyperspace disaster behind them,
Chancellor Lina Soh pushes ahead with the
latest of her GREAT WORKS. The Republic
Fair will be her finest hour, a celebration
of peace, unity, and hope on the frontier
world of Valo.

But an insatiable horror appears on the
horizon. One by one, planets fall as the
carnivorous DRENGIR consume all life in
their path. As Jedi Master AVAR KRISS
leads the battle against this terror, Nihil
forces gather in secret for the next stage of
MARCHION RO'S diabolical plan.

Only the noble JEDI KNIGHTS stand in Ro's
way, but even the protectors of light and life
are not prepared for the terrible darkness
that lies ahead. . . .

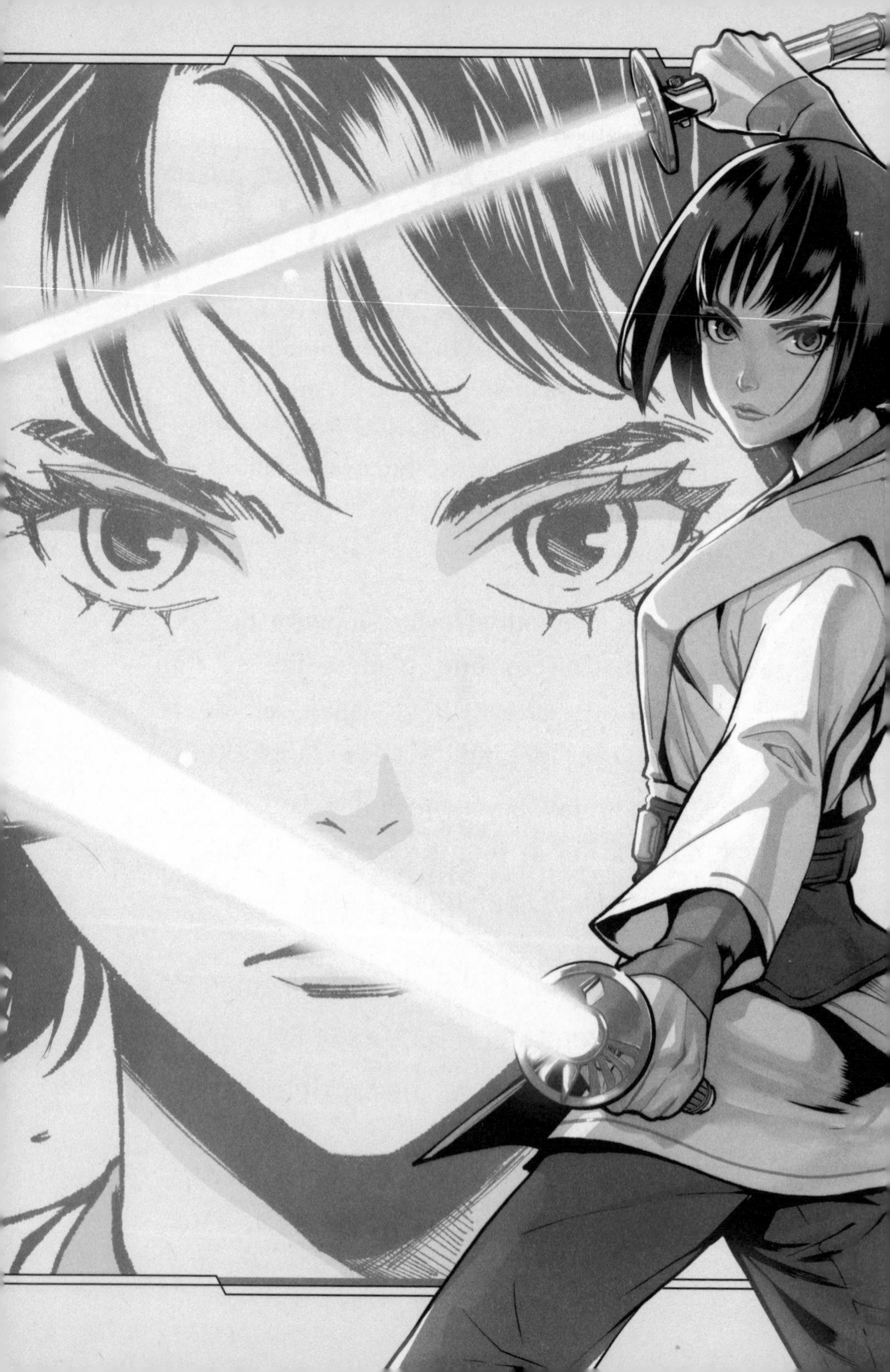

STAR WARS
THE HIGH REPUBLIC

THE EDGE OF BALANCE

1

STORY BY
Shima Shinya &
Justina Ireland

ART BY
Mizuki Sakakibara

ADDITIONAL ART
BY NEZU USUGUMO

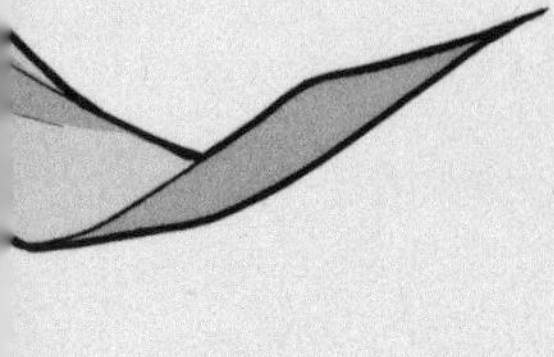

VIZ MEDIA

Disney · LUCASFILM

STAR WARS
THE HIGH REPUBLIC

THE EDGE OF BALANCE
PART ONE

Story by Shima Shinya and Justina Ireland
Art by Mizuki Sakakibara

BONUS CHAPTER
THE BANCHIIANS

Story by Shima Shinya
Storyboarded by Mizuki Sakakibara
Art by Nezu Usugumo

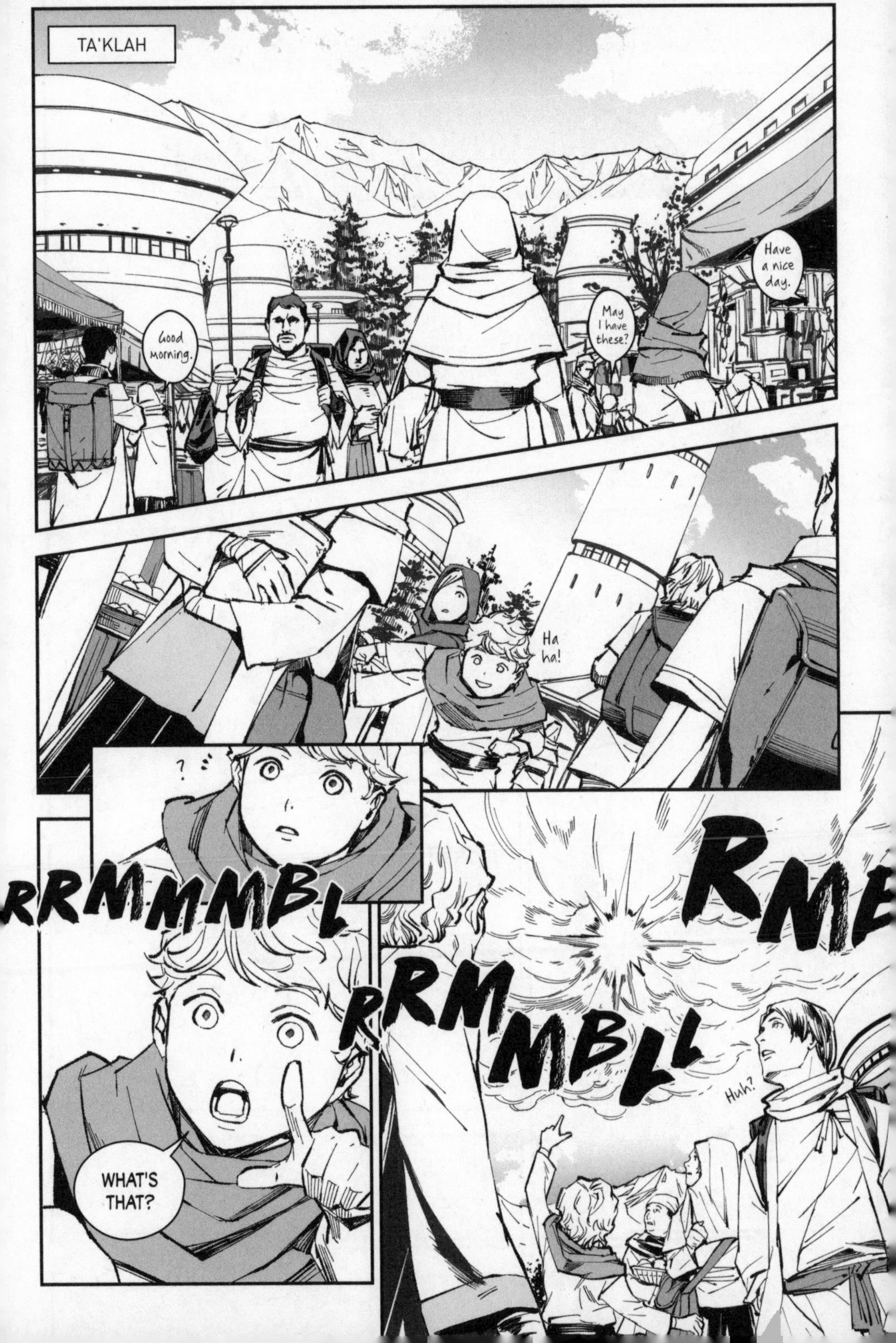
TA'KLAH
Good morning.
May I have these?
Have a nice day.
Ha ha!
? ::
RRMMMBL
RMB
RRMMBLL
Huh?
WHAT'S THAT?

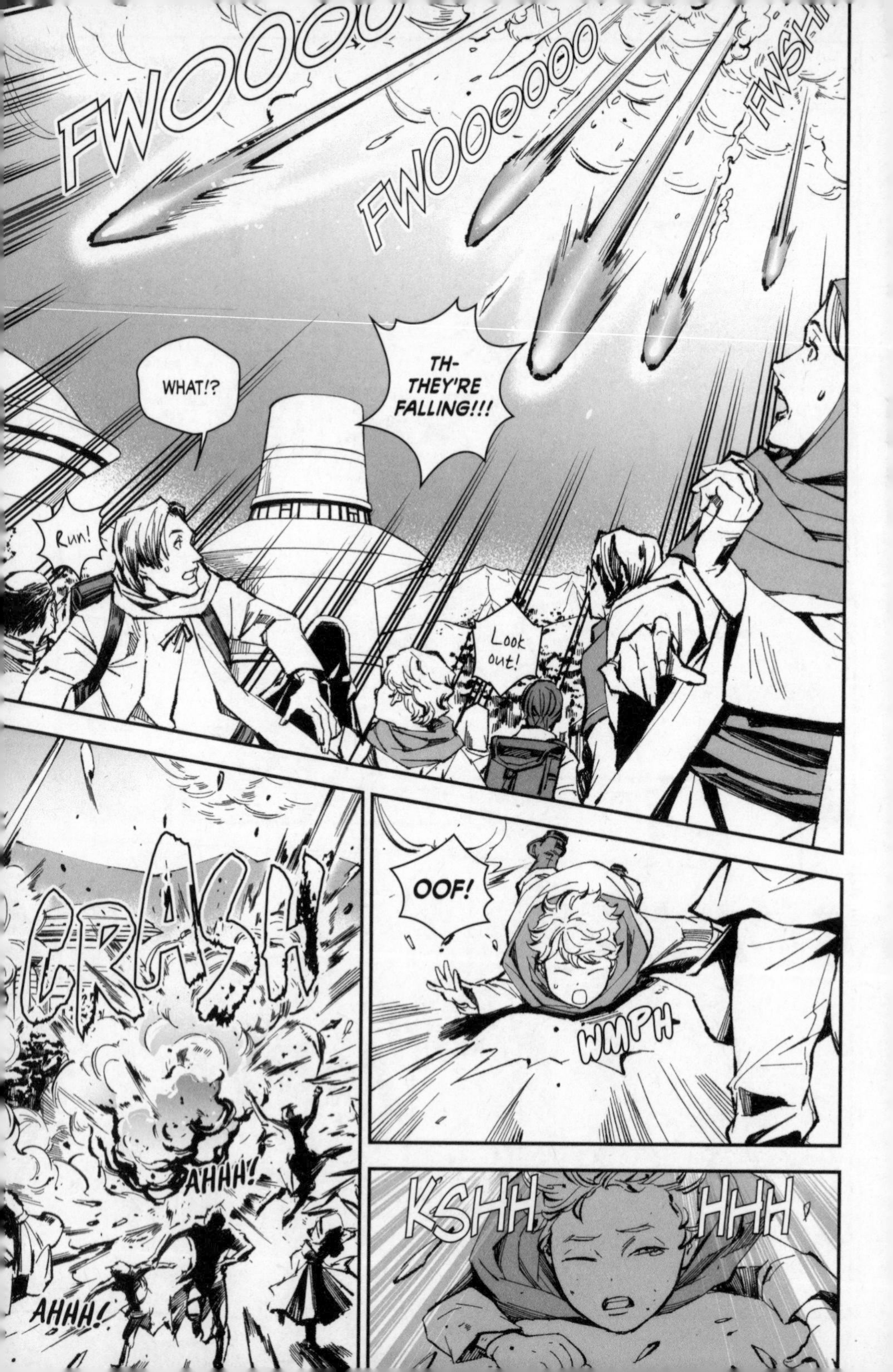
FWOOOO
FWOOOOOOO
FWSH
WHAT!?
TH-
THEY'RE
FALLING!!!
Run!
Look
out!
CRASH
AHHH!
AHHH!
OOF!
WMPH
KSHH HHH

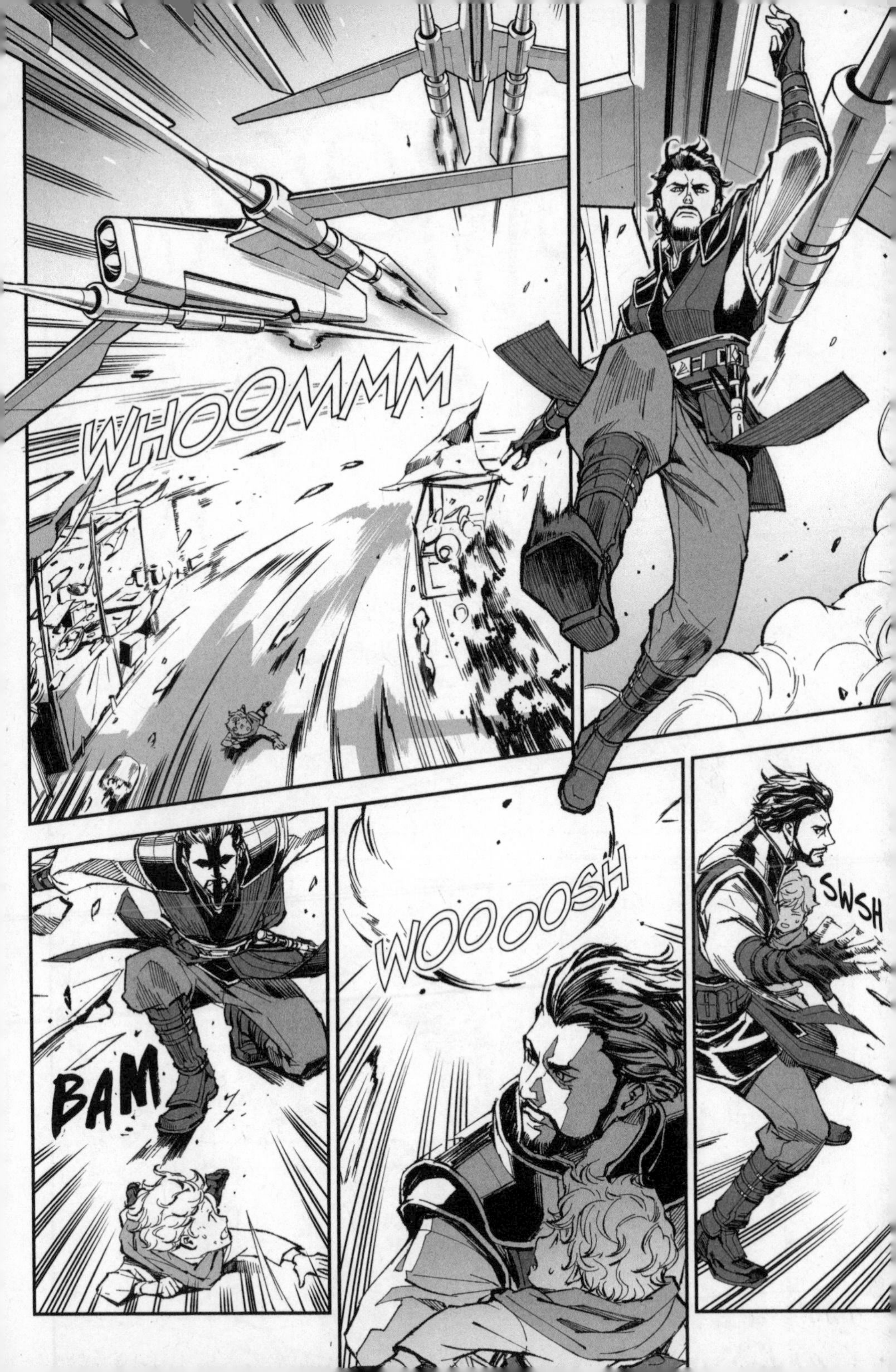
WHOOMMM
SWSH
WOOOOSH
BAM

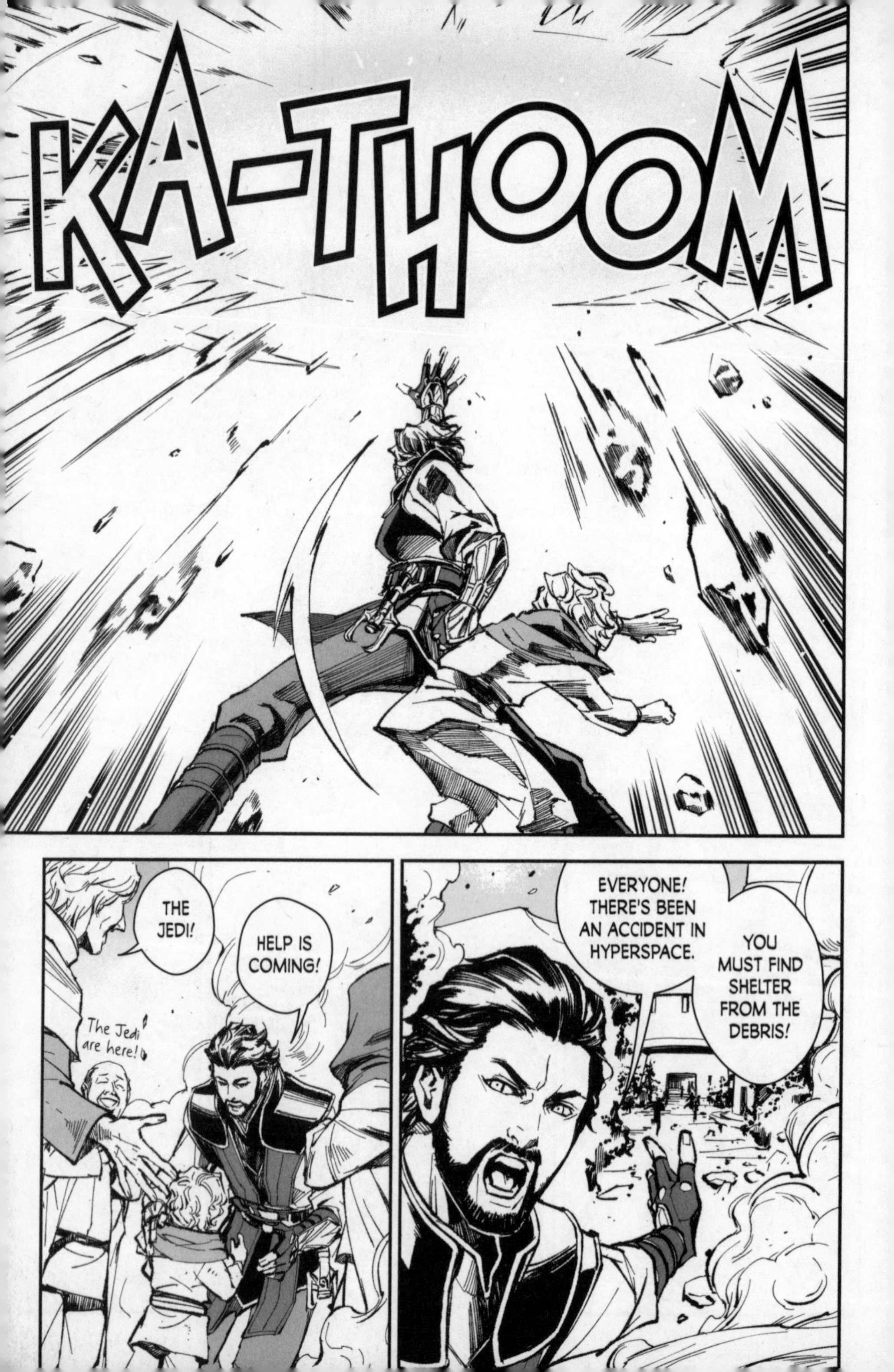
KA-THOOM
THE JEDI!
HELP IS COMING!
The Jedi are here!
EVERYONE! THERE'S BEEN AN ACCIDENT IN HYPERSPACE.
YOU MUST FIND SHELTER FROM THE DEBRIS!

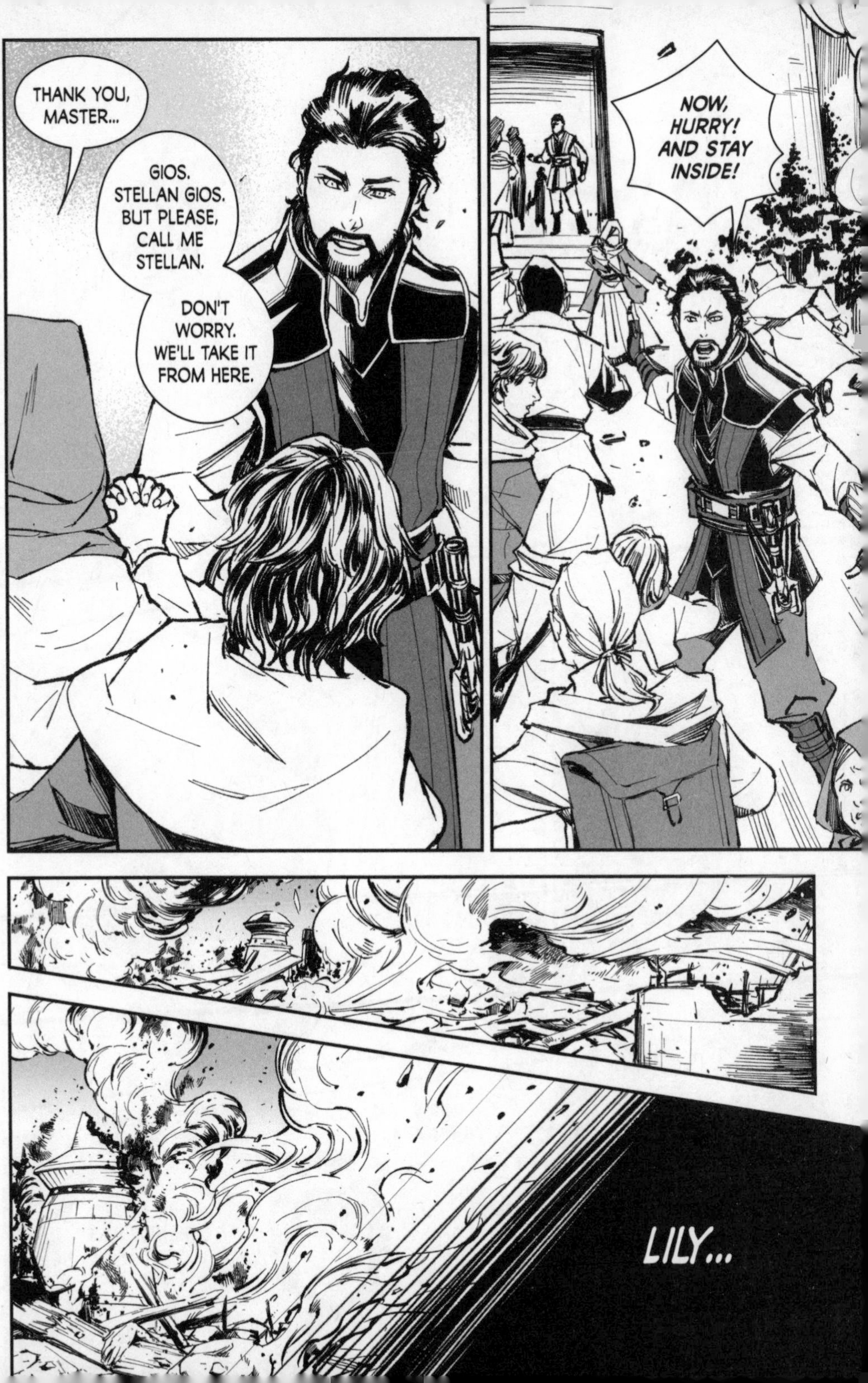
THANK YOU, MASTER...
GIOS. STELLAN GIOS. BUT PLEASE, CALL ME STELLAN.
DON'T WORRY. WE'LL TAKE IT FROM HERE.
NOW, HURRY! AND STAY INSIDE!
LILY...

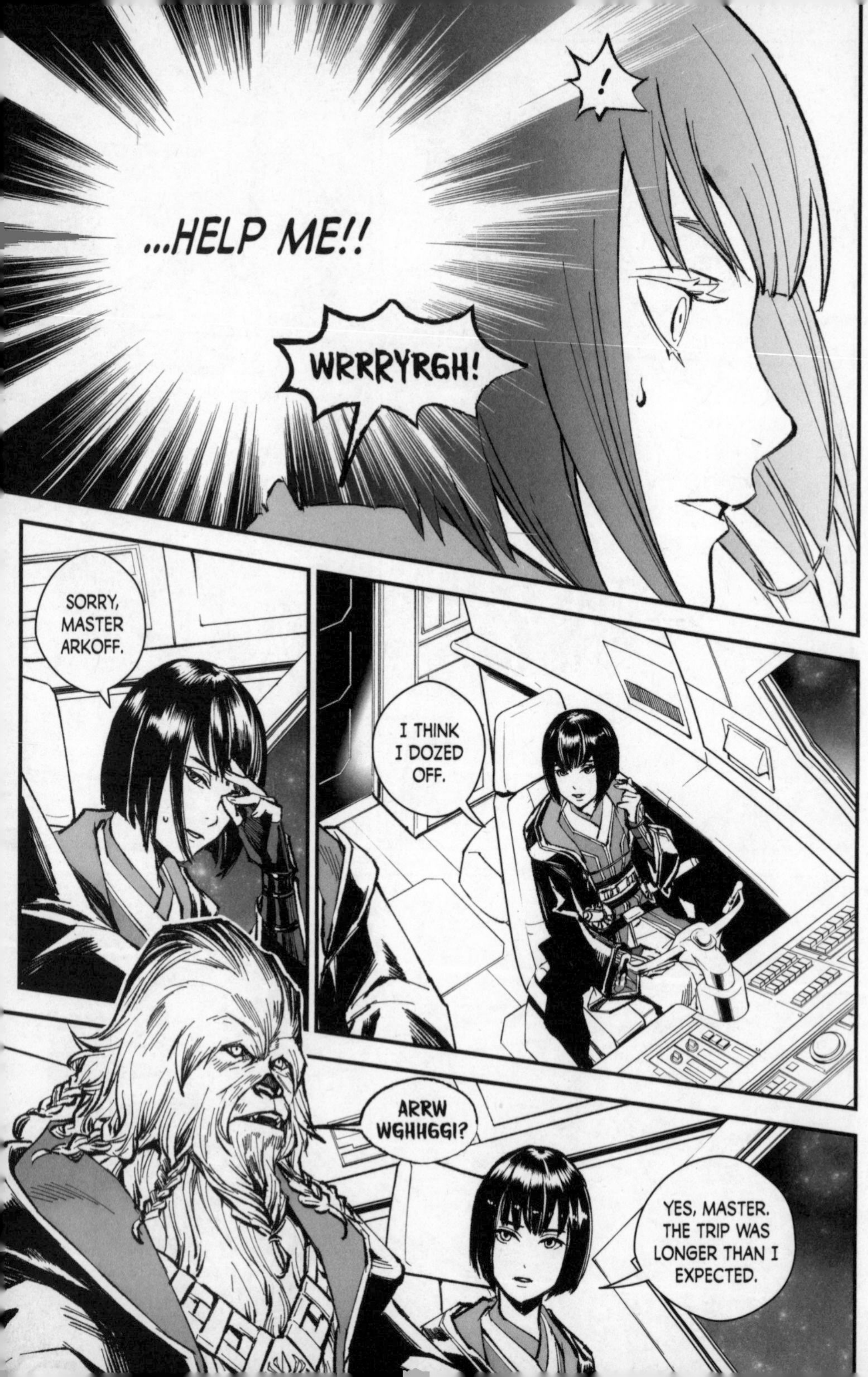
!
...HELP ME!!
WRRRYRGH!
SORRY, MASTER ARKOFF.
I THINK I DOZED OFF.
ARRW WGHHGGI?
YES, MASTER. THE TRIP WAS LONGER THAN I EXPECTED.

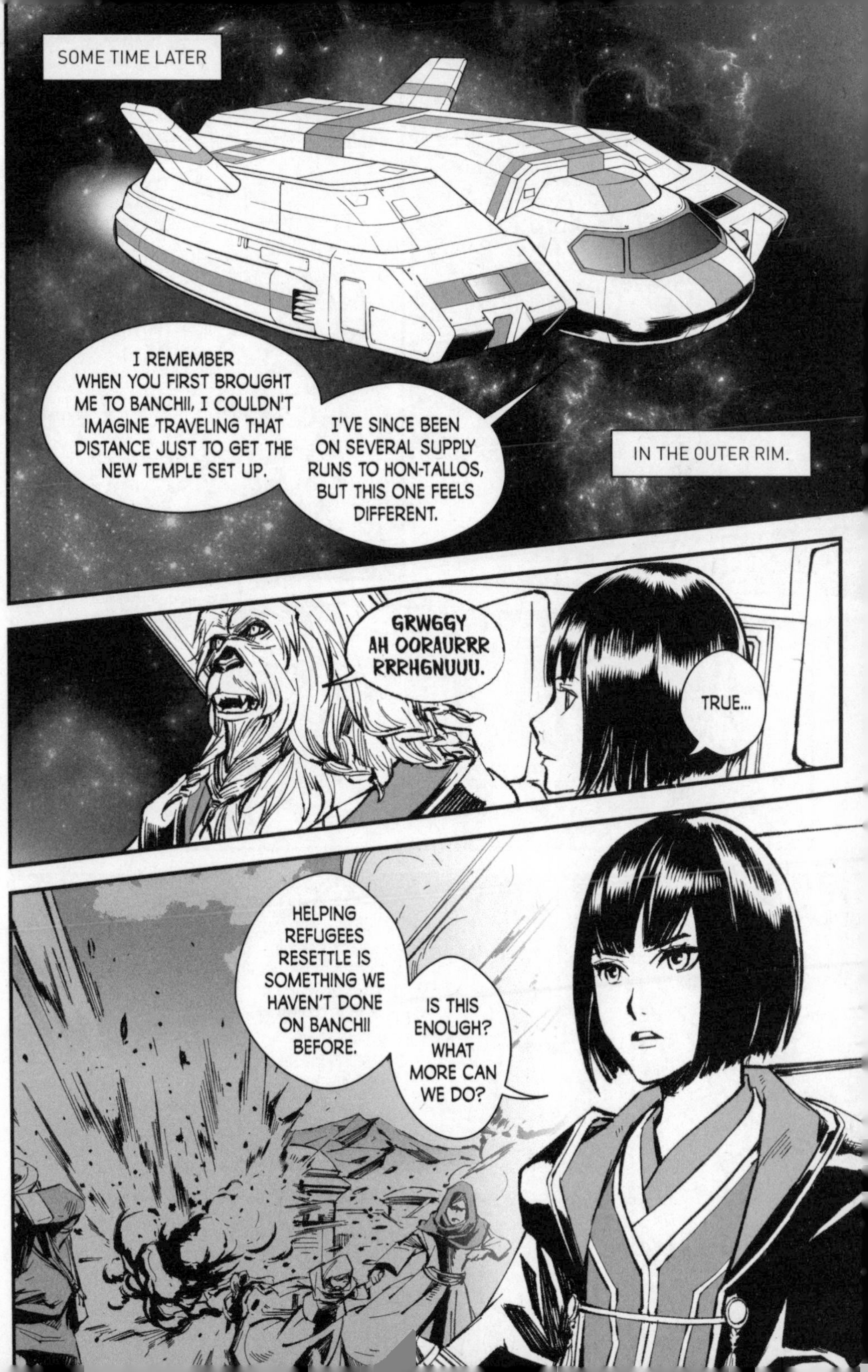
SOME TIME LATER
IN THE OUTER RIM.
I REMEMBER WHEN YOU FIRST BROUGHT ME TO BANCHII, I COULDN'T IMAGINE TRAVELING THAT DISTANCE JUST TO GET THE NEW TEMPLE SET UP.
I'VE SINCE BEEN ON SEVERAL SUPPLY RUNS TO HON-TALLOS, BUT THIS ONE FEELS DIFFERENT.
GRWGGY AH OORAURRR RRRHGNUUU.
TRUE...
HELPING REFUGEES RESETTLE IS SOMETHING WE HAVEN'T DONE ON BANCHII BEFORE.
IS THIS ENOUGH? WHAT MORE CAN WE DO?

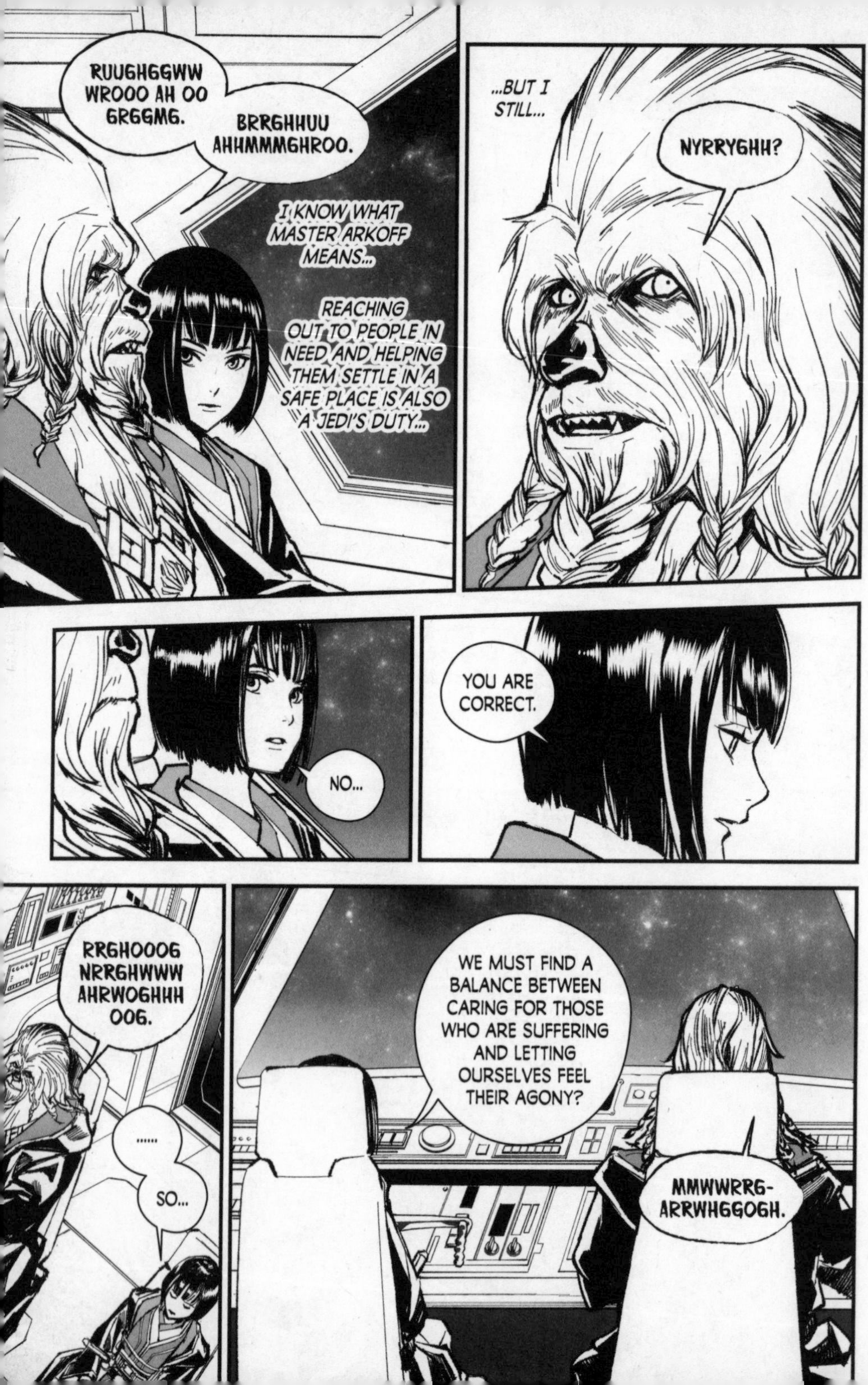
RUUGHGGWW WROOO AH OO GRGGMG.
BRRGHHUU AHHMMMGHROO.
I KNOW WHAT MASTER ARKOFF MEANS...
REACHING OUT TO PEOPLE IN NEED AND HELPING THEM SETTLE IN A SAFE PLACE IS ALSO A JEDI'S DUTY...
...BUT I STILL...
NYRRYGHH?
NO...
YOU ARE CORRECT.
RRGHOOOG NRRGHWWW AHRWOGHHH OOG.
......
SO...
WE MUST FIND A BALANCE BETWEEN CARING FOR THOSE WHO ARE SUFFERING AND LETTING OURSELVES FEEL THEIR AGONY?
MMWWRRG-ARRWHGGOGH.

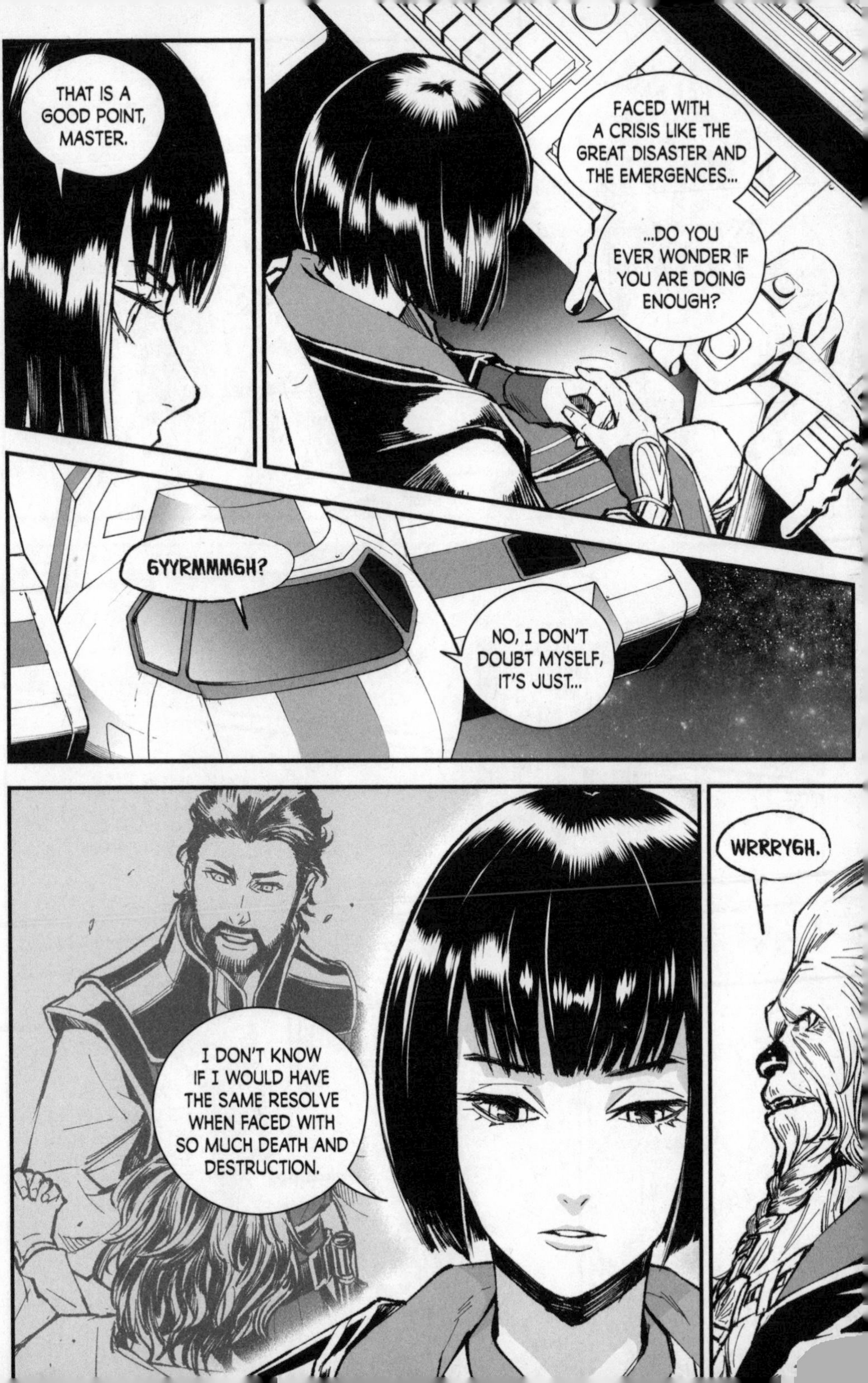
THAT IS A GOOD POINT, MASTER.
FACED WITH A CRISIS LIKE THE GREAT DISASTER AND THE EMERGENCES...
...DO YOU EVER WONDER IF YOU ARE DOING ENOUGH?
GYYRMMMGH?
NO, I DON'T DOUBT MYSELF, IT'S JUST...
I DON'T KNOW IF I WOULD HAVE THE SAME RESOLVE WHEN FACED WITH SO MUCH DEATH AND DESTRUCTION.
WRRRYGH.

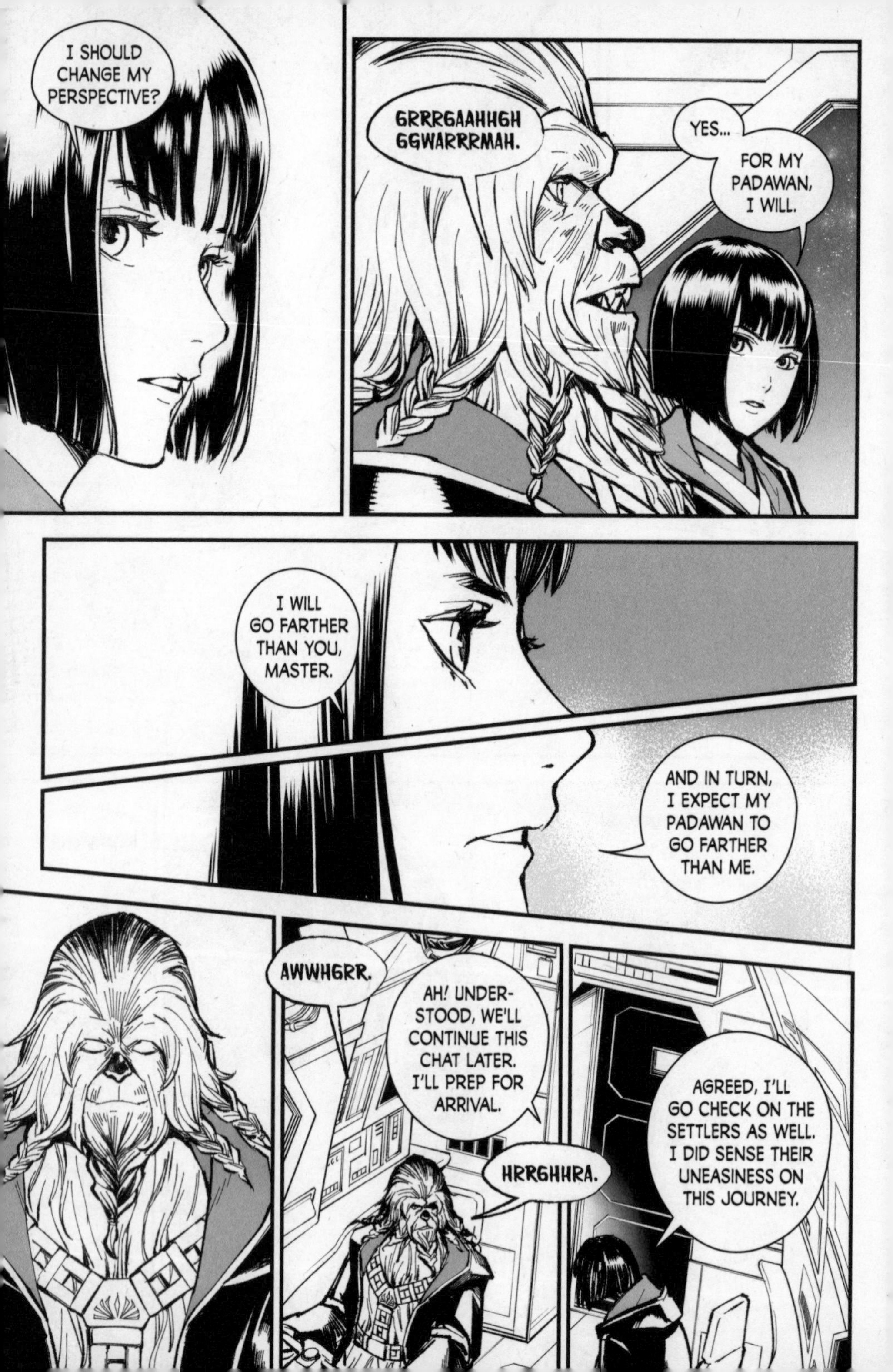
I SHOULD CHANGE MY PERSPECTIVE?
GRRRGAAHHGH GGWARRRMAH.
YES...
FOR MY PADAWAN, I WILL.
I WILL GO FARTHER THAN YOU, MASTER.
AND IN TURN, I EXPECT MY PADAWAN TO GO FARTHER THAN ME.
AWWHGRR.
AH! UNDER-STOOD, WE'LL CONTINUE THIS CHAT LATER. I'LL PREP FOR ARRIVAL.
HRRGHHRA.
AGREED, I'LL GO CHECK ON THE SETTLERS AS WELL. I DID SENSE THEIR UNEASINESS ON THIS JOURNEY.

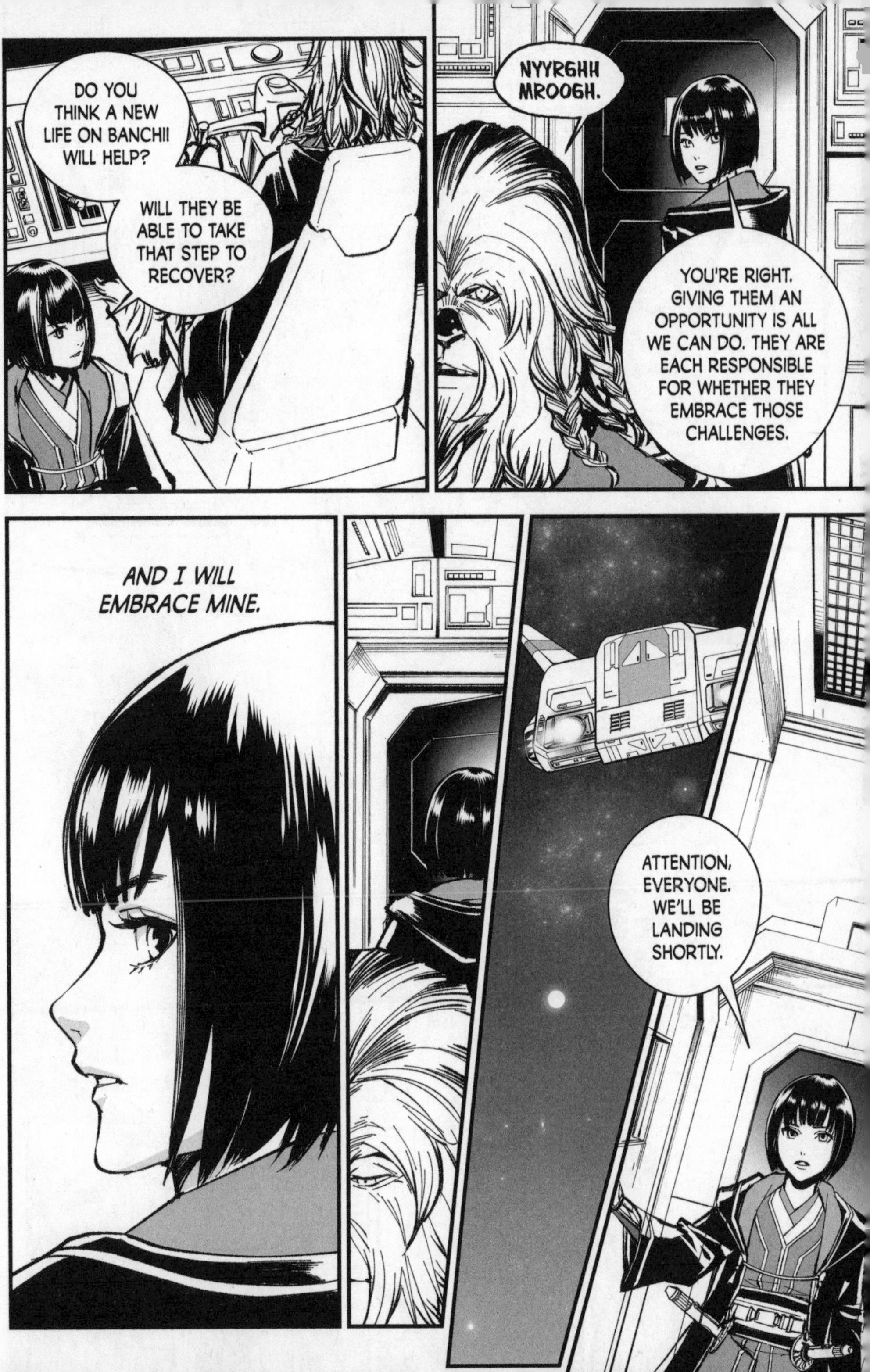
DO YOU THINK A NEW LIFE ON BANCHII WILL HELP?
WILL THEY BE ABLE TO TAKE THAT STEP TO RECOVER?
NYYRGHH MROOGH.
YOU'RE RIGHT. GIVING THEM AN OPPORTUNITY IS ALL WE CAN DO. THEY ARE EACH RESPONSIBLE FOR WHETHER THEY EMBRACE THOSE CHALLENGES.
AND I WILL EMBRACE MINE.
ATTENTION, EVERYONE. WE'LL BE LANDING SHORTLY.

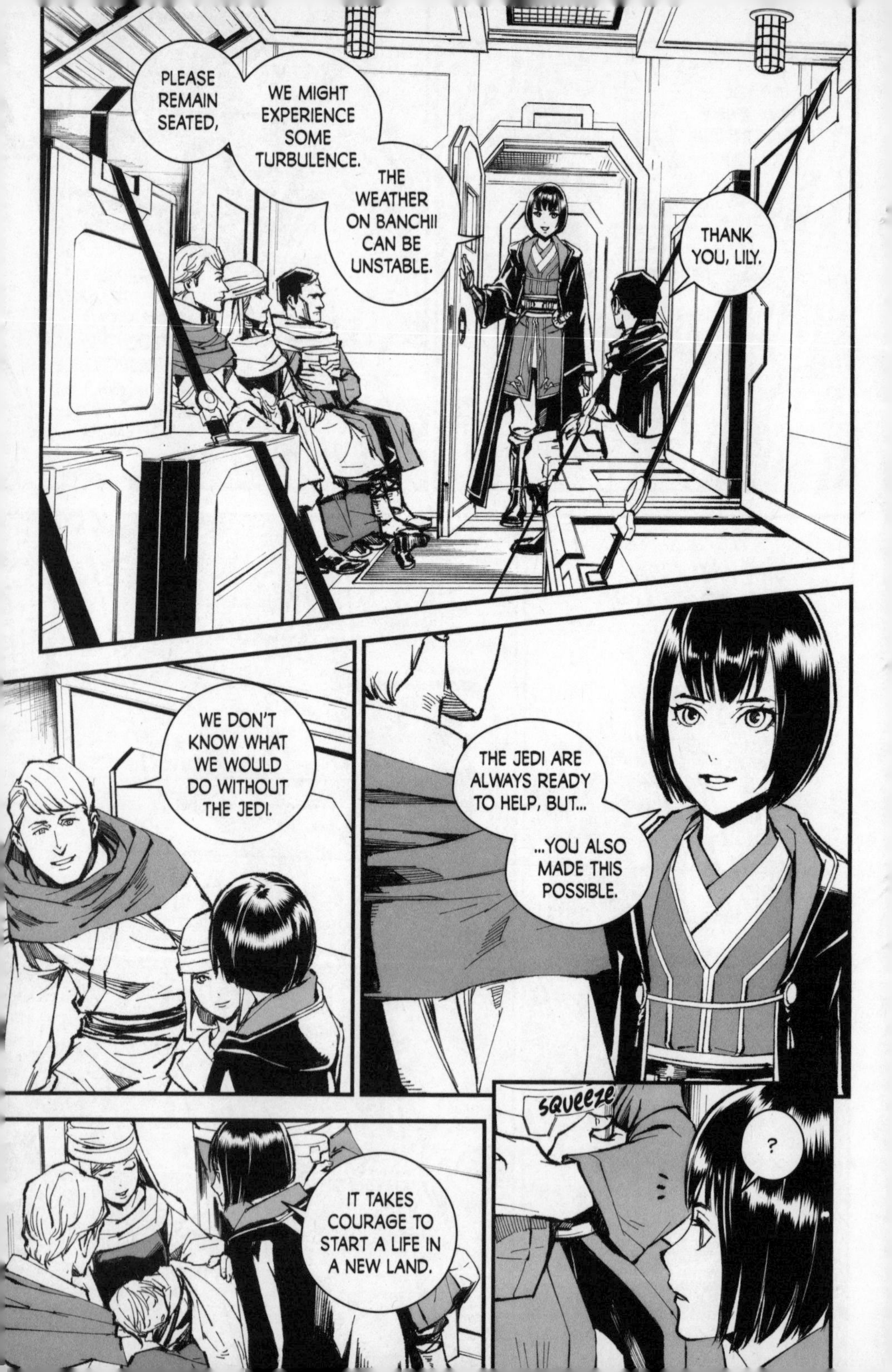
PLEASE REMAIN SEATED,
WE MIGHT EXPERIENCE SOME TURBULENCE.
THE WEATHER ON BANCHII CAN BE UNSTABLE.
THANK YOU, LILY.
WE DON'T KNOW WHAT WE WOULD DO WITHOUT THE JEDI.
THE JEDI ARE ALWAYS READY TO HELP, BUT...
...YOU ALSO MADE THIS POSSIBLE.
IT TAKES COURAGE TO START A LIFE IN A NEW LAND.
SQUEEZE
?

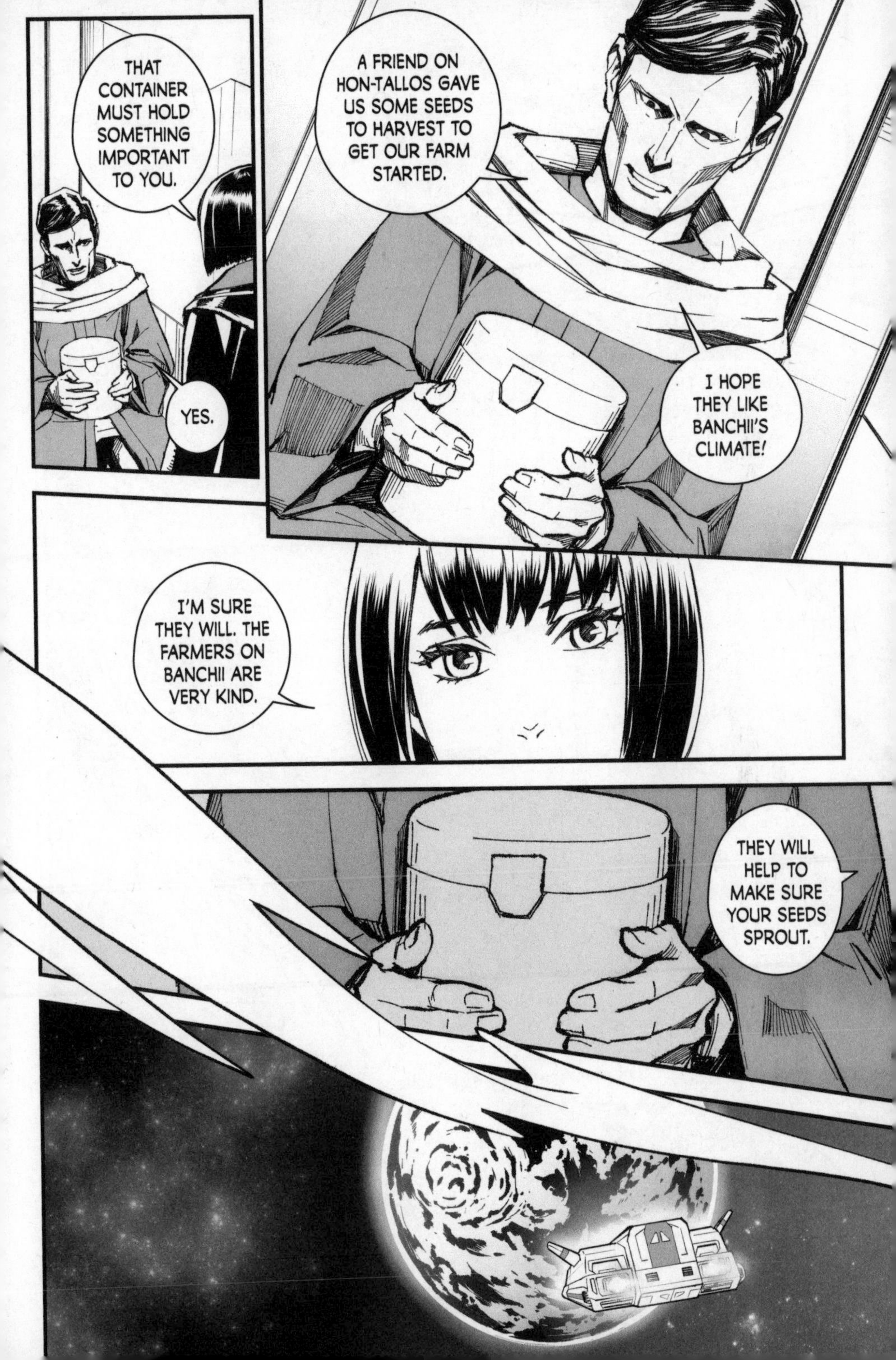
THAT CONTAINER MUST HOLD SOMETHING IMPORTANT TO YOU.
YES.
A FRIEND ON HON-TALLOS GAVE US SOME SEEDS TO HARVEST TO GET OUR FARM STARTED.
I HOPE THEY LIKE BANCHII'S CLIMATE!
I'M SURE THEY WILL. THE FARMERS ON BANCHII ARE VERY KIND.
THEY WILL HELP TO MAKE SURE YOUR SEEDS SPROUT.

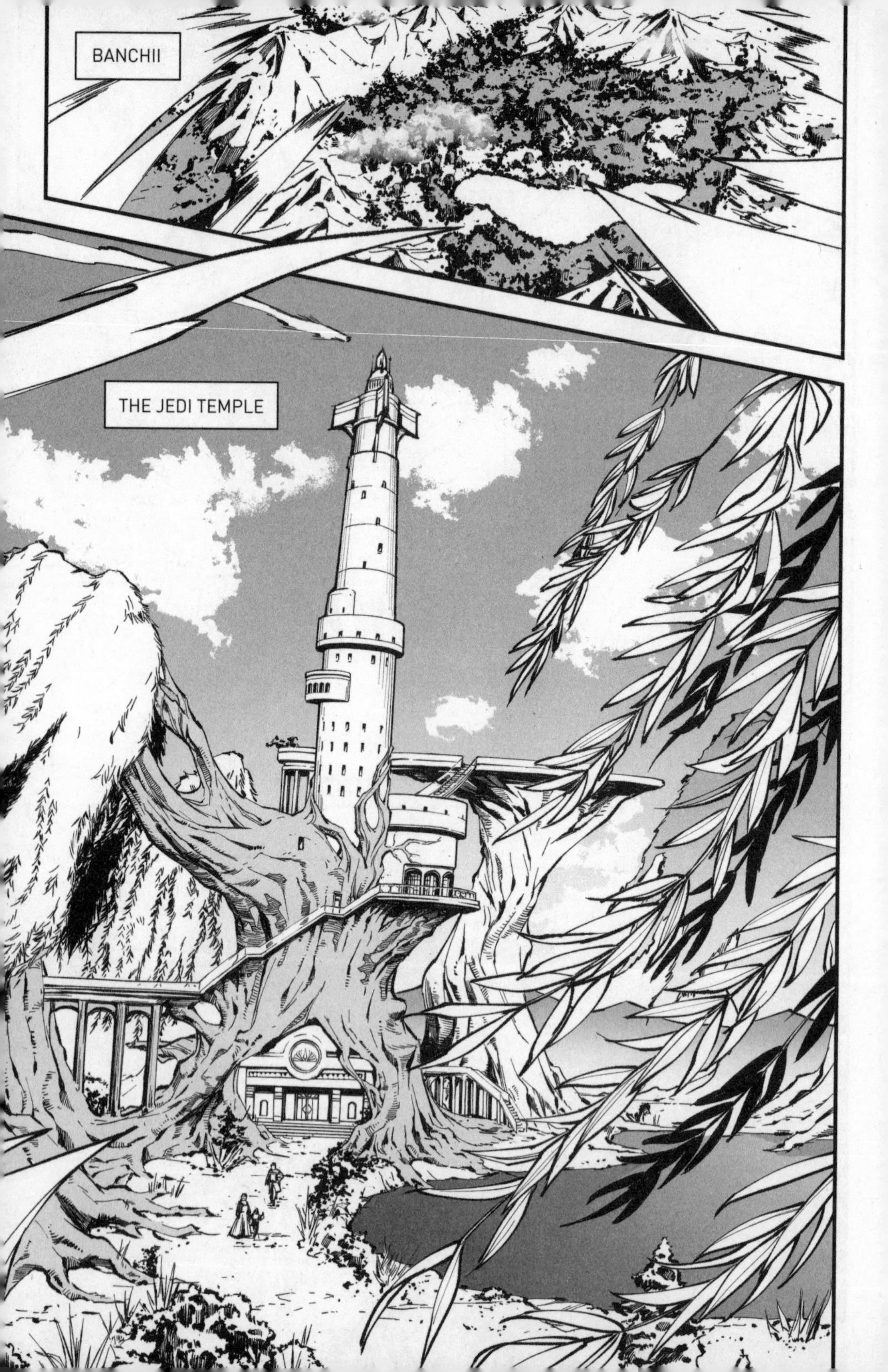
BANCHII
THE JEDI TEMPLE

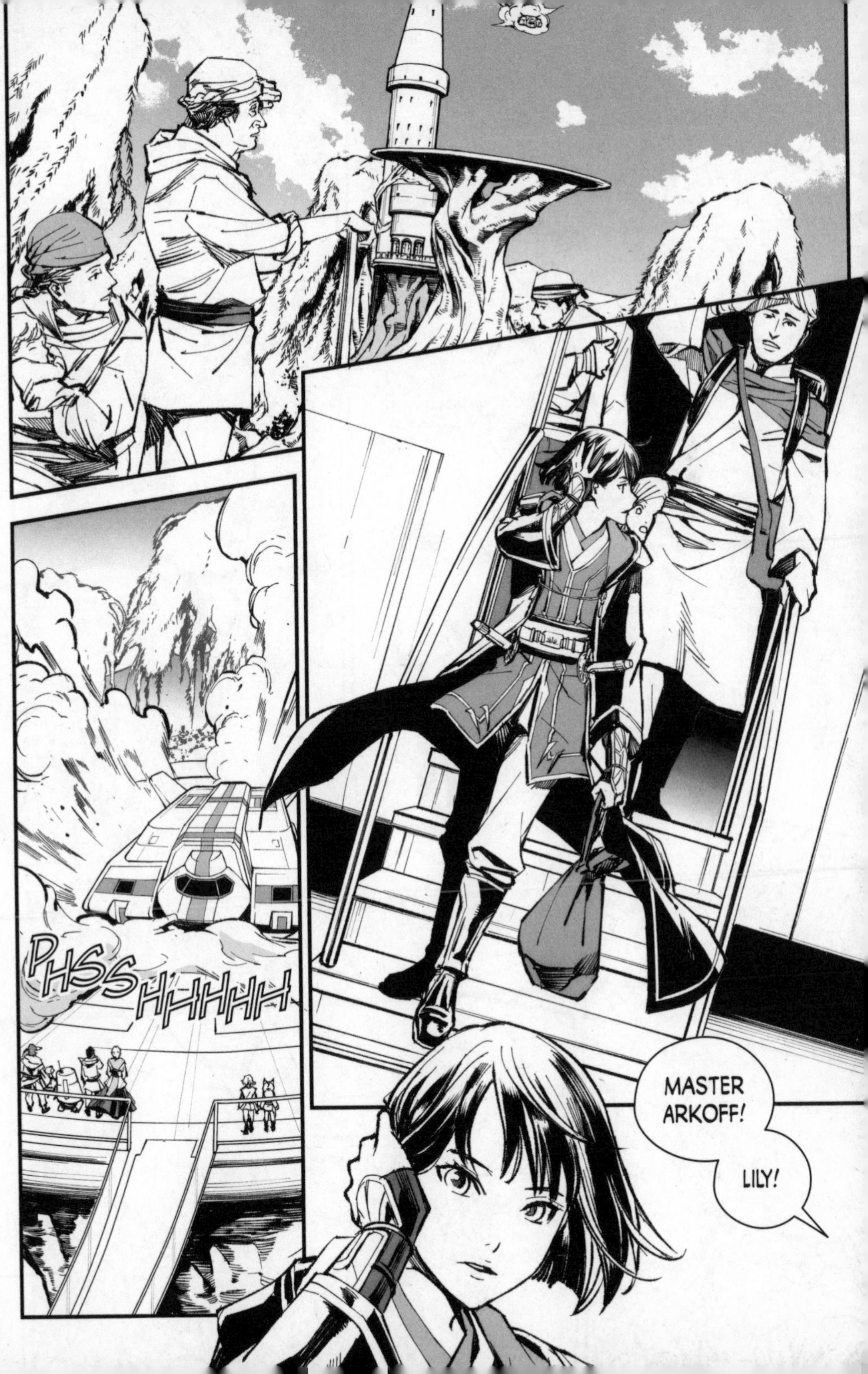
PHSSHHHHHH
MASTER ARKOFF!
LILY!

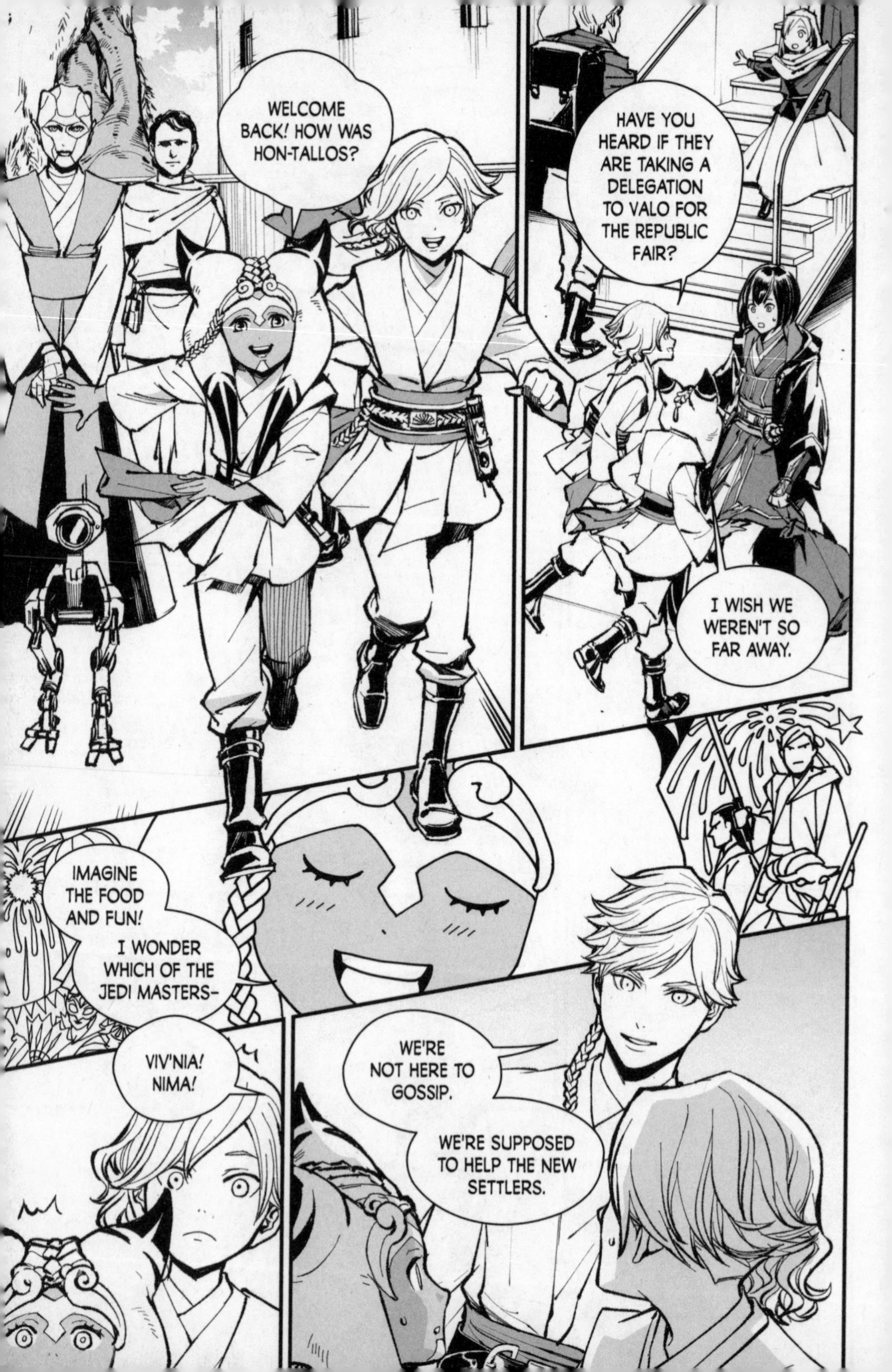
WELCOME BACK! HOW WAS HON-TALLOS?
HAVE YOU HEARD IF THEY ARE TAKING A DELEGATION TO VALO FOR THE REPUBLIC FAIR?
I WISH WE WEREN'T SO FAR AWAY.
IMAGINE THE FOOD AND FUN!
I WONDER WHICH OF THE JEDI MASTERS-
VIV'NIA! NIMA!
WE'RE NOT HERE TO GOSSIP.
WE'RE SUPPOSED TO HELP THE NEW SETTLERS.

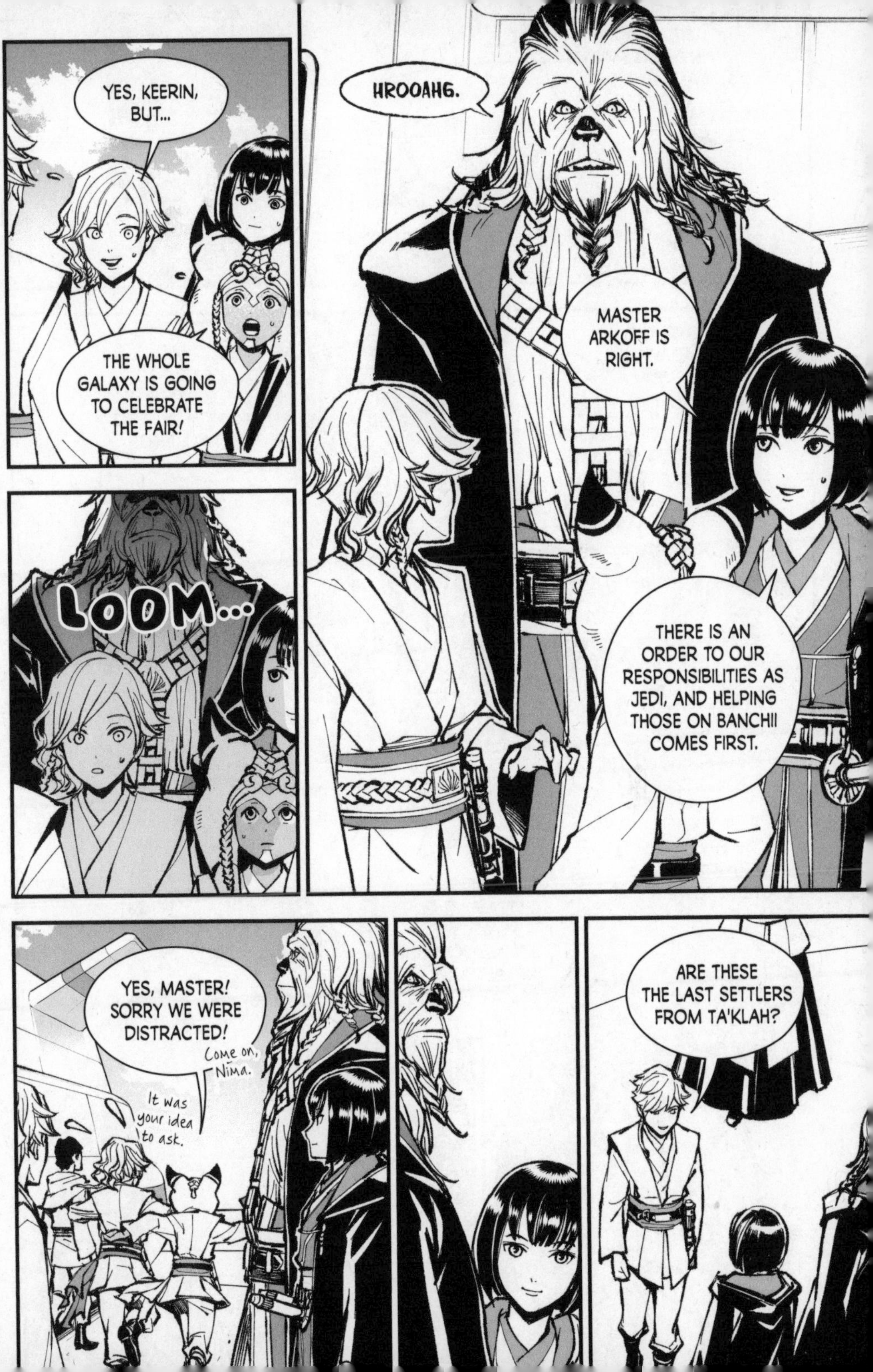
YES, KEERIN, BUT...
THE WHOLE GALAXY IS GOING TO CELEBRATE THE FAIR!
HROOAHG.
MASTER ARKOFF IS RIGHT.
LOOM...
THERE IS AN ORDER TO OUR RESPONSIBILITIES AS JEDI, AND HELPING THOSE ON BANCHII COMES FIRST.
YES, MASTER! SORRY WE WERE DISTRACTED!
Come on, Nima.
It was your idea to ask.
ARE THESE THE LAST SETTLERS FROM TA'KLAH?

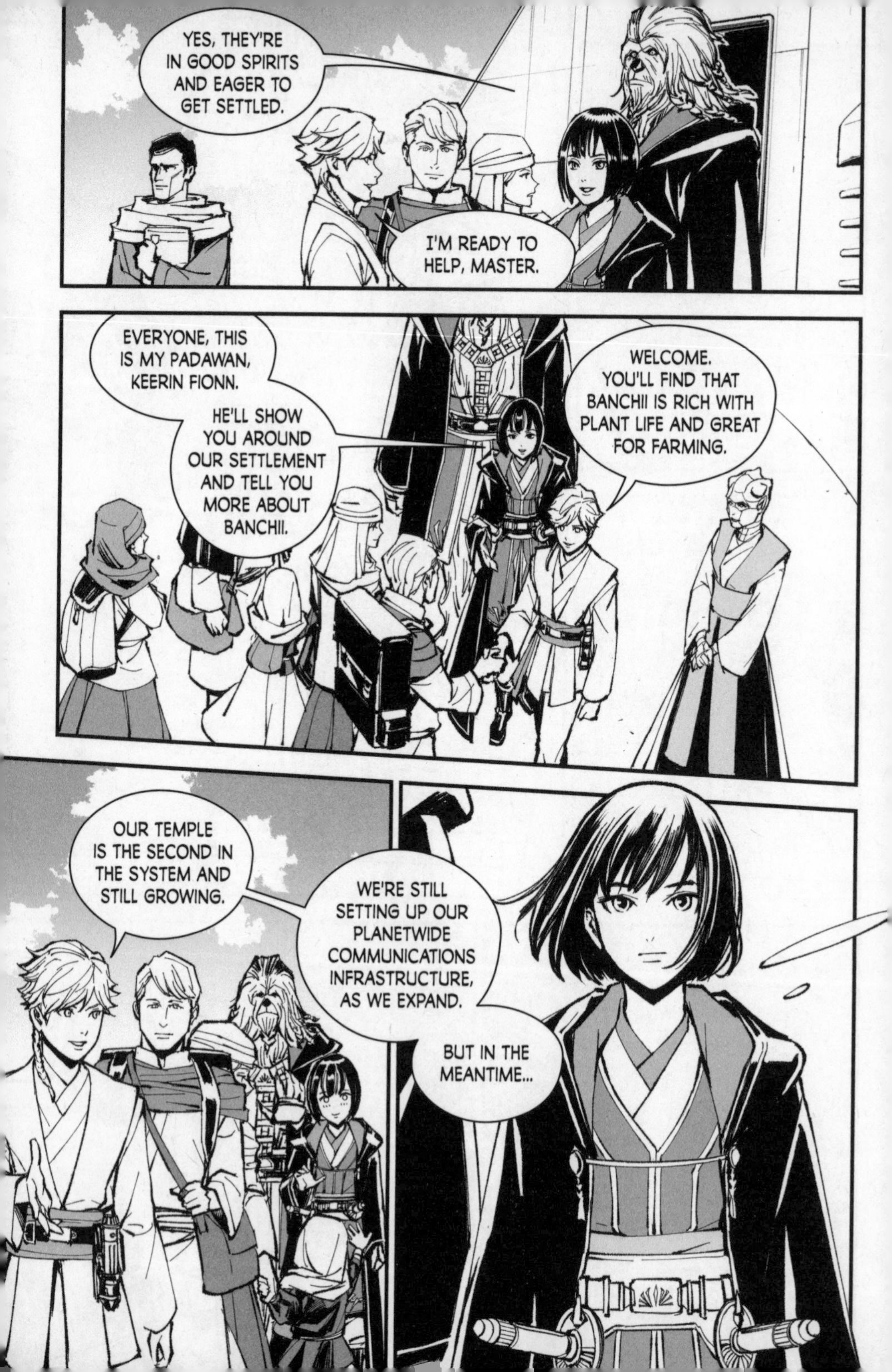

YES, THEY'RE IN GOOD SPIRITS AND EAGER TO GET SETTLED.
I'M READY TO HELP, MASTER.
EVERYONE, THIS IS MY PADAWAN, KEERIN FIONN.
HE'LL SHOW YOU AROUND OUR SETTLEMENT AND TELL YOU MORE ABOUT BANCHII.
WELCOME. YOU'LL FIND THAT BANCHII IS RICH WITH PLANT LIFE AND GREAT FOR FARMING.
OUR TEMPLE IS THE SECOND IN THE SYSTEM AND STILL GROWING.
WE'RE STILL SETTING UP OUR PLANETWIDE COMMUNICATIONS INFRASTRUCTURE, AS WE EXPAND.
BUT IN THE MEANTIME...

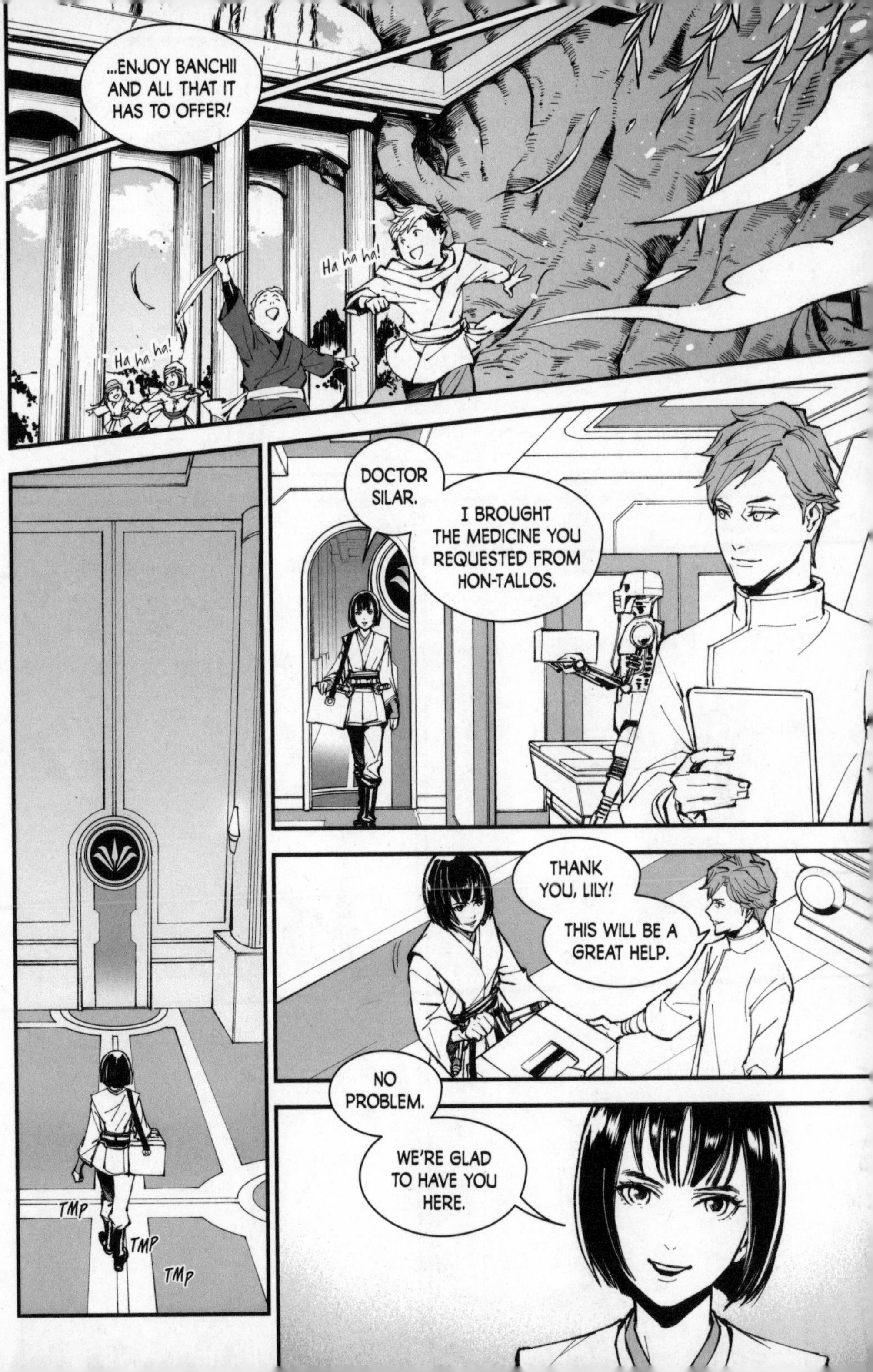
...ENJOY BANCHII AND ALL THAT IT HAS TO OFFER!
Ha ha ha!
Ha ha ha!
DOCTOR SILAR.
I BROUGHT THE MEDICINE YOU REQUESTED FROM HON-TALLOS.
TMP
TMP
TMP
THANK YOU, LILY!
THIS WILL BE A GREAT HELP.
NO PROBLEM.
WE'RE GLAD TO HAVE YOU HERE.

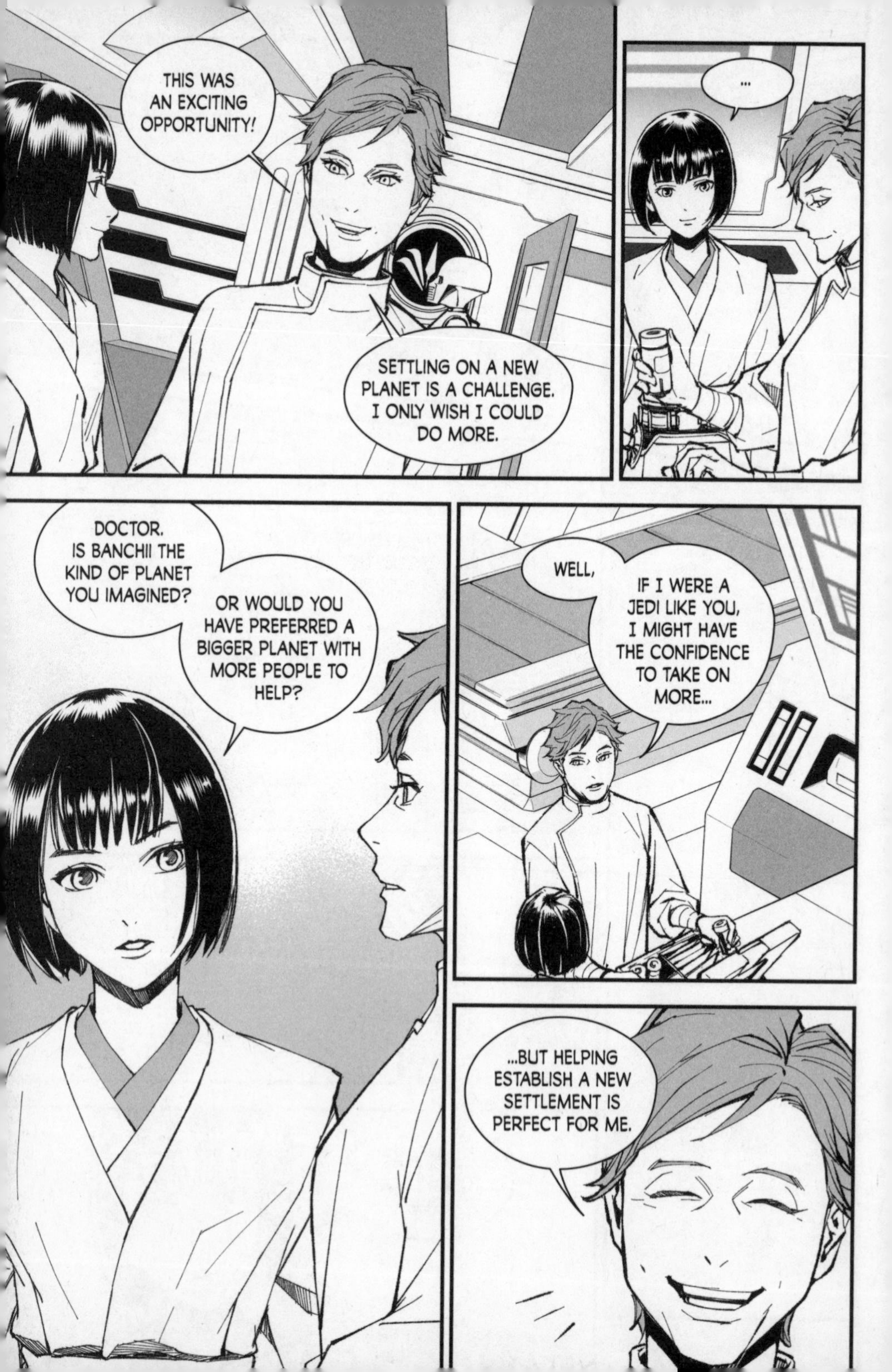
THIS WAS AN EXCITING OPPORTUNITY!
SETTLING ON A NEW PLANET IS A CHALLENGE. I ONLY WISH I COULD DO MORE.
...
DOCTOR. IS BANCHII THE KIND OF PLANET YOU IMAGINED?
OR WOULD YOU HAVE PREFERRED A BIGGER PLANET WITH MORE PEOPLE TO HELP?
WELL,
IF I WERE A JEDI LIKE YOU, I MIGHT HAVE THE CONFIDENCE TO TAKE ON MORE...
...BUT HELPING ESTABLISH A NEW SETTLEMENT IS PERFECT FOR ME.

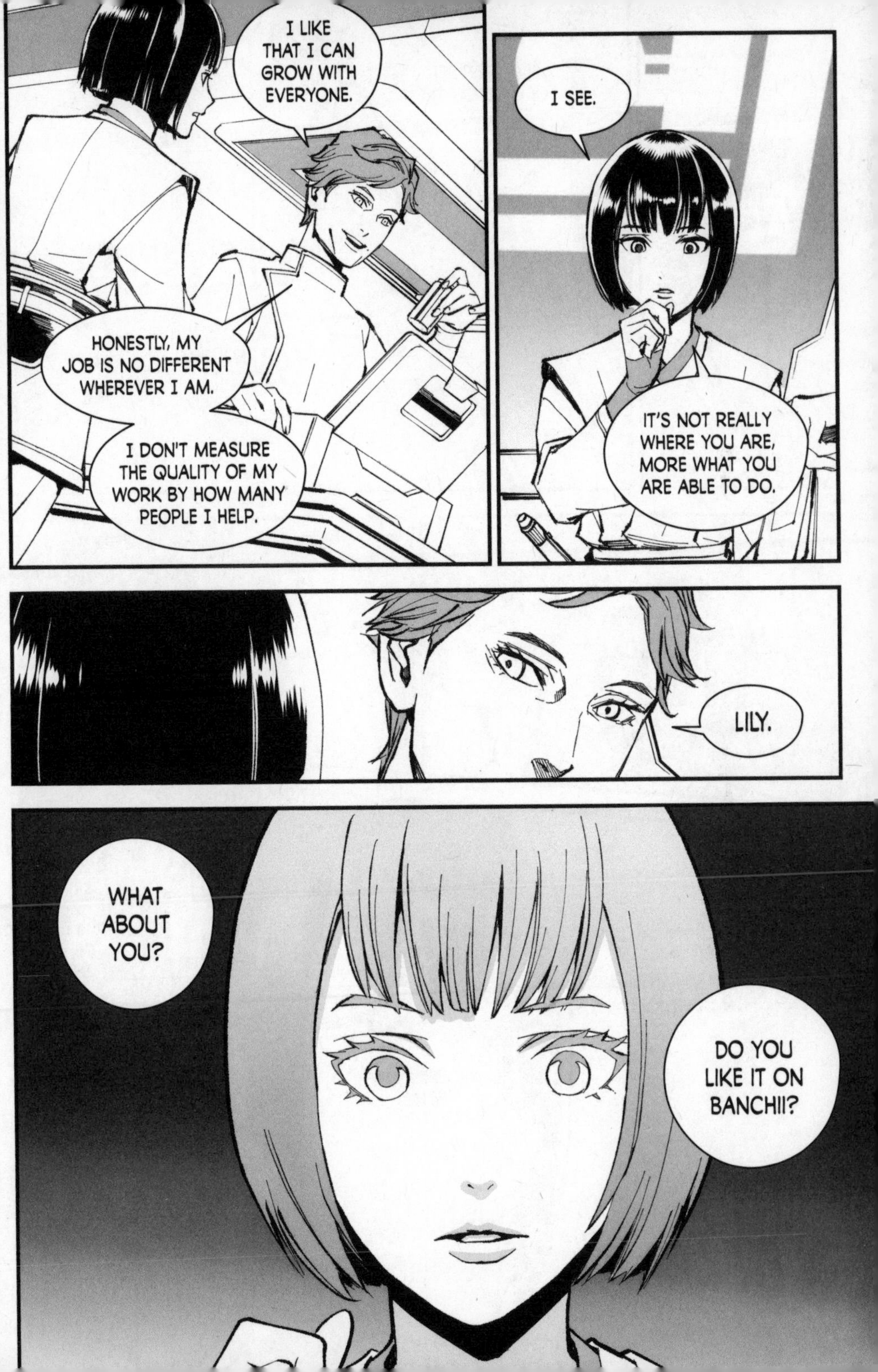
I LIKE THAT I CAN GROW WITH EVERYONE.
HONESTLY, MY JOB IS NO DIFFERENT WHEREVER I AM.
I DON'T MEASURE THE QUALITY OF MY WORK BY HOW MANY PEOPLE I HELP.
I SEE.
IT'S NOT REALLY WHERE YOU ARE, MORE WHAT YOU ARE ABLE TO DO.
LILY.
WHAT ABOUT YOU?
DO YOU LIKE IT ON BANCHII?

OH...

I'VE BEEN SO FOCUSED ON THE SETTLERS...

I'VE ACTUALLY NEVER THOUGHT ABOUT IT.

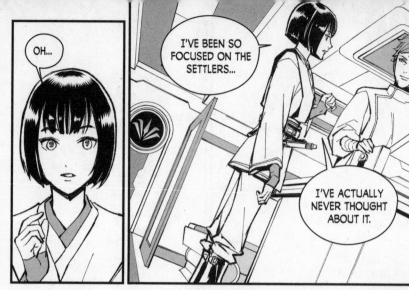

HA HA HA! REALLY?

That's just like you, Lily.

HONEST!

BUT BANCHII HAS BECOME AN IMPORTANT PLACE FOR SO MANY.

MY INSTINCT IS TO PROTECT IT...

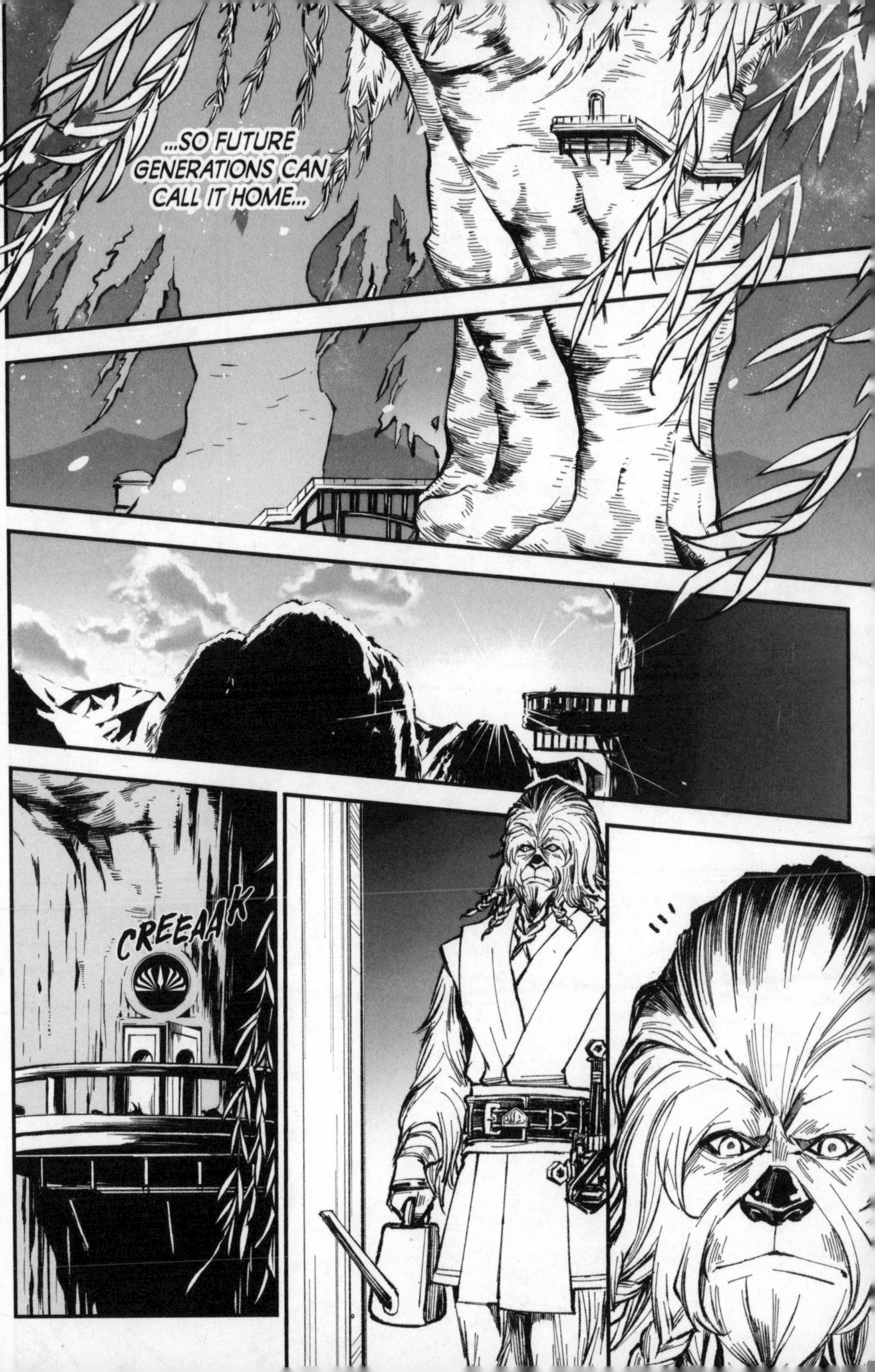
...SO FUTURE GENERATIONS CAN CALL IT HOME...
CREEAAK
!!

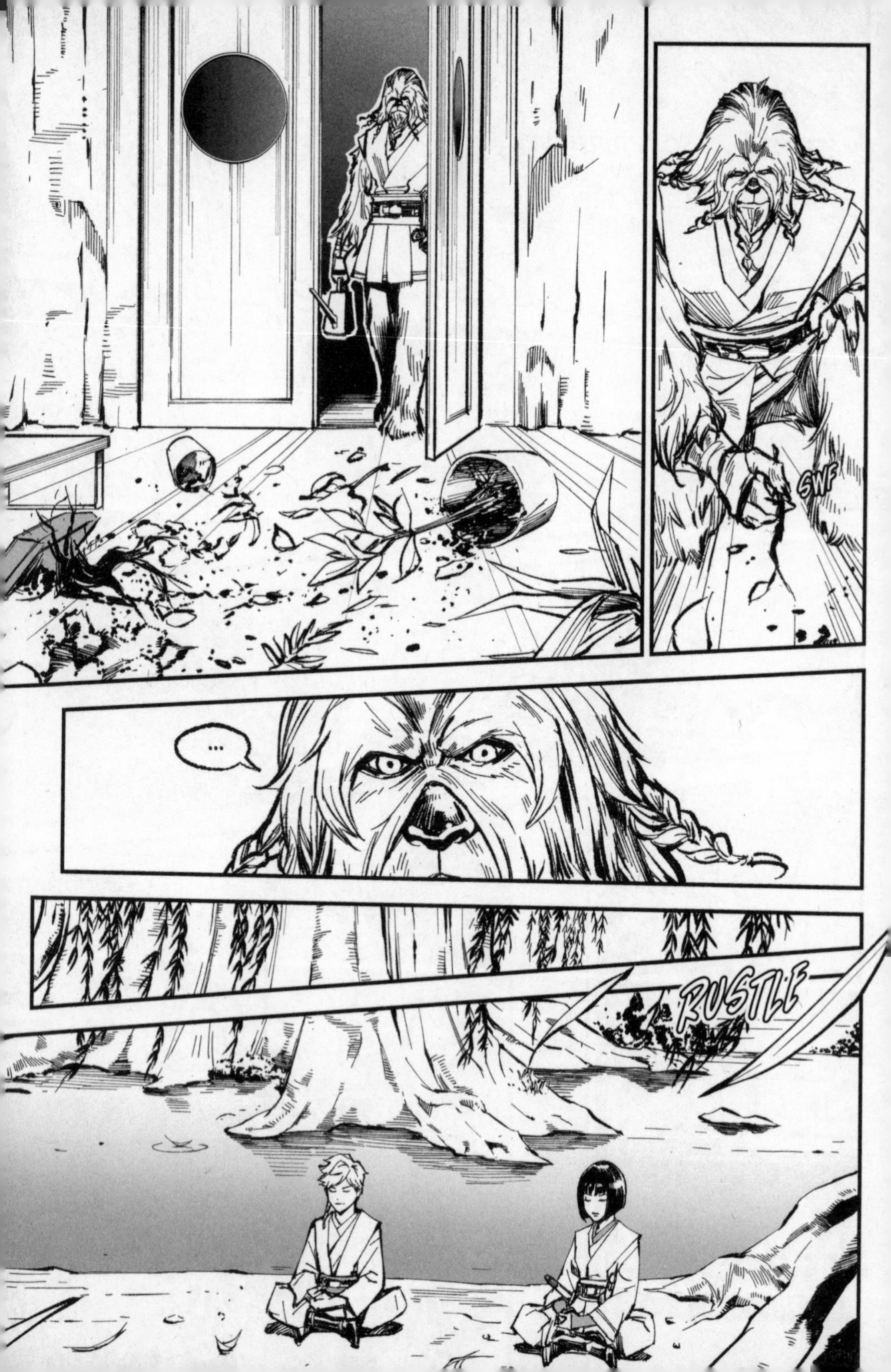
SWF
...
RUSTLE

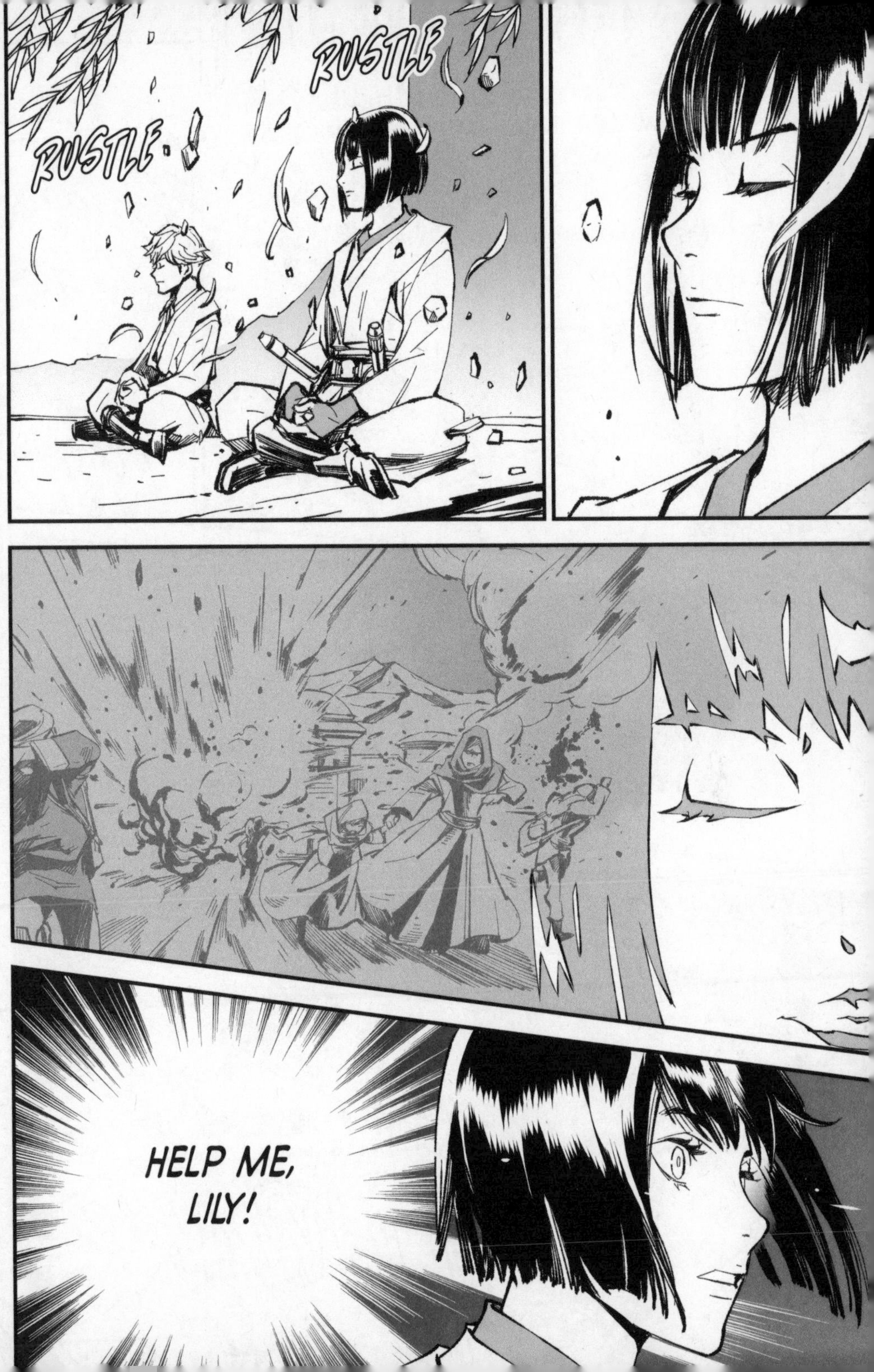
RUSTLE
RUSTLE
HELP ME, LILY!

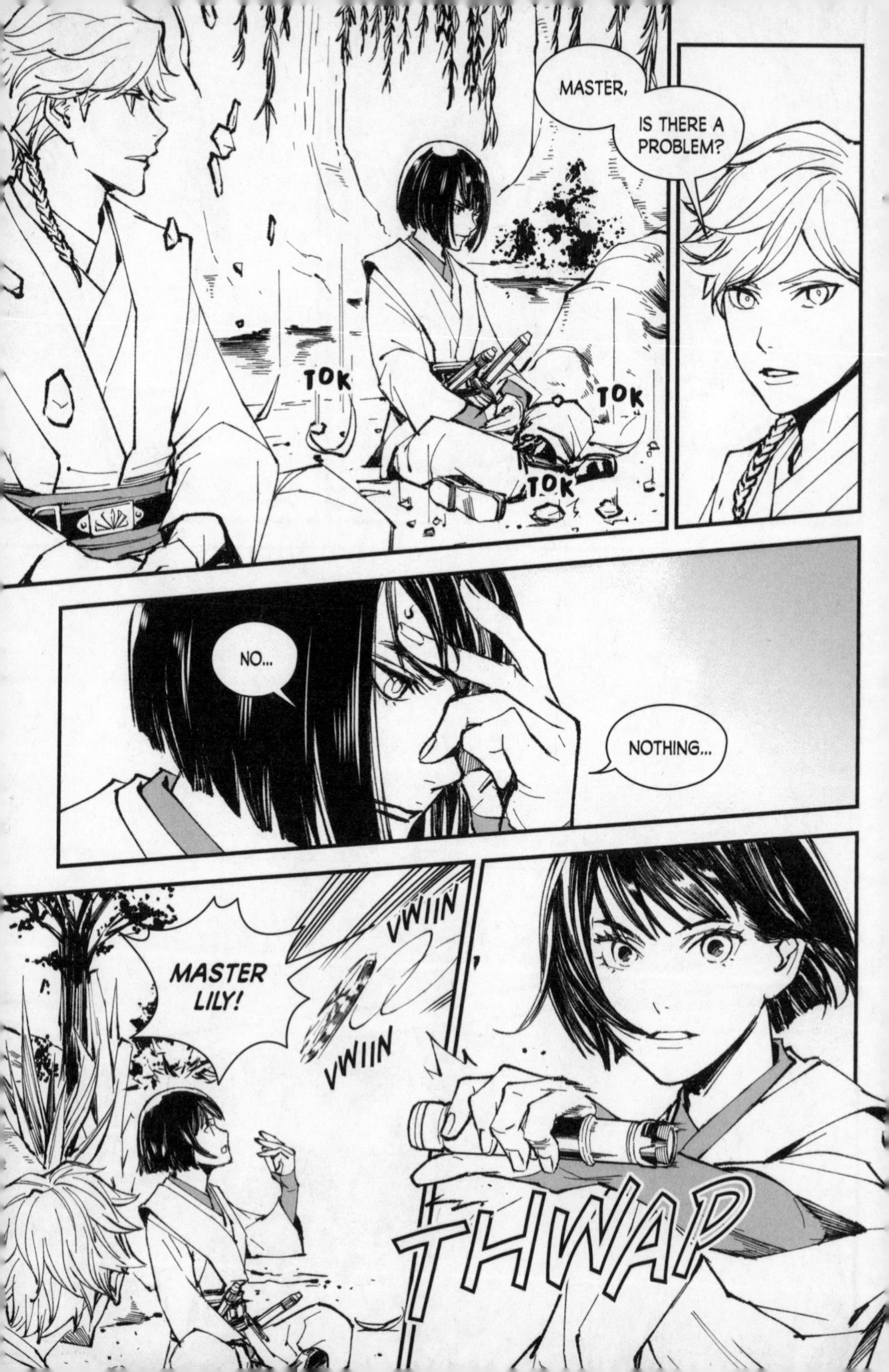
MASTER,
IS THERE A PROBLEM?
TOK
TOK
TOK
NO...
NOTHING...
VWIIN
VWIIN
MASTER LILY!
THWAP

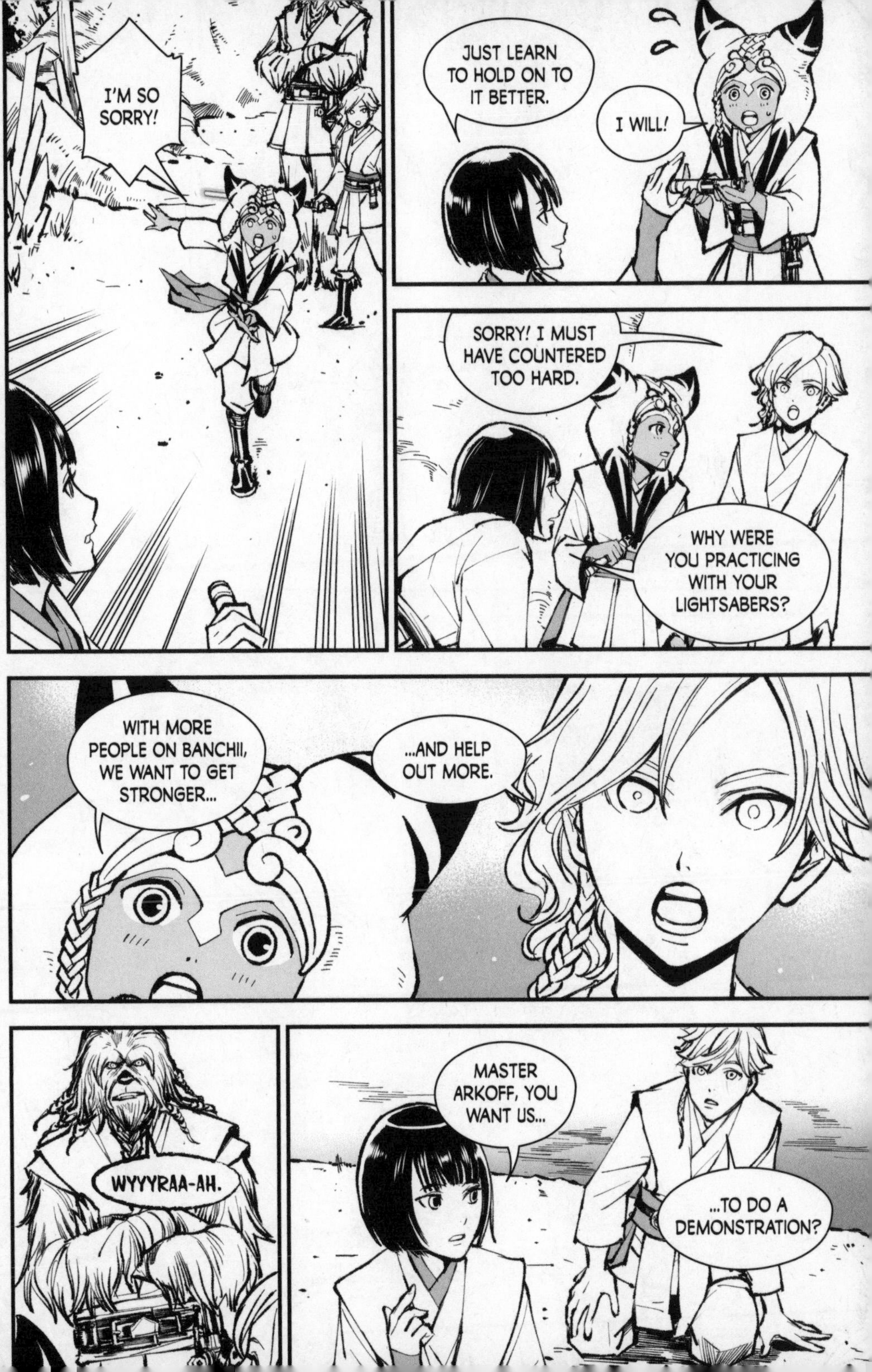
I'M SO SORRY!
JUST LEARN TO HOLD ON TO IT BETTER.
I WILL!
SORRY! I MUST HAVE COUNTERED TOO HARD.
WHY WERE YOU PRACTICING WITH YOUR LIGHTSABERS?
WITH MORE PEOPLE ON BANCHII, WE WANT TO GET STRONGER...
...AND HELP OUT MORE.
WYYYRAA-AH.
MASTER ARKOFF, YOU WANT US...
...TO DO A DEMONSTRATION?

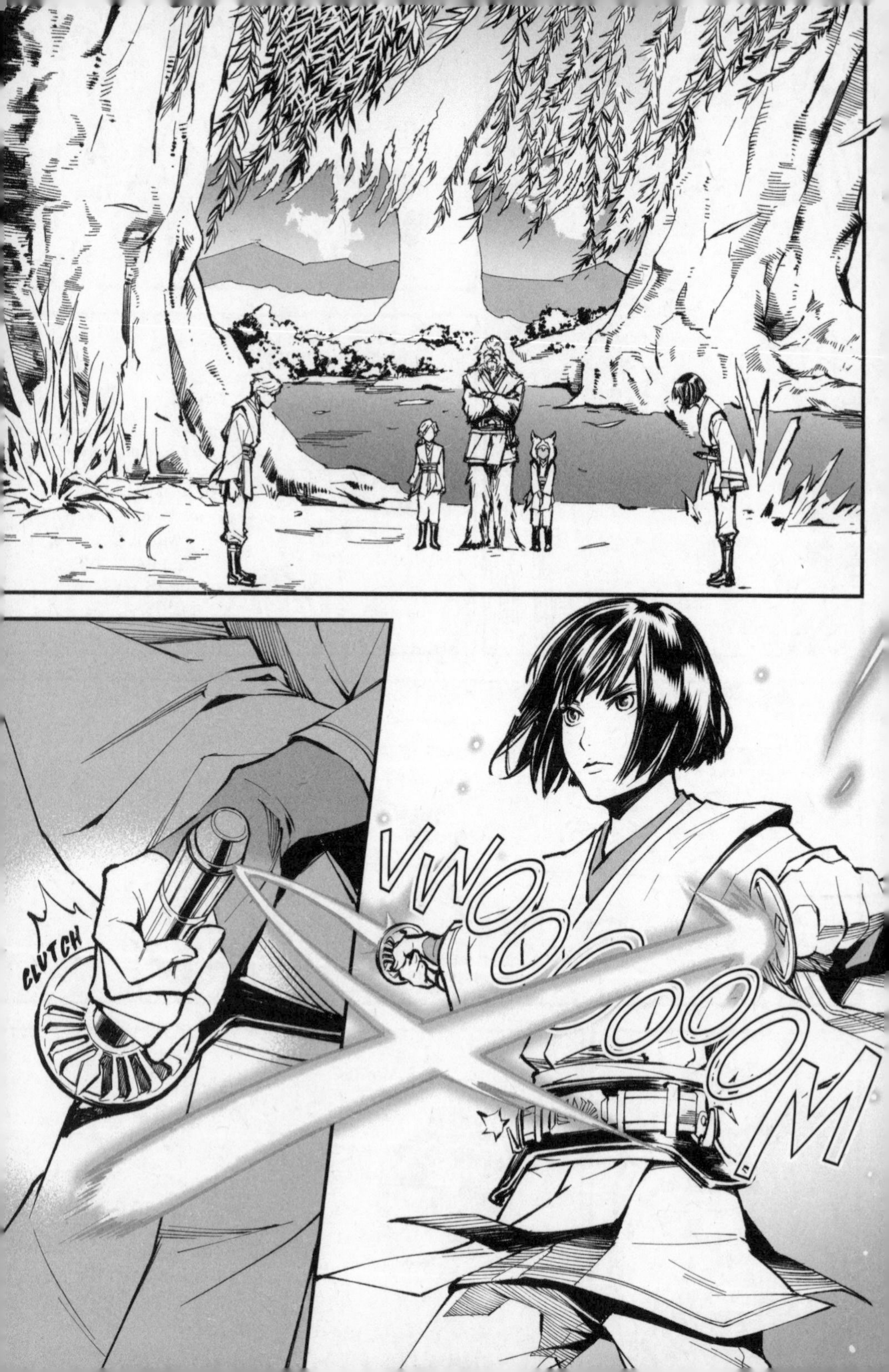

VWOOOOOOM
CLUTCH

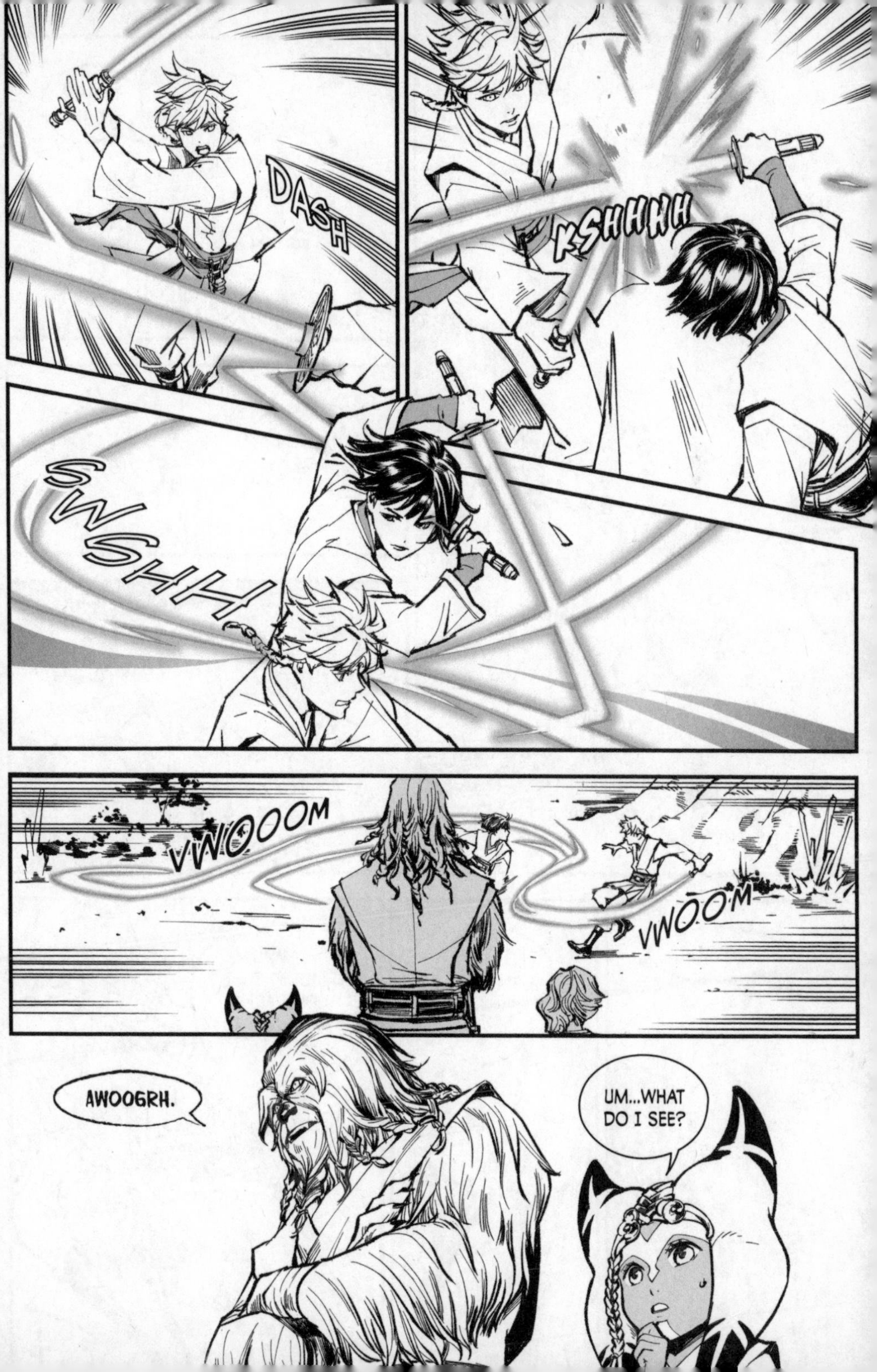
DASH
KSHHHH
SWSHH
VWOOOM
VWOOM
AWOOGRH.
UM...WHAT DO I SEE?

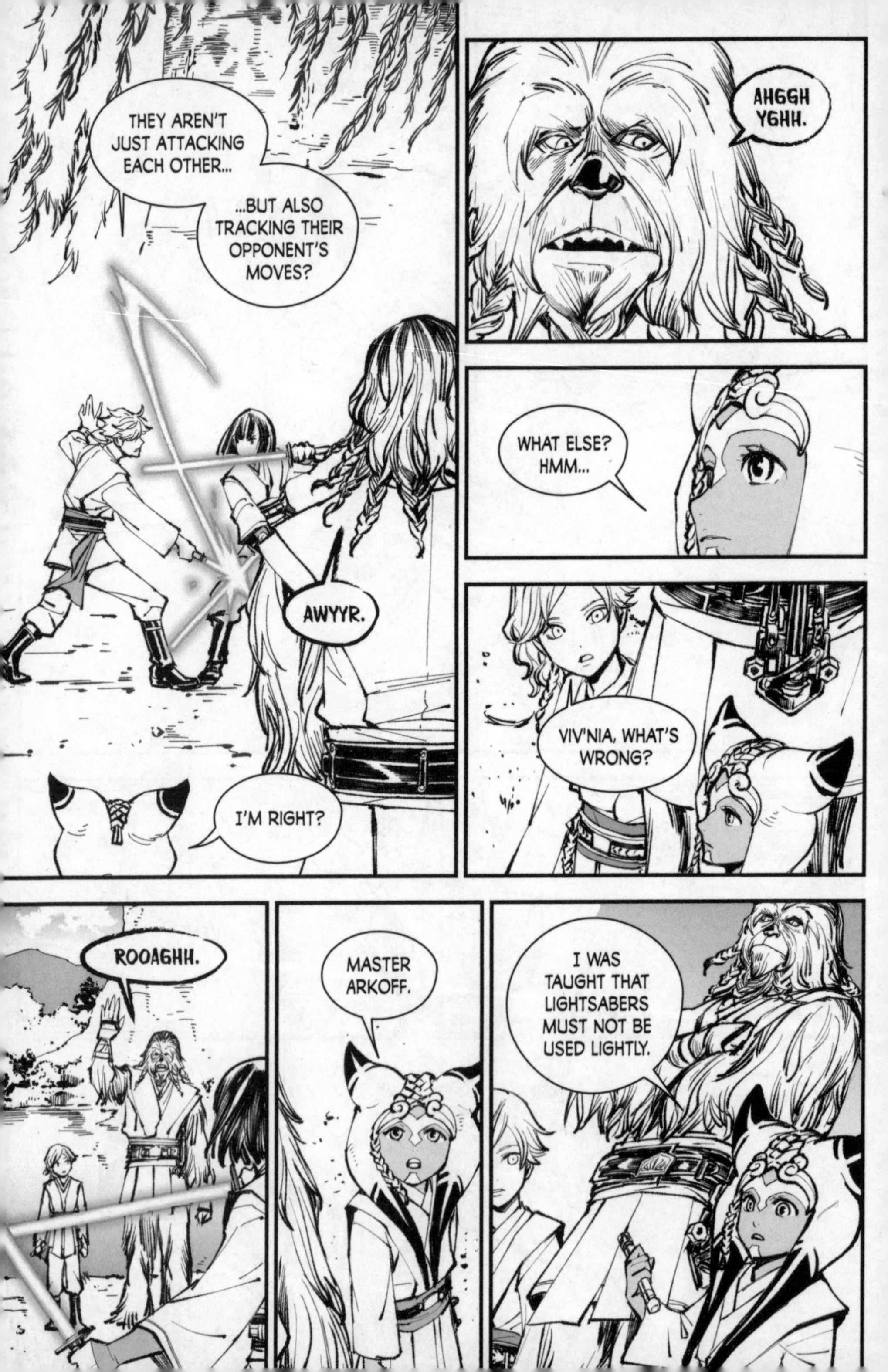
THEY AREN'T JUST ATTACKING EACH OTHER...
...BUT ALSO TRACKING THEIR OPPONENT'S MOVES?
AWYYR.
I'M RIGHT?
AHGGH YGHH.
WHAT ELSE? HMM...
VIV'NIA, WHAT'S WRONG?
ROOAGHH.
MASTER ARKOFF.
I WAS TAUGHT THAT LIGHTSABERS MUST NOT BE USED LIGHTLY.

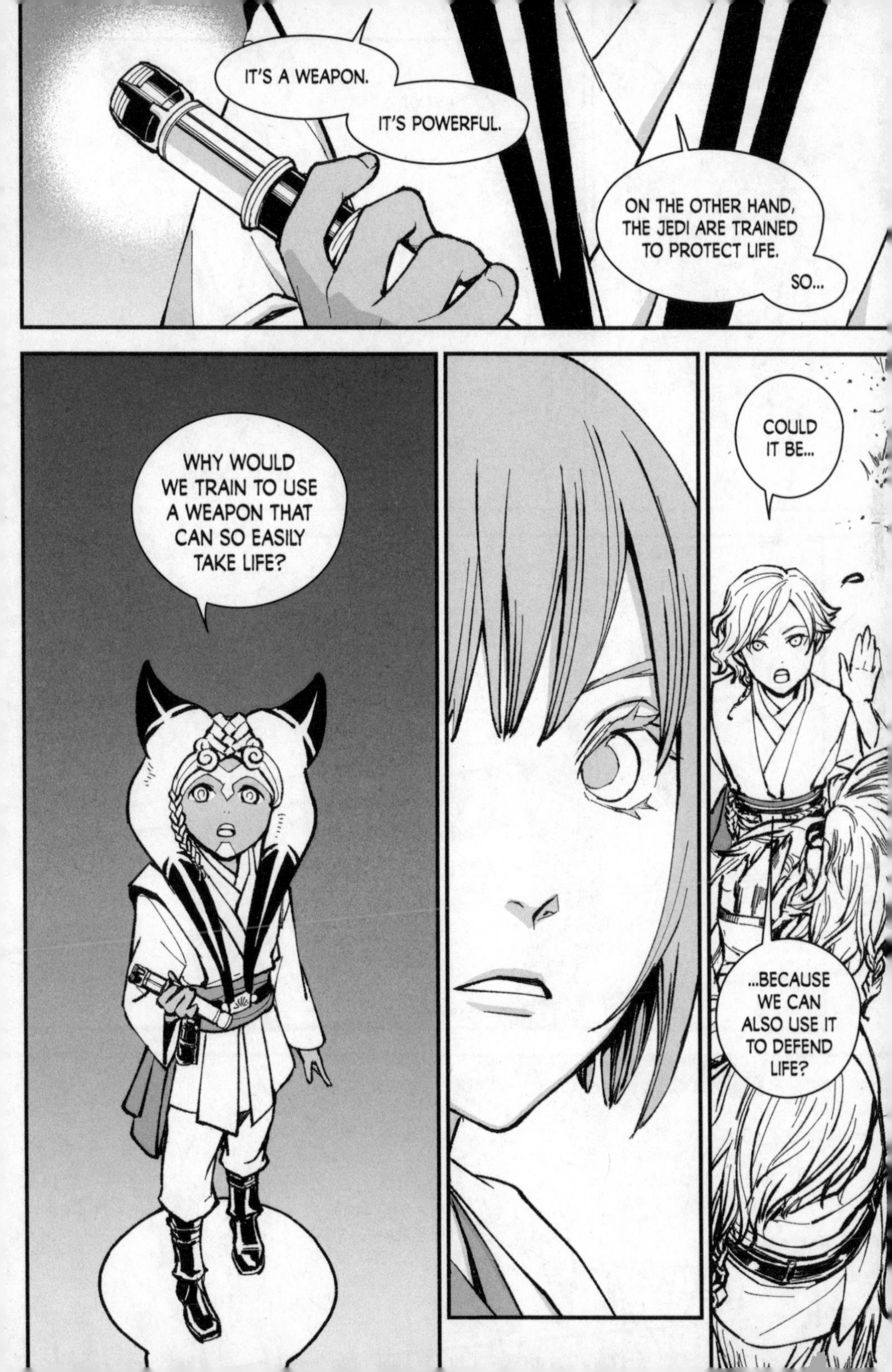
IT'S A WEAPON.
IT'S POWERFUL.
ON THE OTHER HAND, THE JEDI ARE TRAINED TO PROTECT LIFE.
SO...
WHY WOULD WE TRAIN TO USE A WEAPON THAT CAN SO EASILY TAKE LIFE?
COULD IT BE...
...BECAUSE WE CAN ALSO USE IT TO DEFEND LIFE?

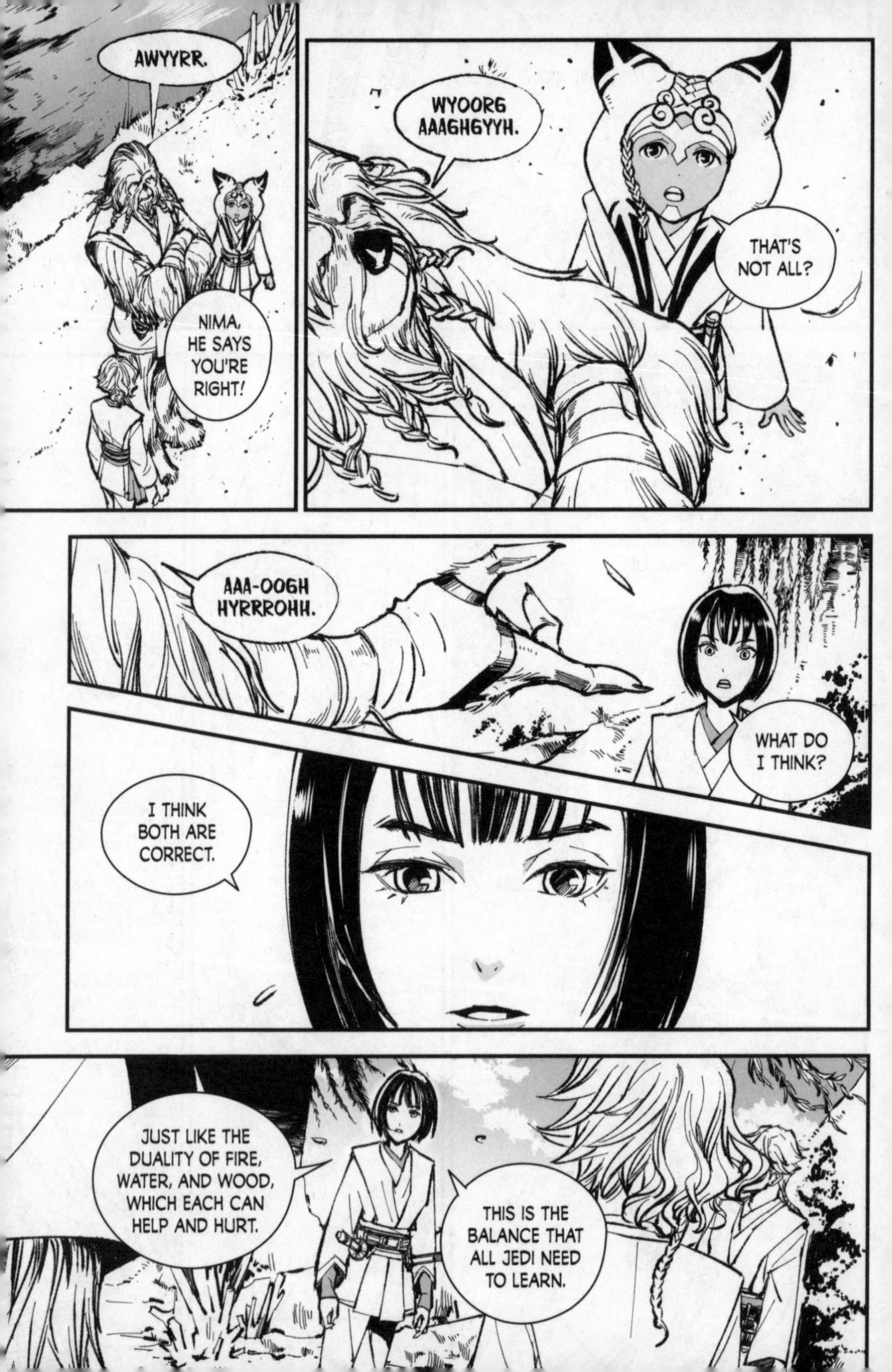

AWYYRR.
NIMA, HE SAYS YOU'RE RIGHT!
WYOORG AAAGHGYYH.
THAT'S NOT ALL?
AAA-OOGH HYRRROHH.
WHAT DO I THINK?
I THINK BOTH ARE CORRECT.
JUST LIKE THE DUALITY OF FIRE, WATER, AND WOOD, WHICH EACH CAN HELP AND HURT.
THIS IS THE BALANCE THAT ALL JEDI NEED TO LEARN.

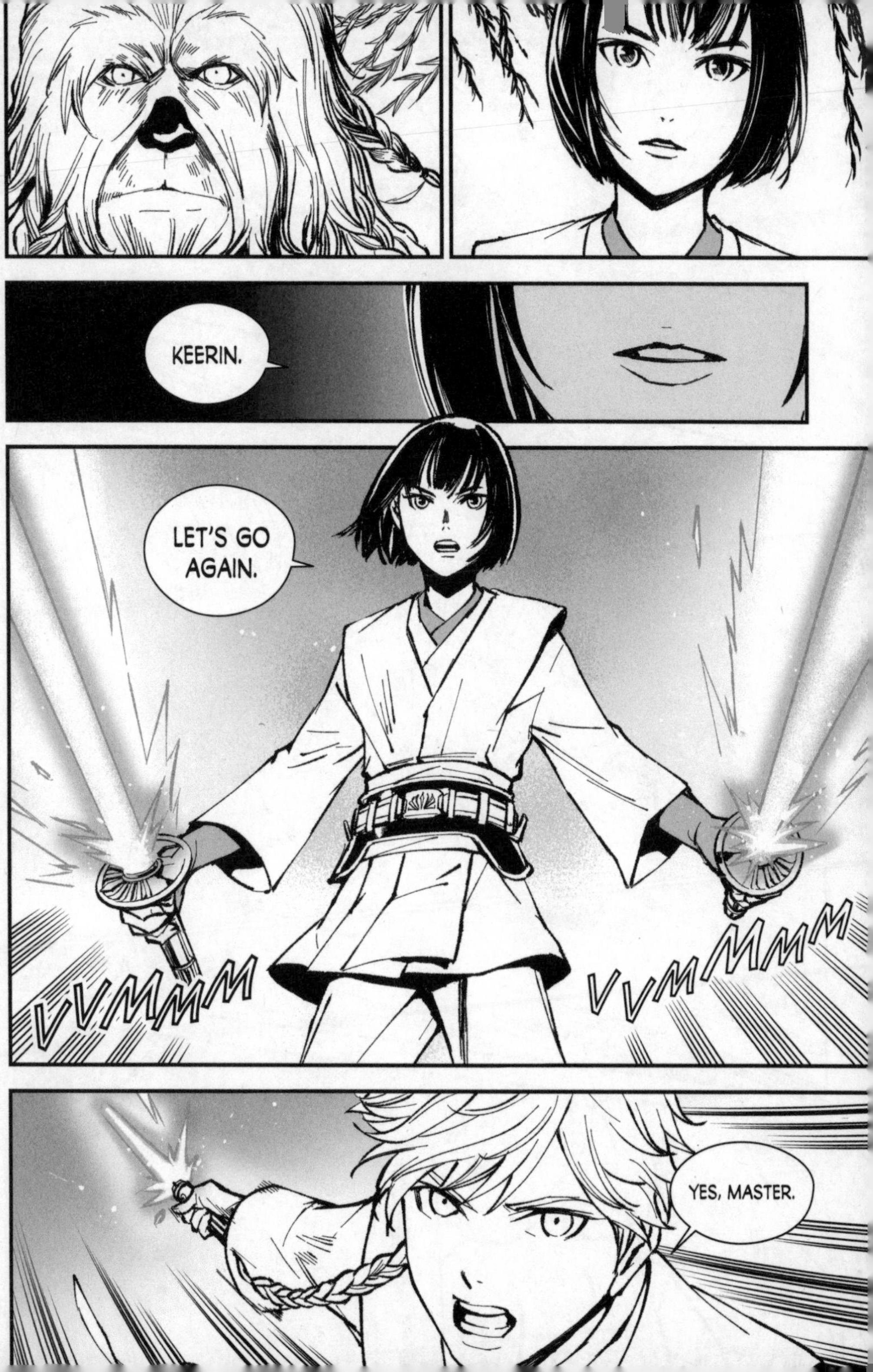
KEERIN.
LET'S GO AGAIN.
VVMMMM
VVMMMMM
YES, MASTER.

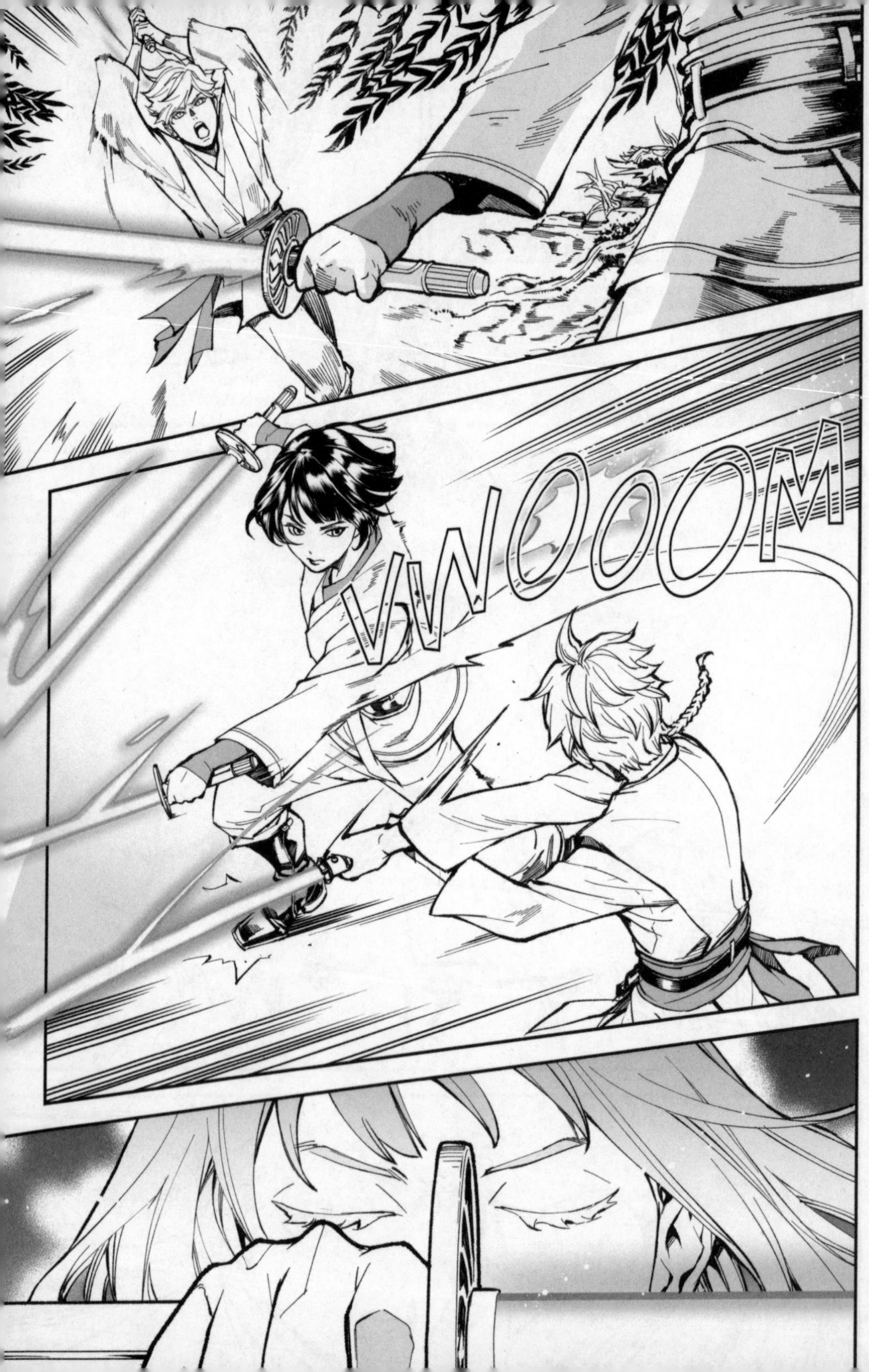
VWOOOM

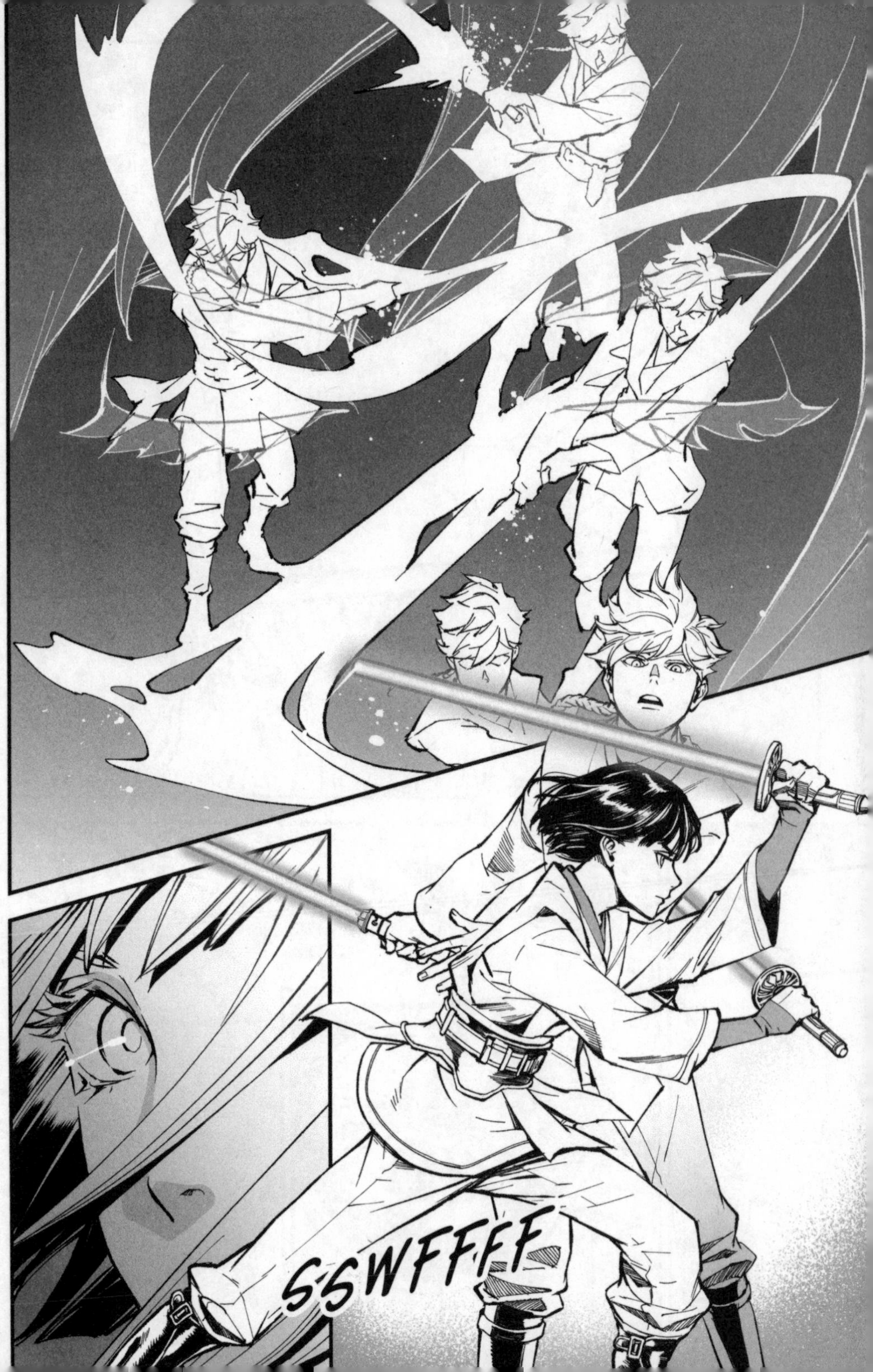
SSWFFFF

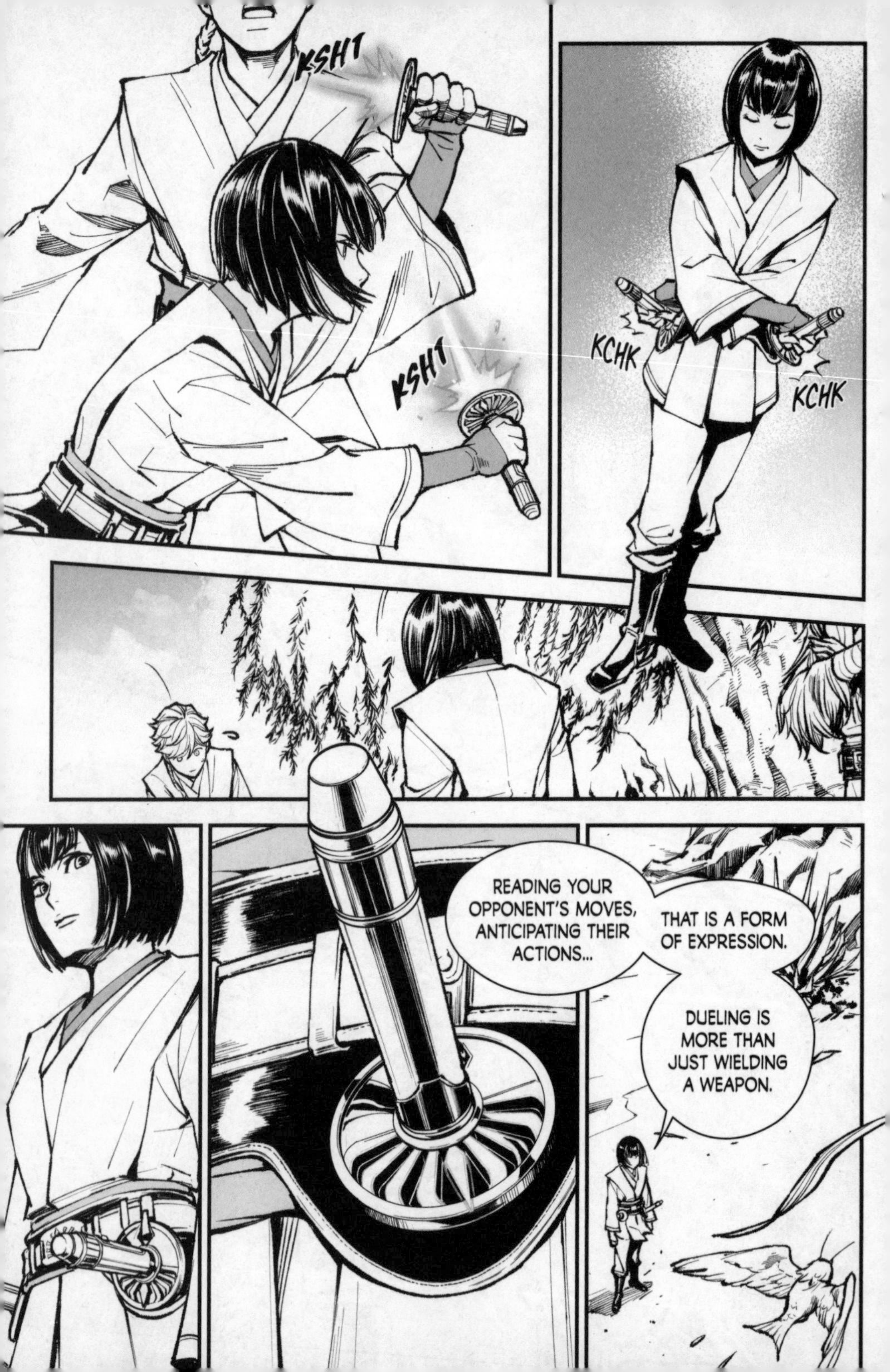

KSHT
KSHT
KCHK
KCHK
READING YOUR OPPONENT'S MOVES, ANTICIPATING THEIR ACTIONS...
THAT IS A FORM OF EXPRESSION.
DUELING IS MORE THAN JUST WIELDING A WEAPON.

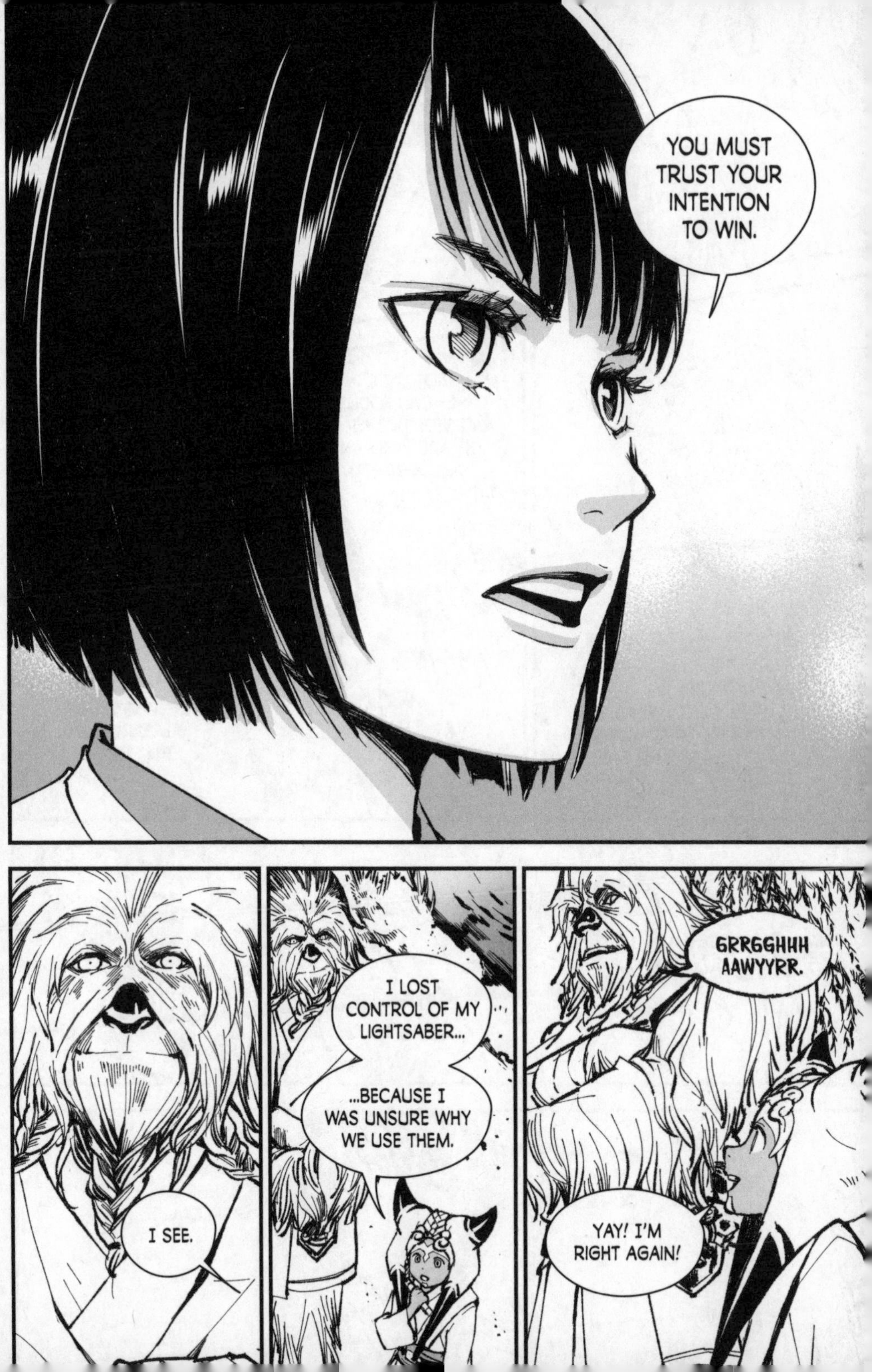

YOU MUST TRUST YOUR INTENTION TO WIN.
I SEE.
I LOST CONTROL OF MY LIGHTSABER...
...BECAUSE I WAS UNSURE WHY WE USE THEM.
GRRGGHHH AAWYYRR.
YAY! I'M RIGHT AGAIN!

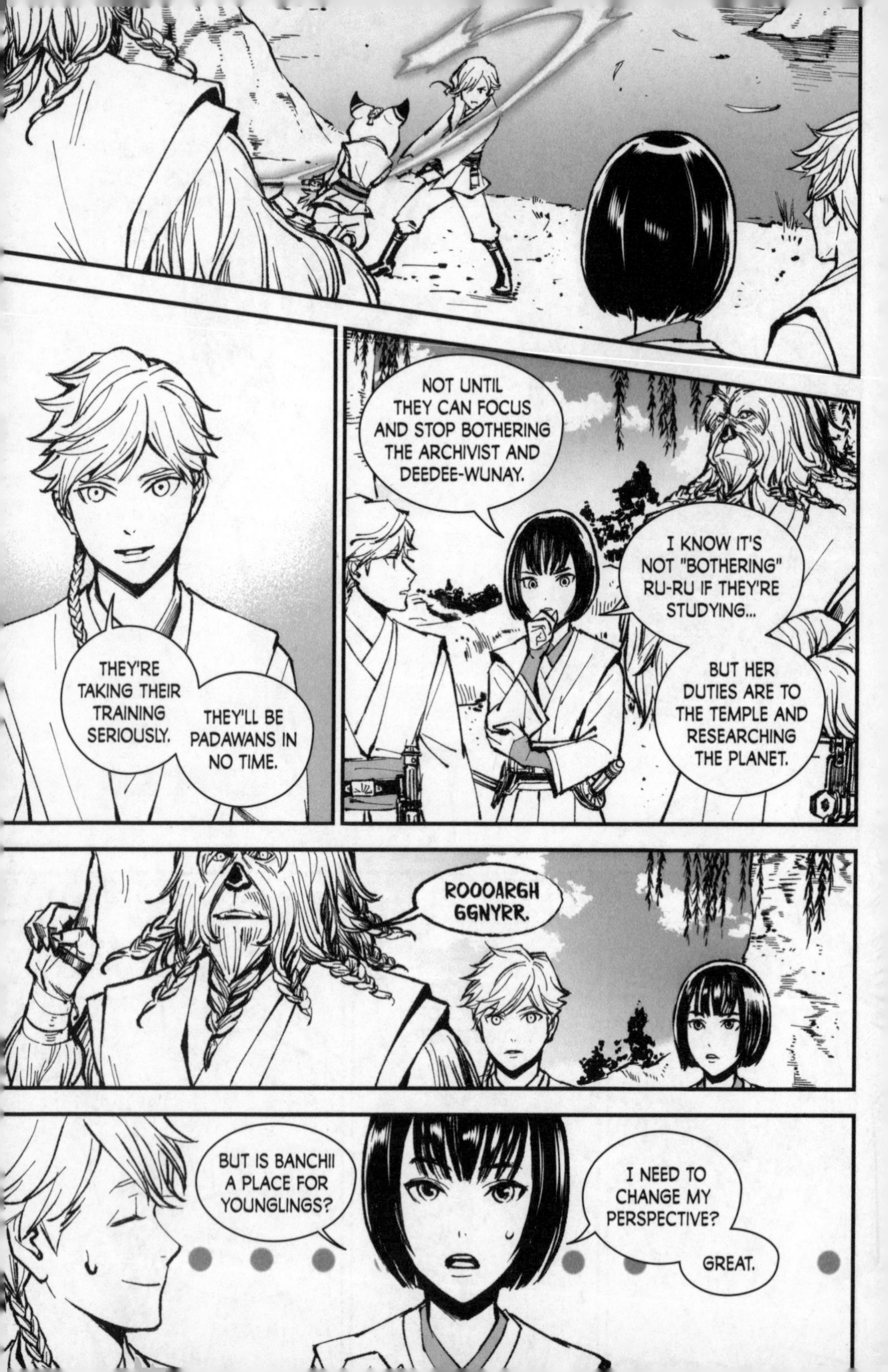
NOT UNTIL THEY CAN FOCUS AND STOP BOTHERING THE ARCHIVIST AND DEEDEE-WUNAY.
THEY'RE TAKING THEIR TRAINING SERIOUSLY.
THEY'LL BE PADAWANS IN NO TIME.
I KNOW IT'S NOT "BOTHERING" RU-RU IF THEY'RE STUDYING...
BUT HER DUTIES ARE TO THE TEMPLE AND RESEARCHING THE PLANET.
ROOOARGH GGNYRR.
BUT IS BANCHII A PLACE FOR YOUNGLINGS?
I NEED TO CHANGE MY PERSPECTIVE?
GREAT.

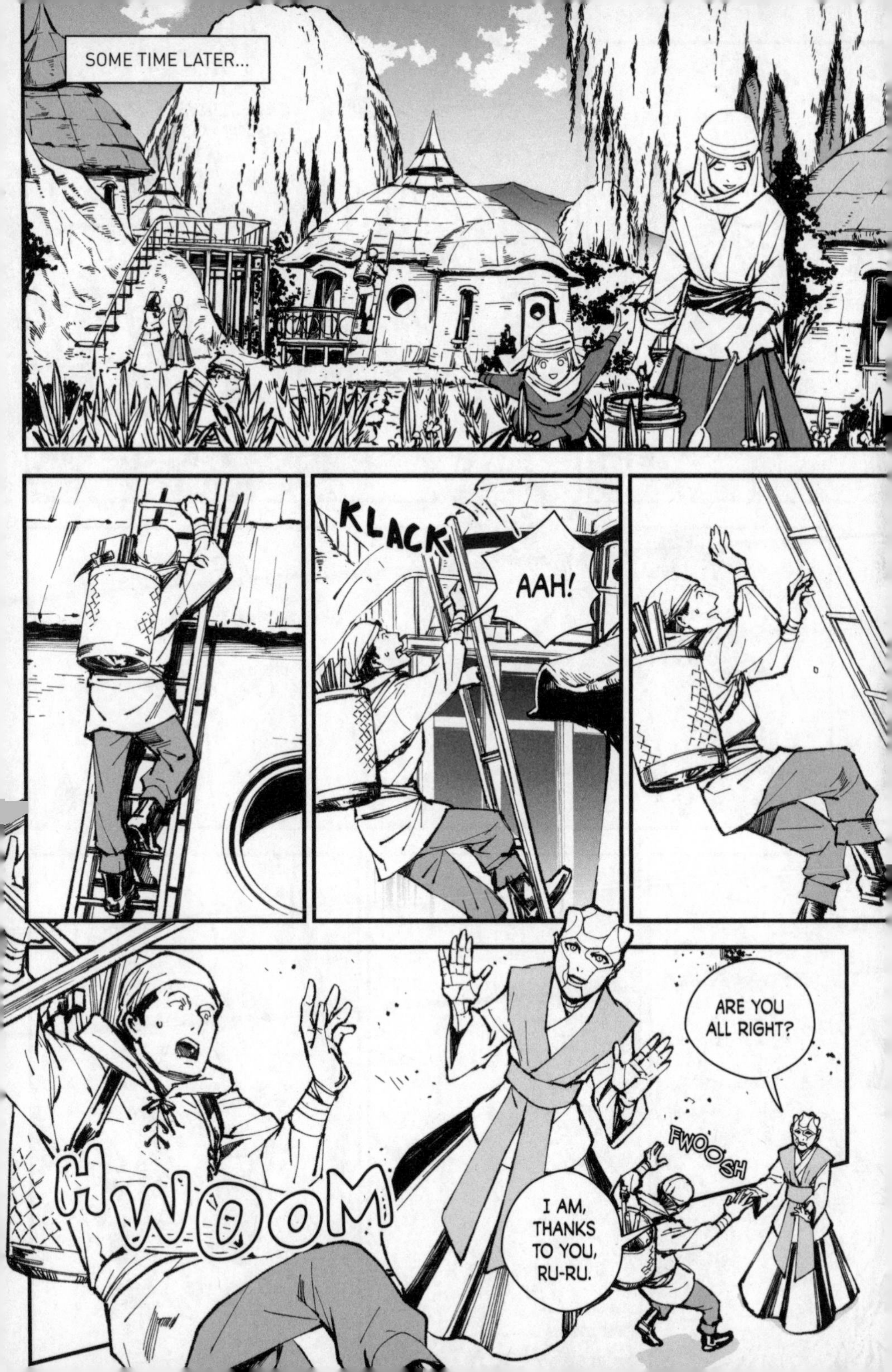
SOME TIME LATER...
KLACK
AAH!
HWOOM
ARE YOU ALL RIGHT?
FWOOSH
I AM, THANKS TO YOU, RU-RU.

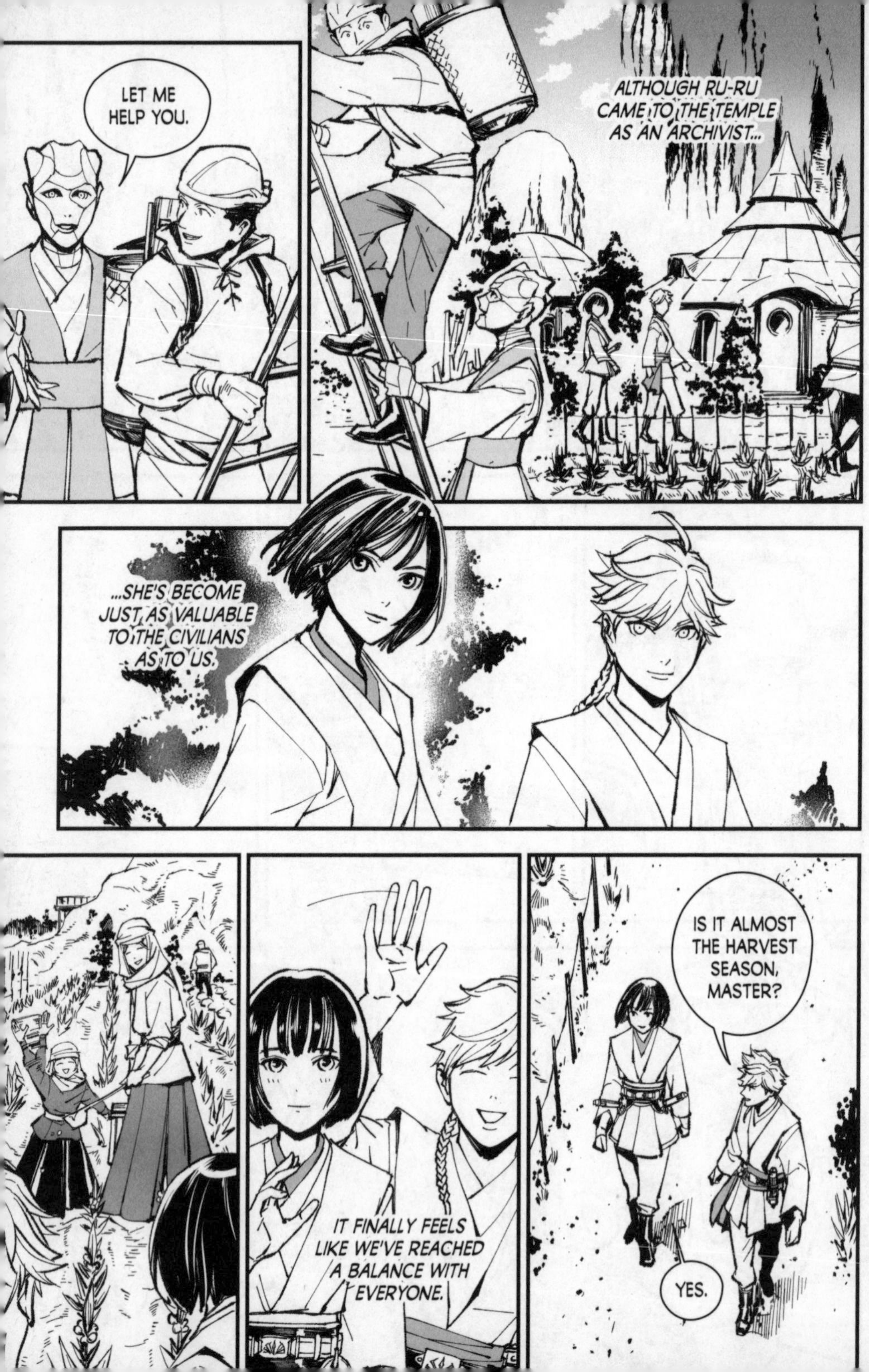
LET ME HELP YOU.
ALTHOUGH RU-RU CAME TO THE TEMPLE AS AN ARCHIVIST...
...SHE'S BECOME JUST AS VALUABLE TO THE CIVILIANS AS TO US.
IT FINALLY FEELS LIKE WE'VE REACHED A BALANCE WITH EVERYONE.
IS IT ALMOST THE HARVEST SEASON, MASTER?
YES.

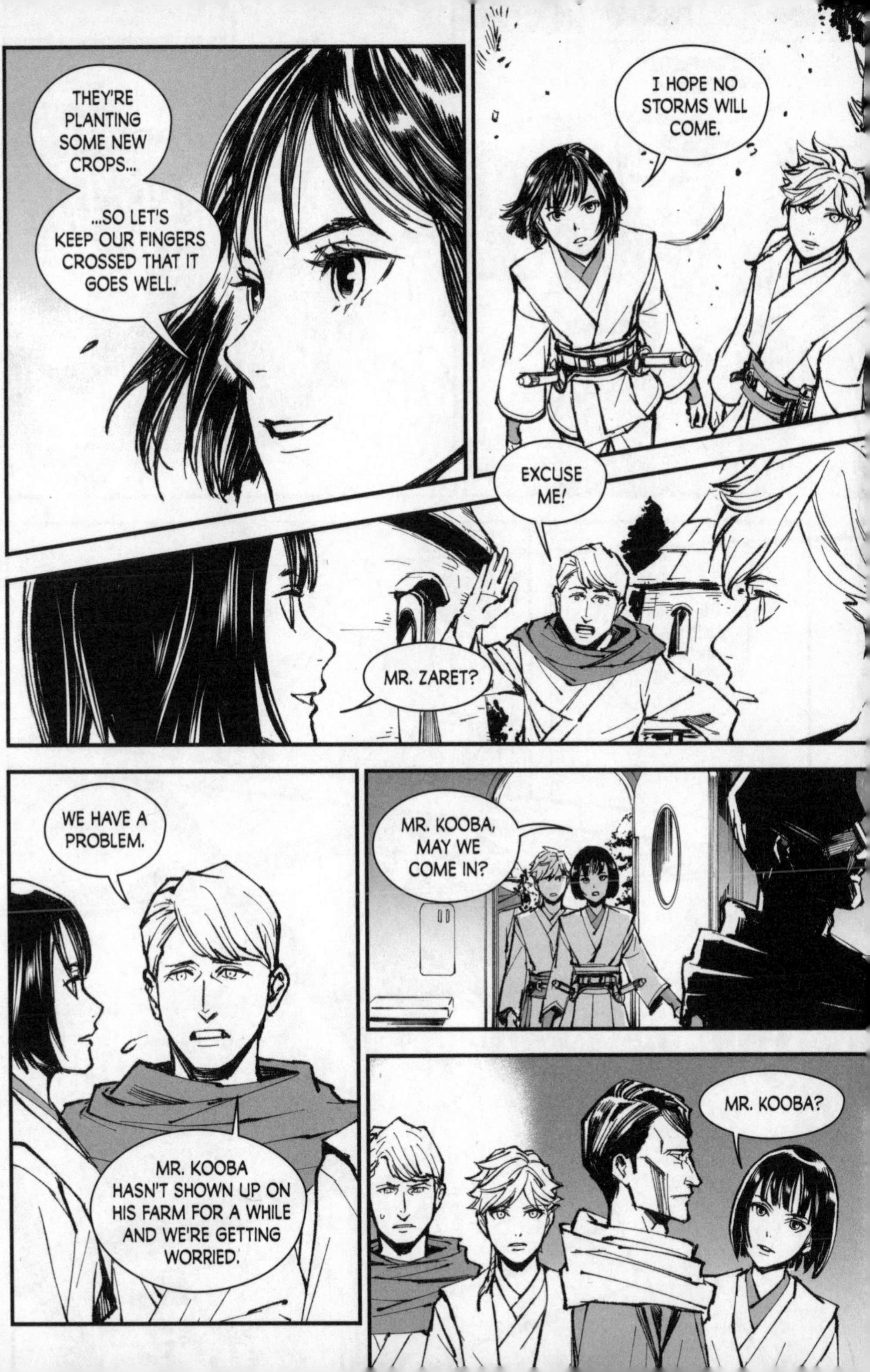
THEY'RE PLANTING SOME NEW CROPS...
...SO LET'S KEEP OUR FINGERS CROSSED THAT IT GOES WELL.
I HOPE NO STORMS WILL COME.
EXCUSE ME!
MR. ZARET?
WE HAVE A PROBLEM.
MR. KOOBA HASN'T SHOWN UP ON HIS FARM FOR A WHILE AND WE'RE GETTING WORRIED.
MR. KOOBA, MAY WE COME IN?
MR. KOOBA?

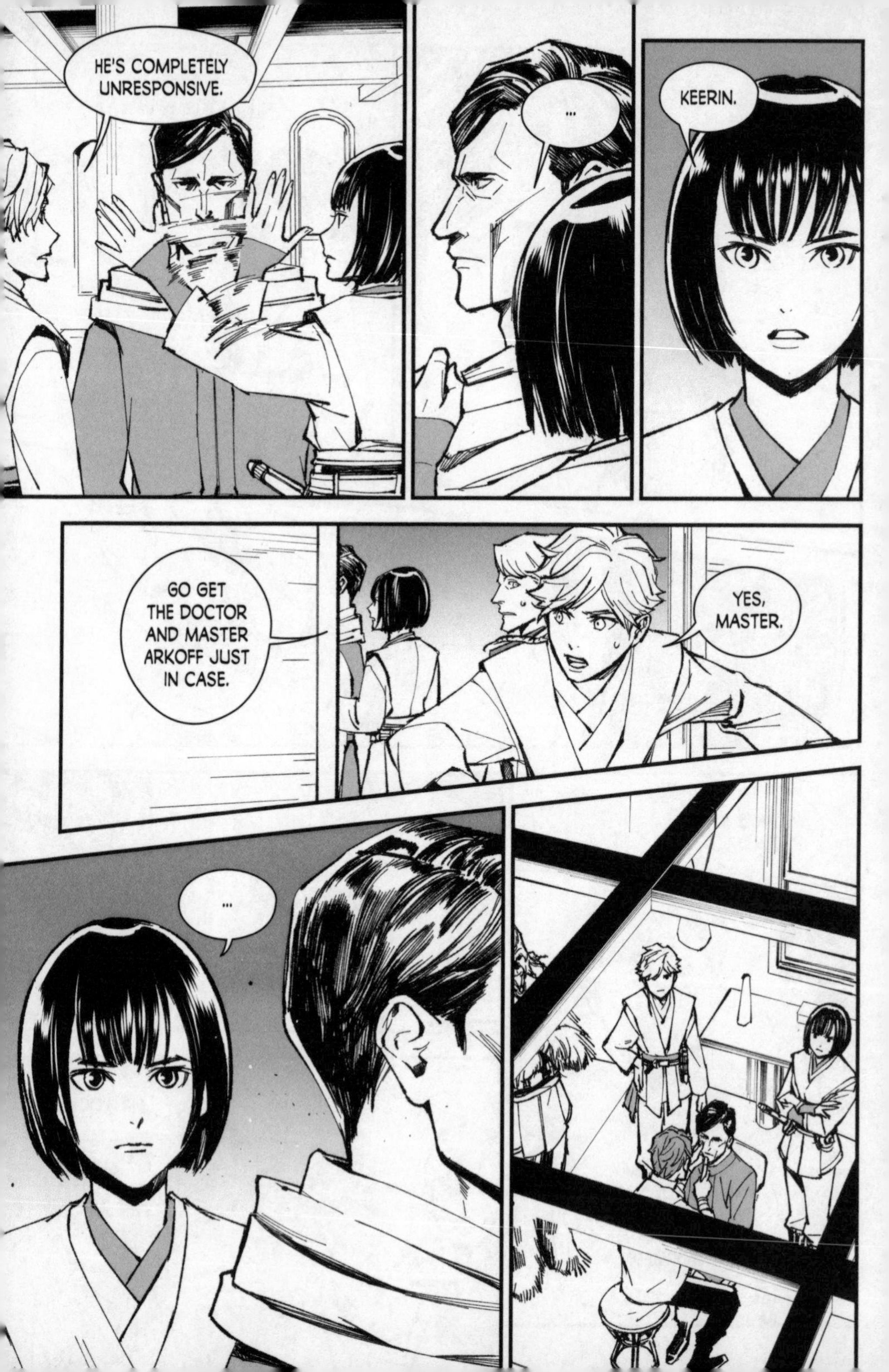
HE'S COMPLETELY UNRESPONSIVE.
...
KEERIN.
GO GET THE DOCTOR AND MASTER ARKOFF JUST IN CASE.
YES, MASTER.
...

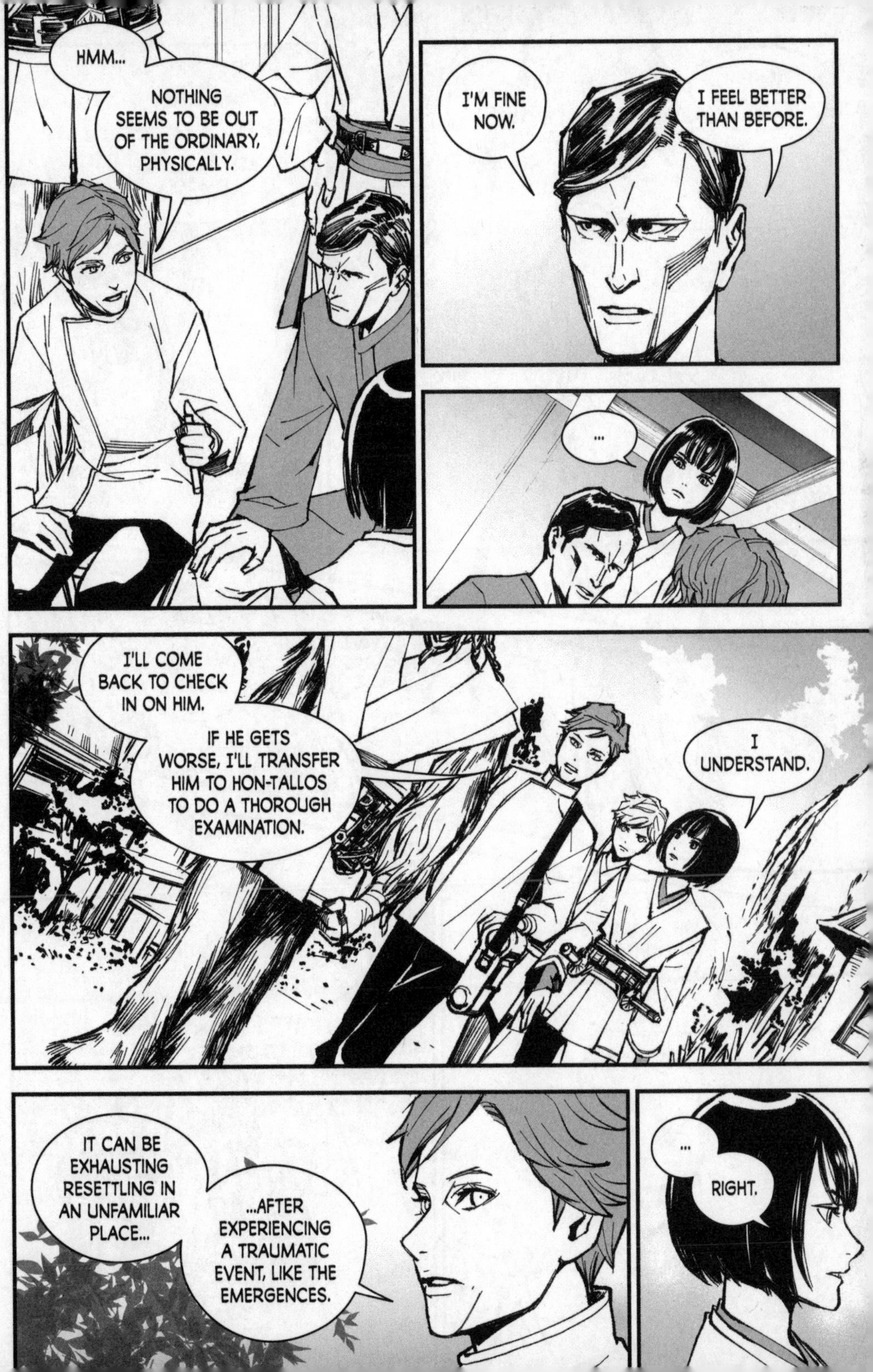
HMM...
NOTHING SEEMS TO BE OUT OF THE ORDINARY, PHYSICALLY.
I'M FINE NOW.
I FEEL BETTER THAN BEFORE.
...
I'LL COME BACK TO CHECK IN ON HIM.
IF HE GETS WORSE, I'LL TRANSFER HIM TO HON-TALLOS TO DO A THOROUGH EXAMINATION.
I UNDERSTAND.
IT CAN BE EXHAUSTING RESETTLING IN AN UNFAMILIAR PLACE...
...AFTER EXPERIENCING A TRAUMATIC EVENT, LIKE THE EMERGENCES.
...
RIGHT.

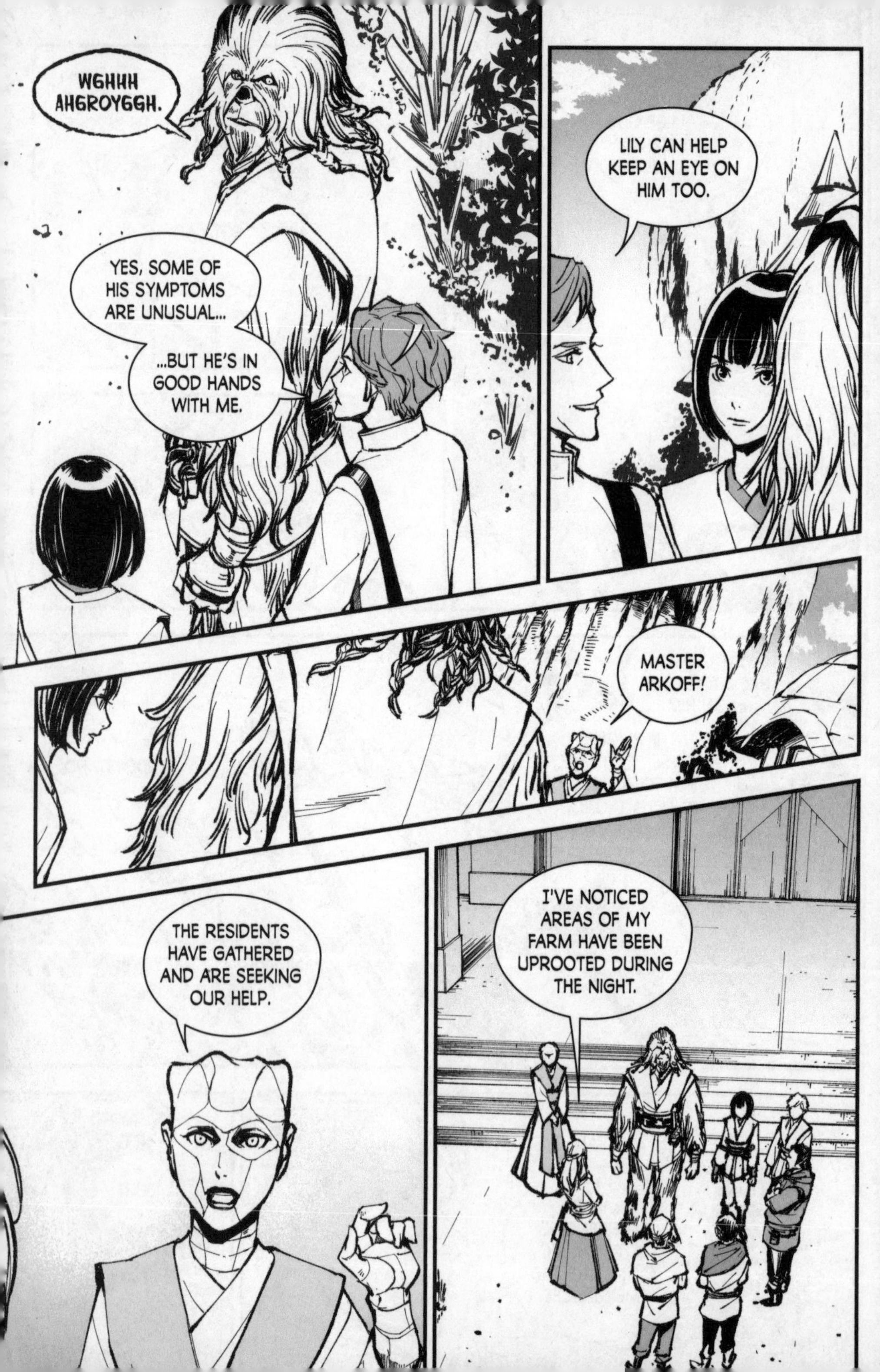
WGHHH AHGROYGGH.
YES, SOME OF HIS SYMPTOMS ARE UNUSUAL...
...BUT HE'S IN GOOD HANDS WITH ME.
LILY CAN HELP KEEP AN EYE ON HIM TOO.
MASTER ARKOFF!
THE RESIDENTS HAVE GATHERED AND ARE SEEKING OUR HELP.
I'VE NOTICED AREAS OF MY FARM HAVE BEEN UPROOTED DURING THE NIGHT.

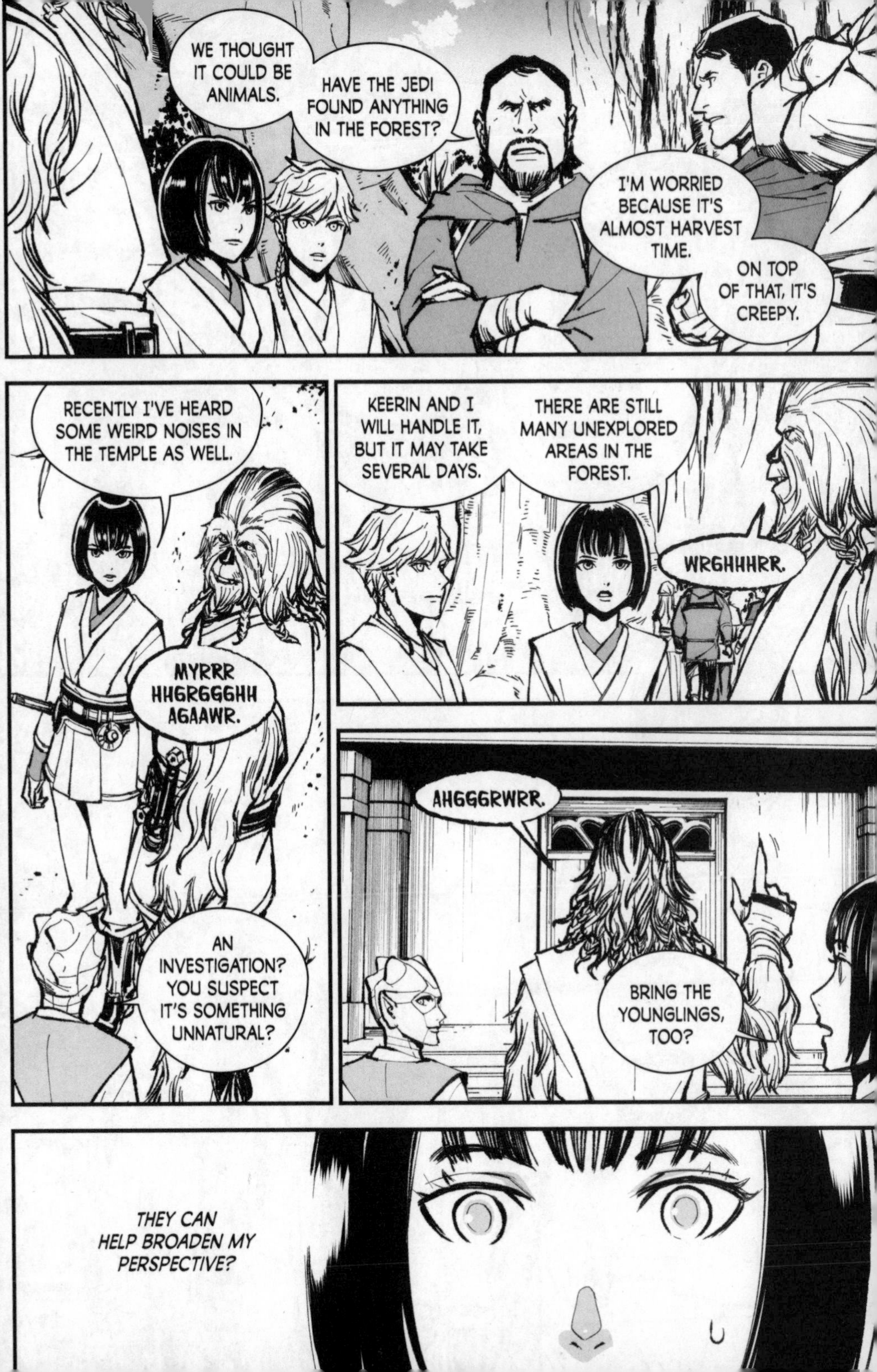
WE THOUGHT IT COULD BE ANIMALS.
HAVE THE JEDI FOUND ANYTHING IN THE FOREST?
I'M WORRIED BECAUSE IT'S ALMOST HARVEST TIME.
ON TOP OF THAT, IT'S CREEPY.
RECENTLY I'VE HEARD SOME WEIRD NOISES IN THE TEMPLE AS WELL.
MYRRR HHGRGGGHH AGAAWR.
AN INVESTIGATION? YOU SUSPECT IT'S SOMETHING UNNATURAL?
KEERIN AND I WILL HANDLE IT, BUT IT MAY TAKE SEVERAL DAYS.
THERE ARE STILL MANY UNEXPLORED AREAS IN THE FOREST.
WRGHHHRR.
AHGGGRWRR.
BRING THE YOUNGLINGS, TOO?
THEY CAN HELP BROADEN MY PERSPECTIVE?

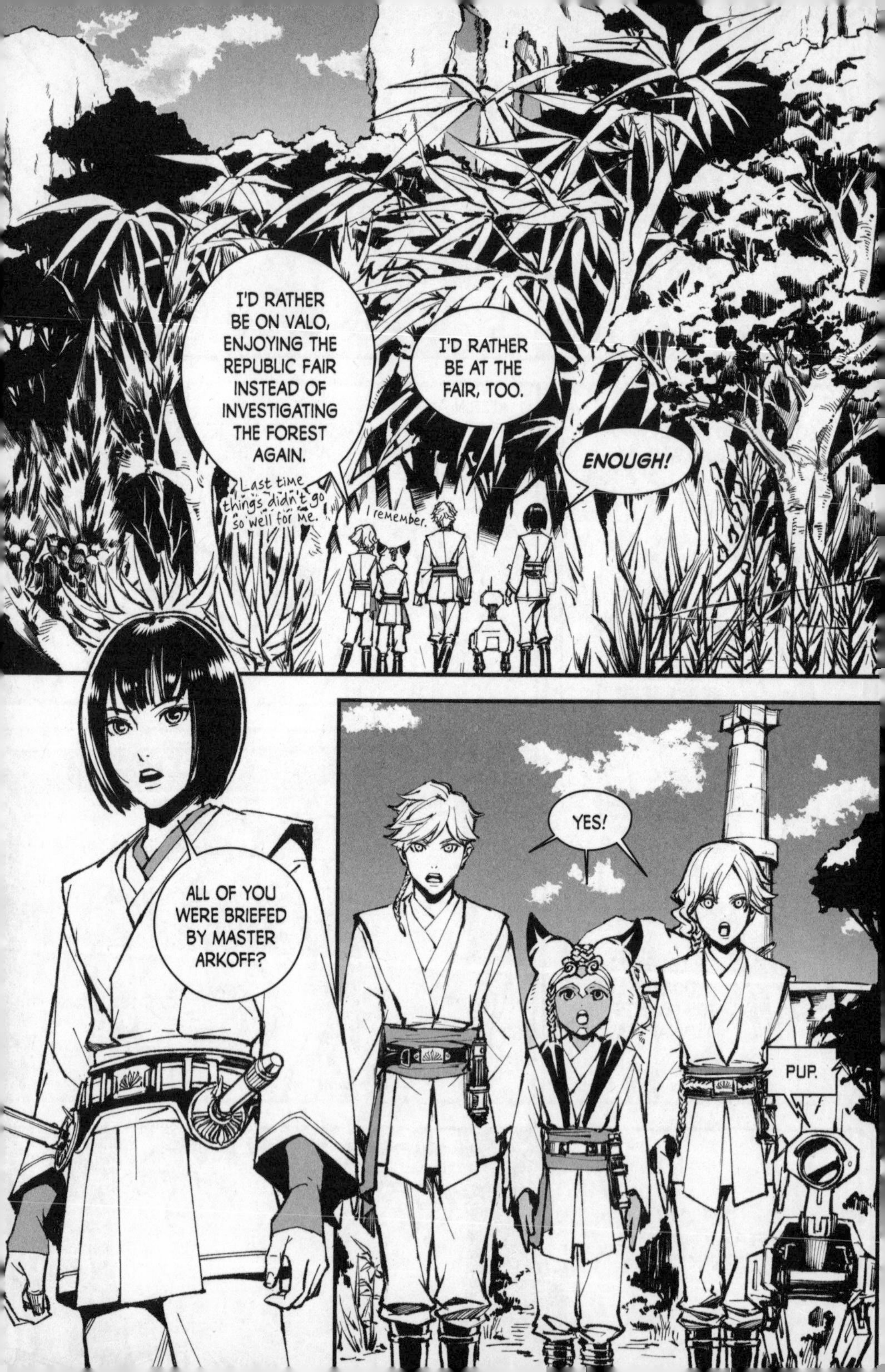
I'D RATHER BE ON VALO, ENJOYING THE REPUBLIC FAIR INSTEAD OF INVESTIGATING THE FOREST AGAIN.
Last time things didn't go so well for me.
I'D RATHER BE AT THE FAIR, TOO.
I remember.
ENOUGH!
ALL OF YOU WERE BRIEFED BY MASTER ARKOFF?
YES!
PUP.

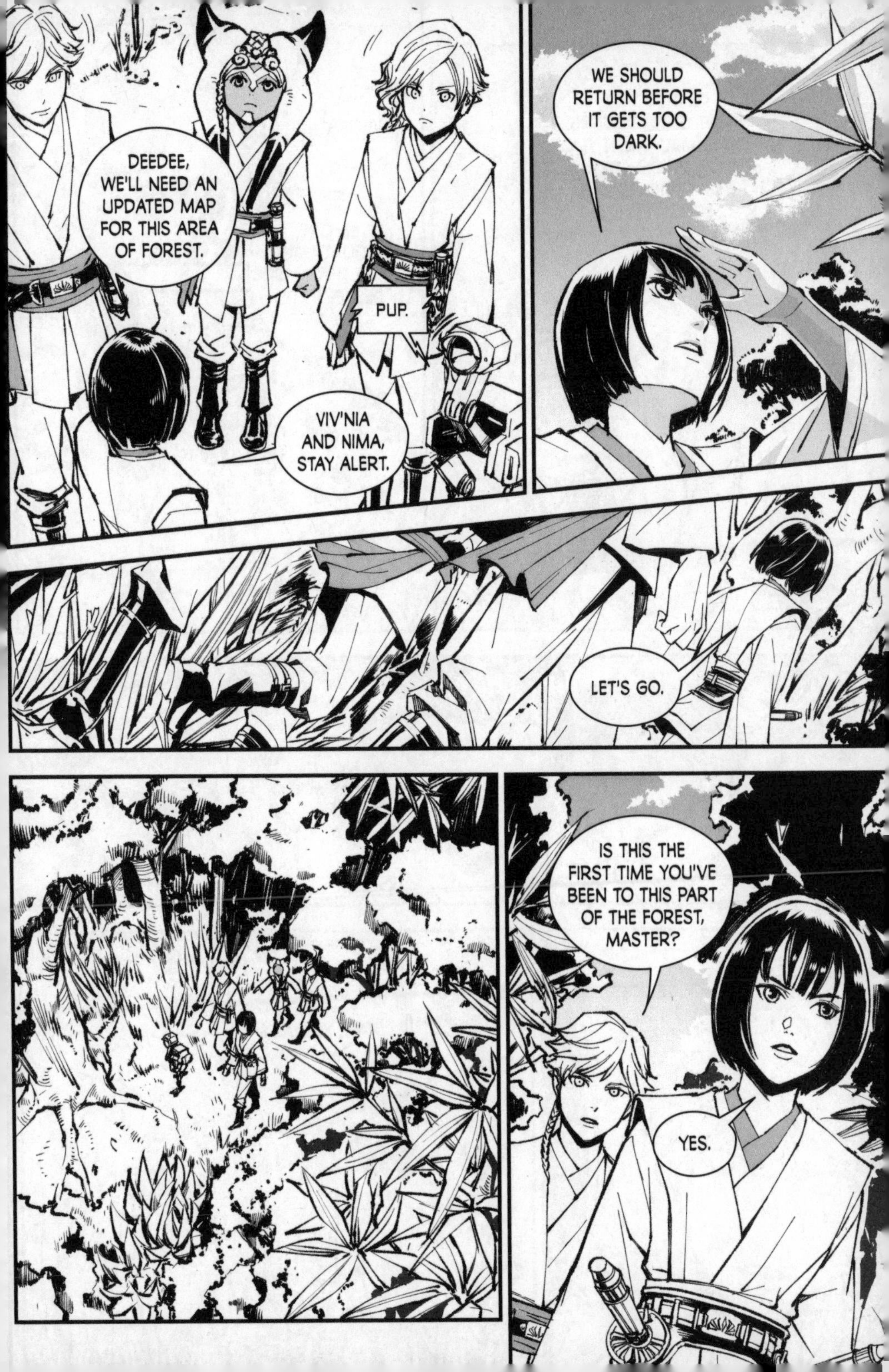
DEEDEE, WE'LL NEED AN UPDATED MAP FOR THIS AREA OF FOREST.
PUP.
VIV'NIA AND NIMA, STAY ALERT.
WE SHOULD RETURN BEFORE IT GETS TOO DARK.
LET'S GO.
IS THIS THE FIRST TIME YOU'VE BEEN TO THIS PART OF THE FOREST, MASTER?
YES.

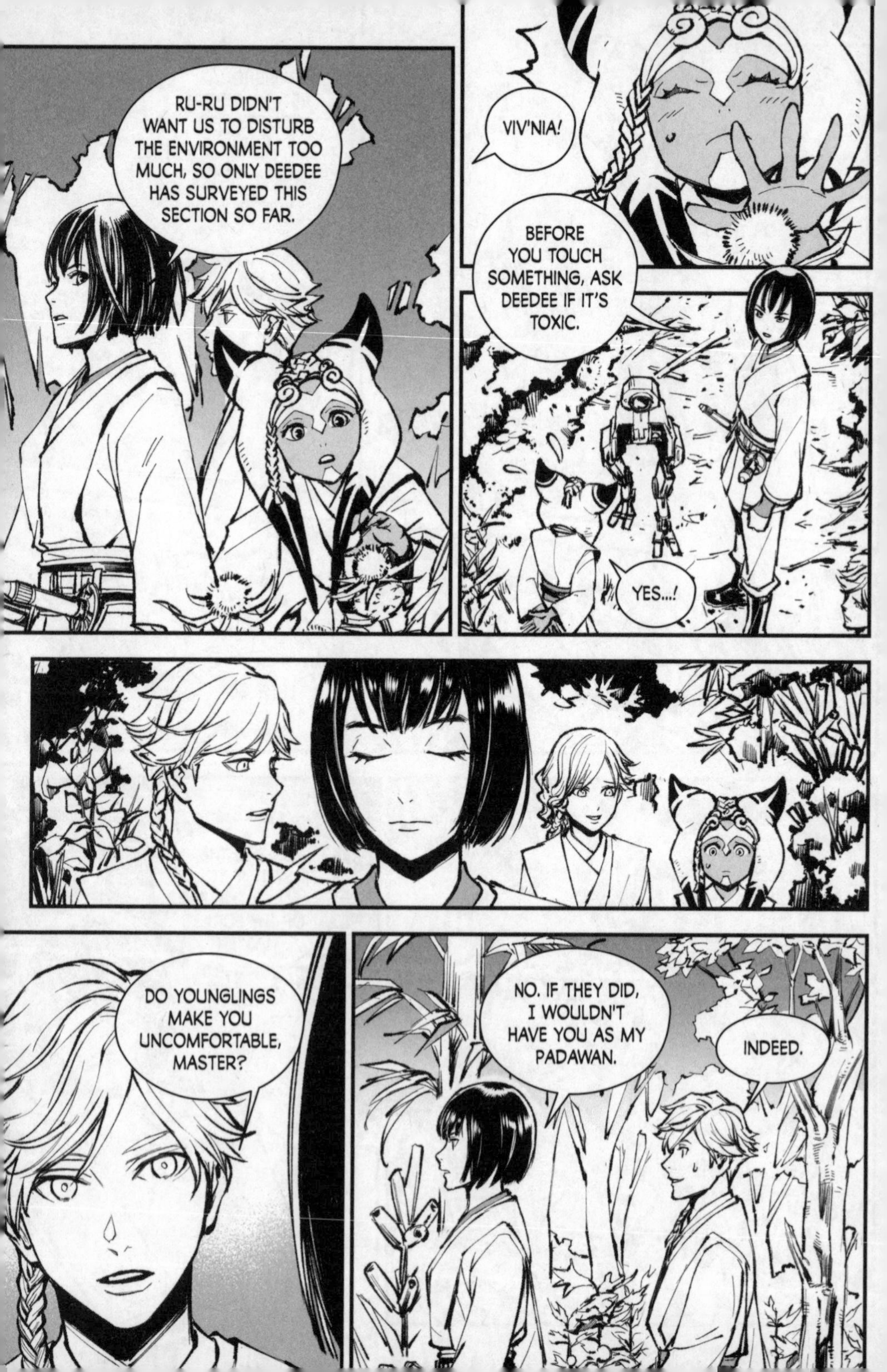
RU-RU DIDN'T WANT US TO DISTURB THE ENVIRONMENT TOO MUCH, SO ONLY DEEDEE HAS SURVEYED THIS SECTION SO FAR.
VIV'NIA!
BEFORE YOU TOUCH SOMETHING, ASK DEEDEE IF IT'S TOXIC.
YES...!
DO YOUNGLINGS MAKE YOU UNCOMFORTABLE, MASTER?
NO. IF THEY DID, I WOULDN'T HAVE YOU AS MY PADAWAN.
INDEED.

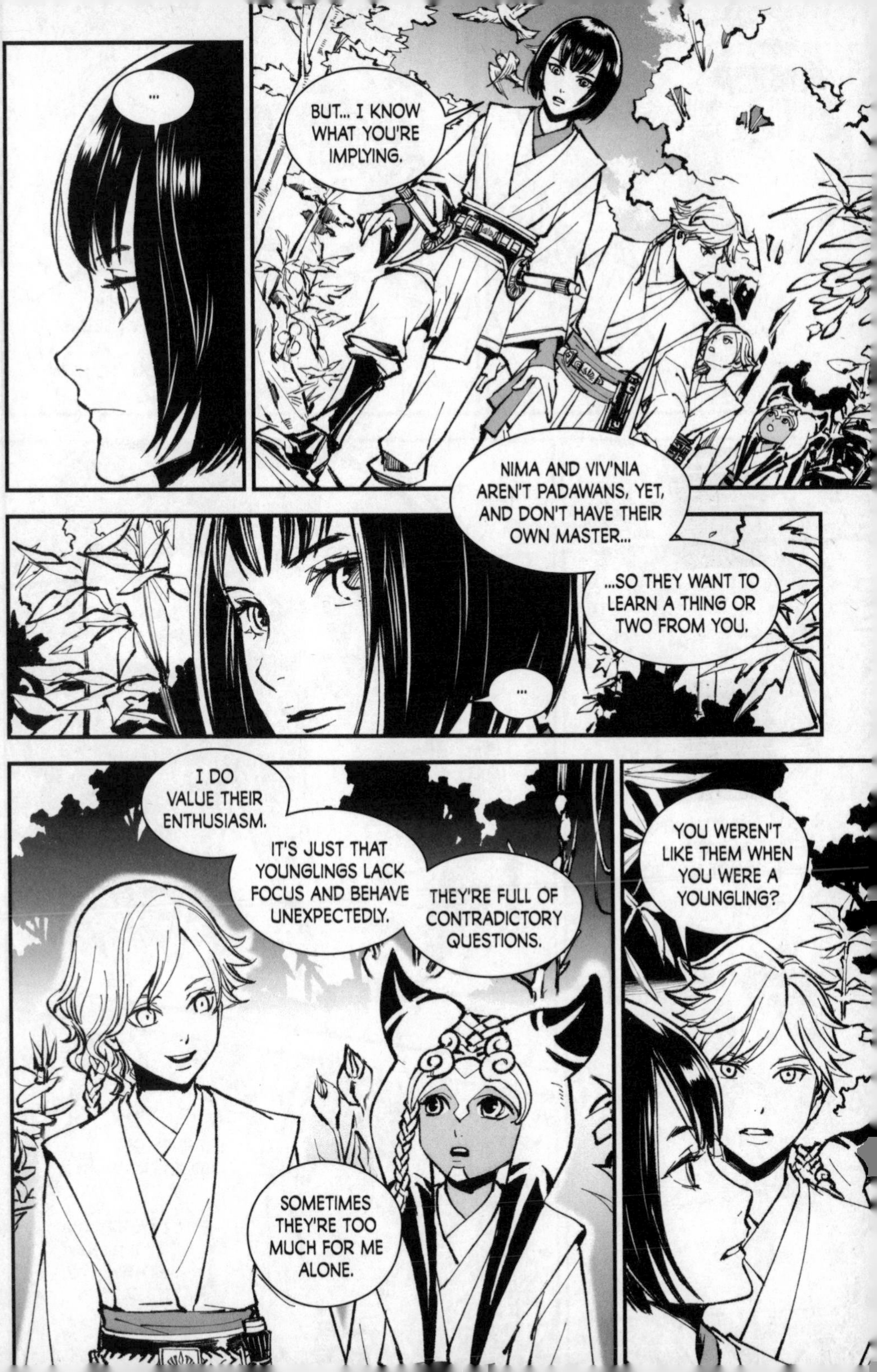
...
BUT... I KNOW WHAT YOU'RE IMPLYING.
NIMA AND VIV'NIA AREN'T PADAWANS, YET, AND DON'T HAVE THEIR OWN MASTER...
...SO THEY WANT TO LEARN A THING OR TWO FROM YOU.
...
I DO VALUE THEIR ENTHUSIASM.
IT'S JUST THAT YOUNGLINGS LACK FOCUS AND BEHAVE UNEXPECTEDLY.
THEY'RE FULL OF CONTRADICTORY QUESTIONS.
SOMETIMES THEY'RE TOO MUCH FOR ME ALONE.
YOU WEREN'T LIKE THEM WHEN YOU WERE A YOUNGLING?

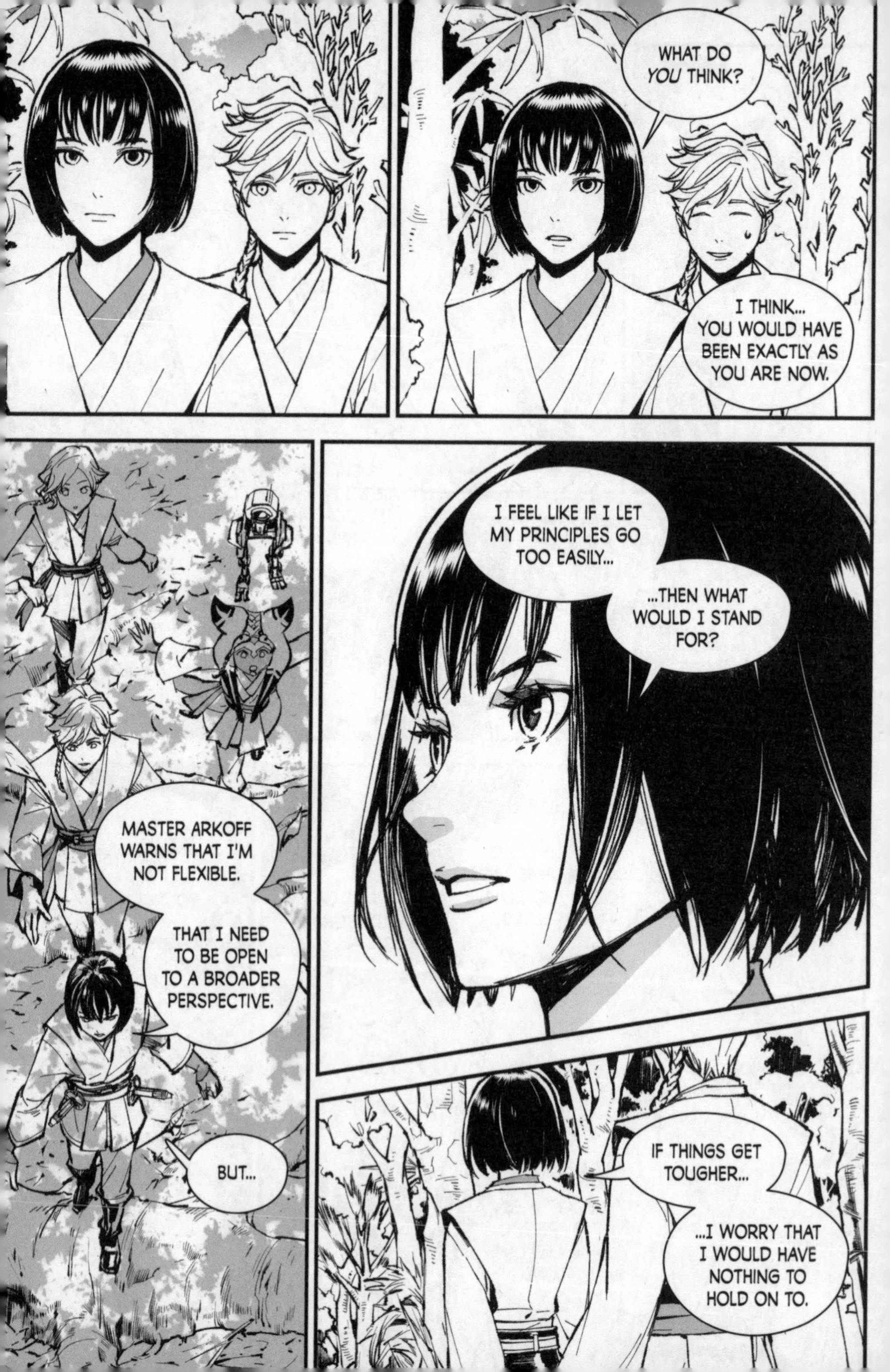
WHAT DO YOU THINK?
I THINK... YOU WOULD HAVE BEEN EXACTLY AS YOU ARE NOW.
MASTER ARKOFF WARNS THAT I'M NOT FLEXIBLE.
THAT I NEED TO BE OPEN TO A BROADER PERSPECTIVE.
BUT...
I FEEL LIKE IF I LET MY PRINCIPLES GO TOO EASILY...
...THEN WHAT WOULD I STAND FOR?
IF THINGS GET TOUGHER...
...I WORRY THAT I WOULD HAVE NOTHING TO HOLD ON TO.

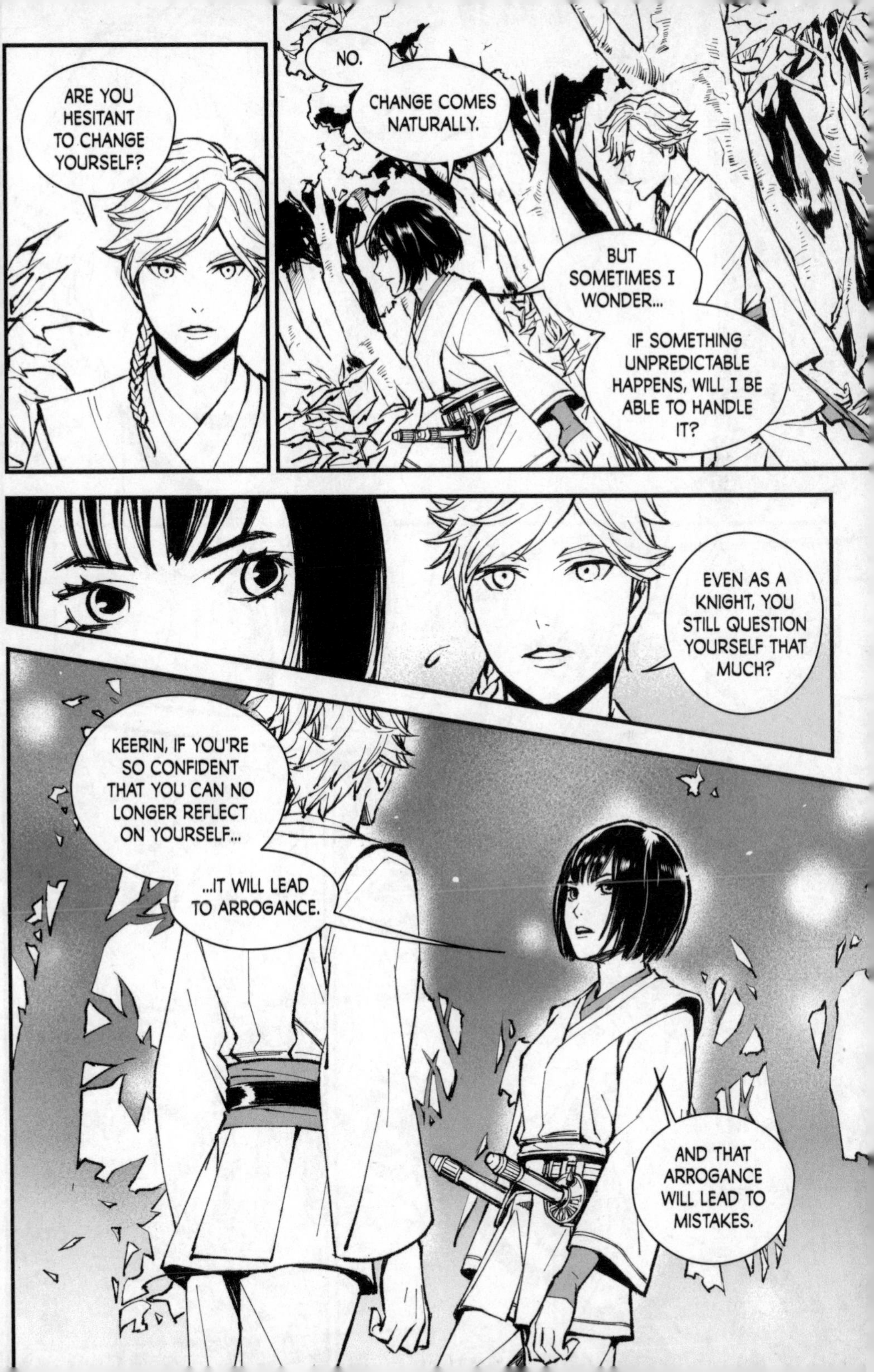
ARE YOU HESITANT TO CHANGE YOURSELF?
NO.
CHANGE COMES NATURALLY.
BUT SOMETIMES I WONDER...
IF SOMETHING UNPREDICTABLE HAPPENS, WILL I BE ABLE TO HANDLE IT?
EVEN AS A KNIGHT, YOU STILL QUESTION YOURSELF THAT MUCH?
KEERIN, IF YOU'RE SO CONFIDENT THAT YOU CAN NO LONGER REFLECT ON YOURSELF...
...IT WILL LEAD TO ARROGANCE.
AND THAT ARROGANCE WILL LEAD TO MISTAKES.

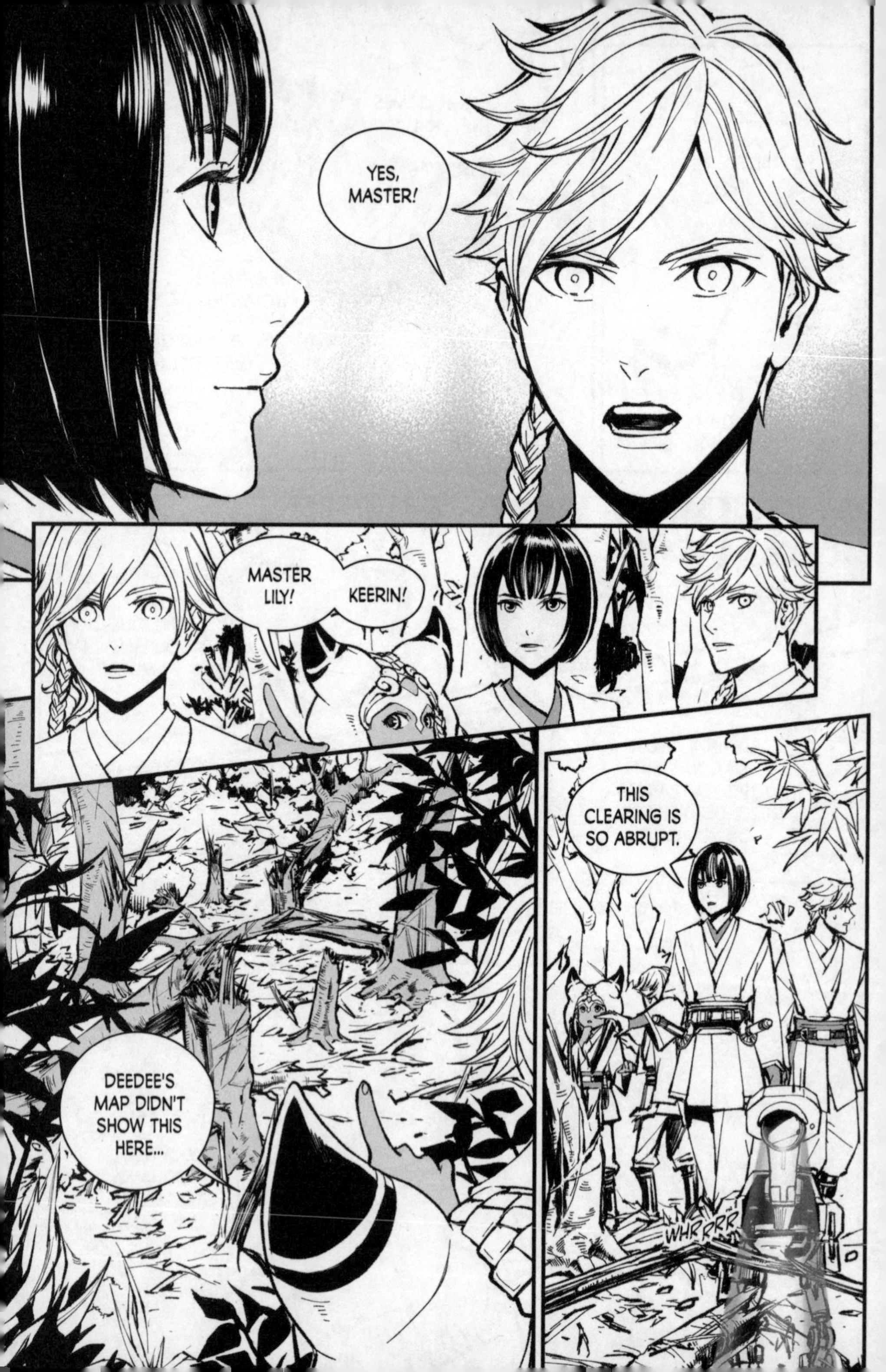
YES, MASTER!
MASTER LILY!
KEERIN!
THIS CLEARING IS SO ABRUPT.
DEEDEE'S MAP DIDN'T SHOW THIS HERE...
WHRRRR

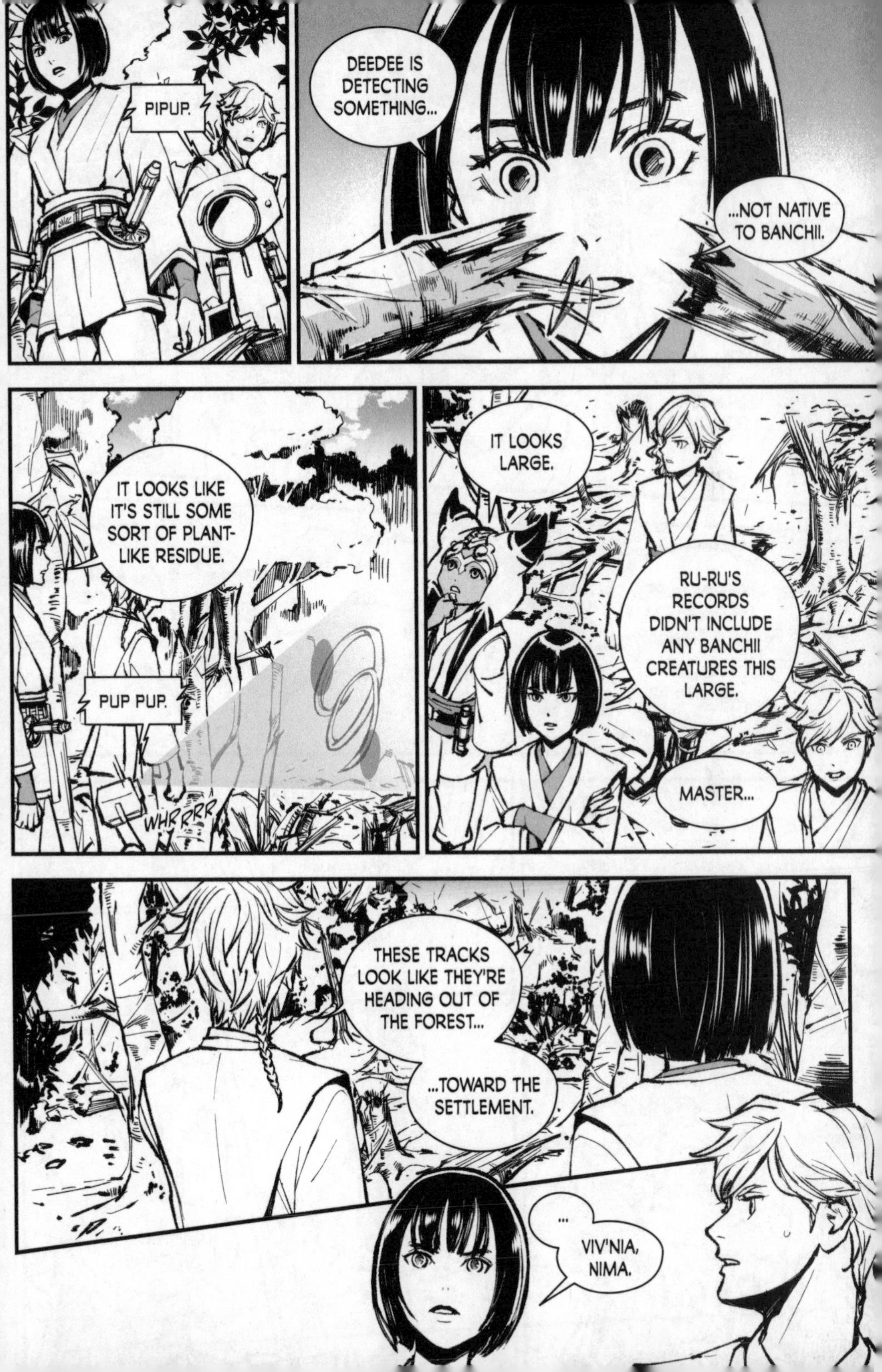
PIPUP.
DEEDEE IS DETECTING SOMETHING...
...NOT NATIVE TO BANCHII.
IT LOOKS LIKE IT'S STILL SOME SORT OF PLANT-LIKE RESIDUE.
PUP PUP.
WHRRRR
IT LOOKS LARGE.
RU-RU'S RECORDS DIDN'T INCLUDE ANY BANCHII CREATURES THIS LARGE.
MASTER...
THESE TRACKS LOOK LIKE THEY'RE HEADING OUT OF THE FOREST...
...TOWARD THE SETTLEMENT.
...
VIV'NIA, NIMA.

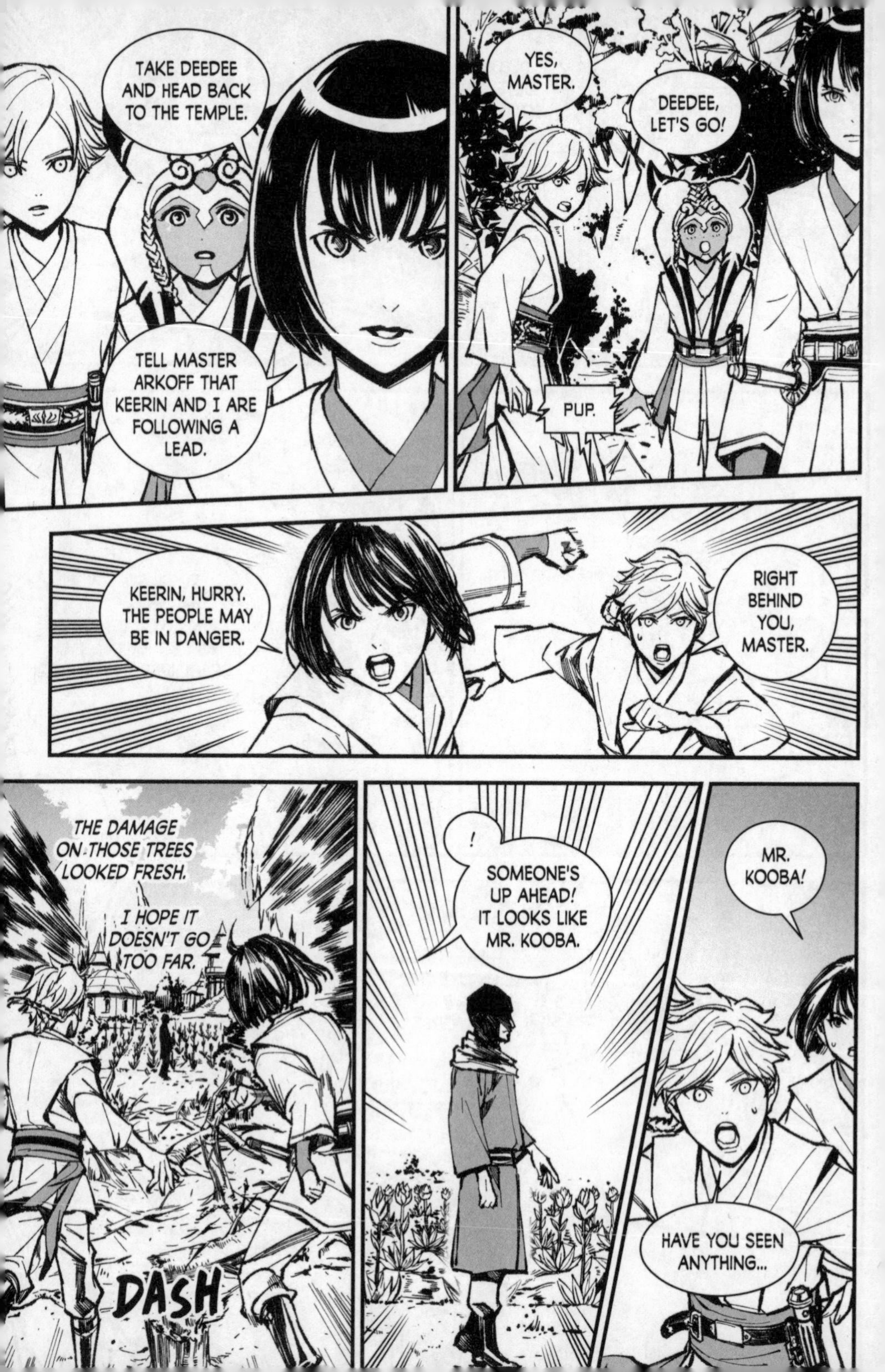
TAKE DEEDEE AND HEAD BACK TO THE TEMPLE.
TELL MASTER ARKOFF THAT KEERIN AND I ARE FOLLOWING A LEAD.
YES, MASTER.
DEEDEE, LET'S GO!
PUP.
KEERIN, HURRY. THE PEOPLE MAY BE IN DANGER.
RIGHT BEHIND YOU, MASTER.
THE DAMAGE ON THOSE TREES LOOKED FRESH.
I HOPE IT DOESN'T GO TOO FAR.
DASH
!
SOMEONE'S UP AHEAD! IT LOOKS LIKE MR. KOOBA.
MR. KOOBA!
HAVE YOU SEEN ANYTHING...

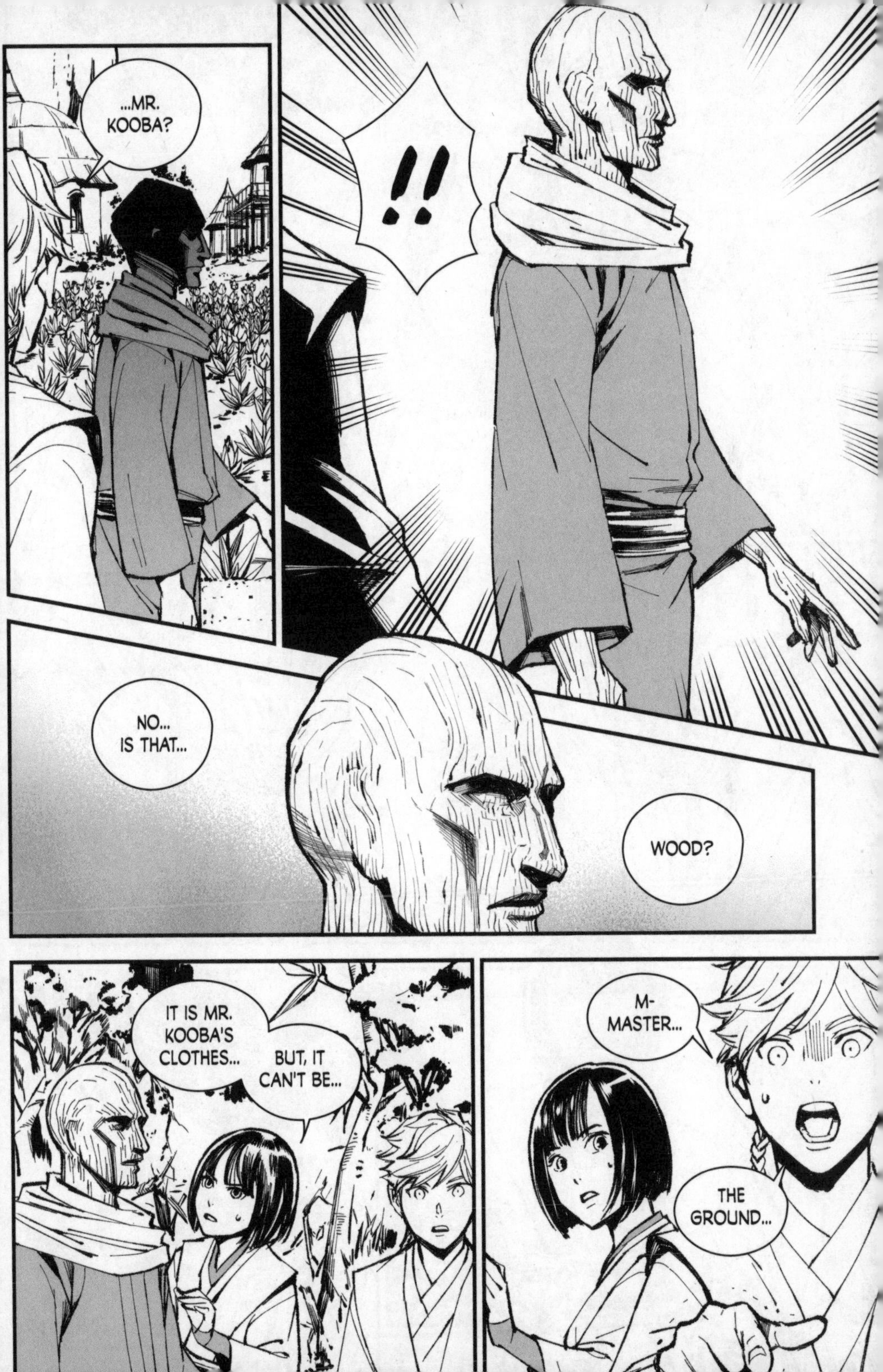
...MR. KOOBA?
!!
NO... IS THAT...
WOOD?
IT IS MR. KOOBA'S CLOTHES...
BUT, IT CAN'T BE...
M-MASTER...
THE GROUND...

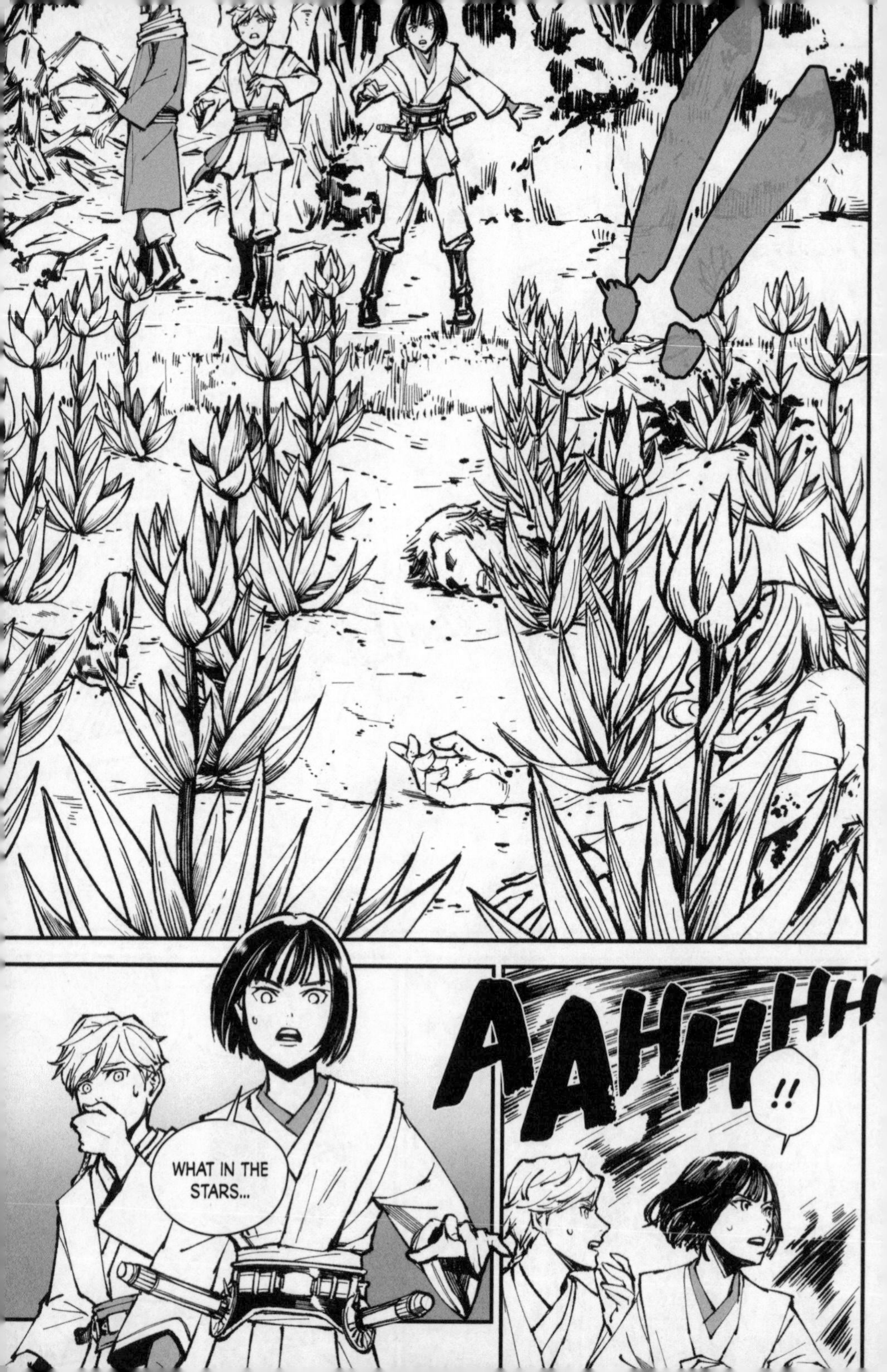
AAHHHH
!!
WHAT IN THE STARS...

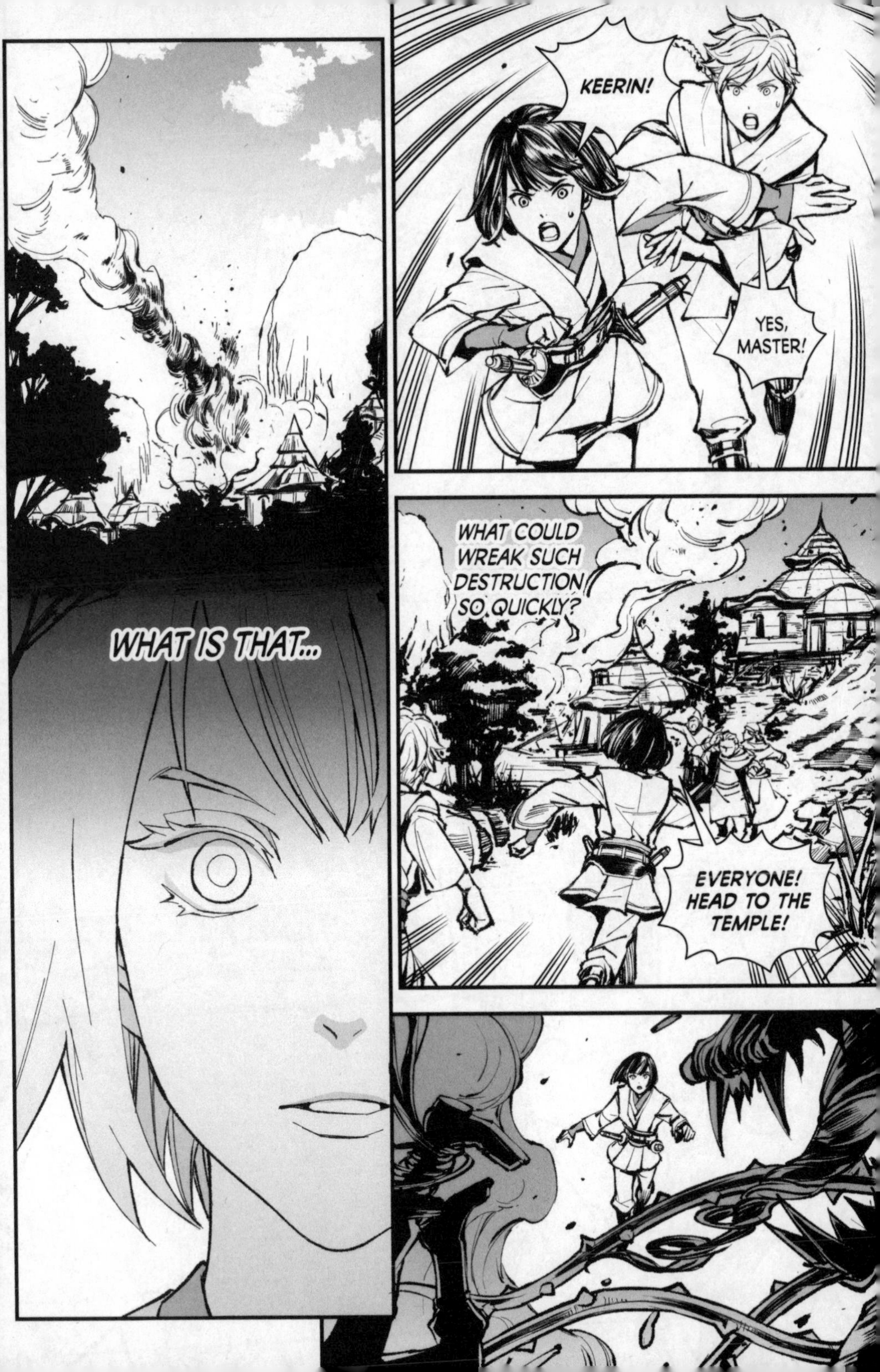
KEERIN!
YES, MASTER!
WHAT COULD WREAK SUCH DESTRUCTION SO QUICKLY?
EVERYONE! HEAD TO THE TEMPLE!
WHAT IS THAT...

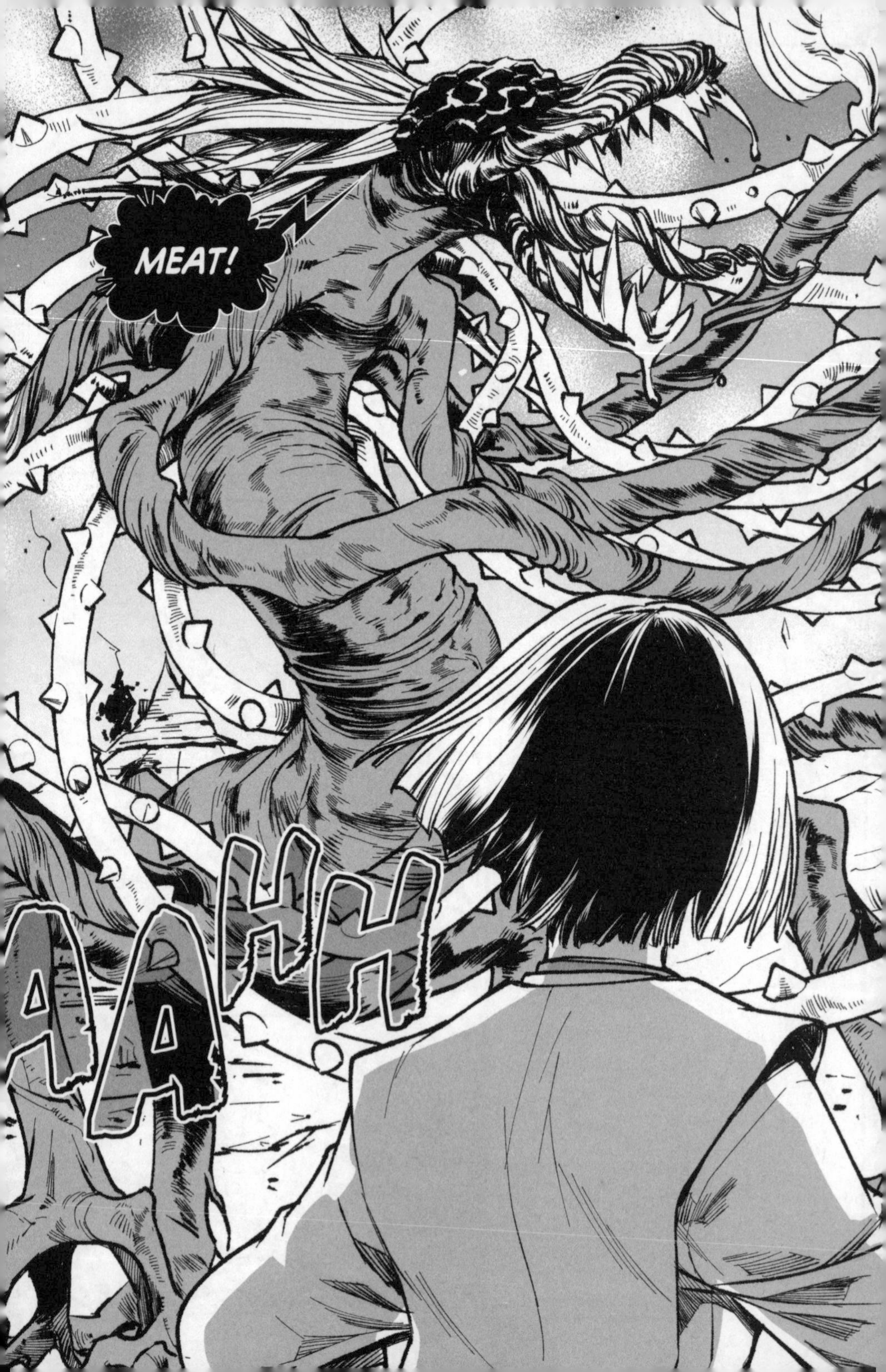
MEAT!
AAHH

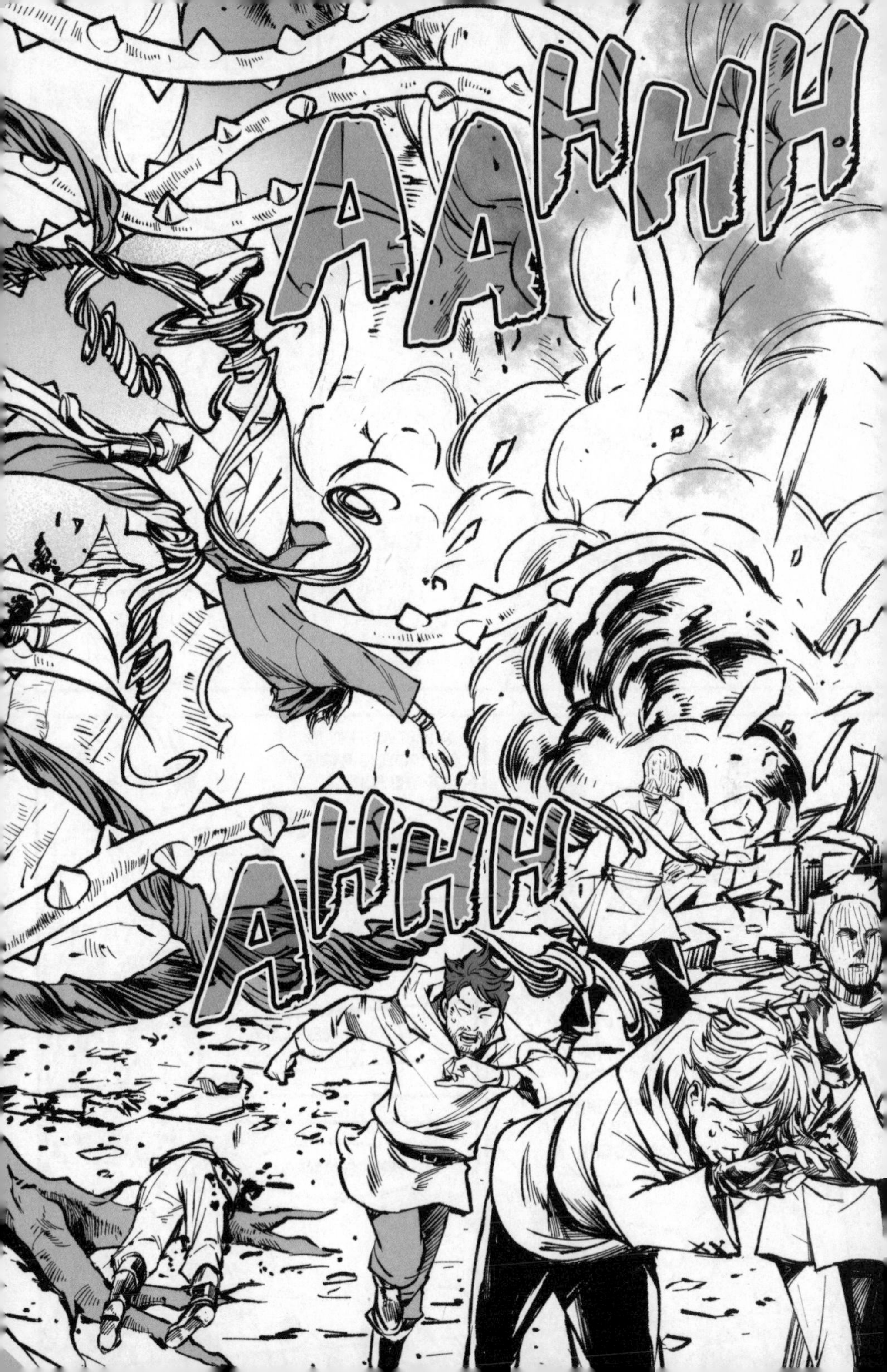
AAHHHH
AHHH

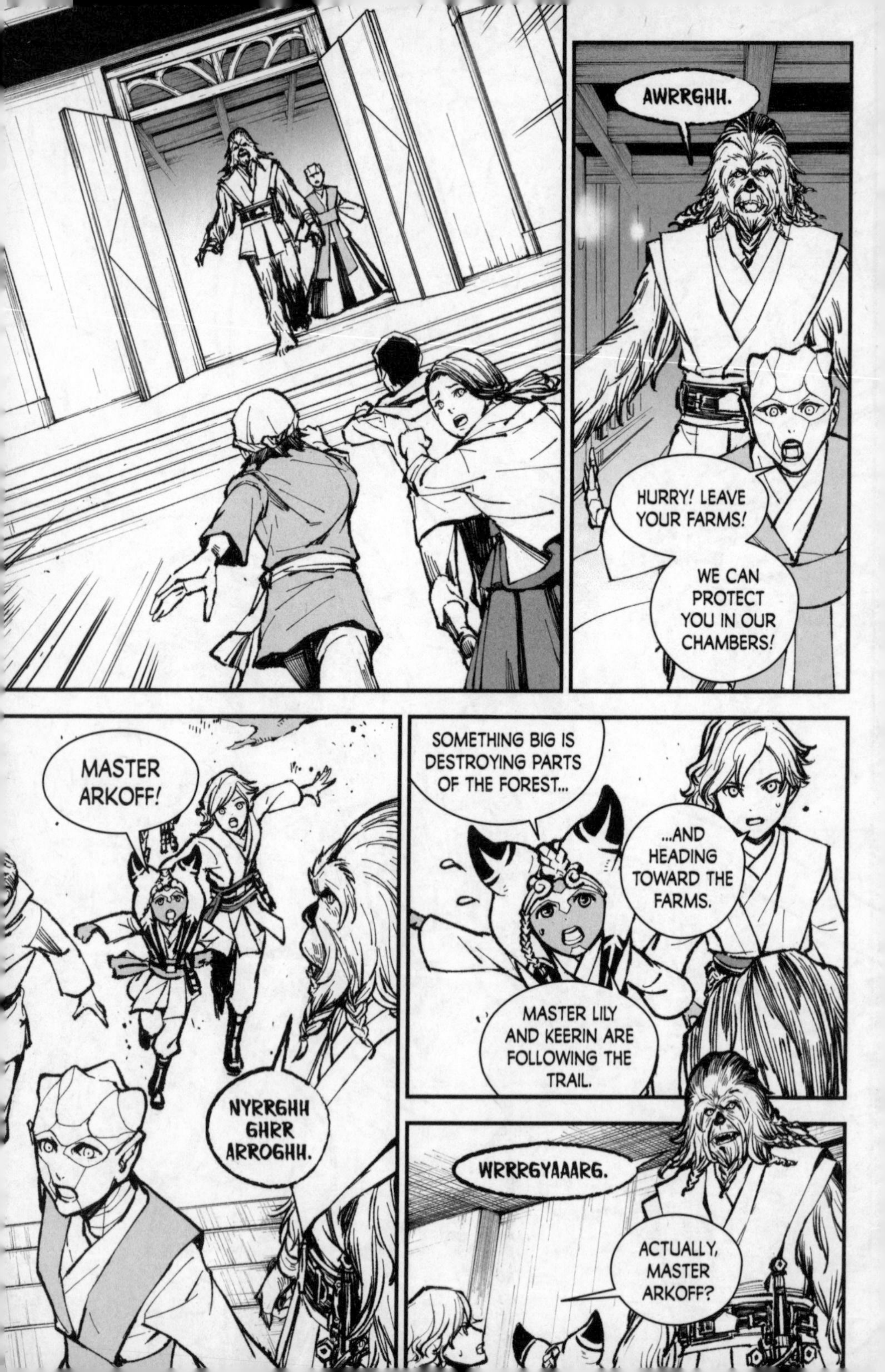
AWRRGHH.
HURRY! LEAVE YOUR FARMS!
WE CAN PROTECT YOU IN OUR CHAMBERS!
MASTER ARKOFF!
NYRRGHH GHRR ARROGHH.
SOMETHING BIG IS DESTROYING PARTS OF THE FOREST...
...AND HEADING TOWARD THE FARMS.
MASTER LILY AND KEERIN ARE FOLLOWING THE TRAIL.
WRRRGYAAARG.
ACTUALLY, MASTER ARKOFF?

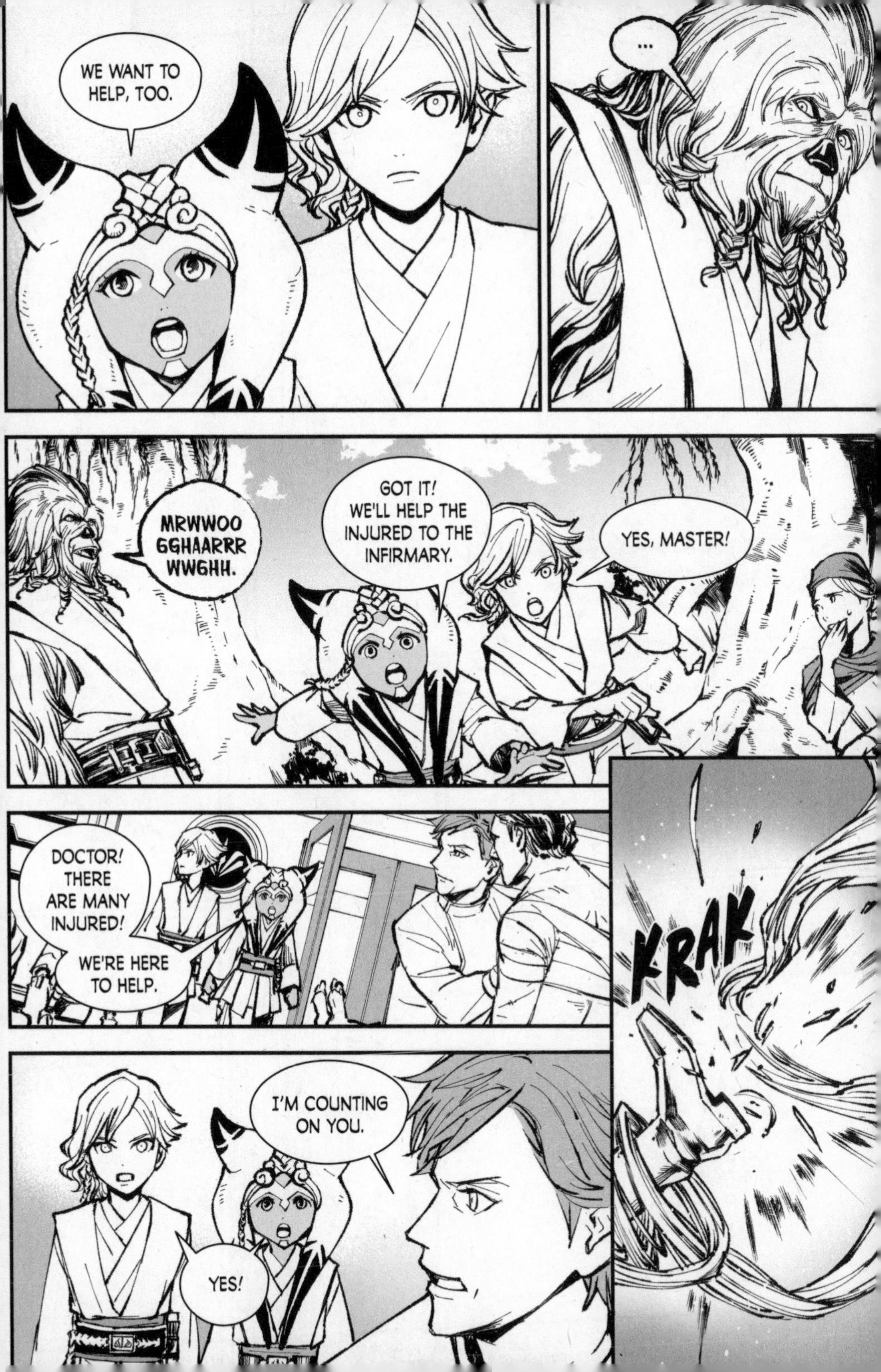
WE WANT TO HELP, TOO.
...
MRWWOO GGHAARRR WWGHH.
GOT IT! WE'LL HELP THE INJURED TO THE INFIRMARY.
YES, MASTER!
DOCTOR! THERE ARE MANY INJURED!
WE'RE HERE TO HELP.
I'M COUNTING ON YOU.
YES!
KRAK

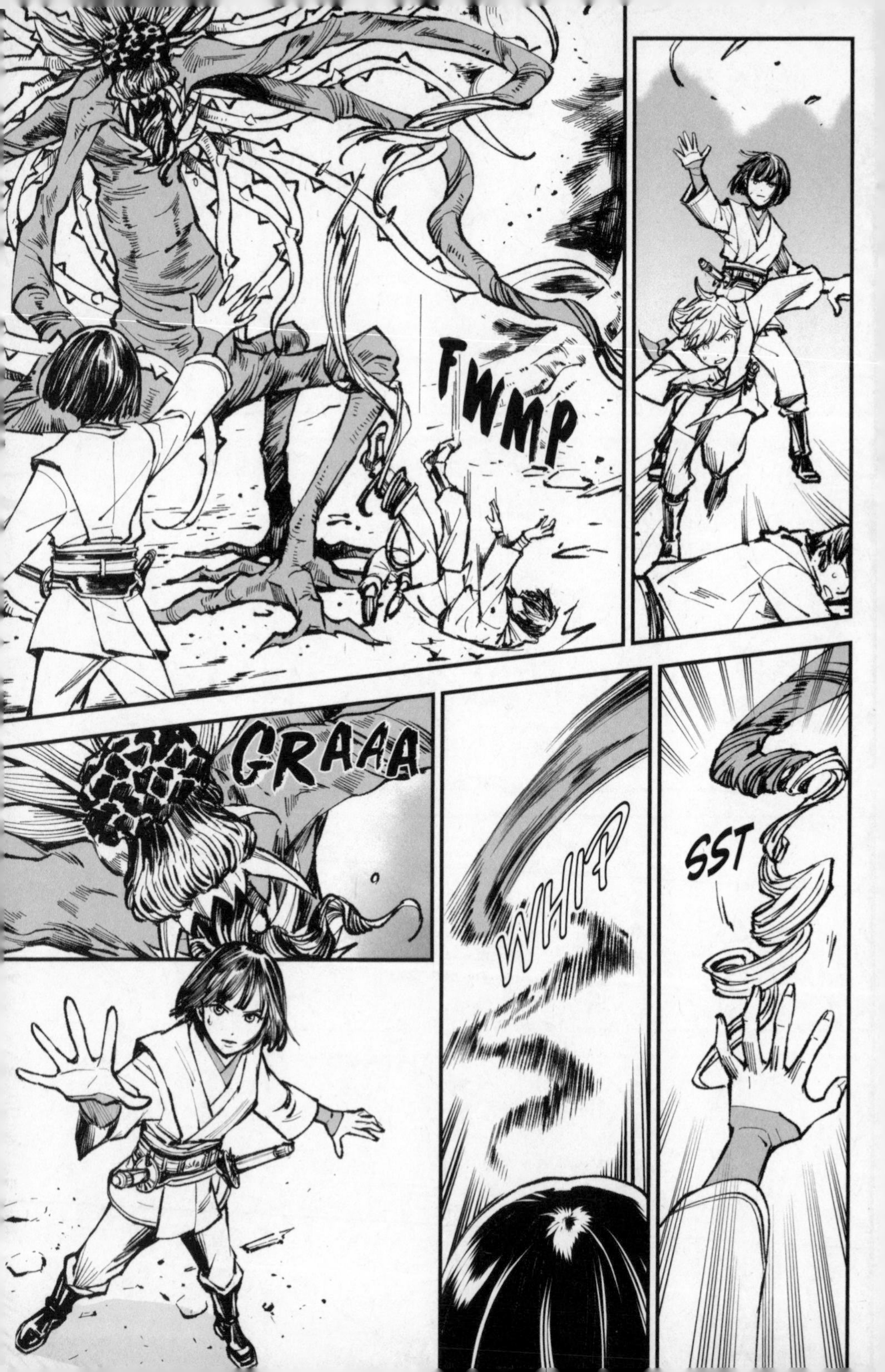
FWMP
GRAAA
WHIP
SST

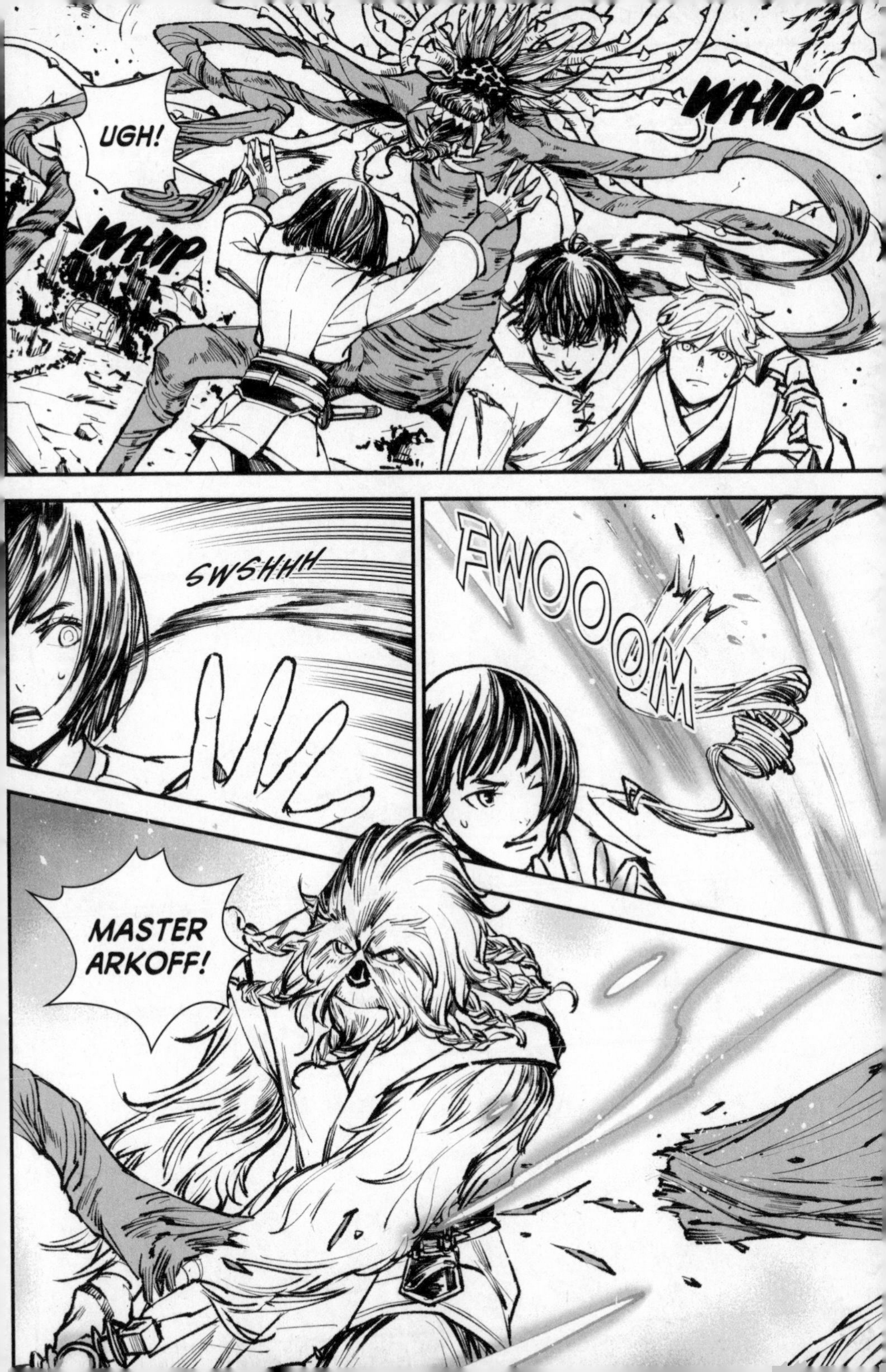
UGH!
WHIP
WHIP
SWSHHH
FWOOOM
MASTER ARKOFF!

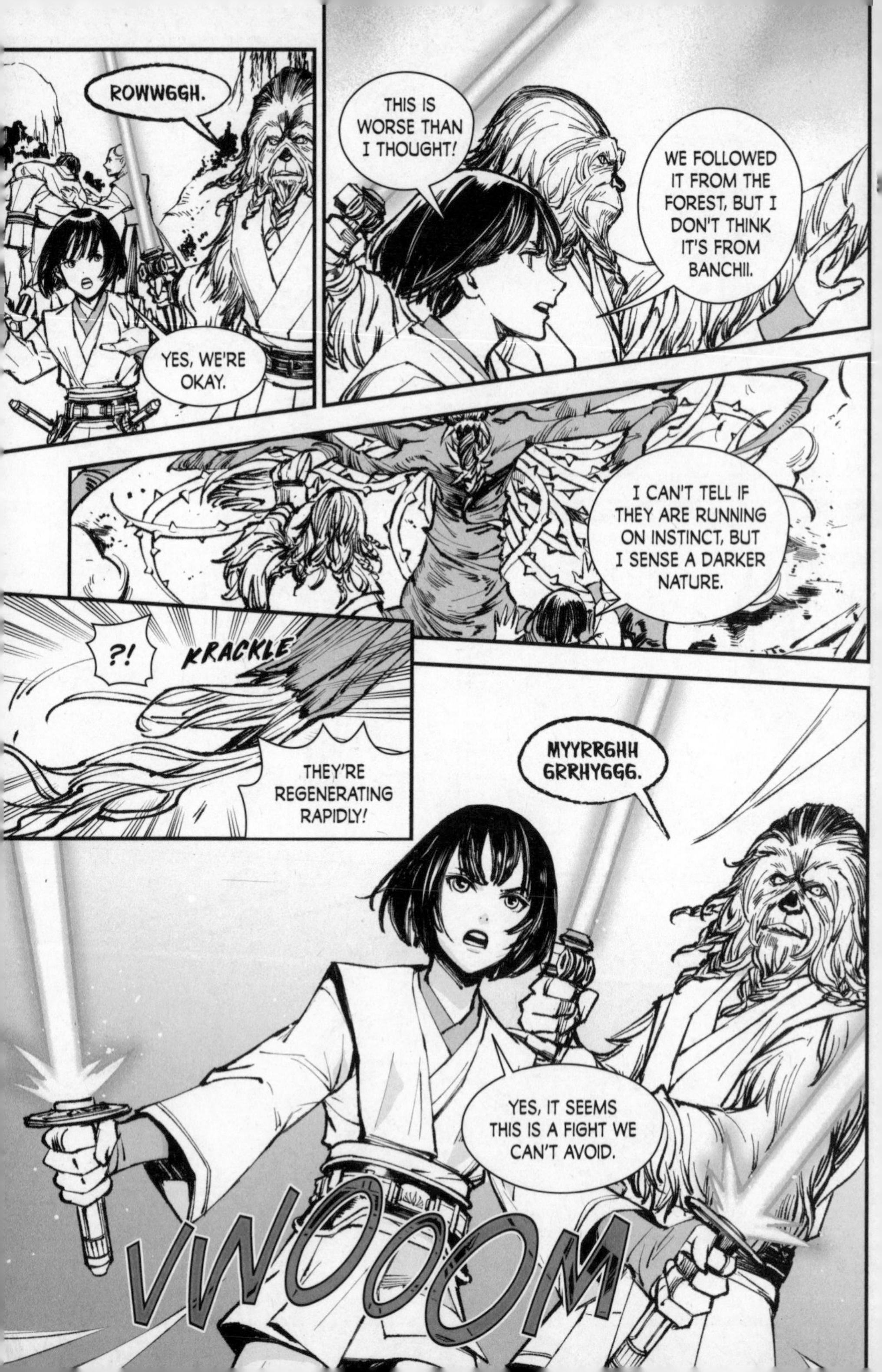
ROWWGGH.
YES, WE'RE OKAY.
THIS IS WORSE THAN I THOUGHT!
WE FOLLOWED IT FROM THE FOREST, BUT I DON'T THINK IT'S FROM BANCHII.
I CAN'T TELL IF THEY ARE RUNNING ON INSTINCT, BUT I SENSE A DARKER NATURE.
?!
KRACKLE
THEY'RE REGENERATING RAPIDLY!
MYYRRGHH GRRHYGGG.
YES, IT SEEMS THIS IS A FIGHT WE CAN'T AVOID.
VWOOOM

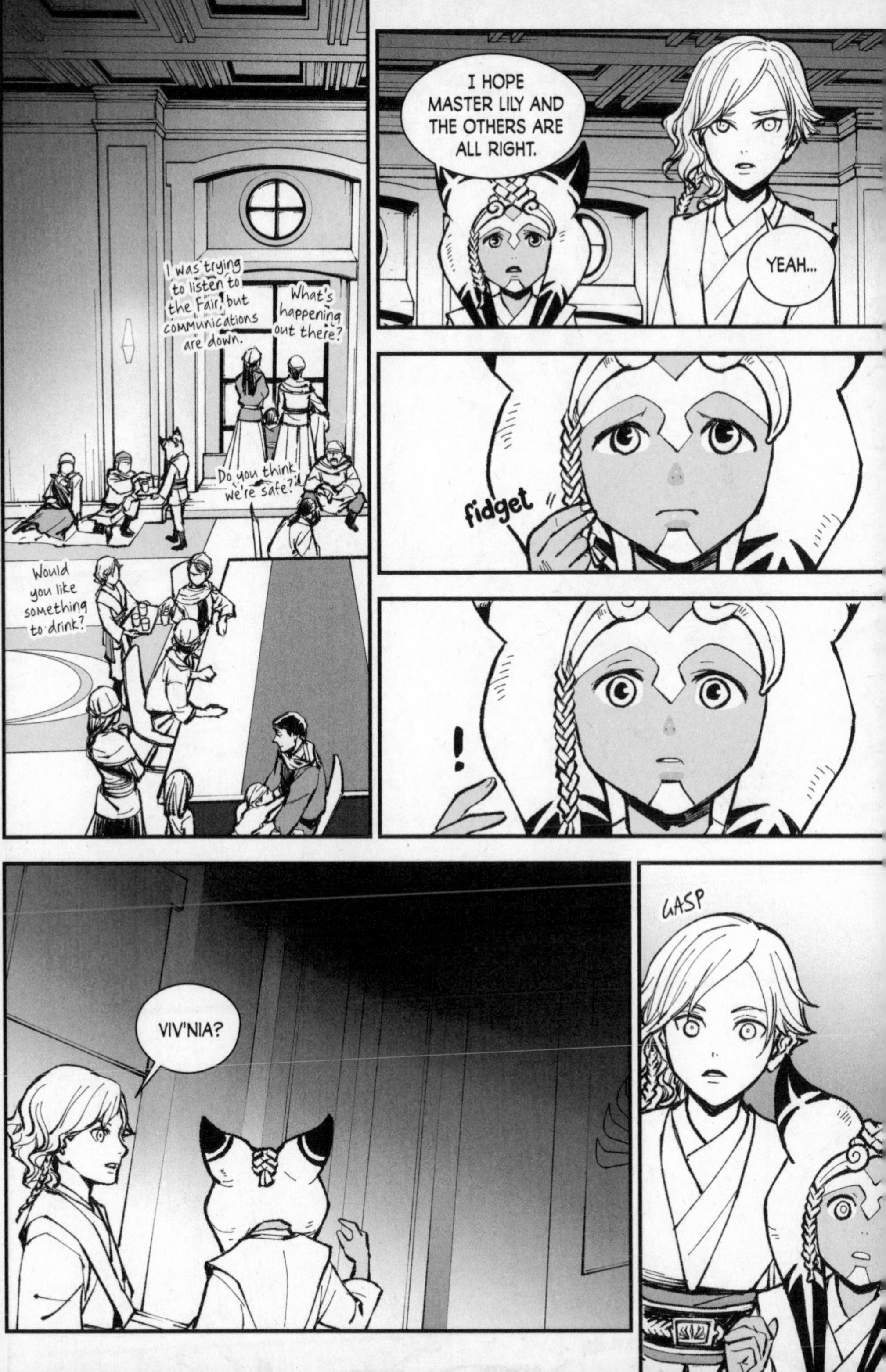

I was trying to listen to the Fair, but communications are down.
What's happening out there?
Do you think we're safe?
Would you like something to drink?
I HOPE MASTER LILY AND THE OTHERS ARE ALL RIGHT.
YEAH...
fidget
!
VIV'NIA?
GASP

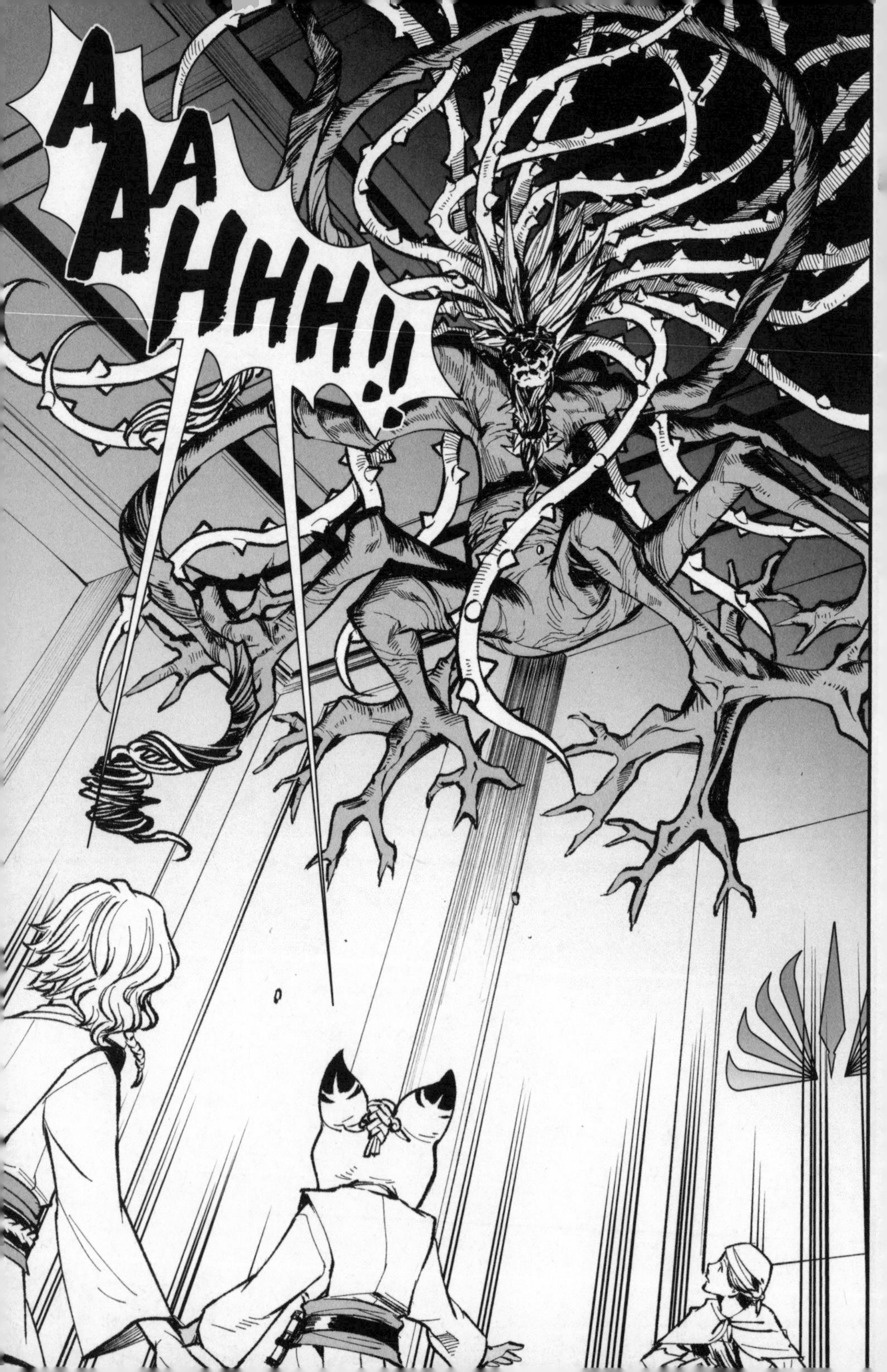
AAAHHHH!!

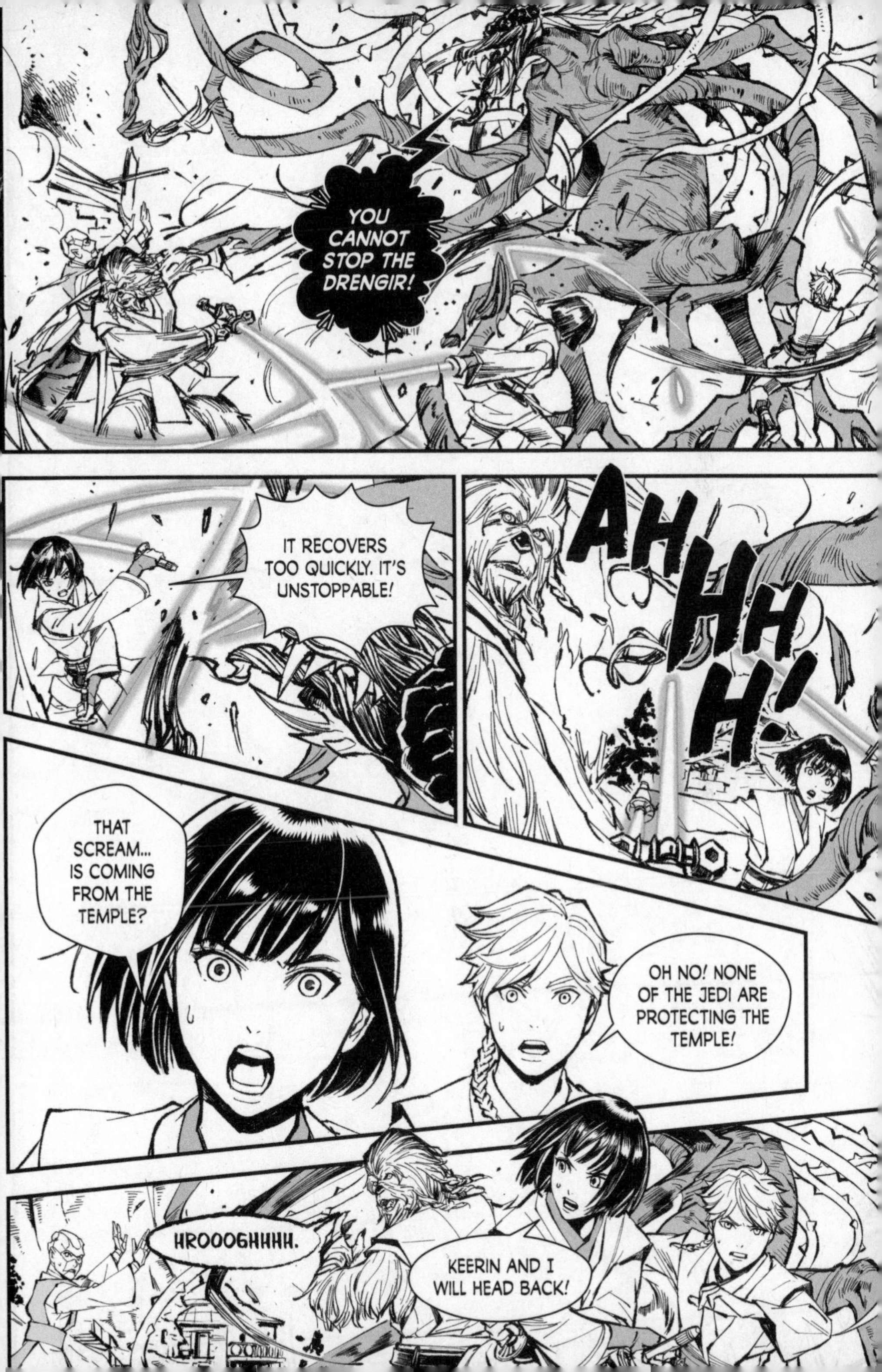
YOU CANNOT STOP THE DRENGIR!
IT RECOVERS TOO QUICKLY. IT'S UNSTOPPABLE!
AHHHHH!
THAT SCREAM... IS COMING FROM THE TEMPLE?
OH NO! NONE OF THE JEDI ARE PROTECTING THE TEMPLE!
HROOOGHHHH.
KEERIN AND I WILL HEAD BACK!

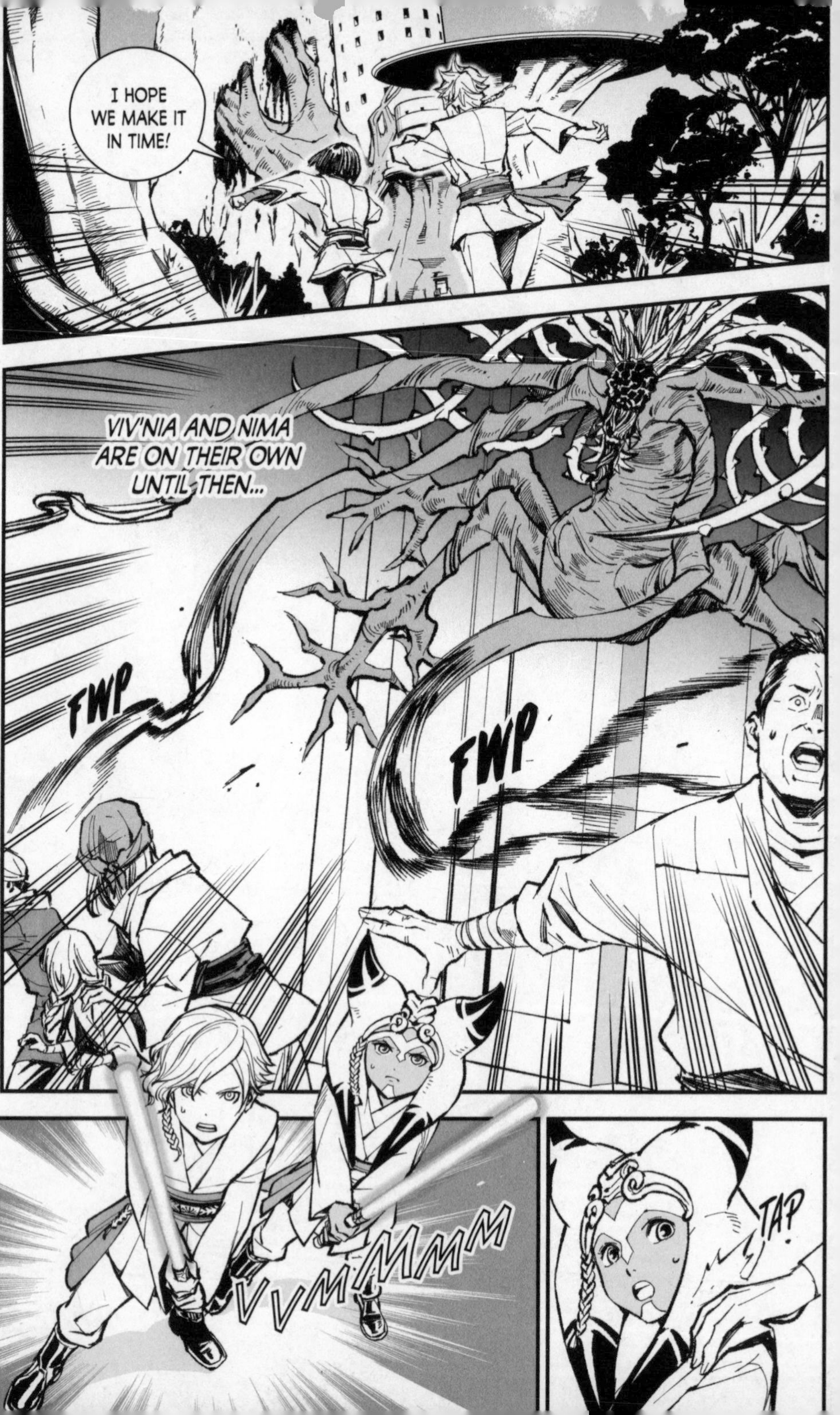
I HOPE WE MAKE IT IN TIME!
VIV'NIA AND NIMA ARE ON THEIR OWN UNTIL THEN...
FWP
FWP
VVMMMMM
TAP

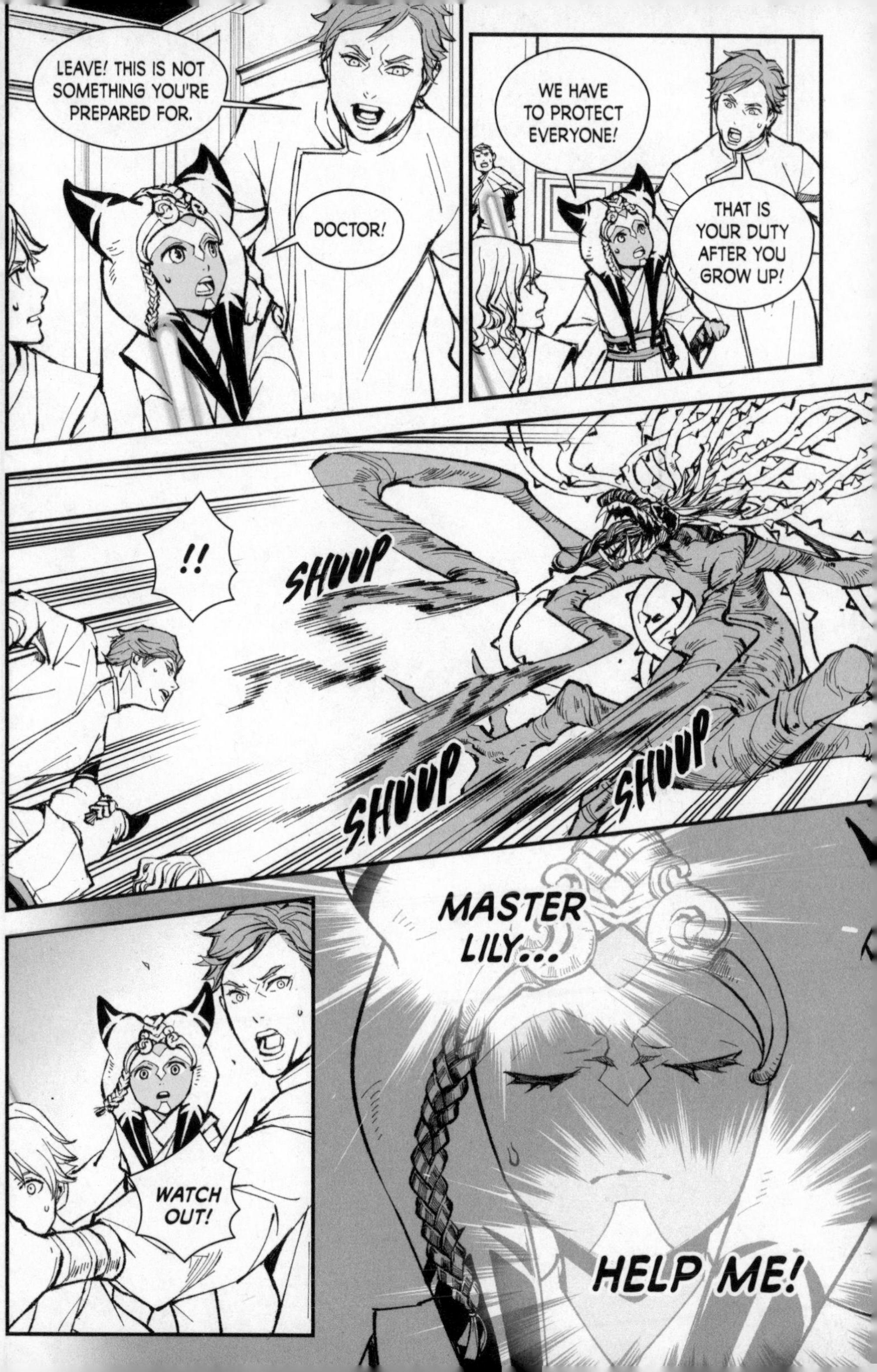
LEAVE! THIS IS NOT SOMETHING YOU'RE PREPARED FOR.
DOCTOR!
WE HAVE TO PROTECT EVERYONE!
THAT IS YOUR DUTY AFTER YOU GROW UP!
!!
SHUUP
SHUUP
SHUUP
MASTER LILY...
HELP ME!
WATCH OUT!

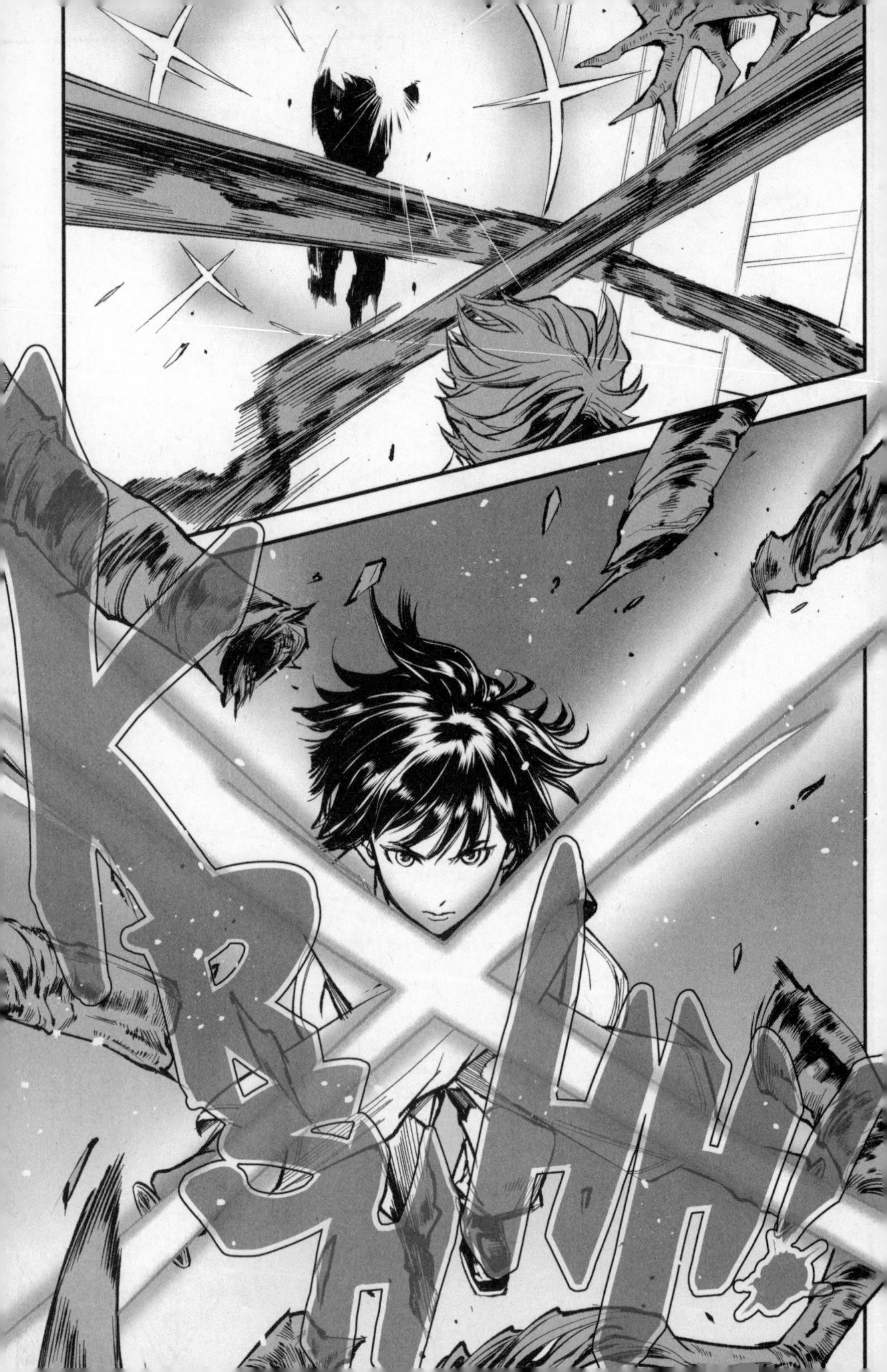

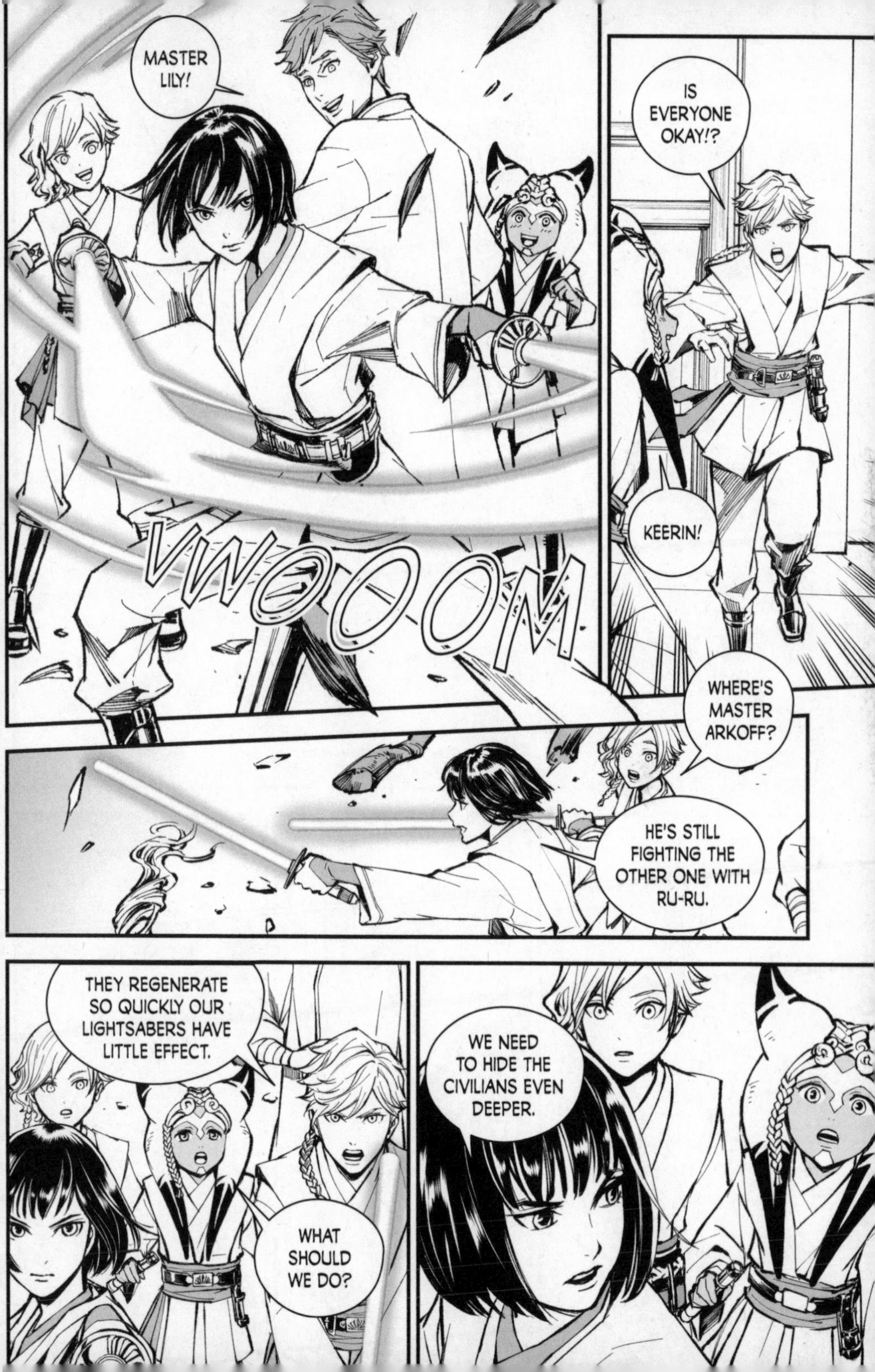
MASTER LILY!
VWOOOOM
IS EVERYONE OKAY!?
KEERIN!
WHERE'S MASTER ARKOFF?
HE'S STILL FIGHTING THE OTHER ONE WITH RU-RU.
THEY REGENERATE SO QUICKLY OUR LIGHTSABERS HAVE LITTLE EFFECT.
WHAT SHOULD WE DO?
WE NEED TO HIDE THE CIVILIANS EVEN DEEPER.

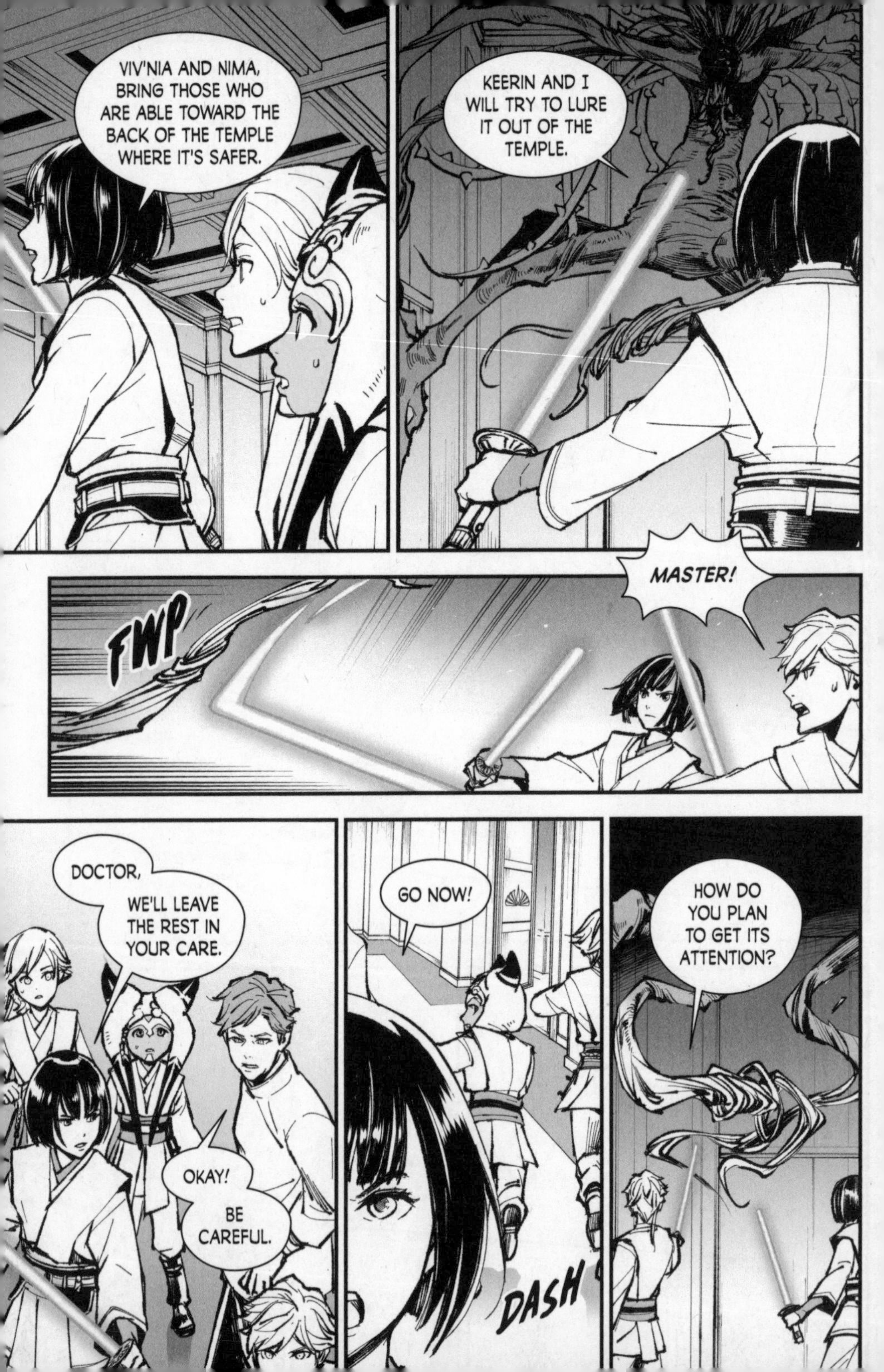
VIV'NIA AND NIMA, BRING THOSE WHO ARE ABLE TOWARD THE BACK OF THE TEMPLE WHERE IT'S SAFER.
KEERIN AND I WILL TRY TO LURE IT OUT OF THE TEMPLE.
FWP
MASTER!
DOCTOR,
WE'LL LEAVE THE REST IN YOUR CARE.
OKAY!
BE CAREFUL.
GO NOW!
DASH
HOW DO YOU PLAN TO GET ITS ATTENTION?

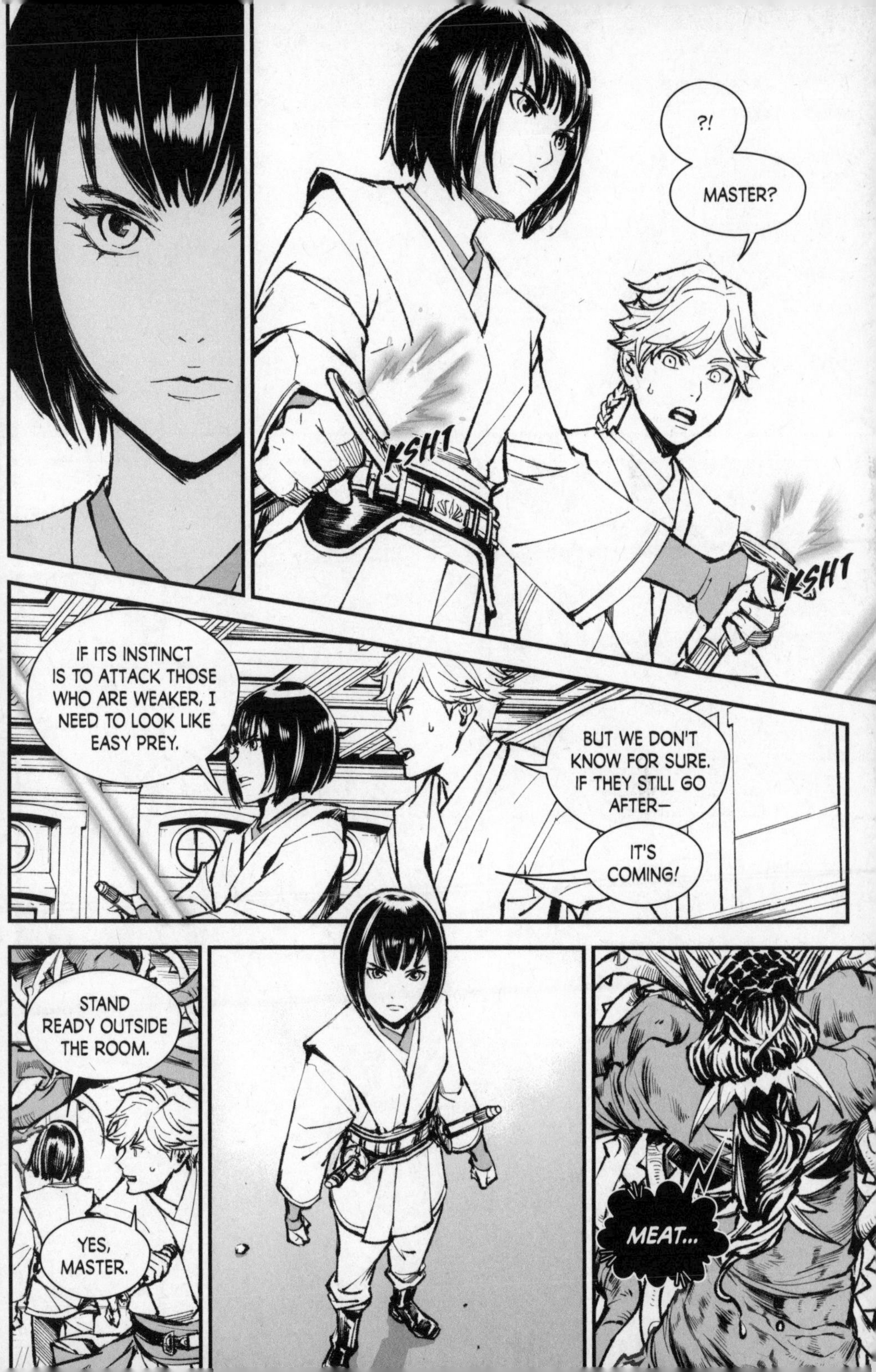
?!
MASTER?
KSHT
KSHT
IF ITS INSTINCT IS TO ATTACK THOSE WHO ARE WEAKER, I NEED TO LOOK LIKE EASY PREY.
BUT WE DON'T KNOW FOR SURE. IF THEY STILL GO AFTER—
IT'S COMING!
STAND READY OUTSIDE THE ROOM.
YES, MASTER.
MEAT...

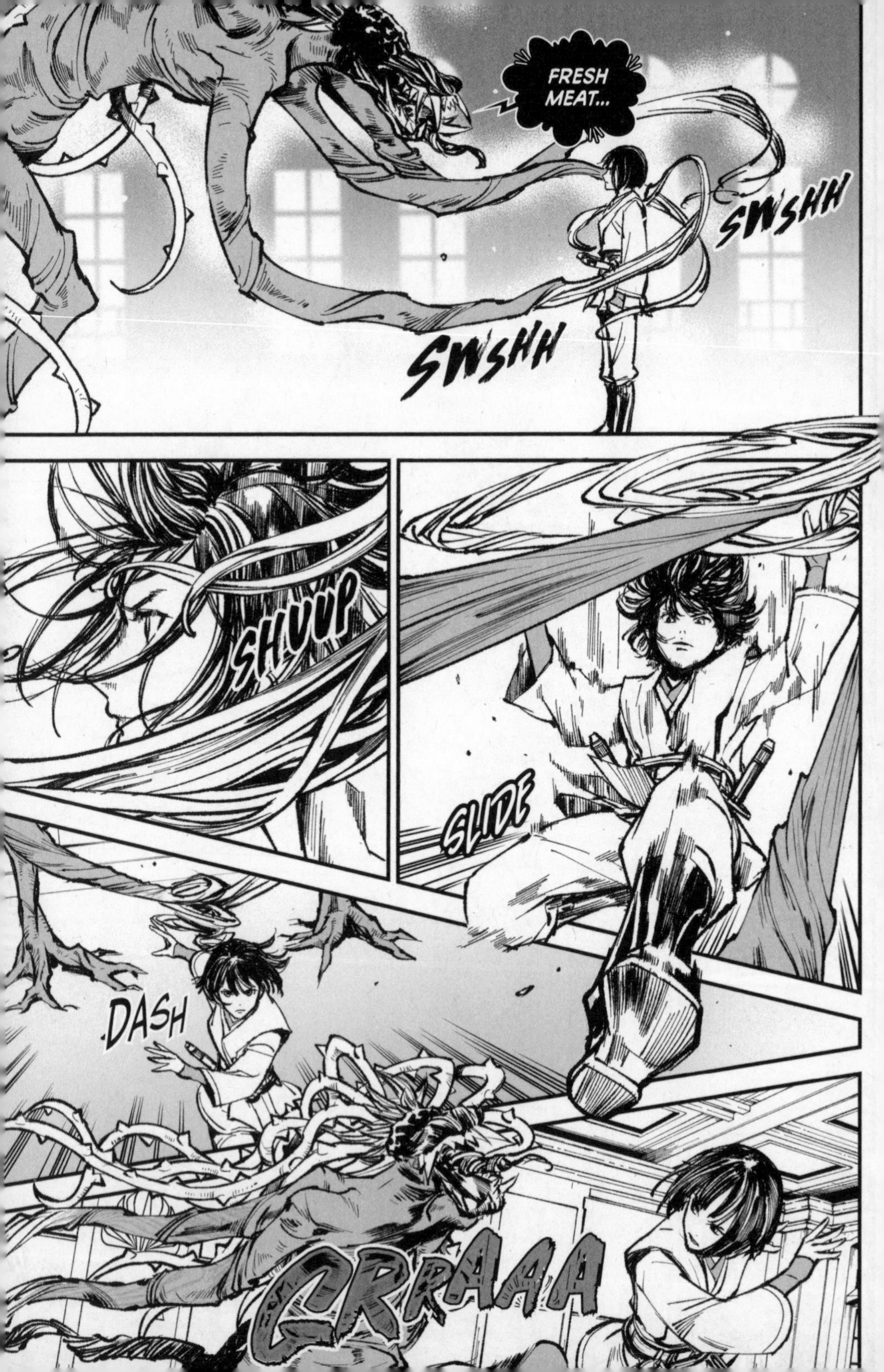
FRESH MEAT...
SWSHH
SWSHH
SLIDE
SHUUP
DASH
CRRAAAA

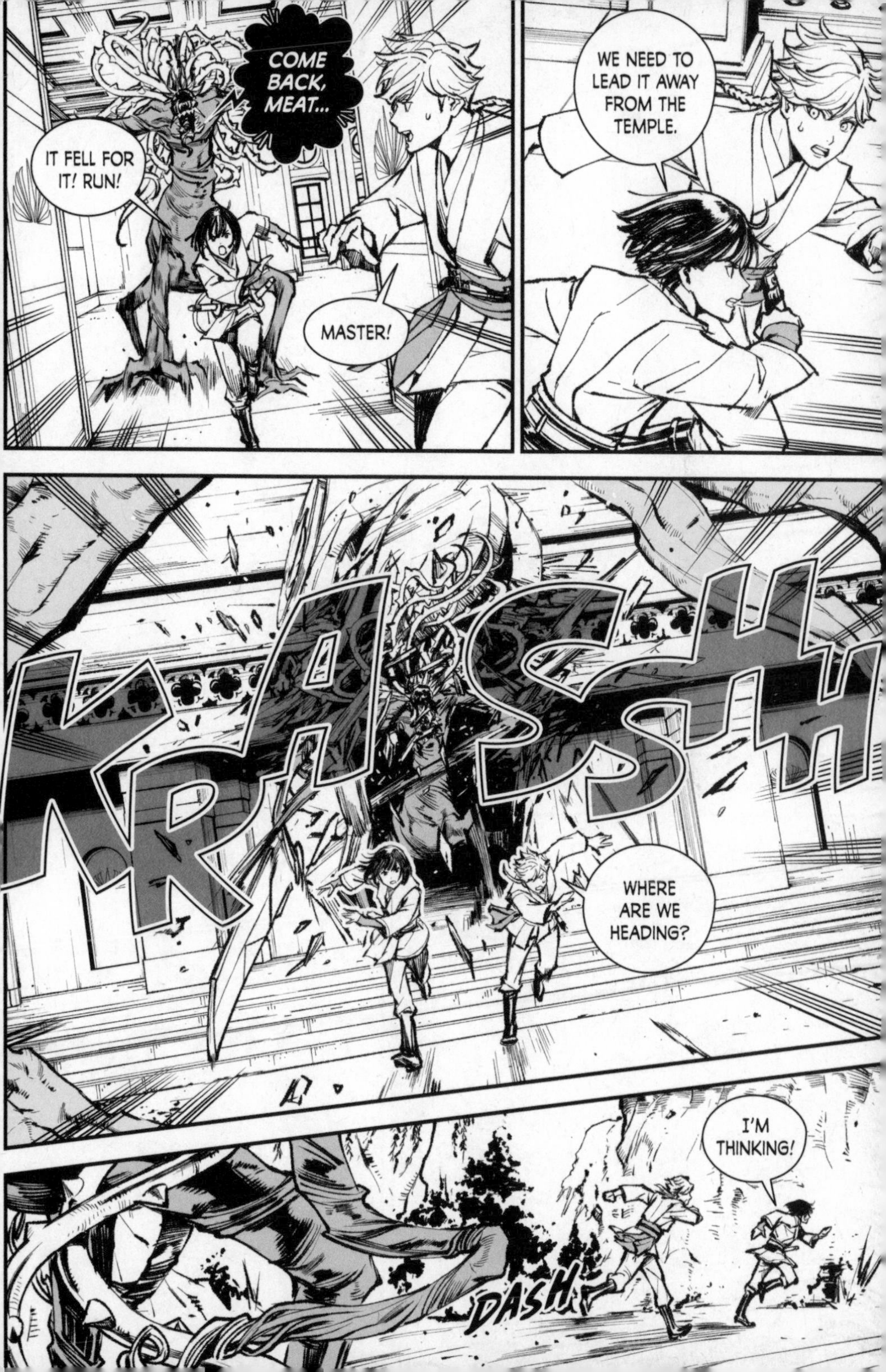
COME BACK, MEAT...
IT FELL FOR IT! RUN!
MASTER!
WE NEED TO LEAD IT AWAY FROM THE TEMPLE.
KRASH
WHERE ARE WE HEADING?
I'M THINKING!
DASH

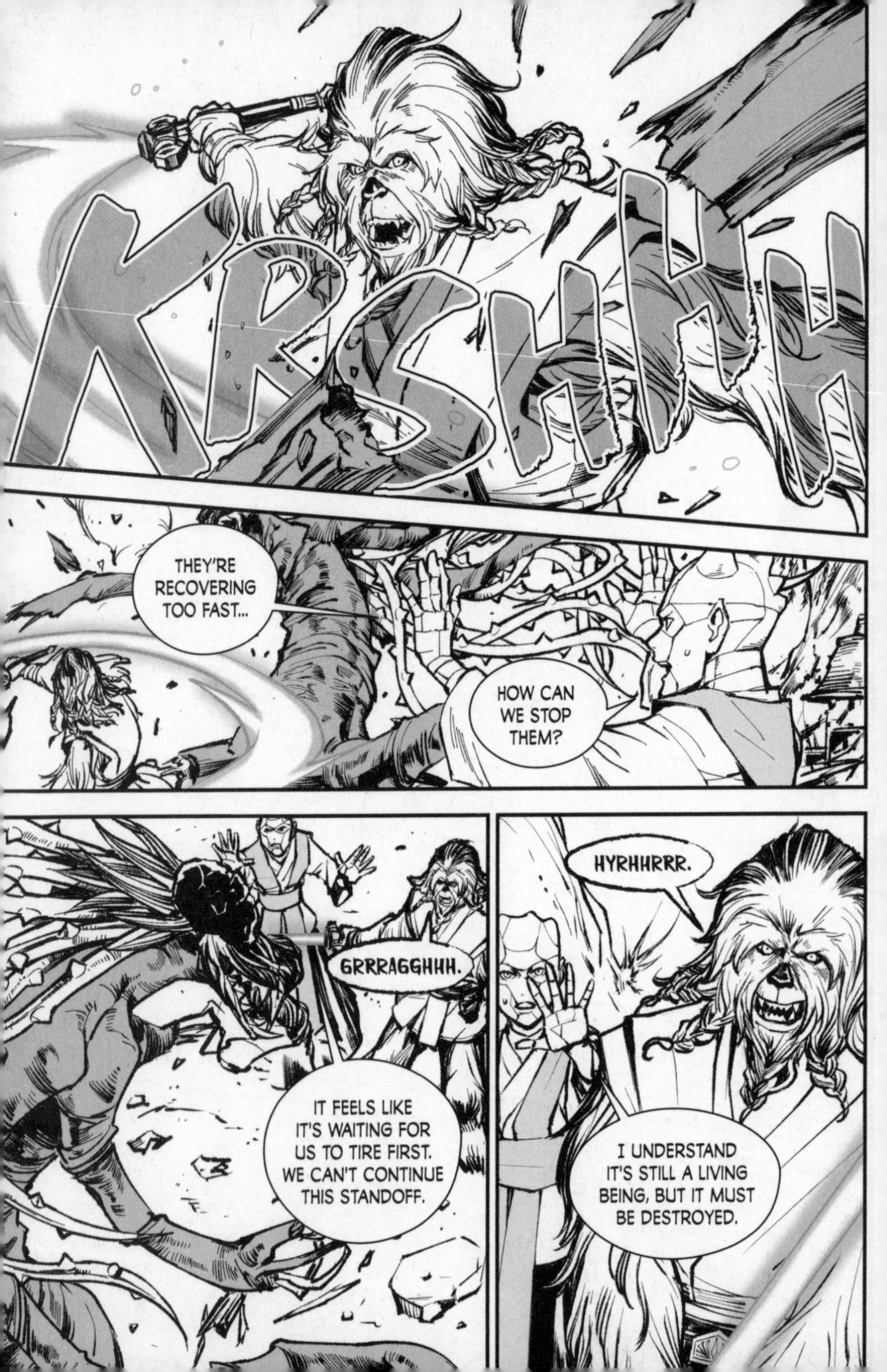
KRSHHH
THEY'RE RECOVERING TOO FAST...
HOW CAN WE STOP THEM?
GRRRAGGHHH.
IT FEELS LIKE IT'S WAITING FOR US TO TIRE FIRST. WE CAN'T CONTINUE THIS STANDOFF.
HYRHHRRR.
I UNDERSTAND IT'S STILL A LIVING BEING, BUT IT MUST BE DESTROYED.

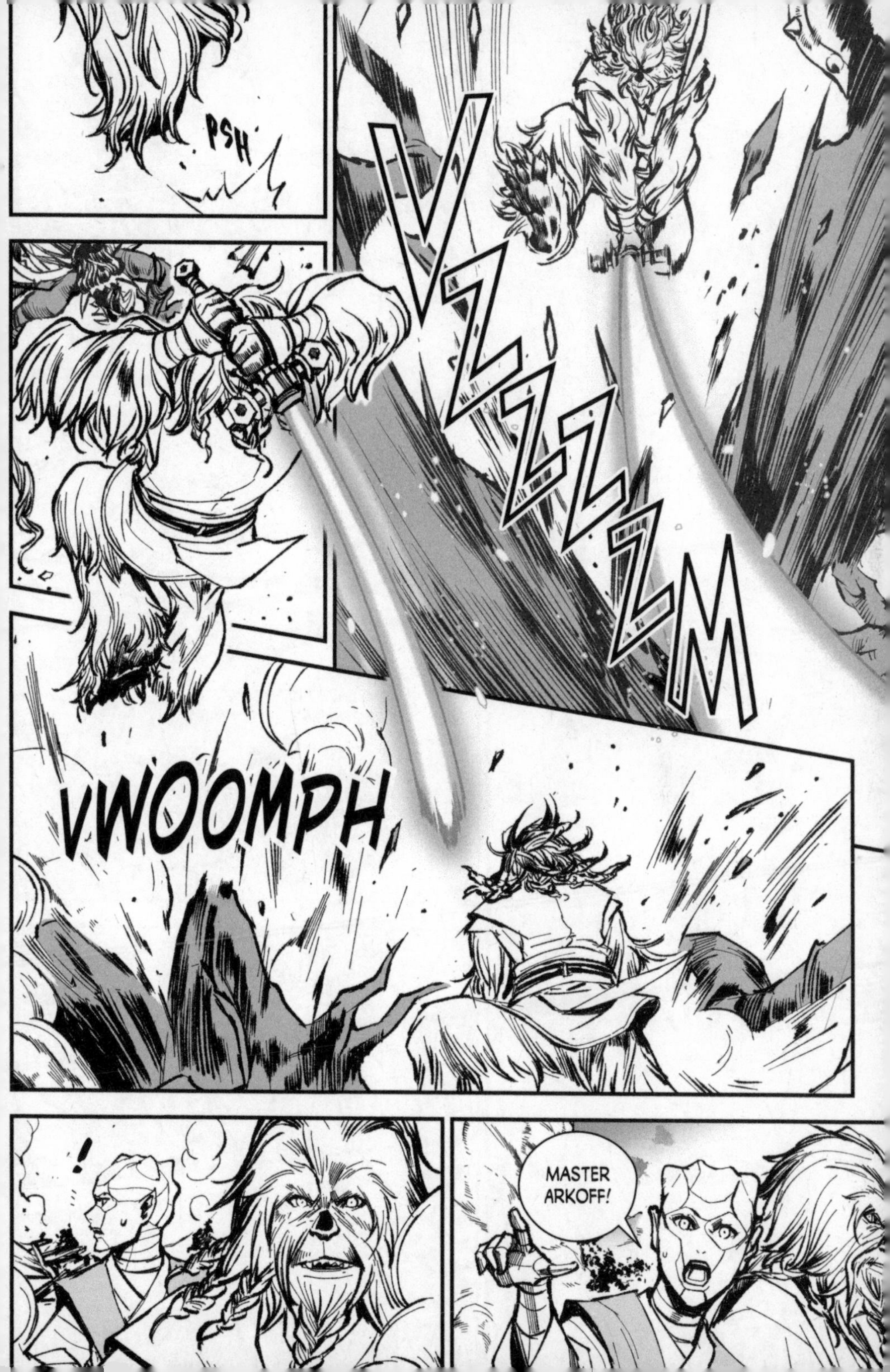
PSH
VZZZZM
VWOOMPH
!
MASTER ARKOFF!

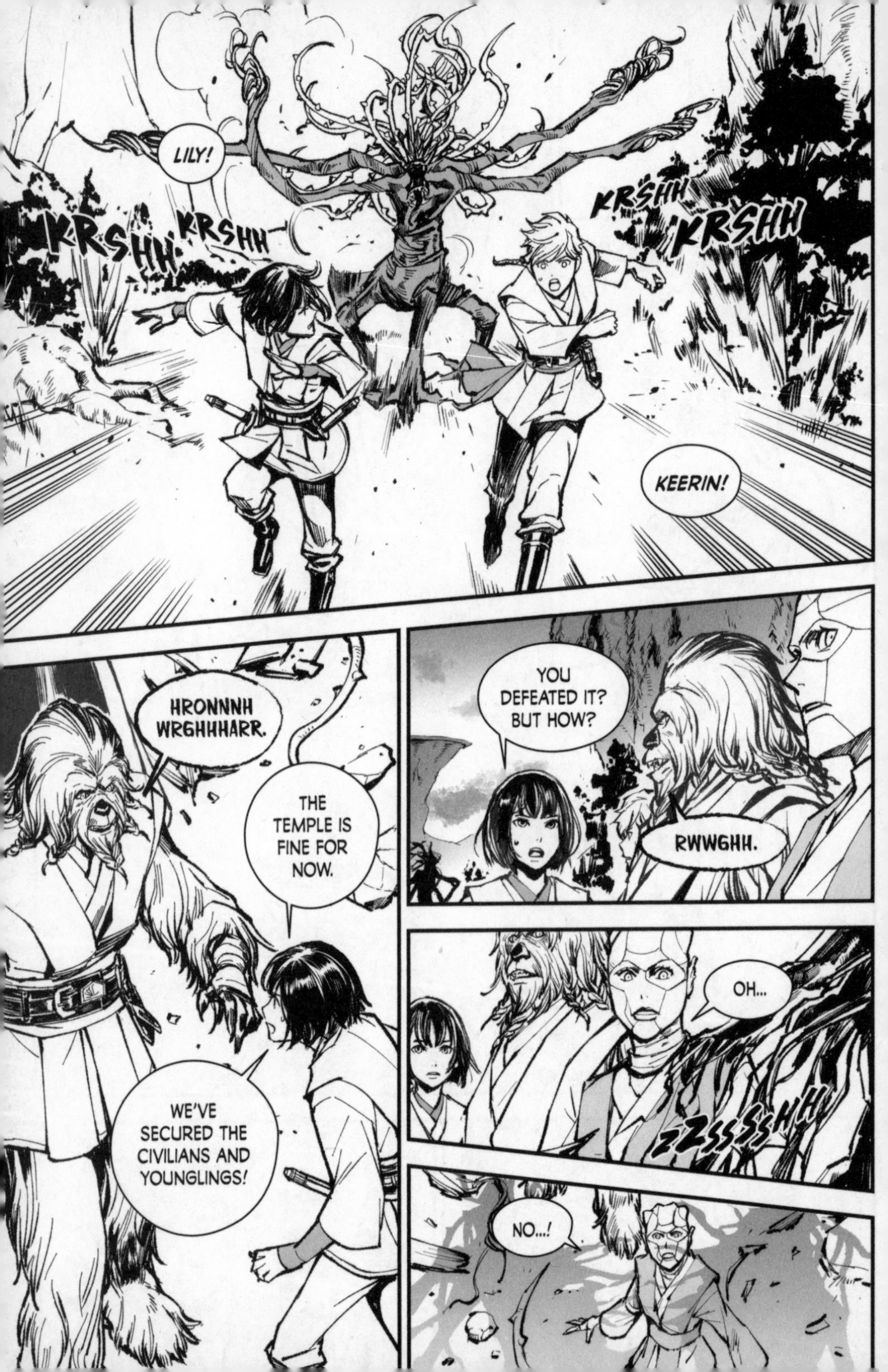
LILY!
KRSHH KRSHH
KRSHH KRSHH
KEERIN!
HRONNNH WRGHHHARR.
THE TEMPLE IS FINE FOR NOW.
WE'VE SECURED THE CIVILIANS AND YOUNGLINGS!
YOU DEFEATED IT? BUT HOW?
RWWGHH.
OH...
ZZSSSSHH
NO...!

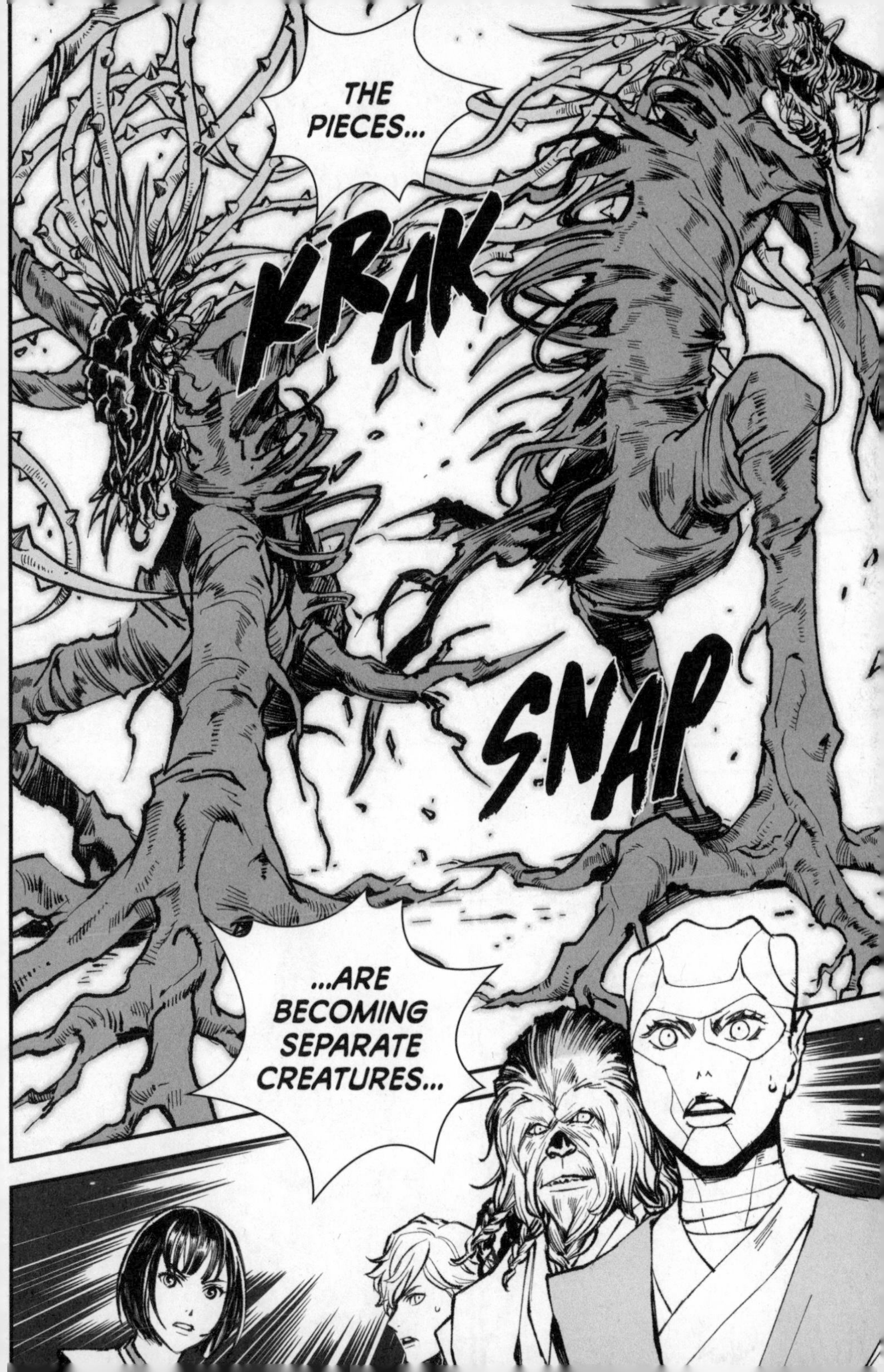
THE PIECES...
KRAK
SNAP
...ARE BECOMING SEPARATE CREATURES...

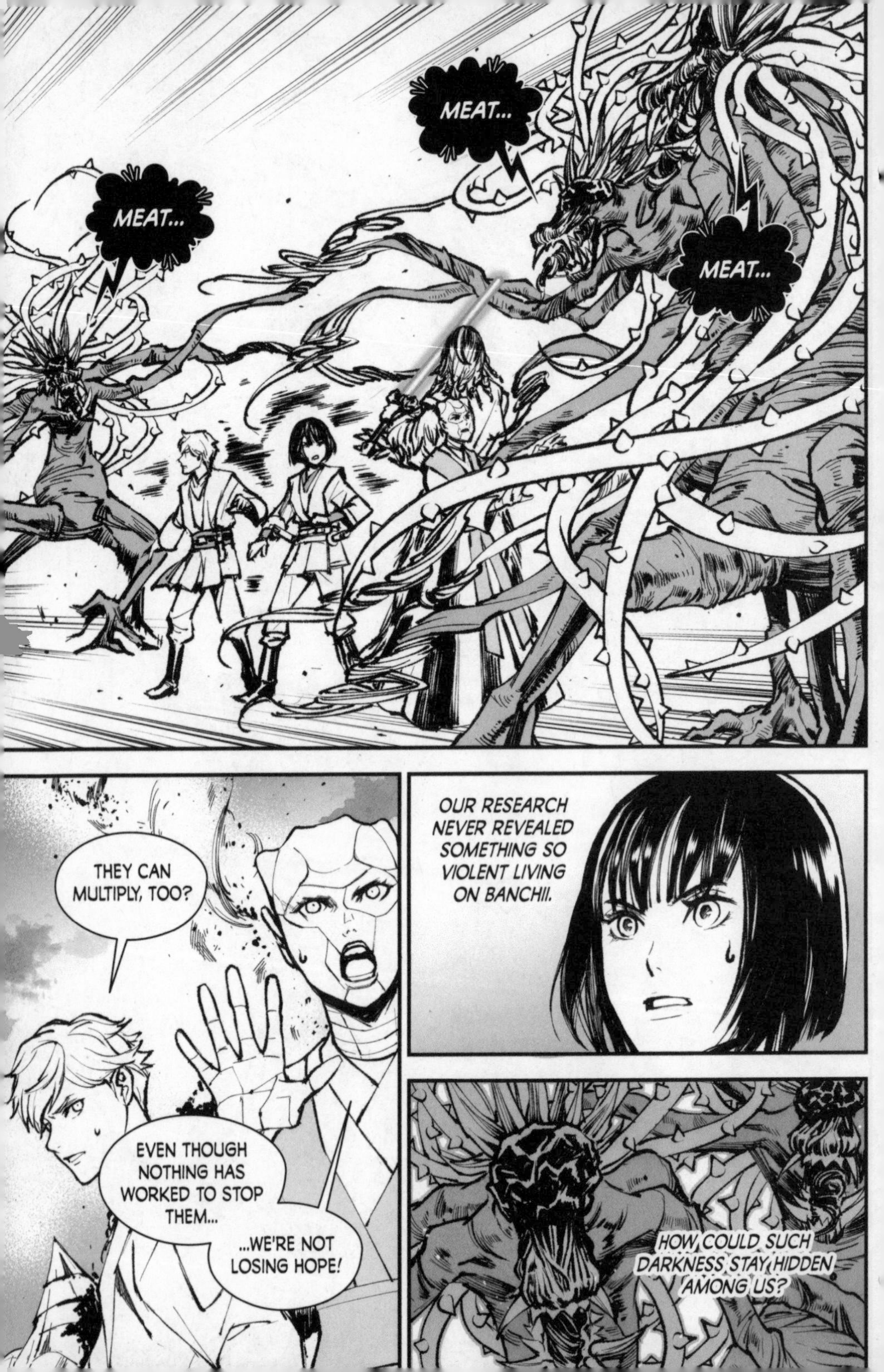
MEAT...
MEAT...
MEAT...
THEY CAN MULTIPLY, TOO?
EVEN THOUGH NOTHING HAS WORKED TO STOP THEM...
...WE'RE NOT LOSING HOPE!
OUR RESEARCH NEVER REVEALED SOMETHING SO VIOLENT LIVING ON BANCHII.
HOW COULD SUCH DARKNESS STAY HIDDEN AMONG US?

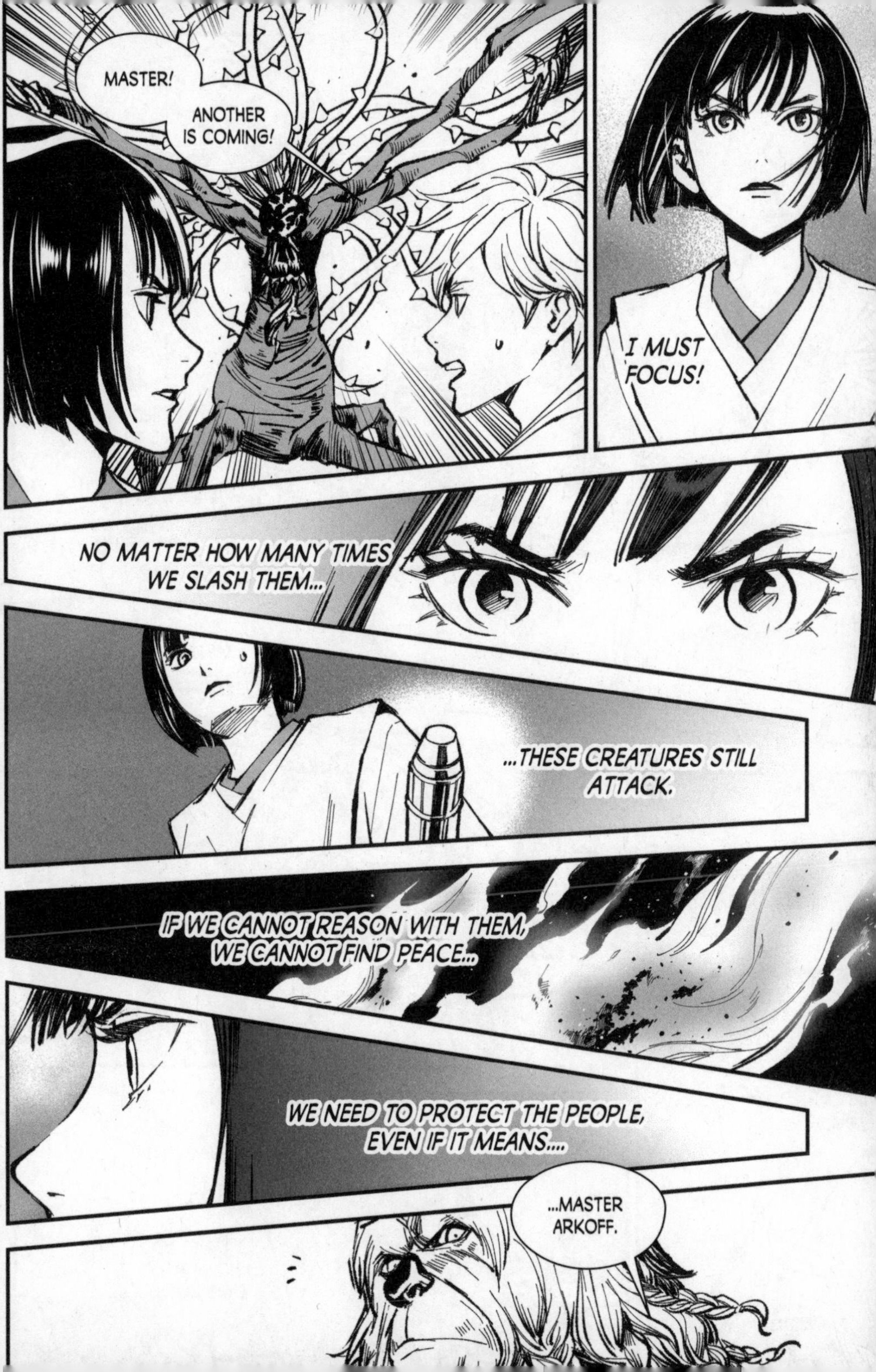
MASTER!
ANOTHER IS COMING!
I MUST FOCUS!
NO MATTER HOW MANY TIMES WE SLASH THEM...
...THESE CREATURES STILL ATTACK.
IF WE CANNOT REASON WITH THEM, WE CANNOT FIND PEACE...
WE NEED TO PROTECT THE PEOPLE, EVEN IF IT MEANS....
...MASTER ARKOFF.

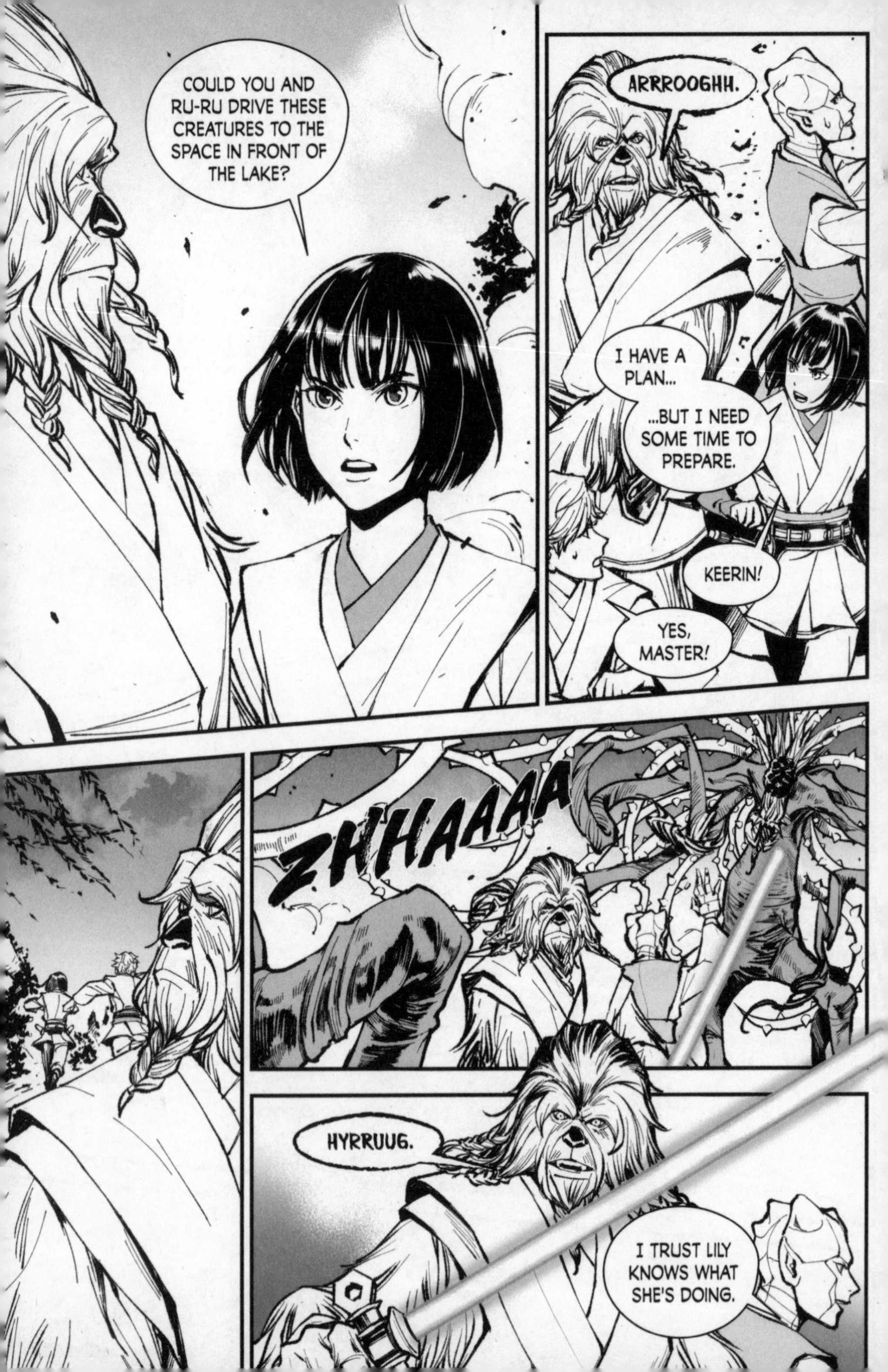
COULD YOU AND RU-RU DRIVE THESE CREATURES TO THE SPACE IN FRONT OF THE LAKE?
ARRROOGHH.
I HAVE A PLAN...
...BUT I NEED SOME TIME TO PREPARE.
KEERIN!
YES, MASTER!
ZHHAAAAA
HYRRUUG.
I TRUST LILY KNOWS WHAT SHE'S DOING.

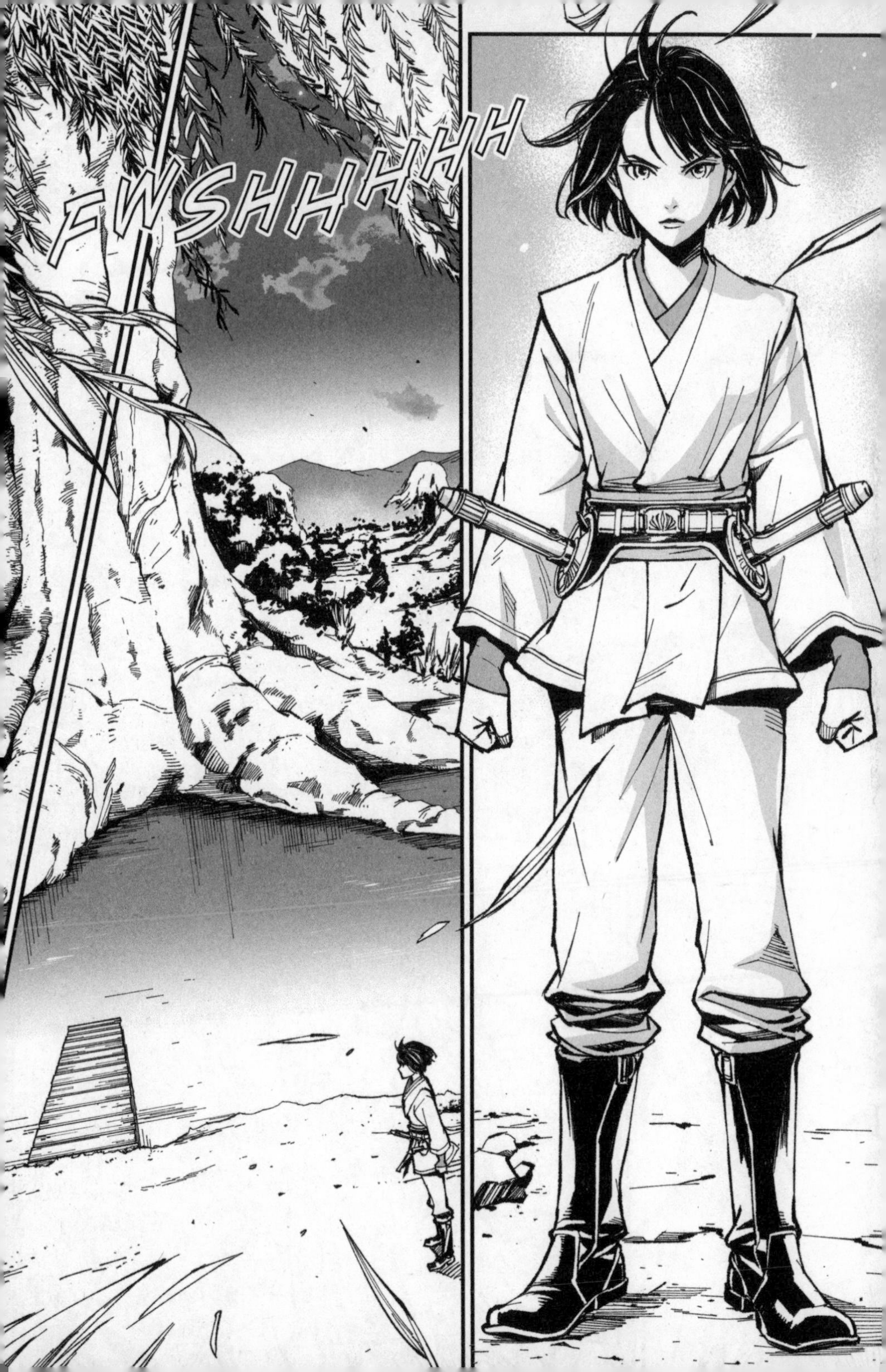
FWSHHHHH

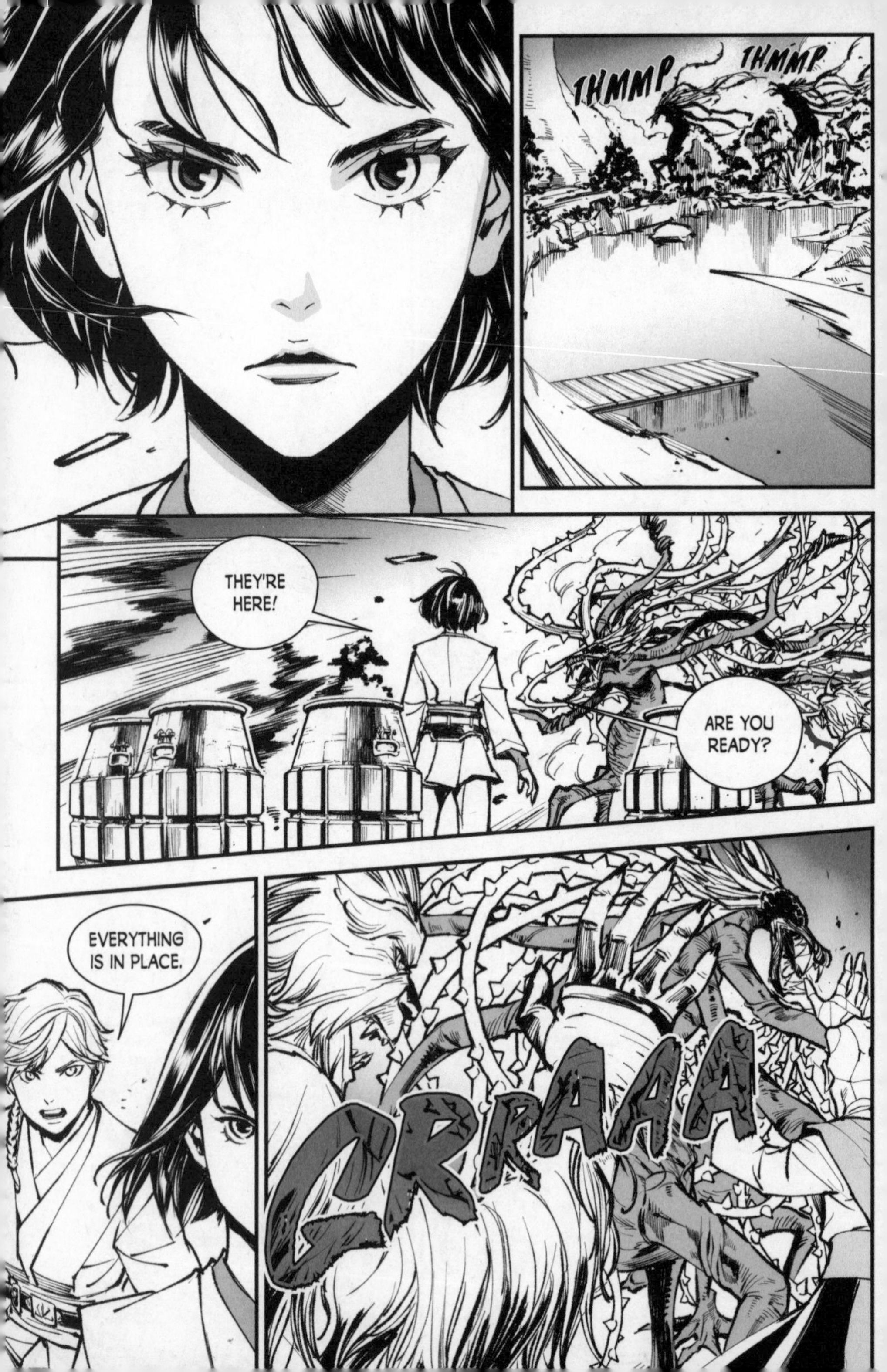
THMMP
THMMP
THEY'RE HERE!
ARE YOU READY?
EVERYTHING IS IN PLACE.
GRRAAAA

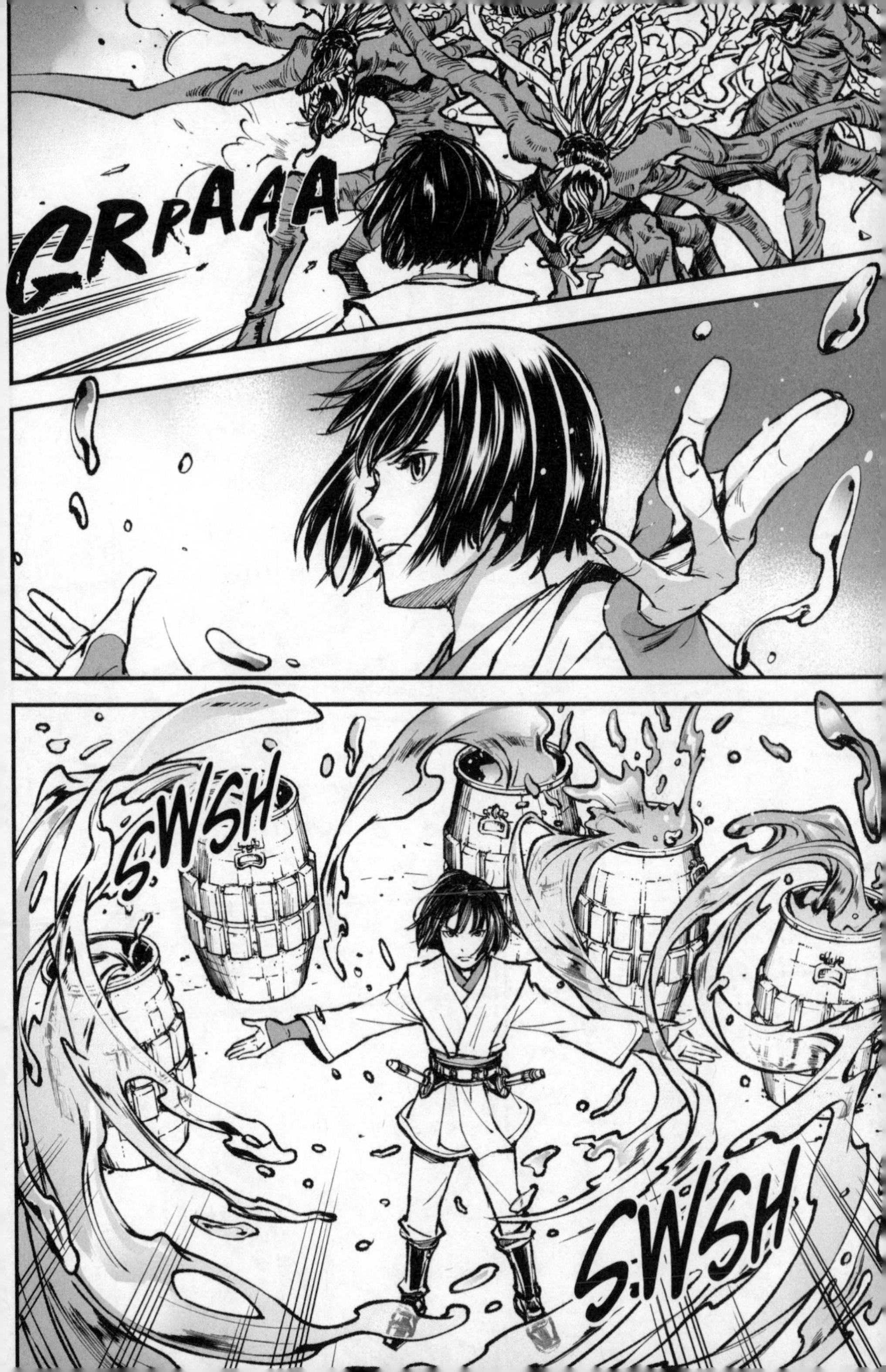
GRRAAA
SWSH
SWSH

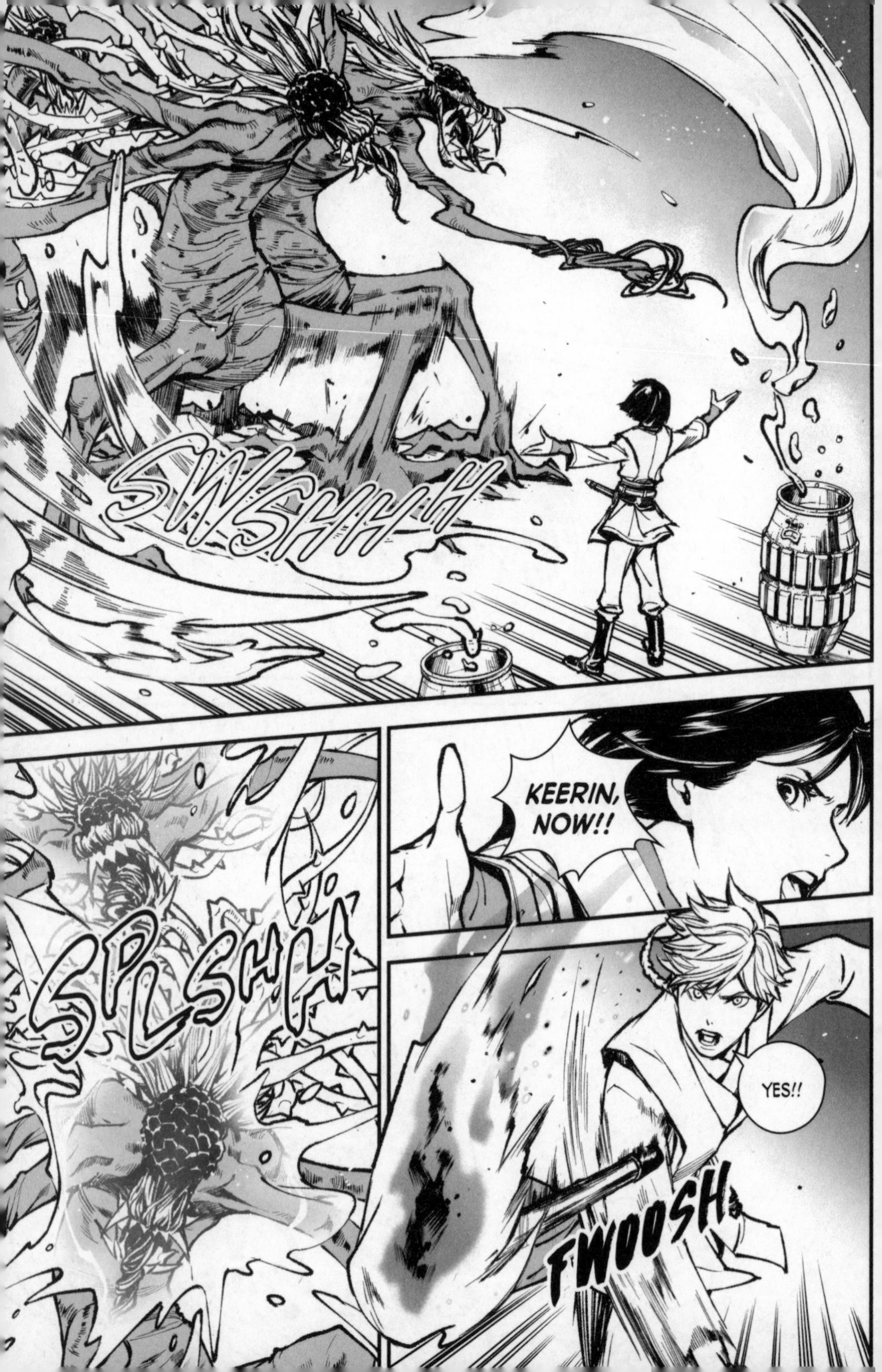
SWSHHH
KEERIN, NOW!!
YES!!
FWOOSH
SPLSHH

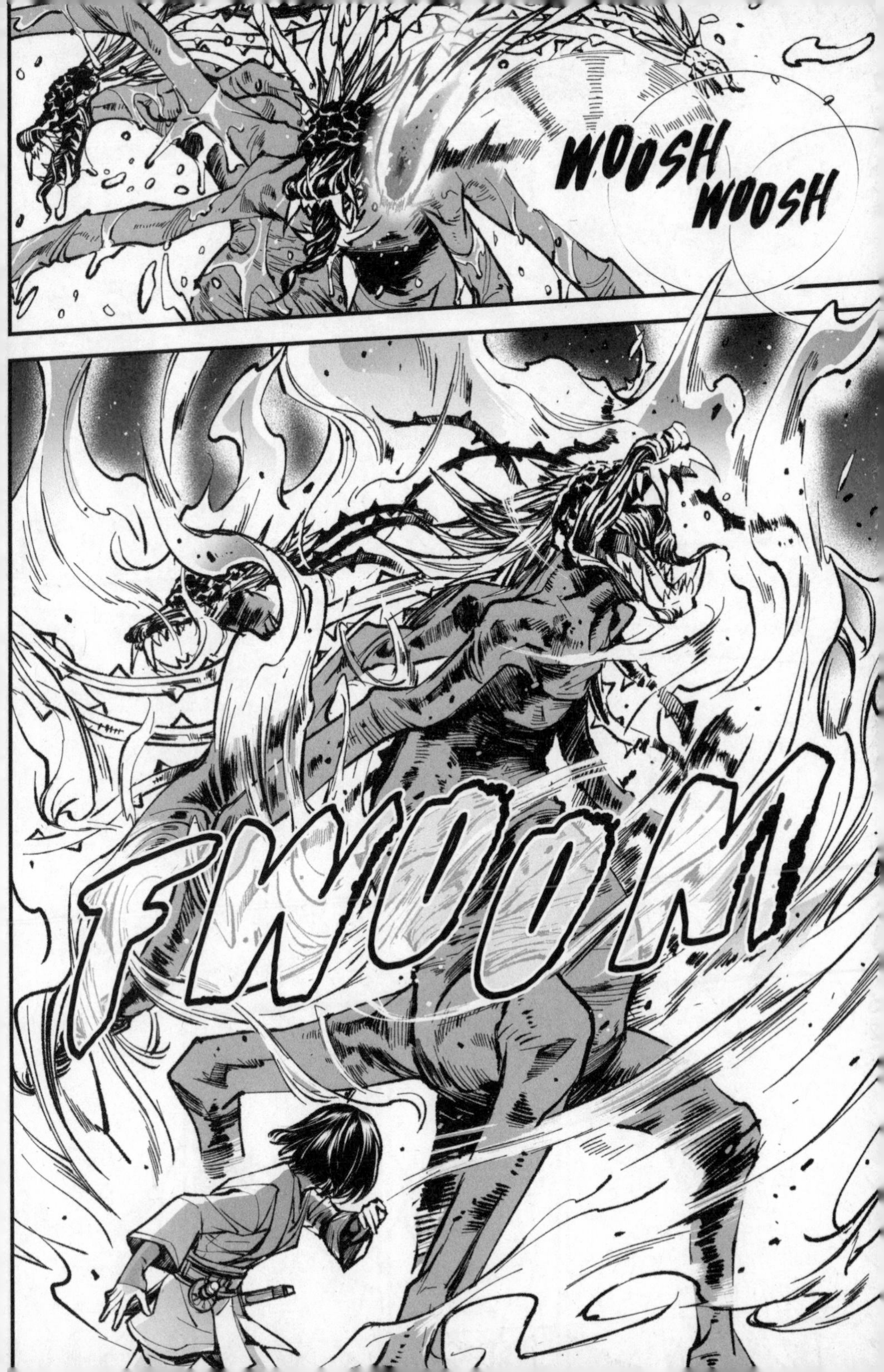
WOOSH
WOOSH
FWOOM

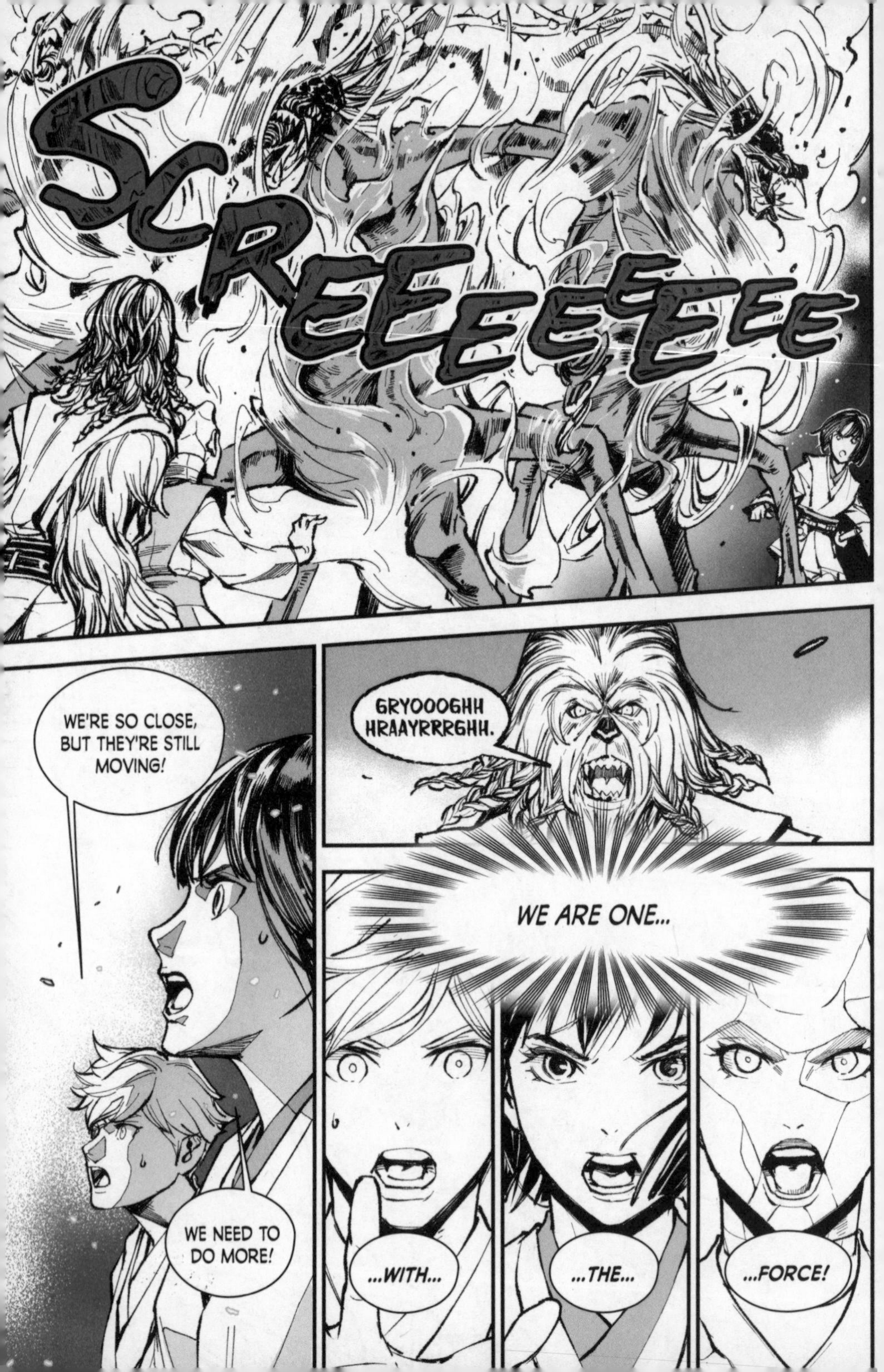
SCREEEEEEEE
WE'RE SO CLOSE, BUT THEY'RE STILL MOVING!
GRYOOOGHH HRAAYRRRGHH.
WE NEED TO DO MORE!
WE ARE ONE...
...WITH...
...THE...
...FORCE!

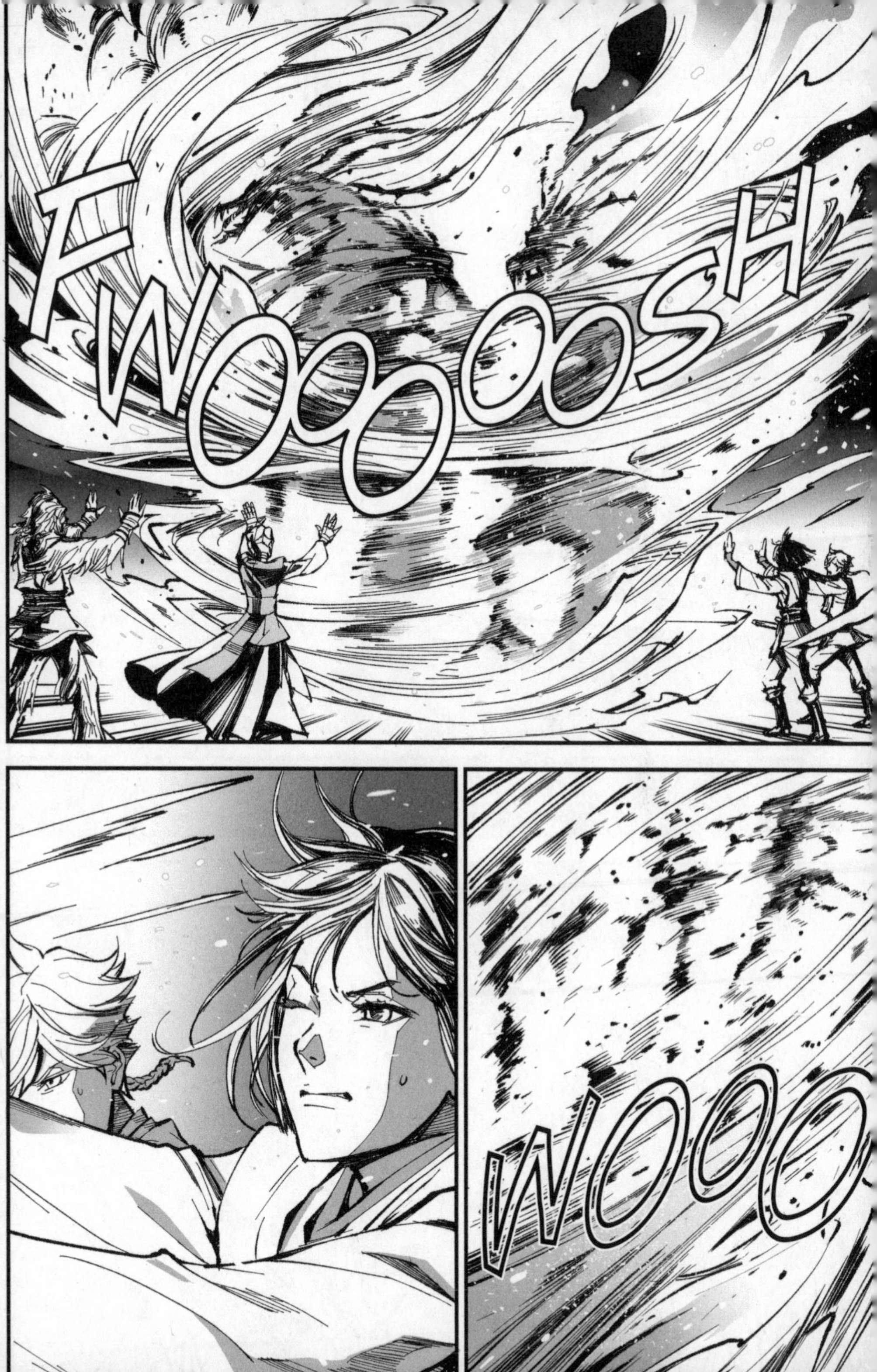
FWOOOOOSH
WOOO

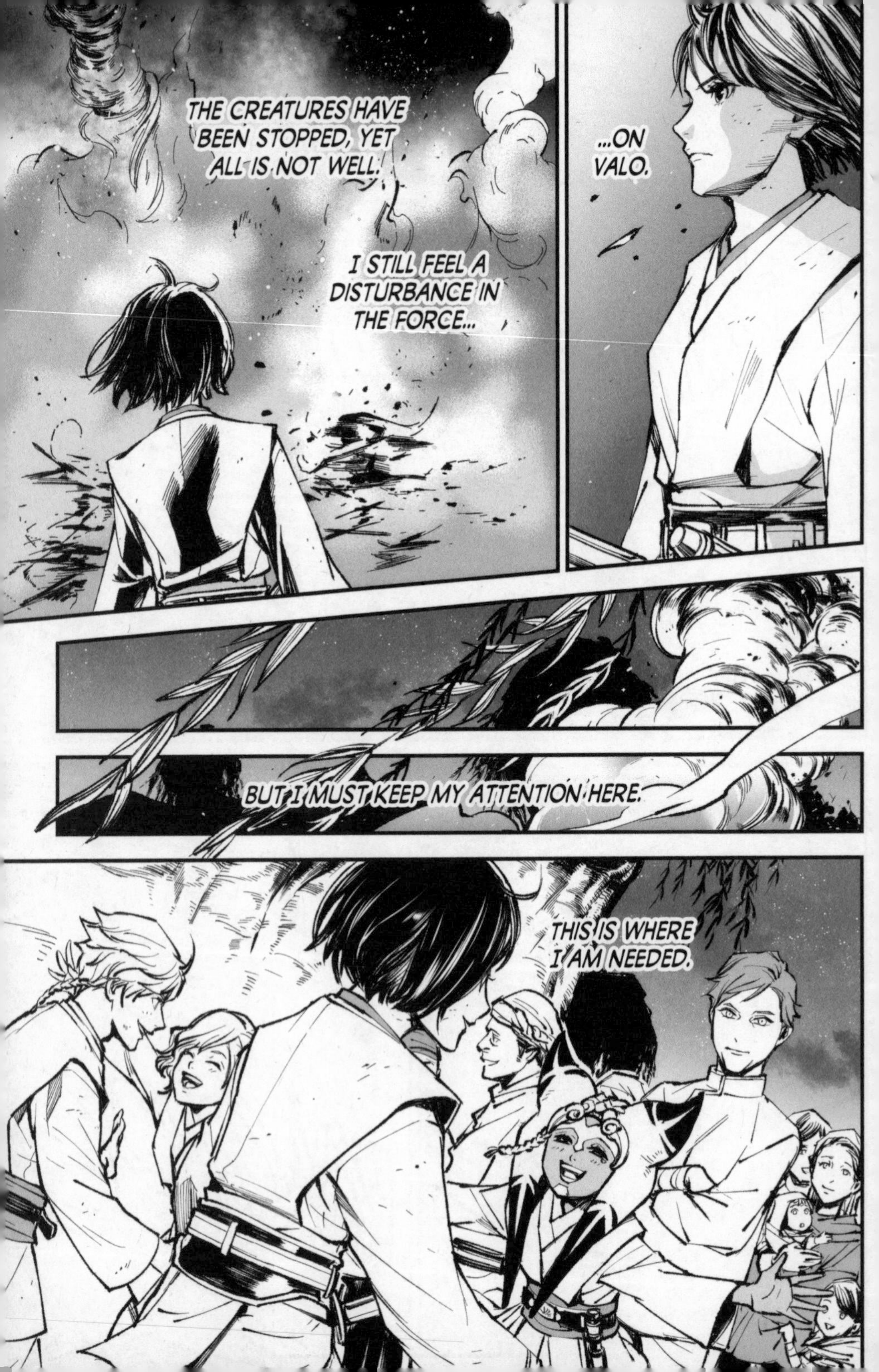
THE CREATURES HAVE BEEN STOPPED, YET ALL IS NOT WELL.
I STILL FEEL A DISTURBANCE IN THE FORCE...
...ON VALO.
BUT I MUST KEEP MY ATTENTION HERE.
THIS IS WHERE I AM NEEDED.

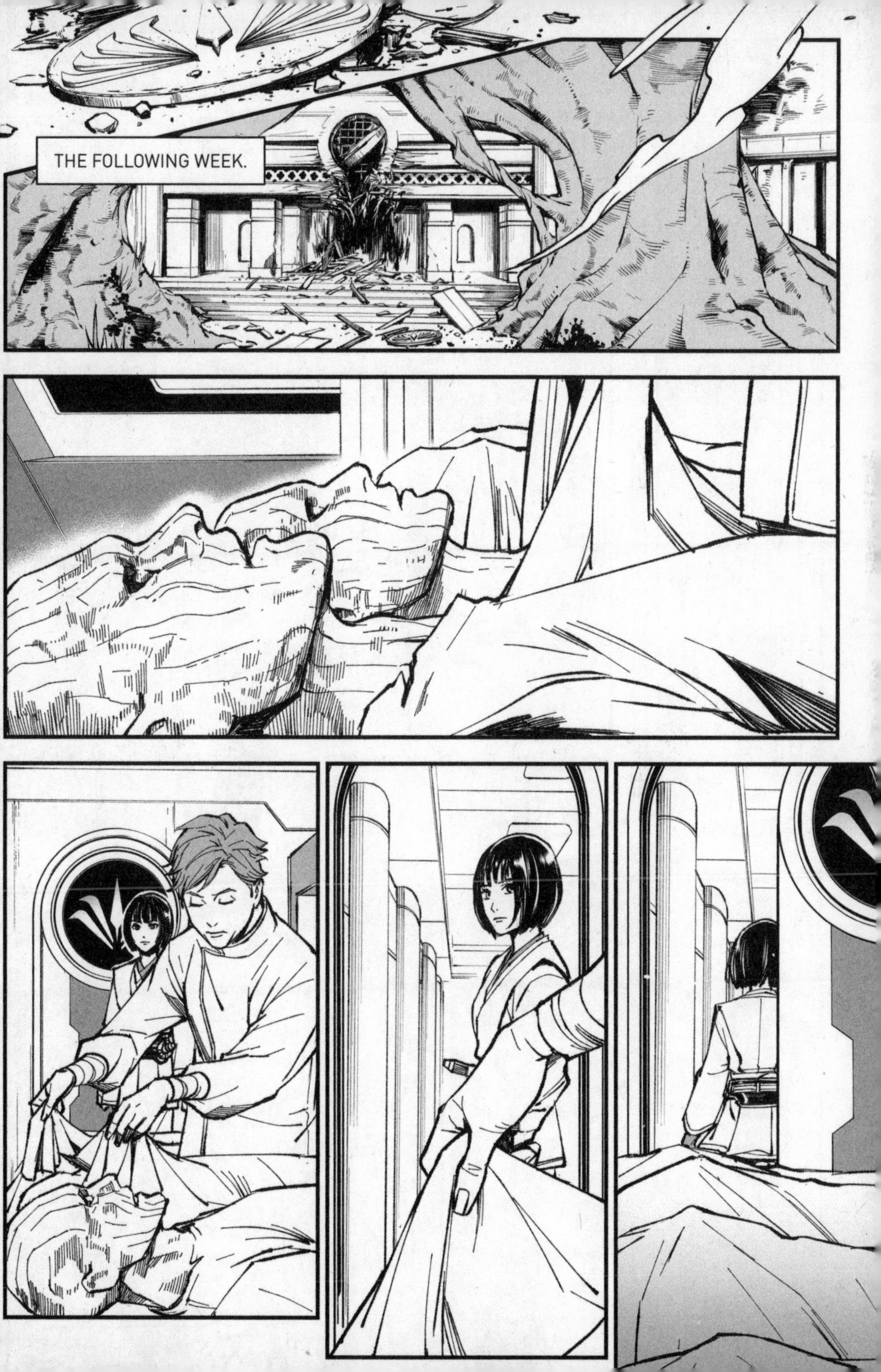
THE FOLLOWING WEEK.

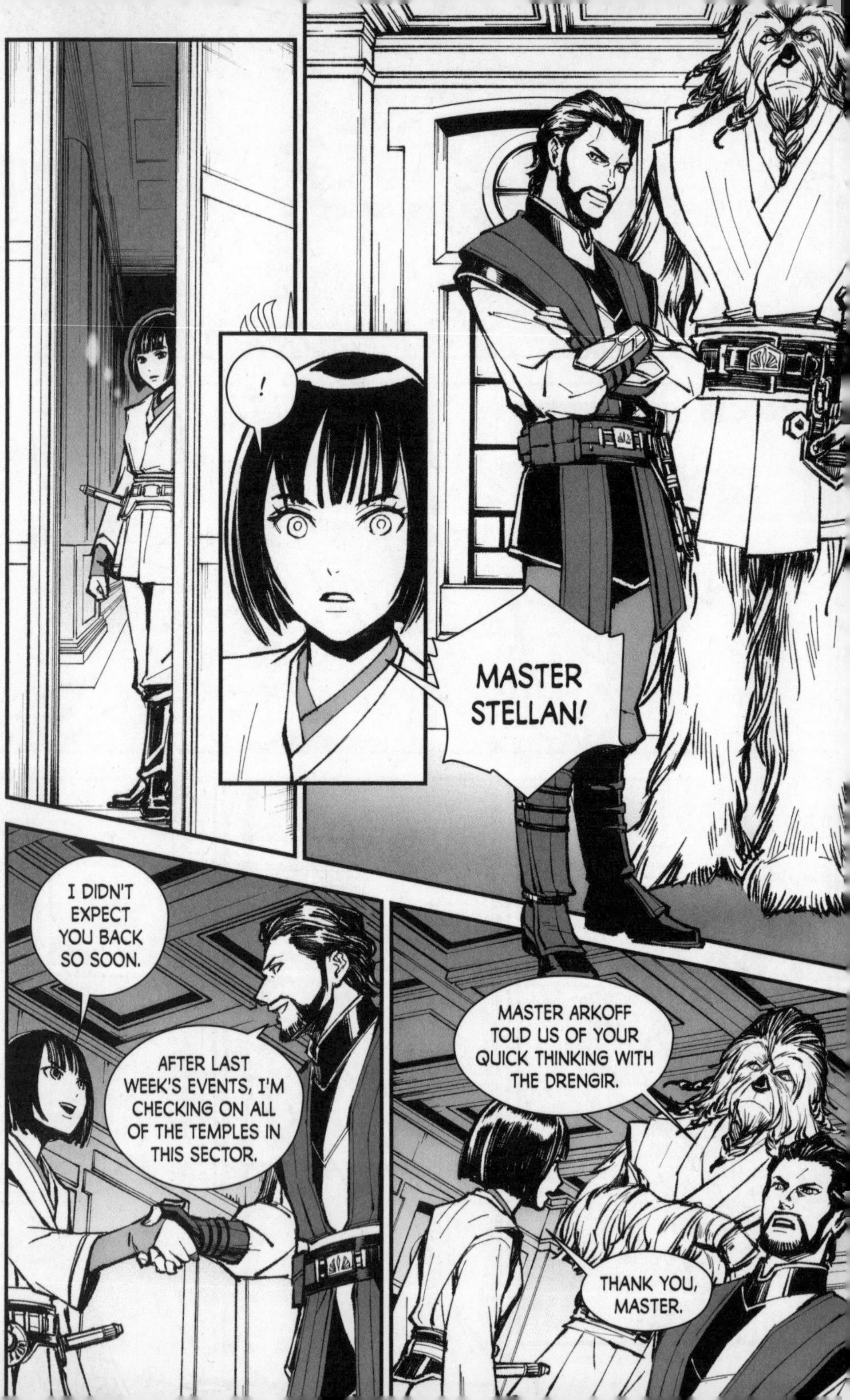
!
MASTER STELLAN!
I DIDN'T EXPECT YOU BACK SO SOON.
AFTER LAST WEEK'S EVENTS, I'M CHECKING ON ALL OF THE TEMPLES IN THIS SECTOR.
MASTER ARKOFF TOLD US OF YOUR QUICK THINKING WITH THE DRENGIR.
THANK YOU, MASTER.

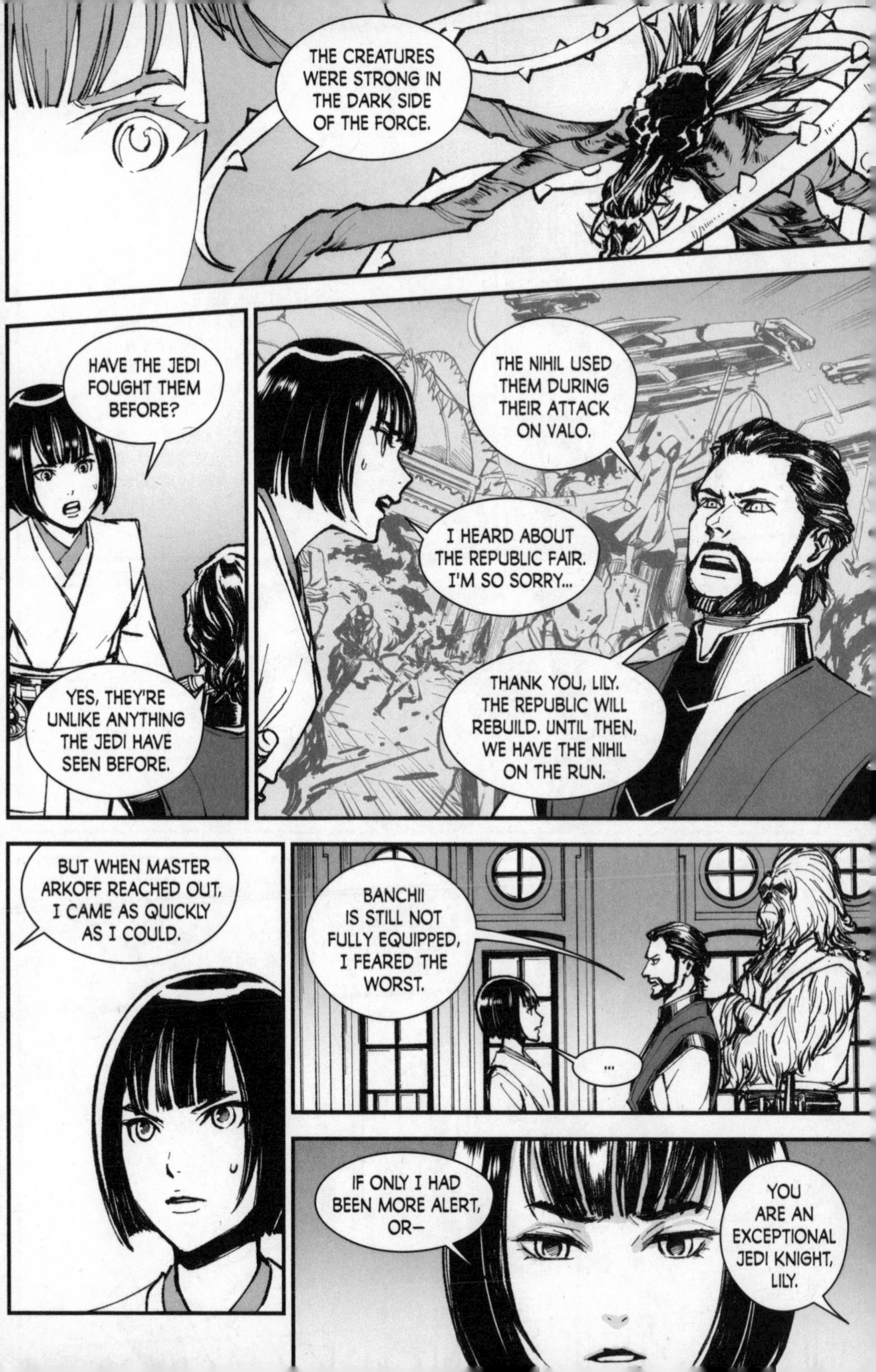
THE CREATURES WERE STRONG IN THE DARK SIDE OF THE FORCE.
HAVE THE JEDI FOUGHT THEM BEFORE?
YES, THEY'RE UNLIKE ANYTHING THE JEDI HAVE SEEN BEFORE.
THE NIHIL USED THEM DURING THEIR ATTACK ON VALO.
I HEARD ABOUT THE REPUBLIC FAIR. I'M SO SORRY...
THANK YOU, LILY. THE REPUBLIC WILL REBUILD. UNTIL THEN, WE HAVE THE NIHIL ON THE RUN.
BUT WHEN MASTER ARKOFF REACHED OUT, I CAME AS QUICKLY AS I COULD.
BANCHII IS STILL NOT FULLY EQUIPPED, I FEARED THE WORST.
...
IF ONLY I HAD BEEN MORE ALERT, OR–
YOU ARE AN EXCEPTIONAL JEDI KNIGHT, LILY.

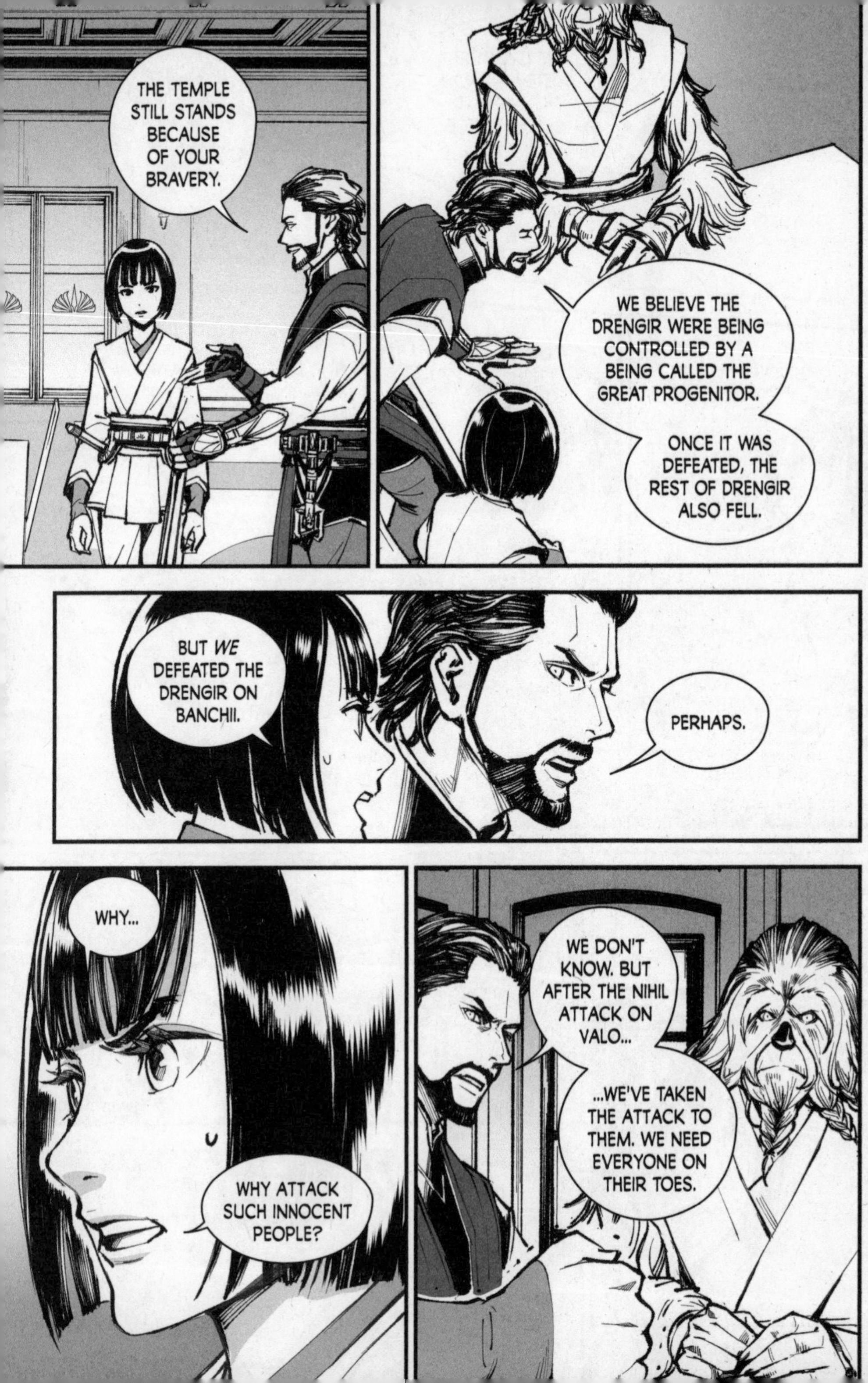
THE TEMPLE STILL STANDS BECAUSE OF YOUR BRAVERY.
WE BELIEVE THE DRENGIR WERE BEING CONTROLLED BY A BEING CALLED THE GREAT PROGENITOR.
ONCE IT WAS DEFEATED, THE REST OF DRENGIR ALSO FELL.
BUT *WE* DEFEATED THE DRENGIR ON BANCHII.
PERHAPS.
WHY...
WHY ATTACK SUCH INNOCENT PEOPLE?
WE DON'T KNOW. BUT AFTER THE NIHIL ATTACK ON VALO...
...WE'VE TAKEN THE ATTACK TO THEM. WE NEED EVERYONE ON THEIR TOES.

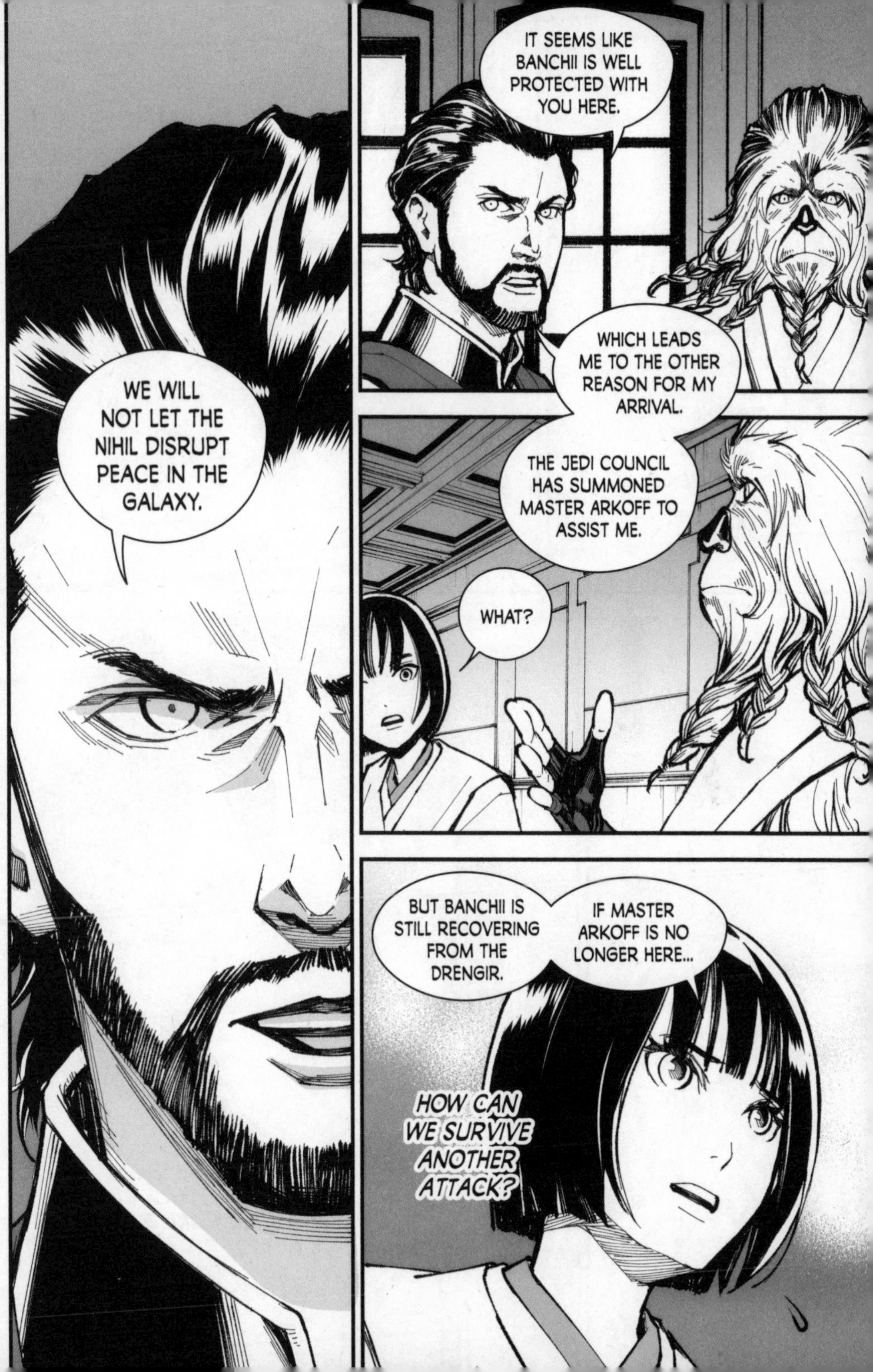
WE WILL NOT LET THE NIHIL DISRUPT PEACE IN THE GALAXY.
IT SEEMS LIKE BANCHII IS WELL PROTECTED WITH YOU HERE.
WHICH LEADS ME TO THE OTHER REASON FOR MY ARRIVAL.
THE JEDI COUNCIL HAS SUMMONED MASTER ARKOFF TO ASSIST ME.
WHAT?
IF MASTER ARKOFF IS NO LONGER HERE...
BUT BANCHII IS STILL RECOVERING FROM THE DRENGIR.
HOW CAN WE SURVIVE ANOTHER ATTACK?

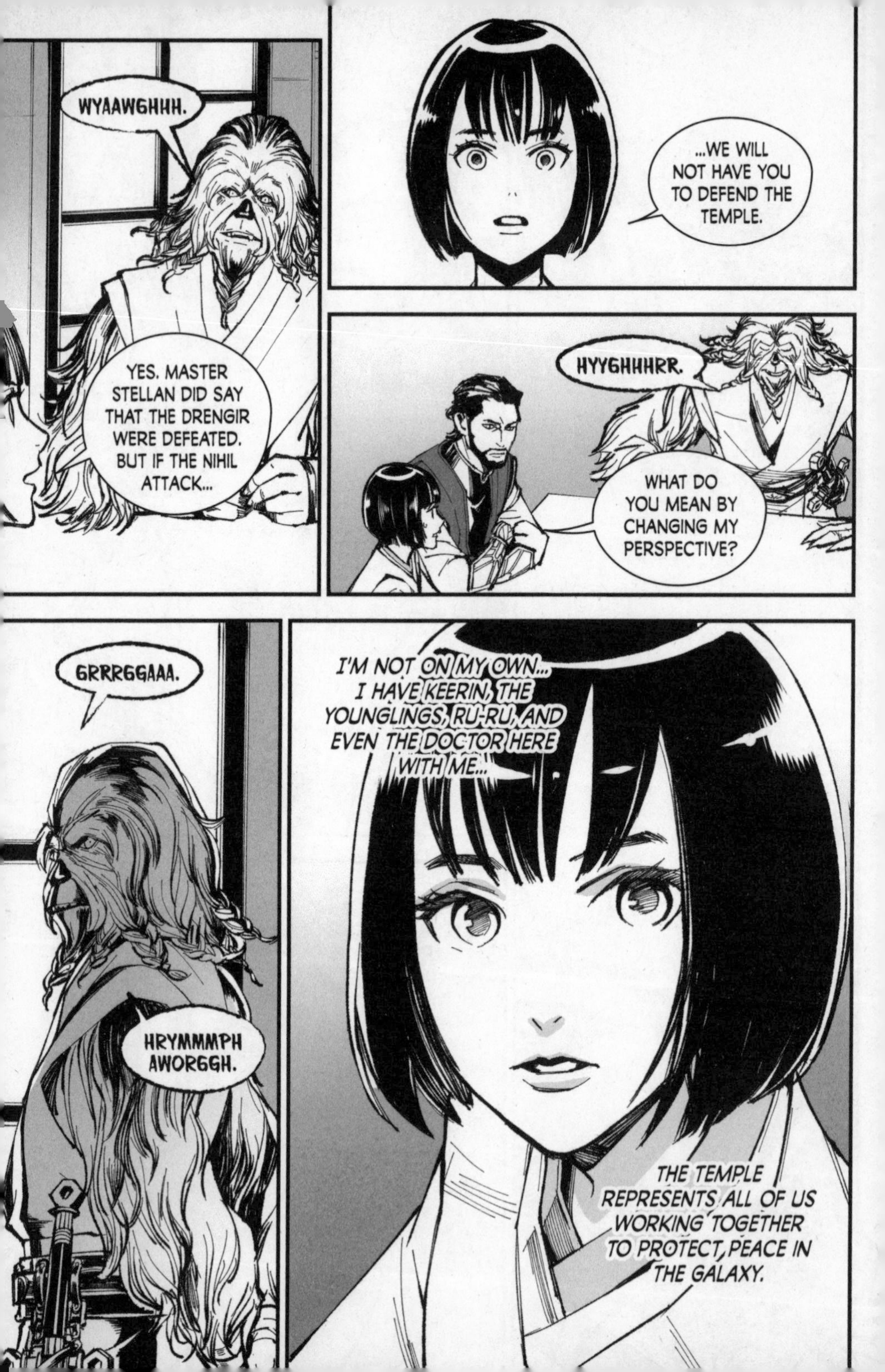
WYAAWGHHH.
YES. MASTER STELLAN DID SAY THAT THE DRENGIR WERE DEFEATED. BUT IF THE NIHIL ATTACK...
...WE WILL NOT HAVE YOU TO DEFEND THE TEMPLE.
HYYGHHHRR.
WHAT DO YOU MEAN BY CHANGING MY PERSPECTIVE?
GRRRGGAAA.
HRYMMMPH AWORGGH.
I'M NOT ON MY OWN... I HAVE KEERIN, THE YOUNGLINGS, RU-RU, AND EVEN THE DOCTOR HERE WITH ME...
THE TEMPLE REPRESENTS ALL OF US WORKING TOGETHER TO PROTECT PEACE IN THE GALAXY.

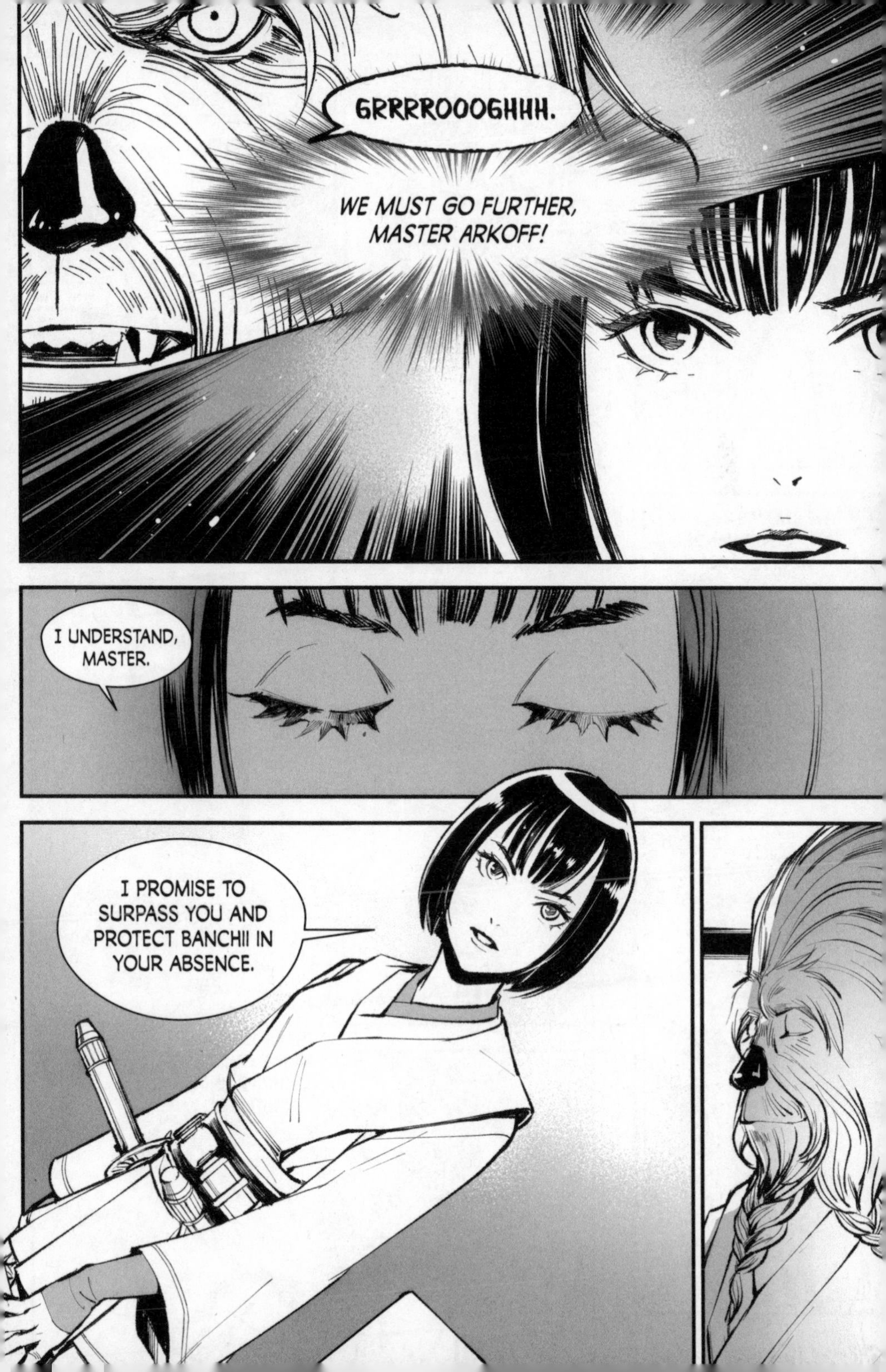
GRRRROOOGHHH.
WE MUST GO FURTHER, MASTER ARKOFF!
I UNDERSTAND, MASTER.
I PROMISE TO SURPASS YOU AND PROTECT BANCHII IN YOUR ABSENCE.

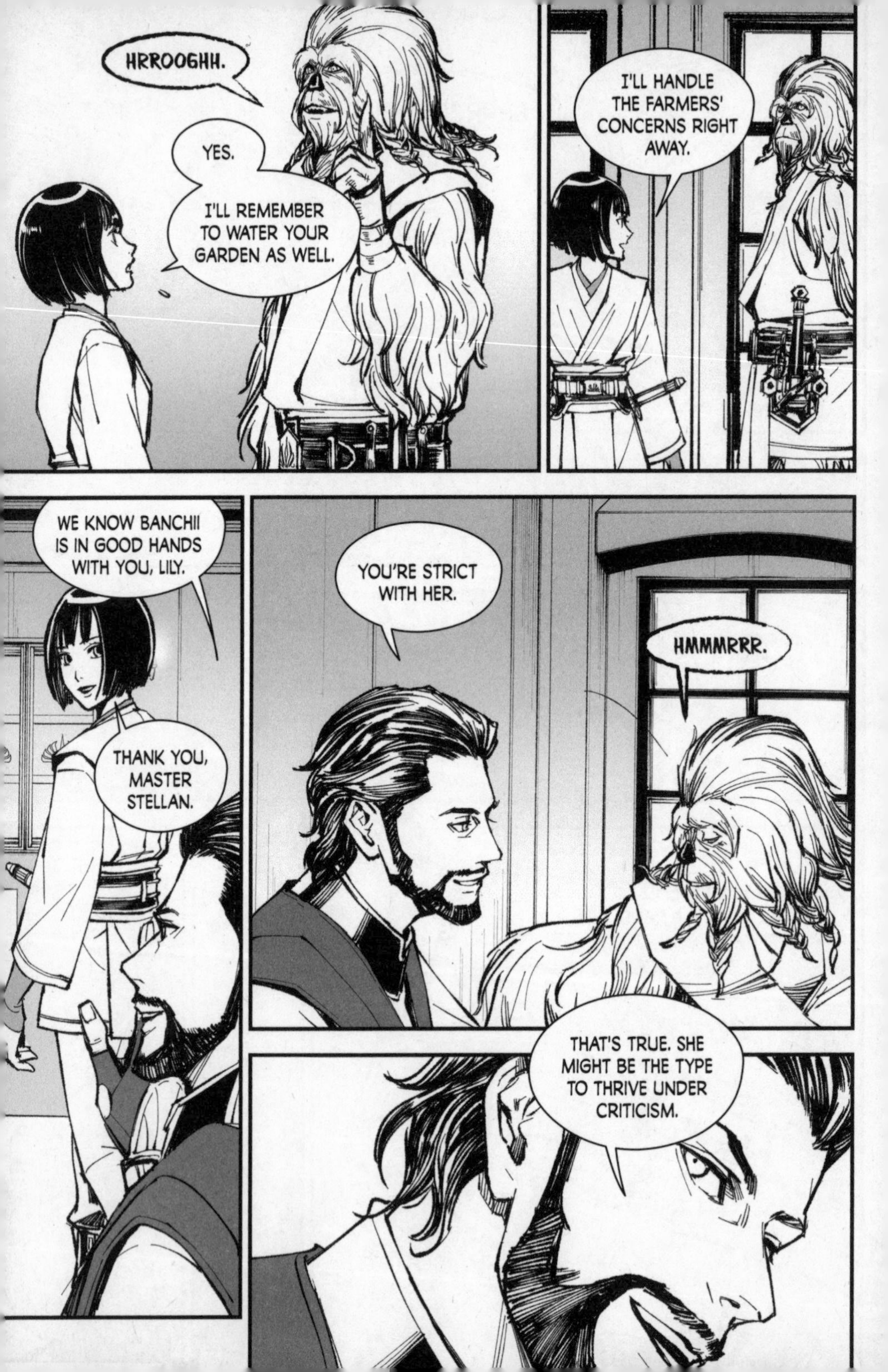
HRROOGHH.
YES.
I'LL REMEMBER TO WATER YOUR GARDEN AS WELL.
I'LL HANDLE THE FARMERS' CONCERNS RIGHT AWAY.
WE KNOW BANCHII IS IN GOOD HANDS WITH YOU, LILY.
THANK YOU, MASTER STELLAN.
YOU'RE STRICT WITH HER.
HMMMRRR.
THAT'S TRUE. SHE MIGHT BE THE TYPE TO THRIVE UNDER CRITICISM.

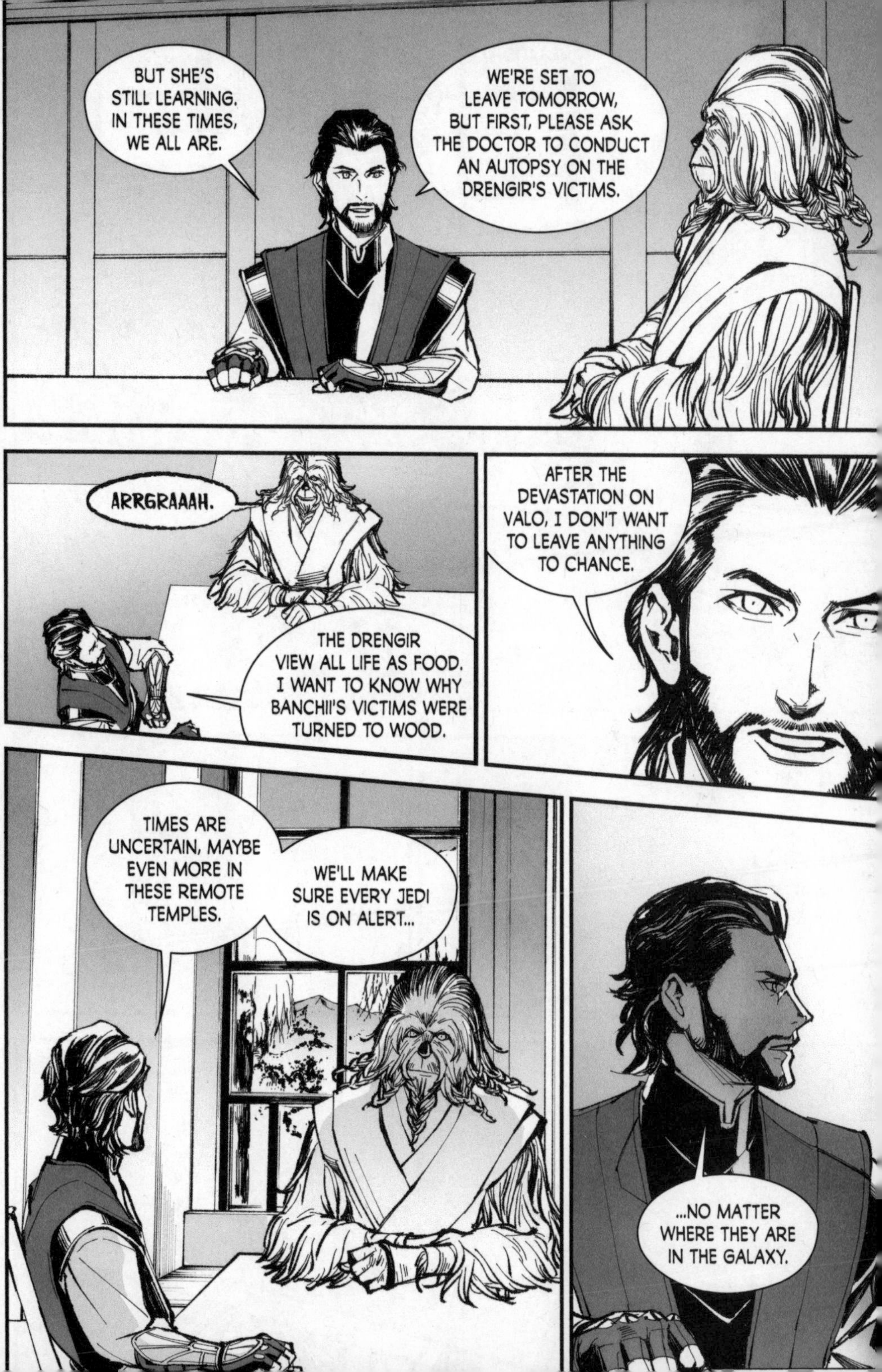
BUT SHE'S STILL LEARNING. IN THESE TIMES, WE ALL ARE.
WE'RE SET TO LEAVE TOMORROW, BUT FIRST, PLEASE ASK THE DOCTOR TO CONDUCT AN AUTOPSY ON THE DRENGIR'S VICTIMS.
ARRGRAAAH.
THE DRENGIR VIEW ALL LIFE AS FOOD. I WANT TO KNOW WHY BANCHII'S VICTIMS WERE TURNED TO WOOD.
AFTER THE DEVASTATION ON VALO, I DON'T WANT TO LEAVE ANYTHING TO CHANCE.
TIMES ARE UNCERTAIN, MAYBE EVEN MORE IN THESE REMOTE TEMPLES.
WE'LL MAKE SURE EVERY JEDI IS ON ALERT...
...NO MATTER WHERE THEY ARE IN THE GALAXY.

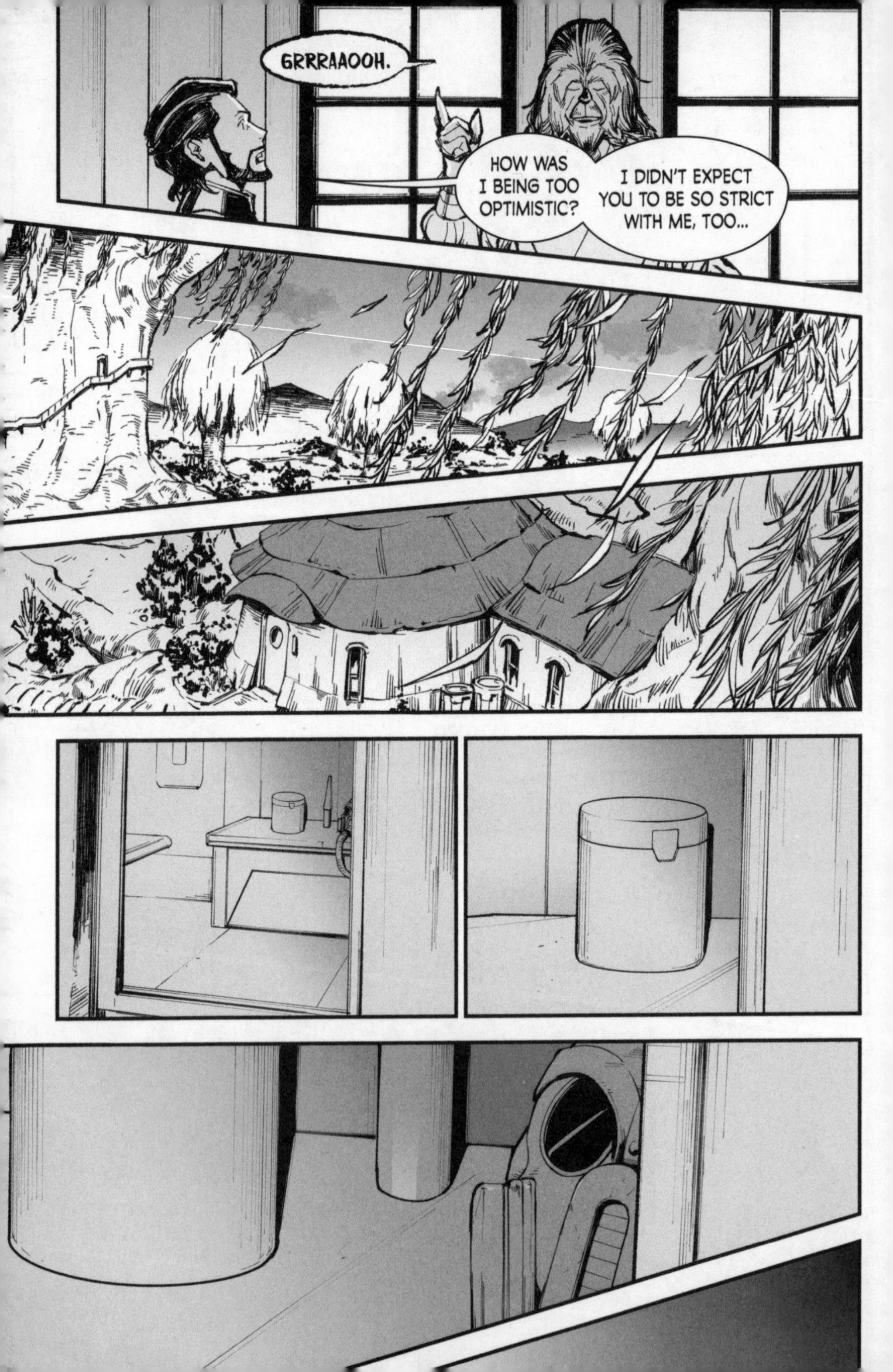
I DIDN'T EXPECT YOU TO BE SO STRICT WITH ME, TOO...
GRRRAAOOH.
HOW WAS I BEING TOO OPTIMISTIC?

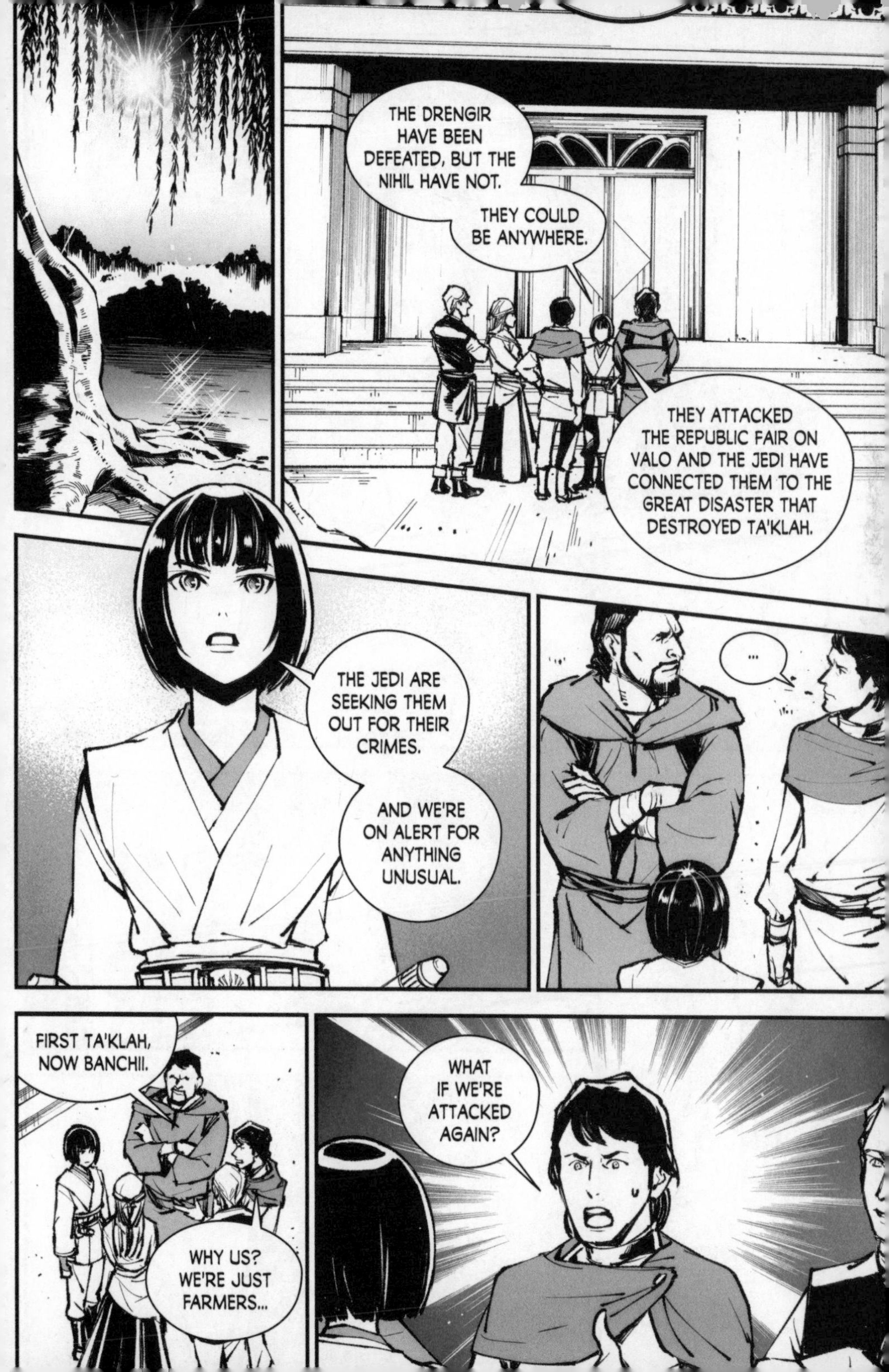

THE DRENGIR HAVE BEEN DEFEATED, BUT THE NIHIL HAVE NOT.
THEY COULD BE ANYWHERE.
THEY ATTACKED THE REPUBLIC FAIR ON VALO AND THE JEDI HAVE CONNECTED THEM TO THE GREAT DISASTER THAT DESTROYED TA'KLAH.
THE JEDI ARE SEEKING THEM OUT FOR THEIR CRIMES.
AND WE'RE ON ALERT FOR ANYTHING UNUSUAL.
...
FIRST TA'KLAH, NOW BANCHII.
WHY US? WE'RE JUST FARMERS...
WHAT IF WE'RE ATTACKED AGAIN?

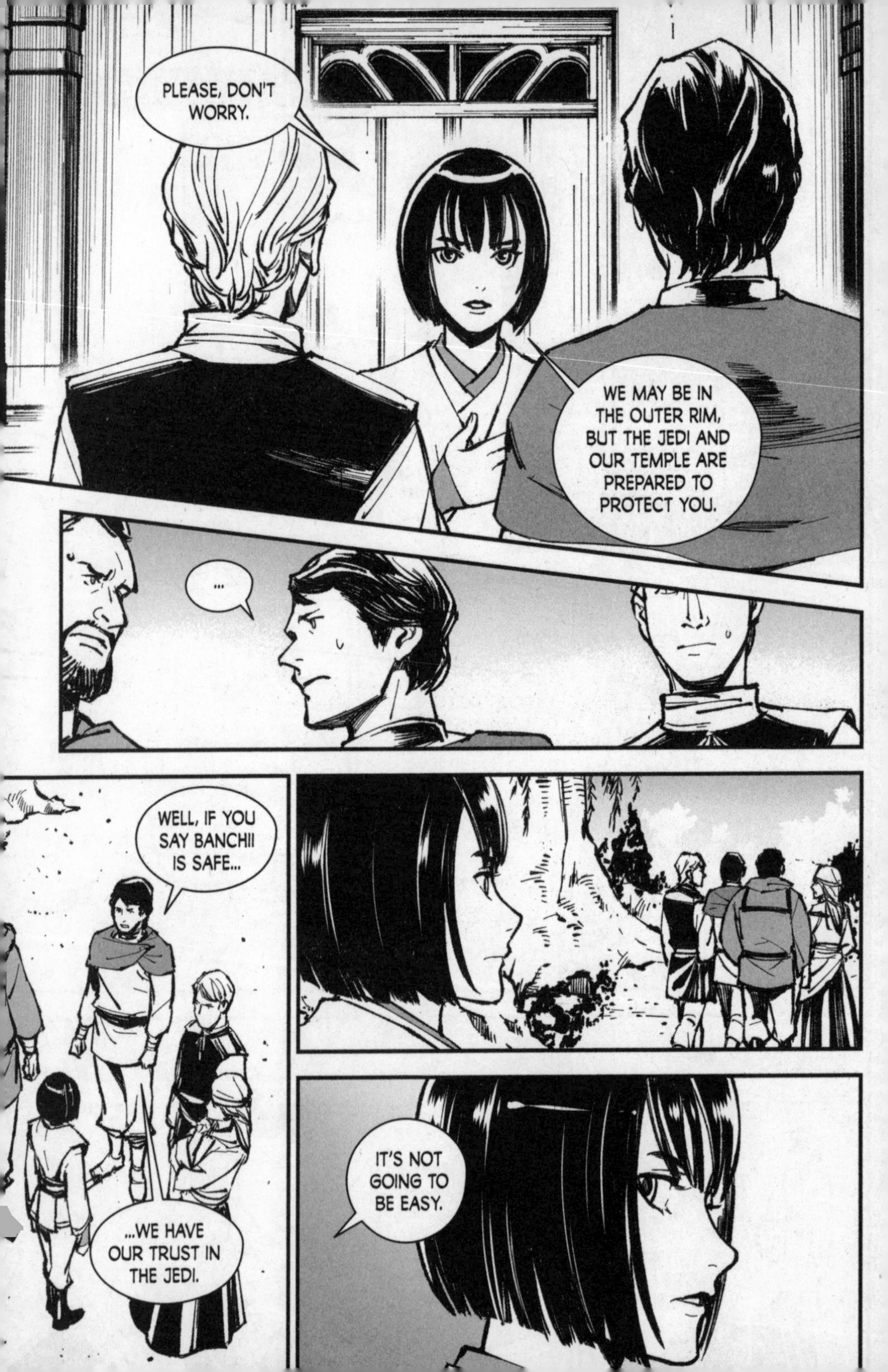
PLEASE, DON'T WORRY.
WE MAY BE IN THE OUTER RIM, BUT THE JEDI AND OUR TEMPLE ARE PREPARED TO PROTECT YOU.
...
WELL, IF YOU SAY BANCHII IS SAFE...
...WE HAVE OUR TRUST IN THE JEDI.
IT'S NOT GOING TO BE EASY.

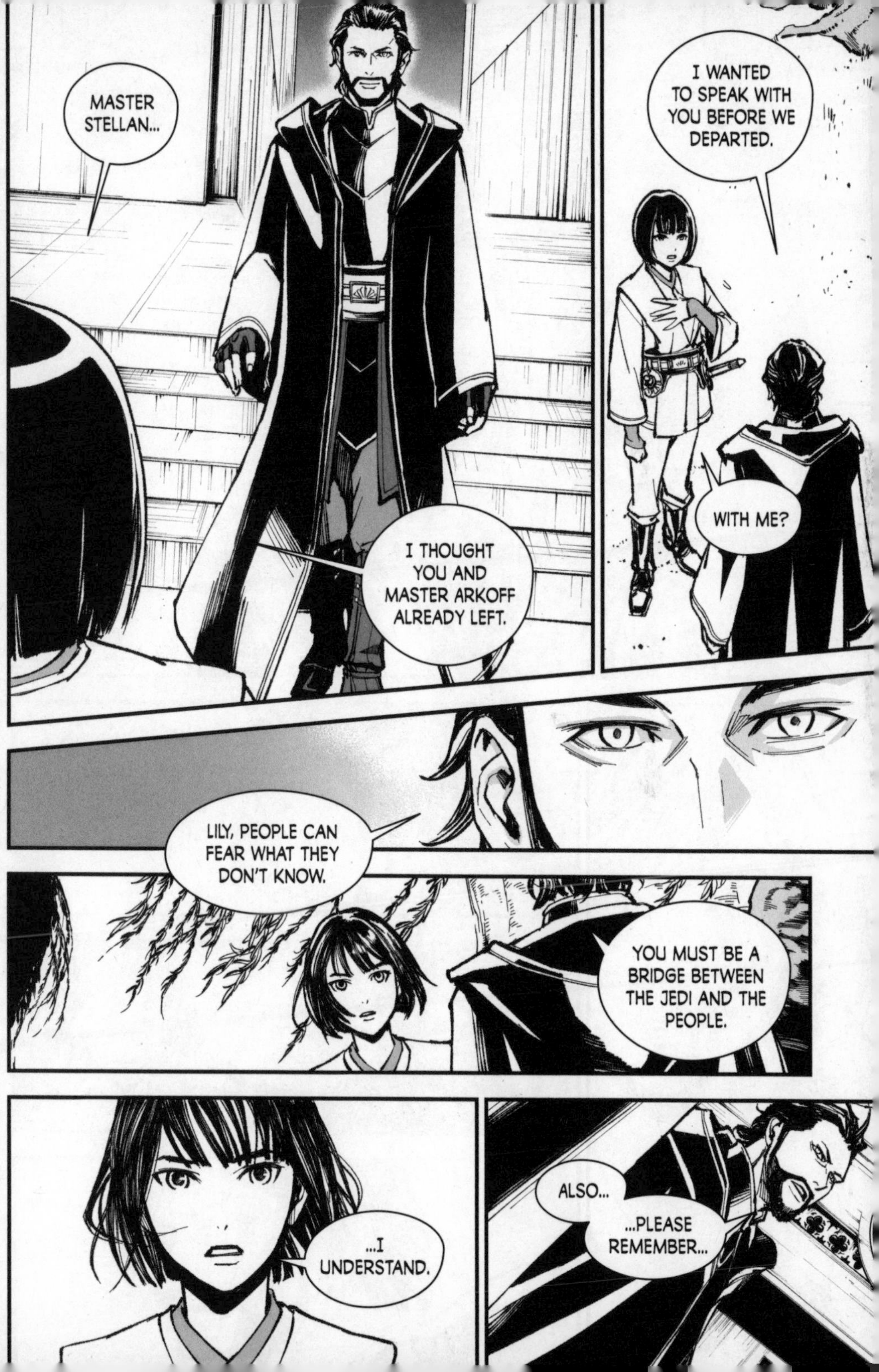
MASTER STELLAN...
I THOUGHT YOU AND MASTER ARKOFF ALREADY LEFT.
I WANTED TO SPEAK WITH YOU BEFORE WE DEPARTED.
WITH ME?
LILY, PEOPLE CAN FEAR WHAT THEY DON'T KNOW.
YOU MUST BE A BRIDGE BETWEEN THE JEDI AND THE PEOPLE.
...I UNDERSTAND.
ALSO...
...PLEASE REMEMBER...

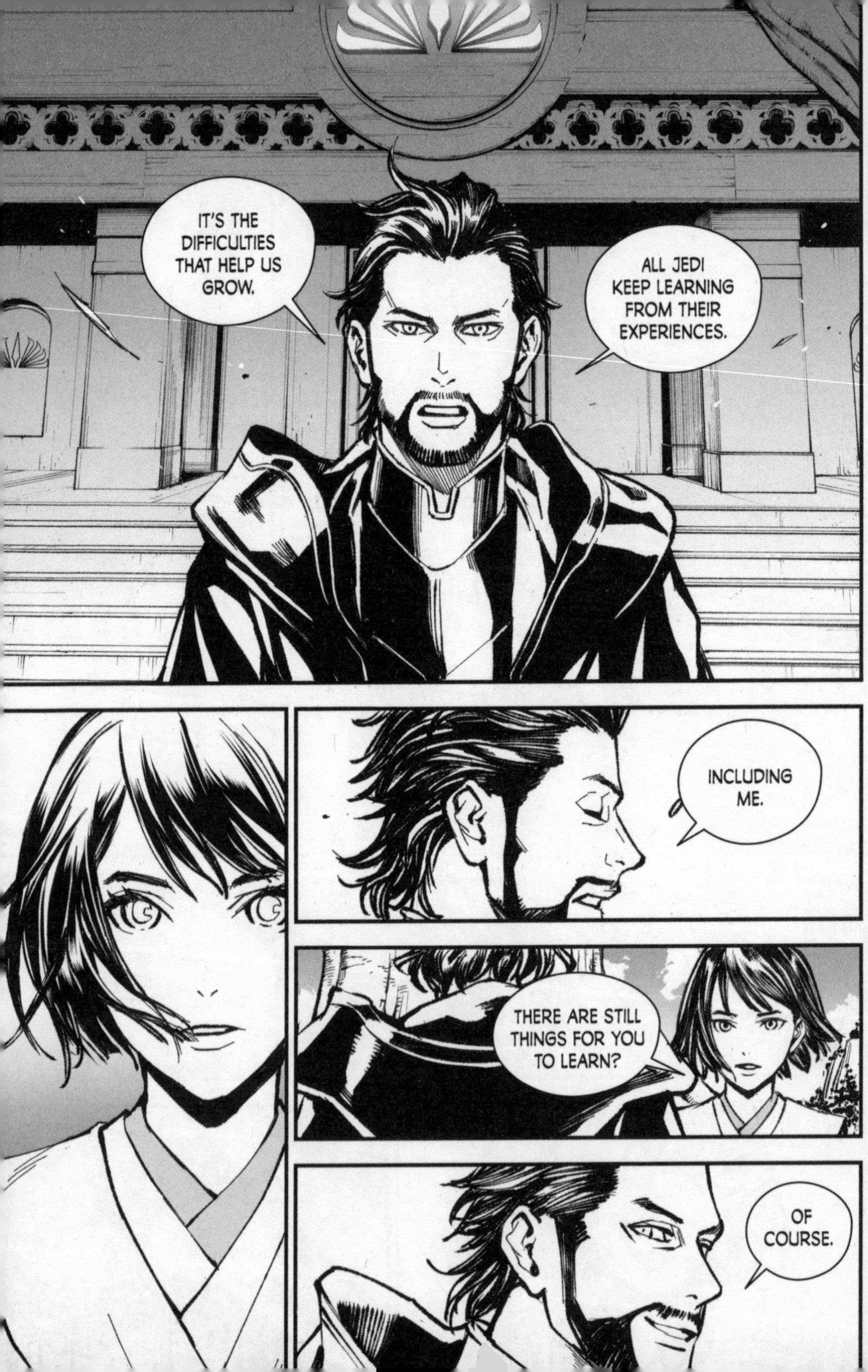
IT'S THE DIFFICULTIES THAT HELP US GROW.
ALL JEDI KEEP LEARNING FROM THEIR EXPERIENCES.
INCLUDING ME.
THERE ARE STILL THINGS FOR YOU TO LEARN?
OF COURSE.

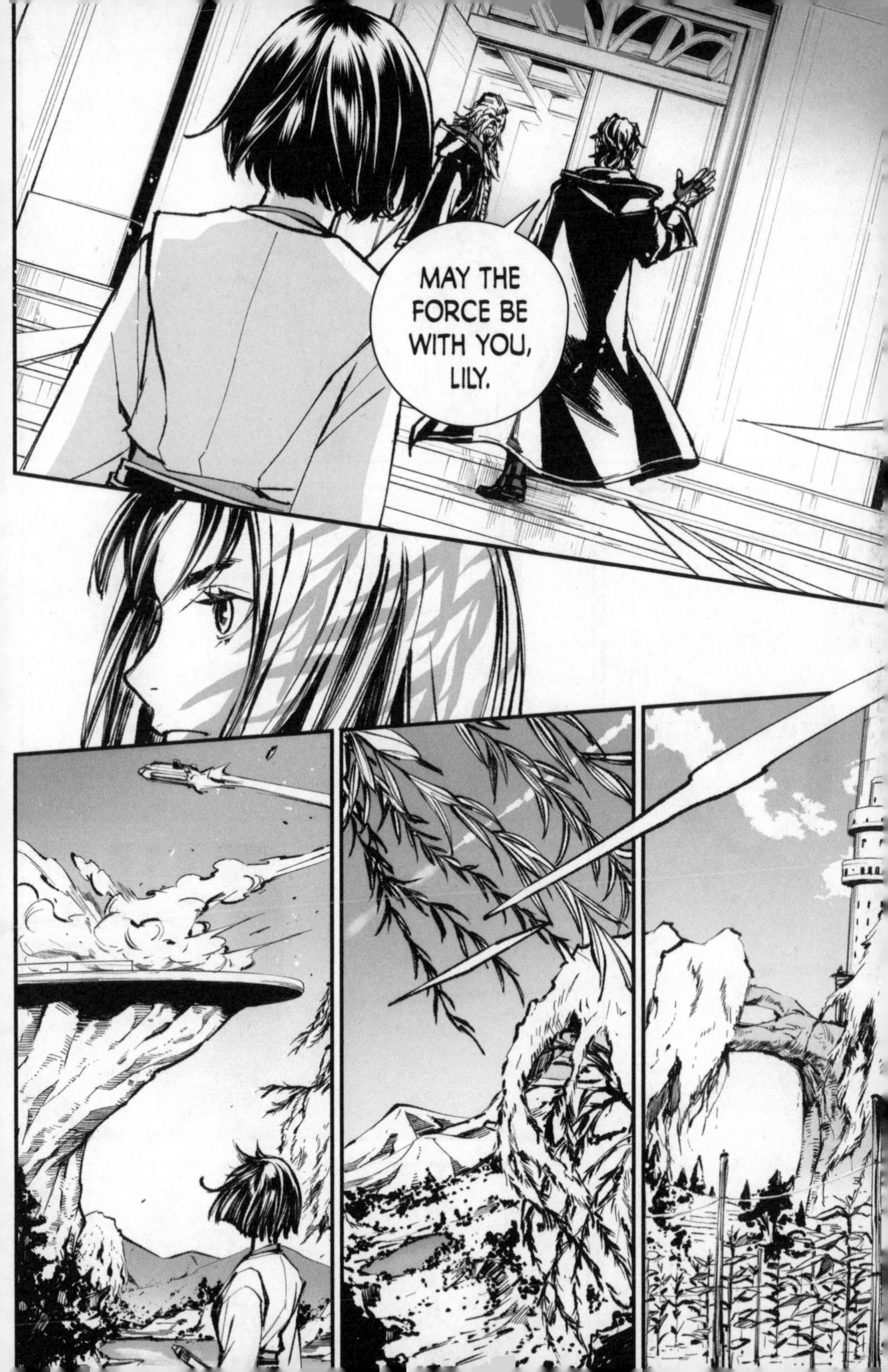
MAY THE FORCE BE WITH YOU, LILY.

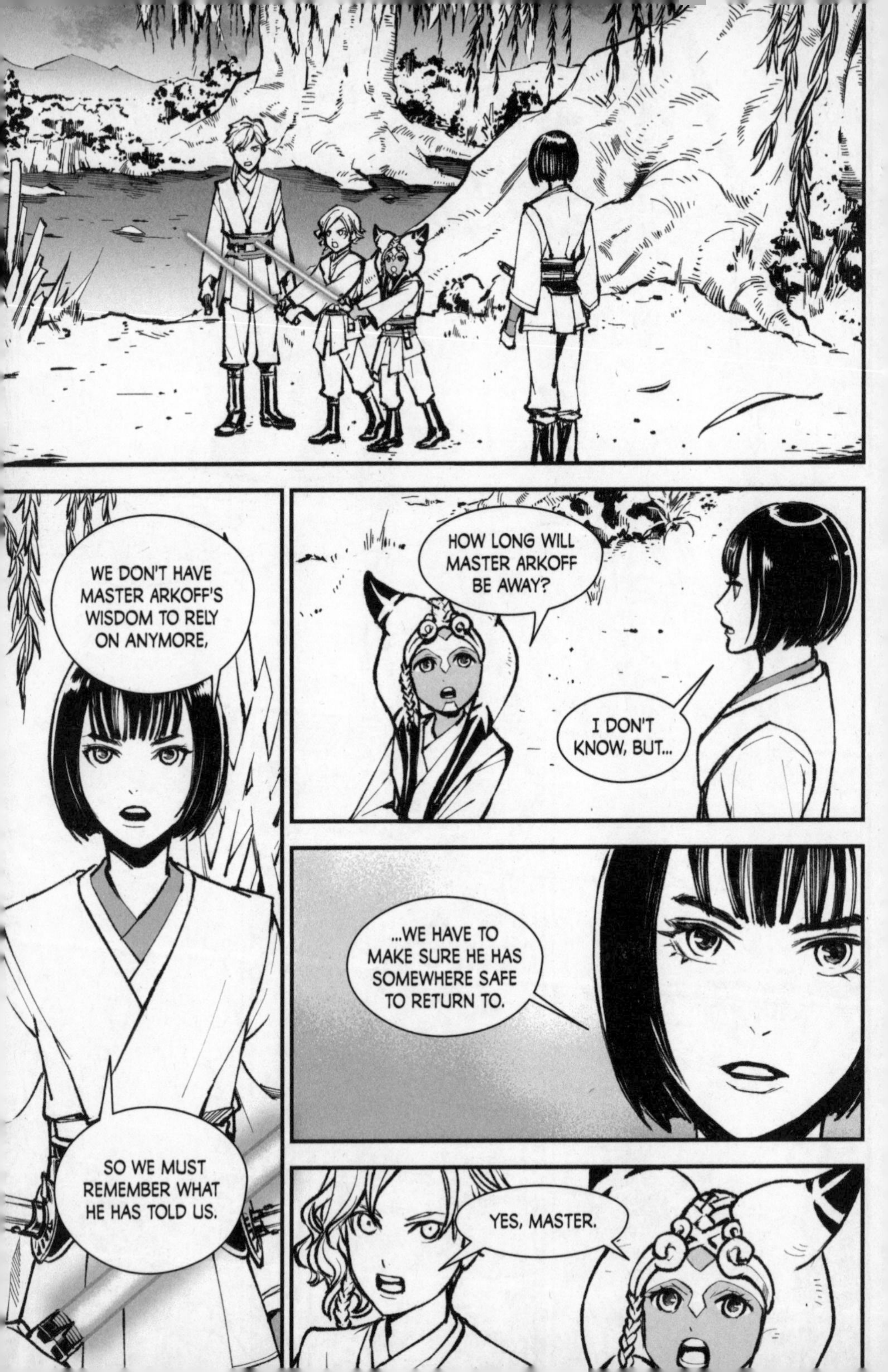
WE DON'T HAVE MASTER ARKOFF'S WISDOM TO RELY ON ANYMORE,
SO WE MUST REMEMBER WHAT HE HAS TOLD US.
HOW LONG WILL MASTER ARKOFF BE AWAY?
I DON'T KNOW, BUT...
...WE HAVE TO MAKE SURE HE HAS SOMEWHERE SAFE TO RETURN TO.
YES, MASTER.

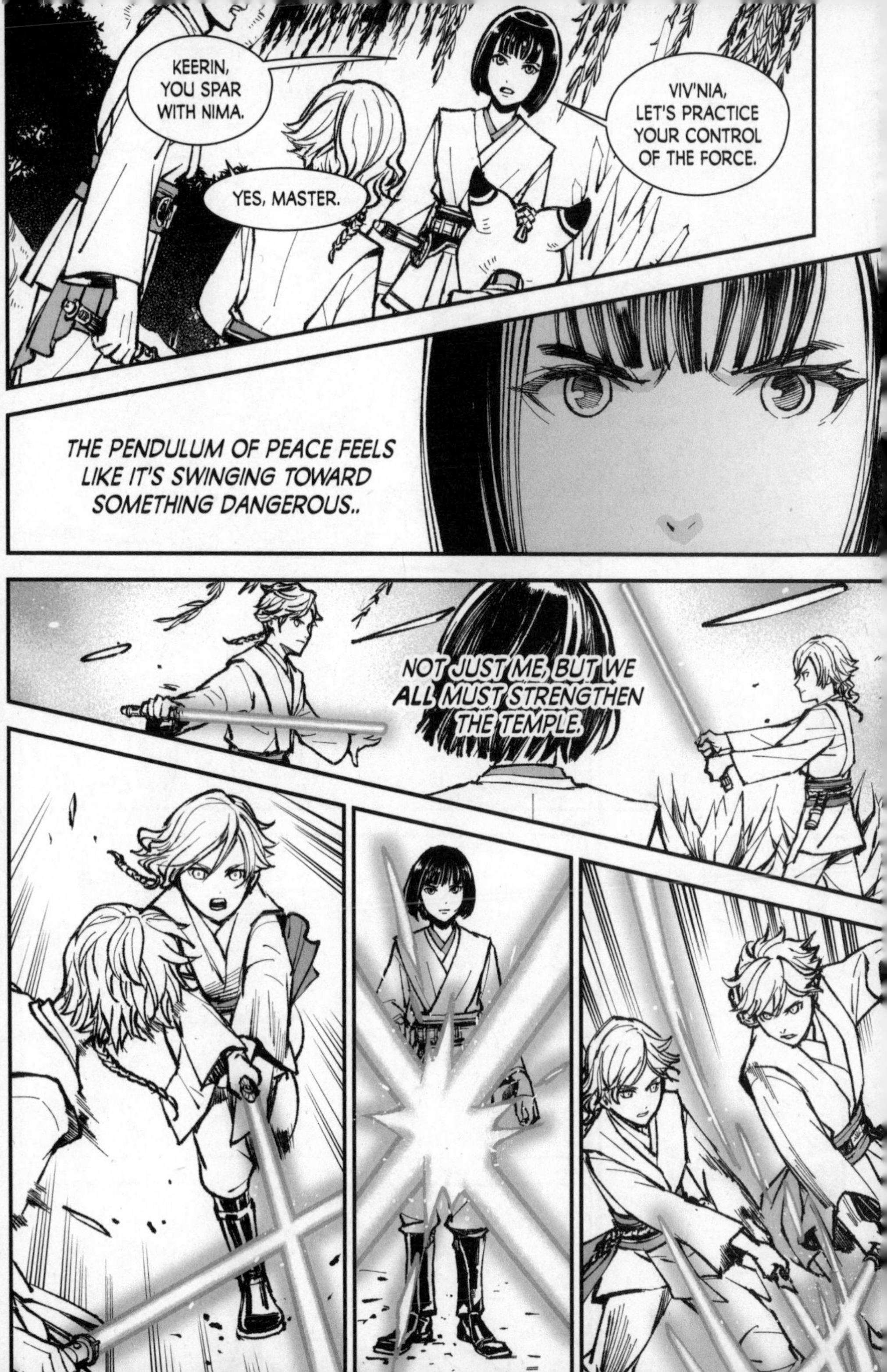
VIV'NIA, LET'S PRACTICE YOUR CONTROL OF THE FORCE.
KEERIN, YOU SPAR WITH NIMA.
YES, MASTER.
THE PENDULUM OF PEACE FEELS LIKE IT'S SWINGING TOWARD SOMETHING DANGEROUS..
NOT JUST ME, BUT WE ALL MUST STRENGTHEN THE TEMPLE.

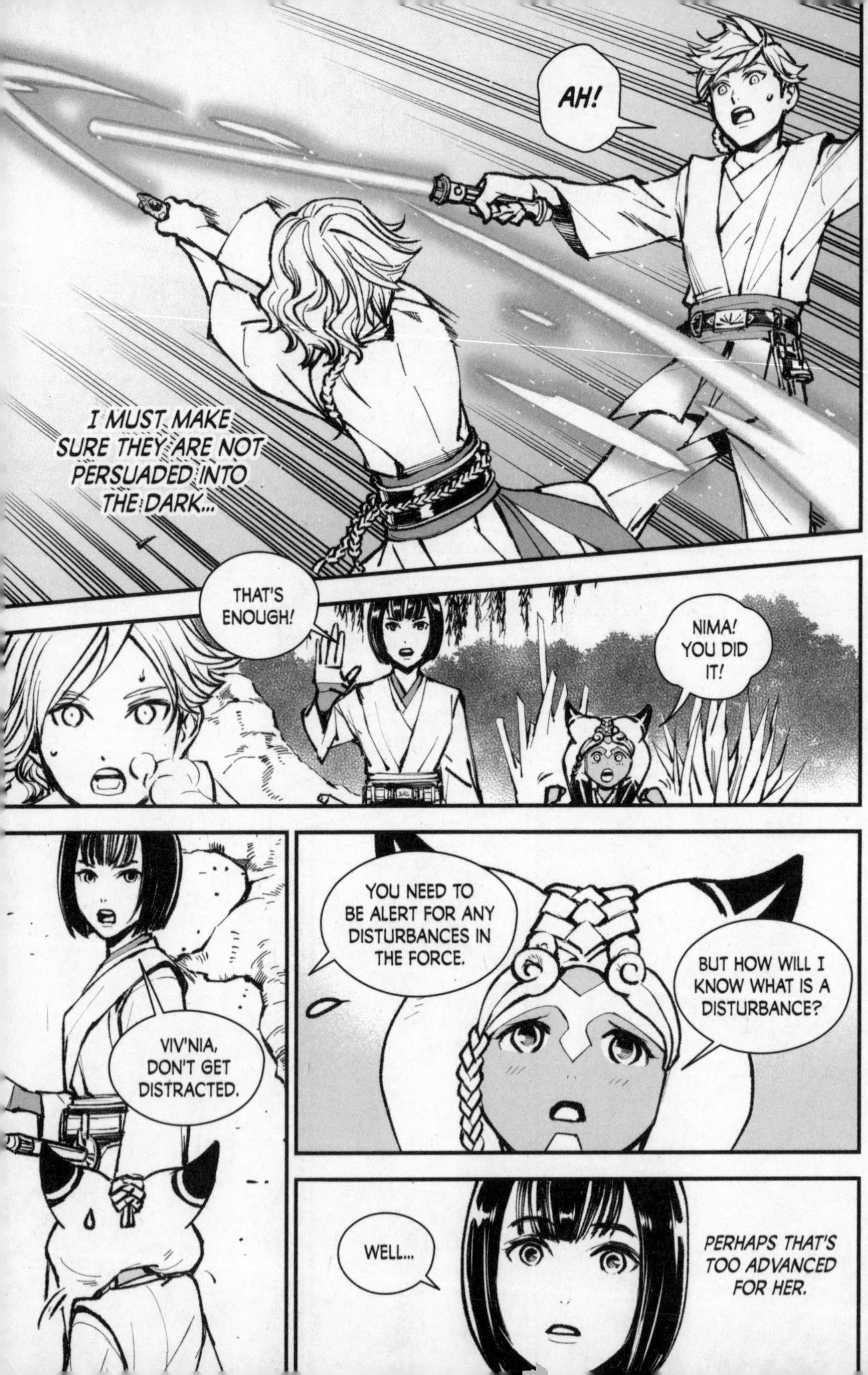
AH!
I MUST MAKE SURE THEY ARE NOT PERSUADED INTO THE DARK...
THAT'S ENOUGH!
NIMA! YOU DID IT!
VIV'NIA, DON'T GET DISTRACTED.
YOU NEED TO BE ALERT FOR ANY DISTURBANCES IN THE FORCE.
BUT HOW WILL I KNOW WHAT IS A DISTURBANCE?
WELL...
PERHAPS THAT'S TOO ADVANCED FOR HER.

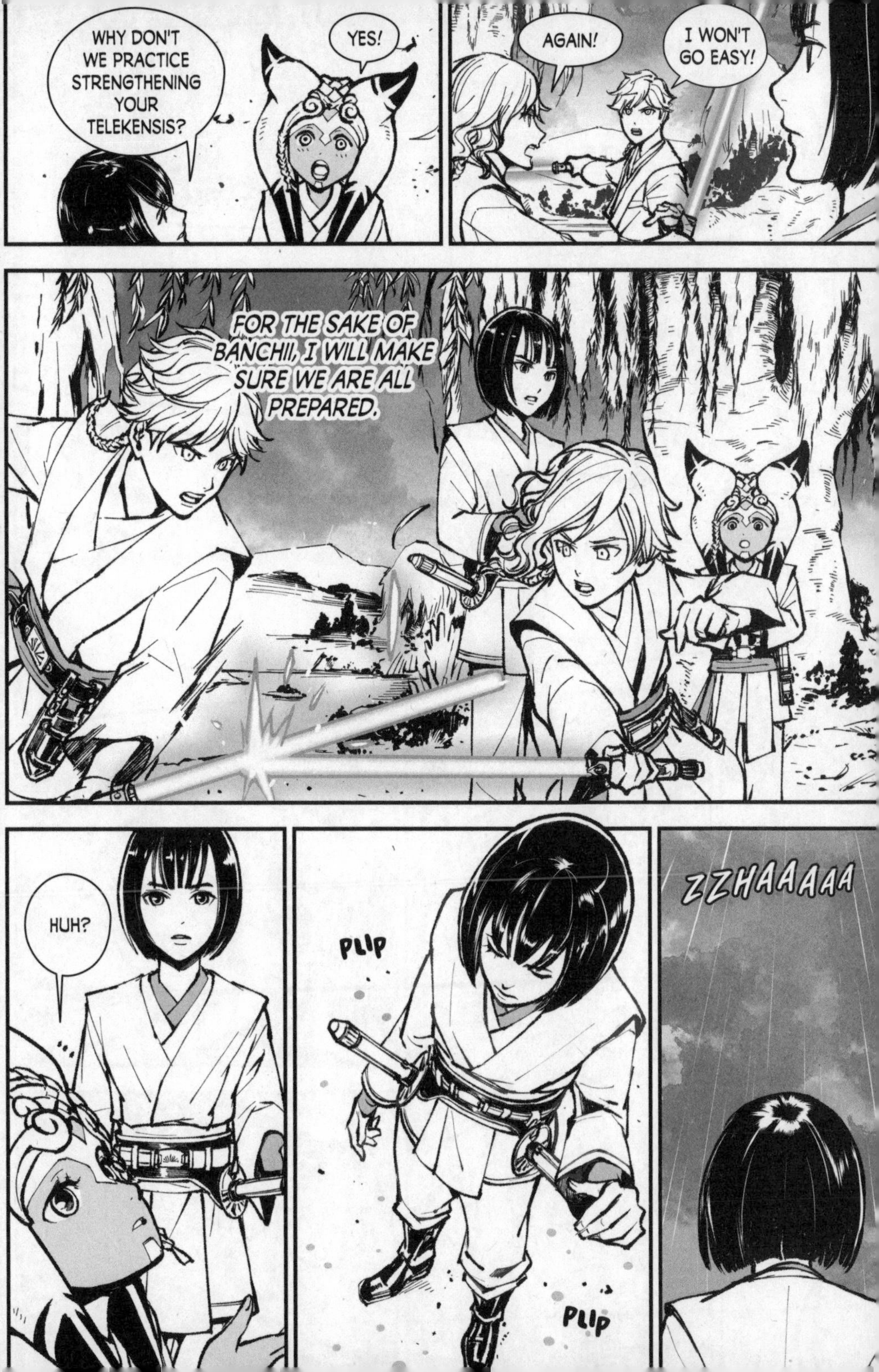
WHY DON'T WE PRACTICE STRENGTHENING YOUR TELEKENSIS?
YES!
AGAIN!
I WON'T GO EASY!
FOR THE SAKE OF BANCHII, I WILL MAKE SURE WE ARE ALL PREPARED.
HUH?
...
PLIP
PLIP
ZZHAAAAAA

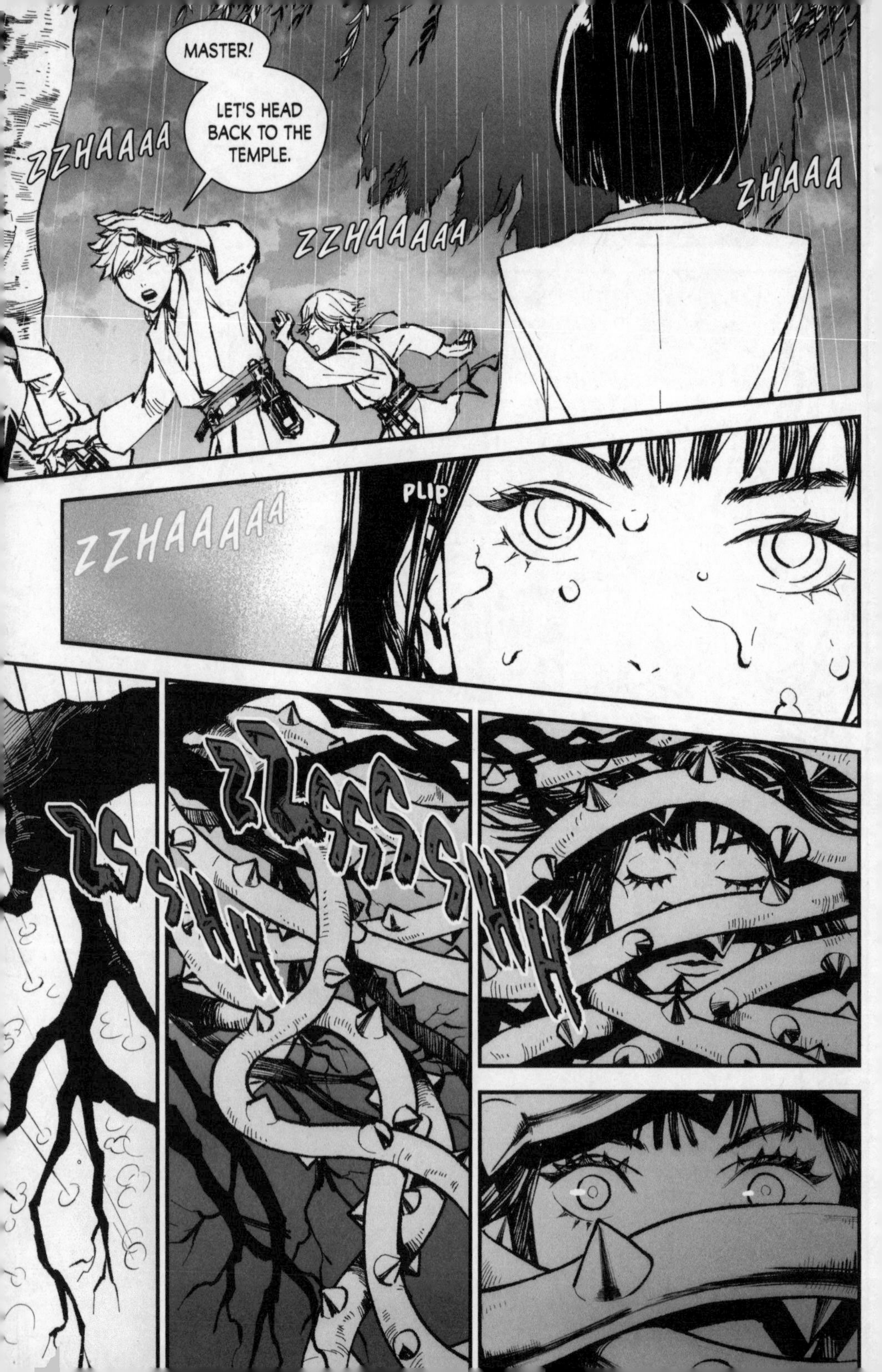
MASTER!
LET'S HEAD BACK TO THE TEMPLE.
ZZHAAAA
ZZHAAAAAA
ZHAAA
PLIP
ZZHAAAAAA
ZZSSSSHHH
ZZSSSHH

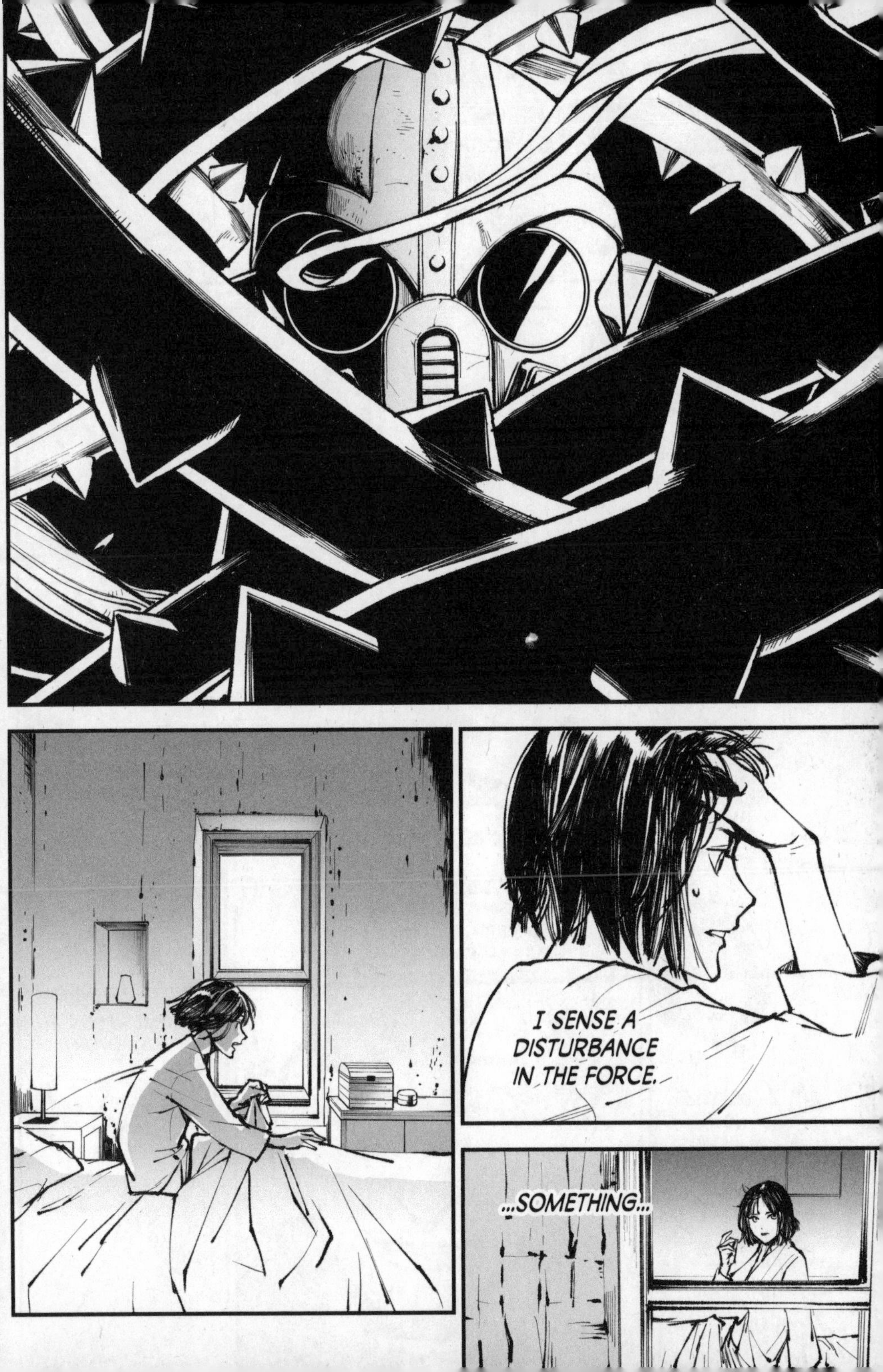
I SENSE A DISTURBANCE IN THE FORCE.
...SOMETHING...

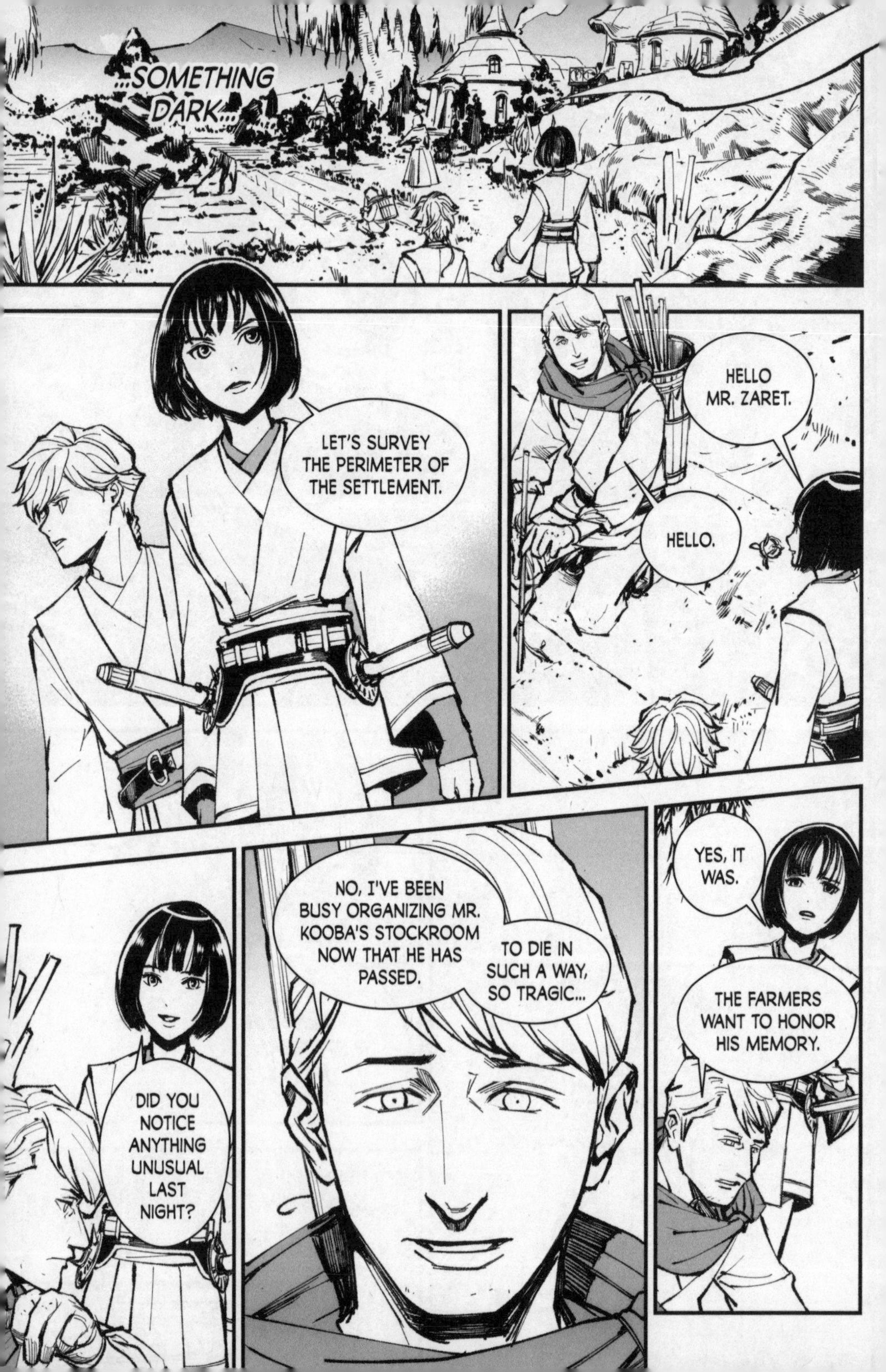
...SOMETHING DARK...
LET'S SURVEY THE PERIMETER OF THE SETTLEMENT.
HELLO MR. ZARET.
HELLO.
DID YOU NOTICE ANYTHING UNUSUAL LAST NIGHT?
NO, I'VE BEEN BUSY ORGANIZING MR. KOOBA'S STOCKROOM NOW THAT HE HAS PASSED.
TO DIE IN SUCH A WAY, SO TRAGIC...
YES, IT WAS.
THE FARMERS WANT TO HONOR HIS MEMORY.

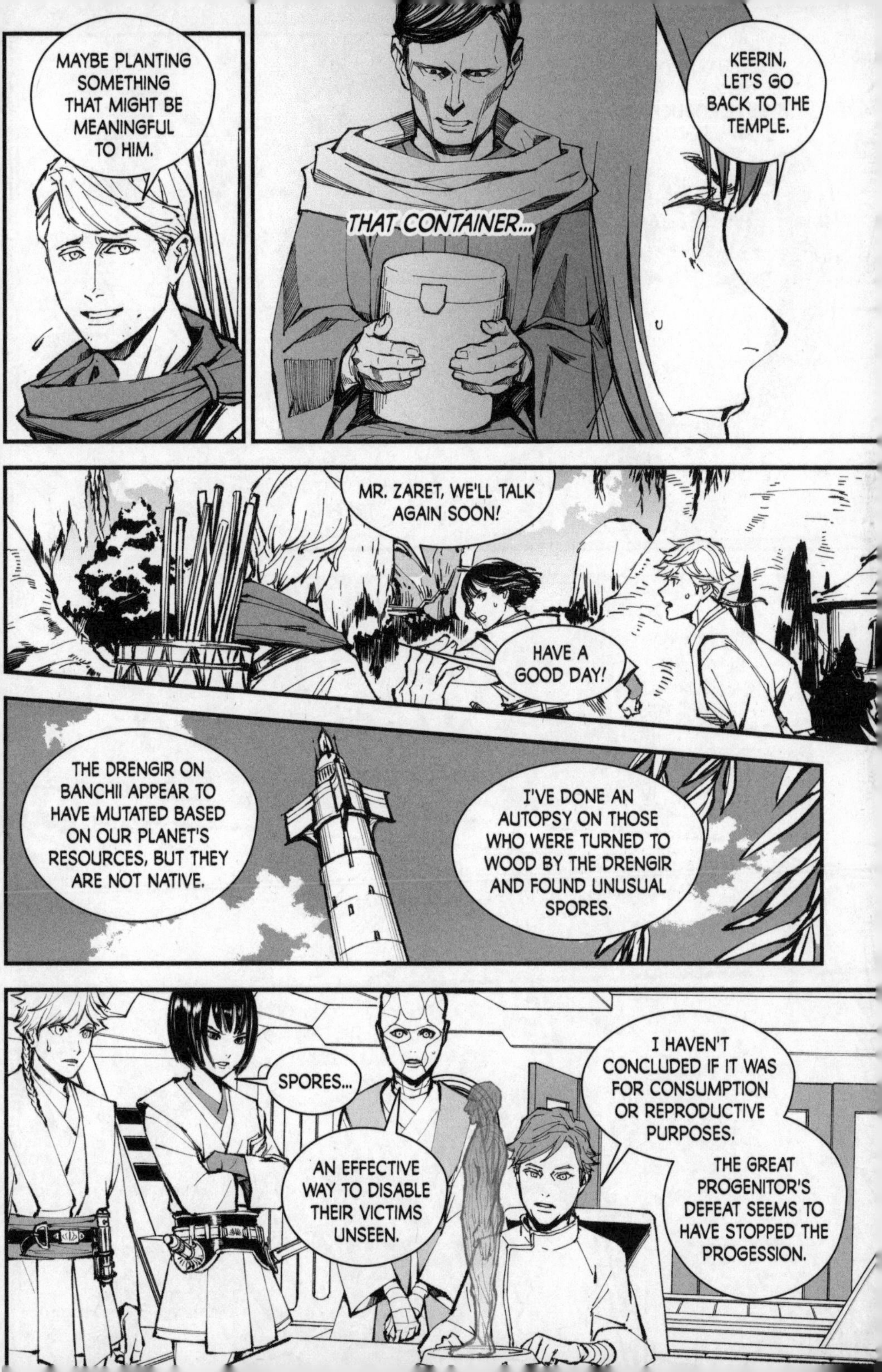
MAYBE PLANTING SOMETHING THAT MIGHT BE MEANINGFUL TO HIM.
THAT CONTAINER...
KEERIN, LET'S GO BACK TO THE TEMPLE.
MR. ZARET, WE'LL TALK AGAIN SOON!
HAVE A GOOD DAY!
THE DRENGIR ON BANCHII APPEAR TO HAVE MUTATED BASED ON OUR PLANET'S RESOURCES, BUT THEY ARE NOT NATIVE.
I'VE DONE AN AUTOPSY ON THOSE WHO WERE TURNED TO WOOD BY THE DRENGIR AND FOUND UNUSUAL SPORES.
SPORES...
AN EFFECTIVE WAY TO DISABLE THEIR VICTIMS UNSEEN.
I HAVEN'T CONCLUDED IF IT WAS FOR CONSUMPTION OR REPRODUCTIVE PURPOSES.
THE GREAT PROGENITOR'S DEFEAT SEEMS TO HAVE STOPPED THE PROGESSION.

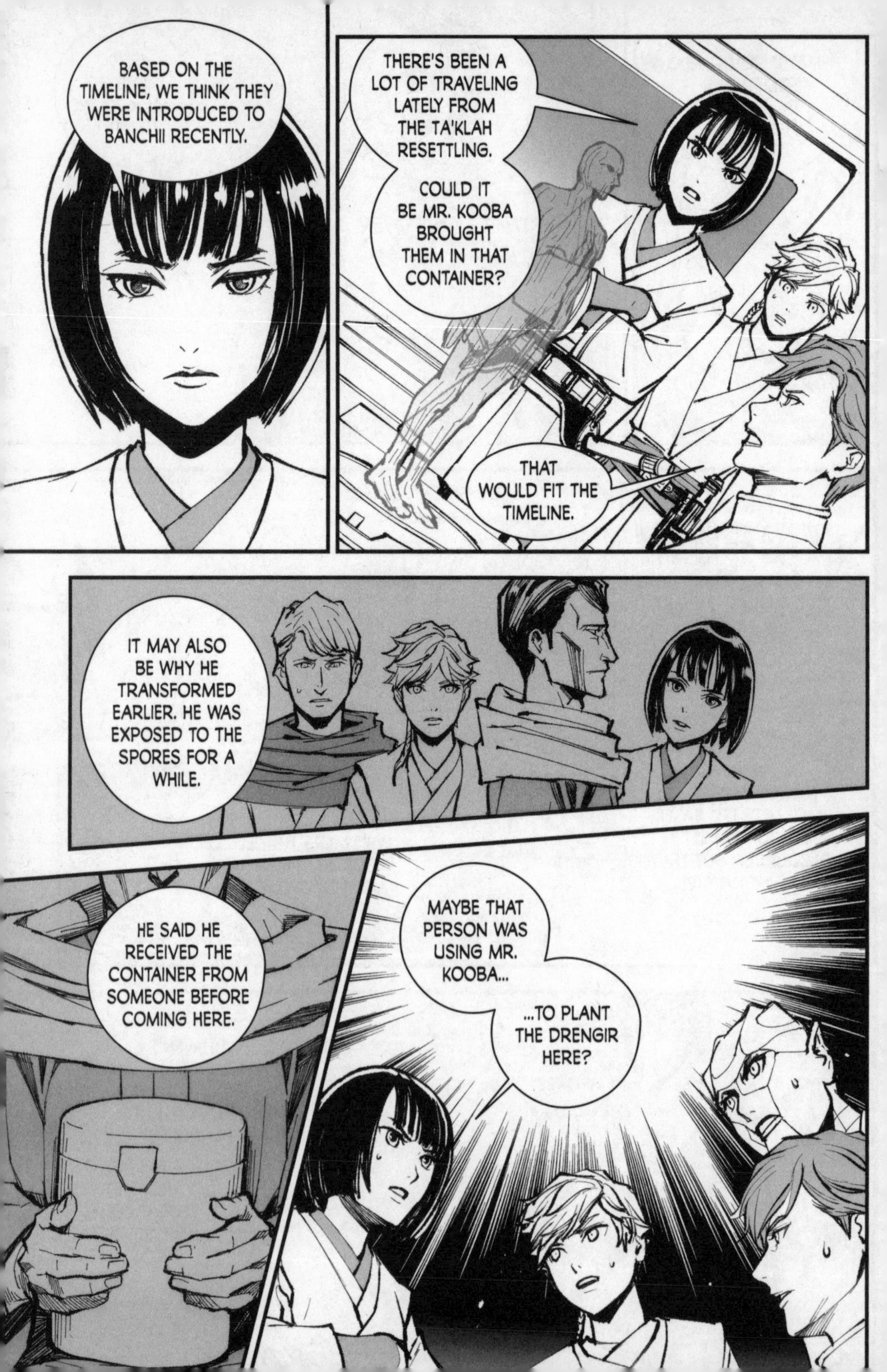
BASED ON THE TIMELINE, WE THINK THEY WERE INTRODUCED TO BANCHII RECENTLY.
THERE'S BEEN A LOT OF TRAVELING LATELY FROM THE TA'KLAH RESETTLING.
COULD IT BE MR. KOOBA BROUGHT THEM IN THAT CONTAINER?
THAT WOULD FIT THE TIMELINE.
IT MAY ALSO BE WHY HE TRANSFORMED EARLIER. HE WAS EXPOSED TO THE SPORES FOR A WHILE.
HE SAID HE RECEIVED THE CONTAINER FROM SOMEONE BEFORE COMING HERE.
MAYBE THAT PERSON WAS USING MR. KOOBA...
...TO PLANT THE DRENGIR HERE?

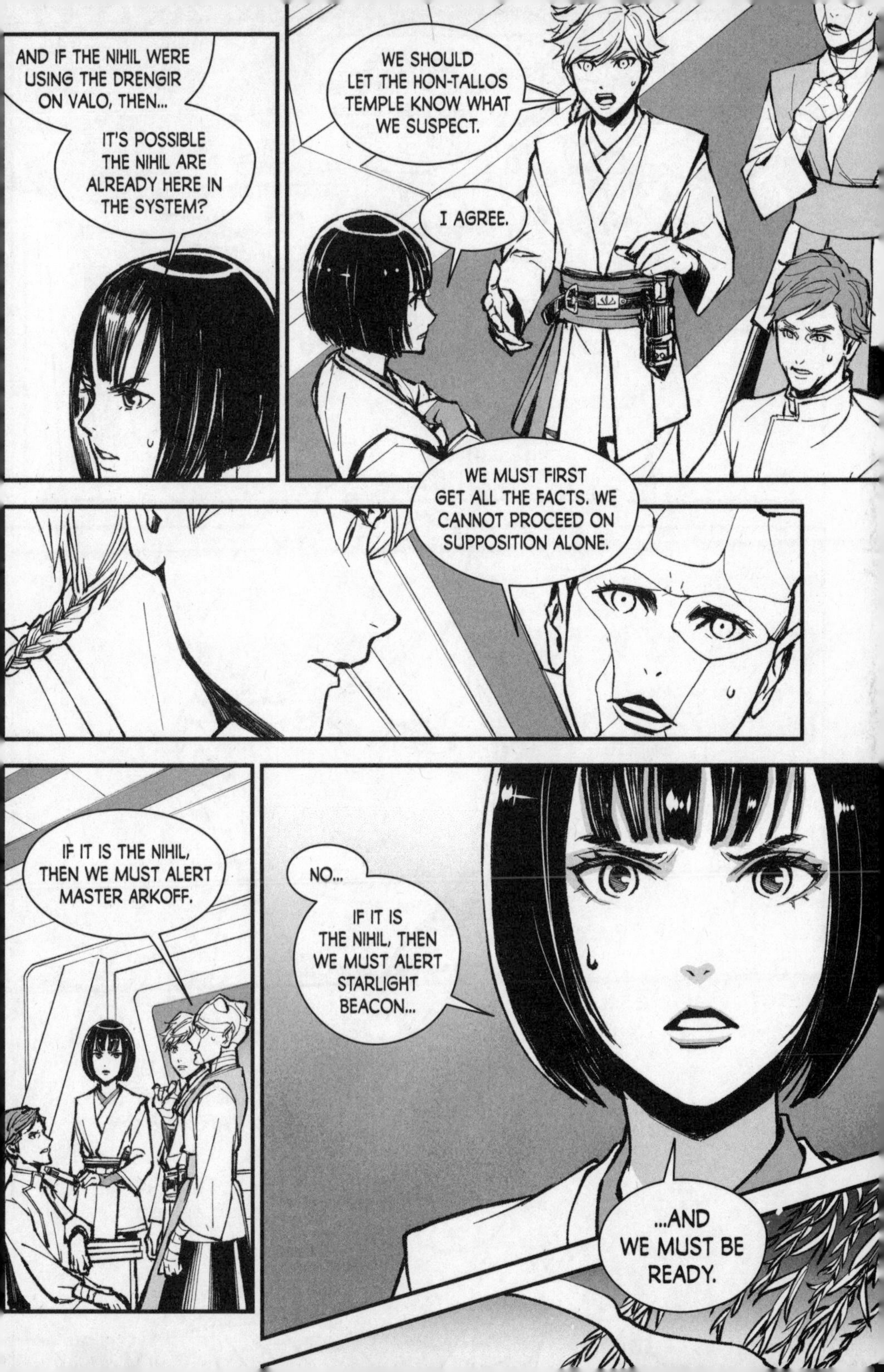
AND IF THE NIHIL WERE USING THE DRENGIR ON VALO, THEN...
IT'S POSSIBLE THE NIHIL ARE ALREADY HERE IN THE SYSTEM?
WE SHOULD LET THE HON-TALLOS TEMPLE KNOW WHAT WE SUSPECT.
I AGREE.
WE MUST FIRST GET ALL THE FACTS. WE CANNOT PROCEED ON SUPPOSITION ALONE.
IF IT IS THE NIHIL, THEN WE MUST ALERT MASTER ARKOFF.
NO...
IF IT IS THE NIHIL, THEN WE MUST ALERT STARLIGHT BEACON...
...AND WE MUST BE READY.

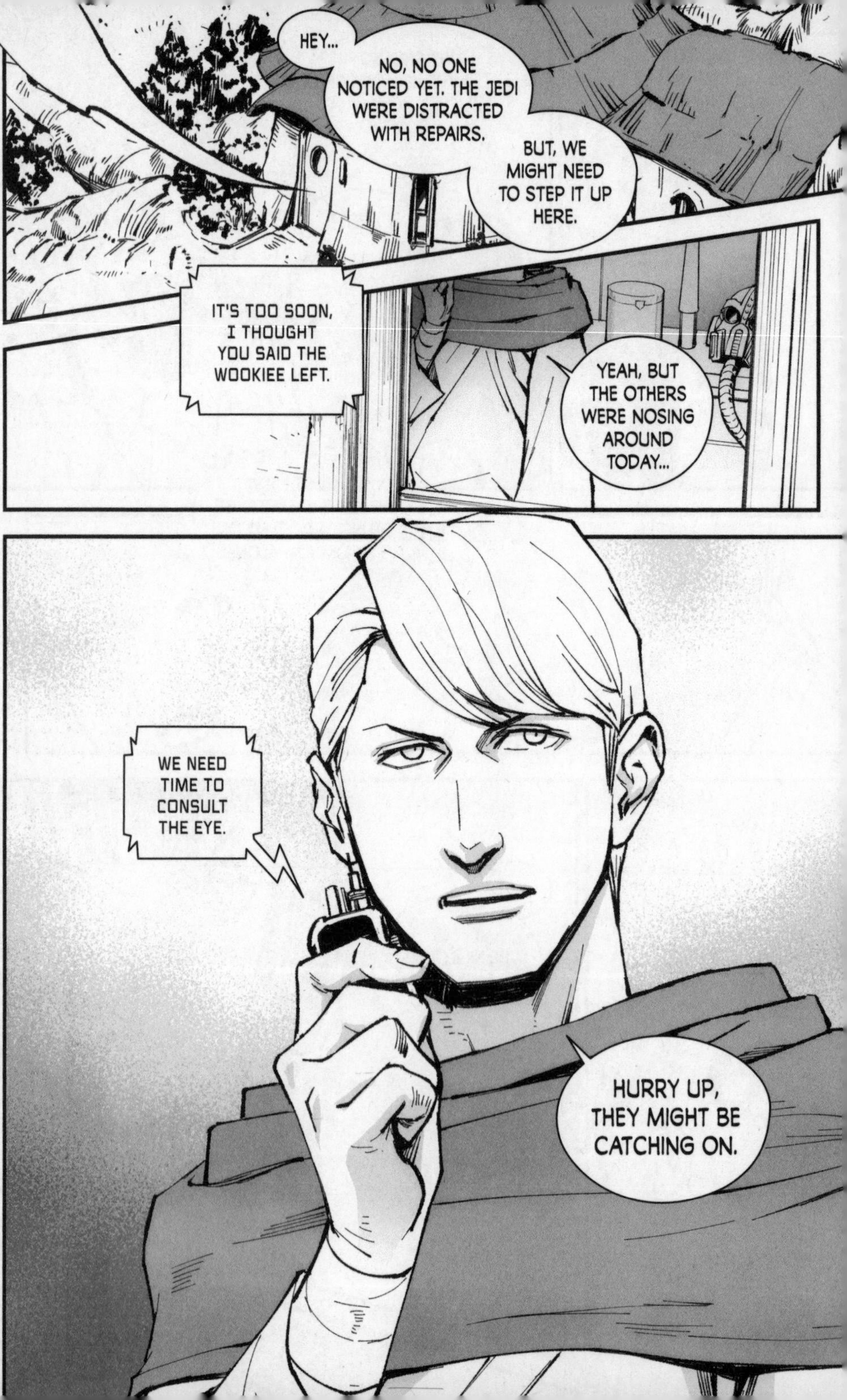
HEY...
NO, NO ONE NOTICED YET. THE JEDI WERE DISTRACTED WITH REPAIRS.
BUT, WE MIGHT NEED TO STEP IT UP HERE.
IT'S TOO SOON, I THOUGHT YOU SAID THE WOOKIEE LEFT.
YEAH, BUT THE OTHERS WERE NOSING AROUND TODAY...
WE NEED TIME TO CONSULT THE EYE.
HURRY UP, THEY MIGHT BE CATCHING ON.

TO BE CONTINUED IN

THE EDGE OF
BALANCE

BONUS CHAPTER
THE BANCHIIANS

Story by Shima Shinya
Storyboarded by Mizuki Sakakibara
Art by Nezu Usugumo

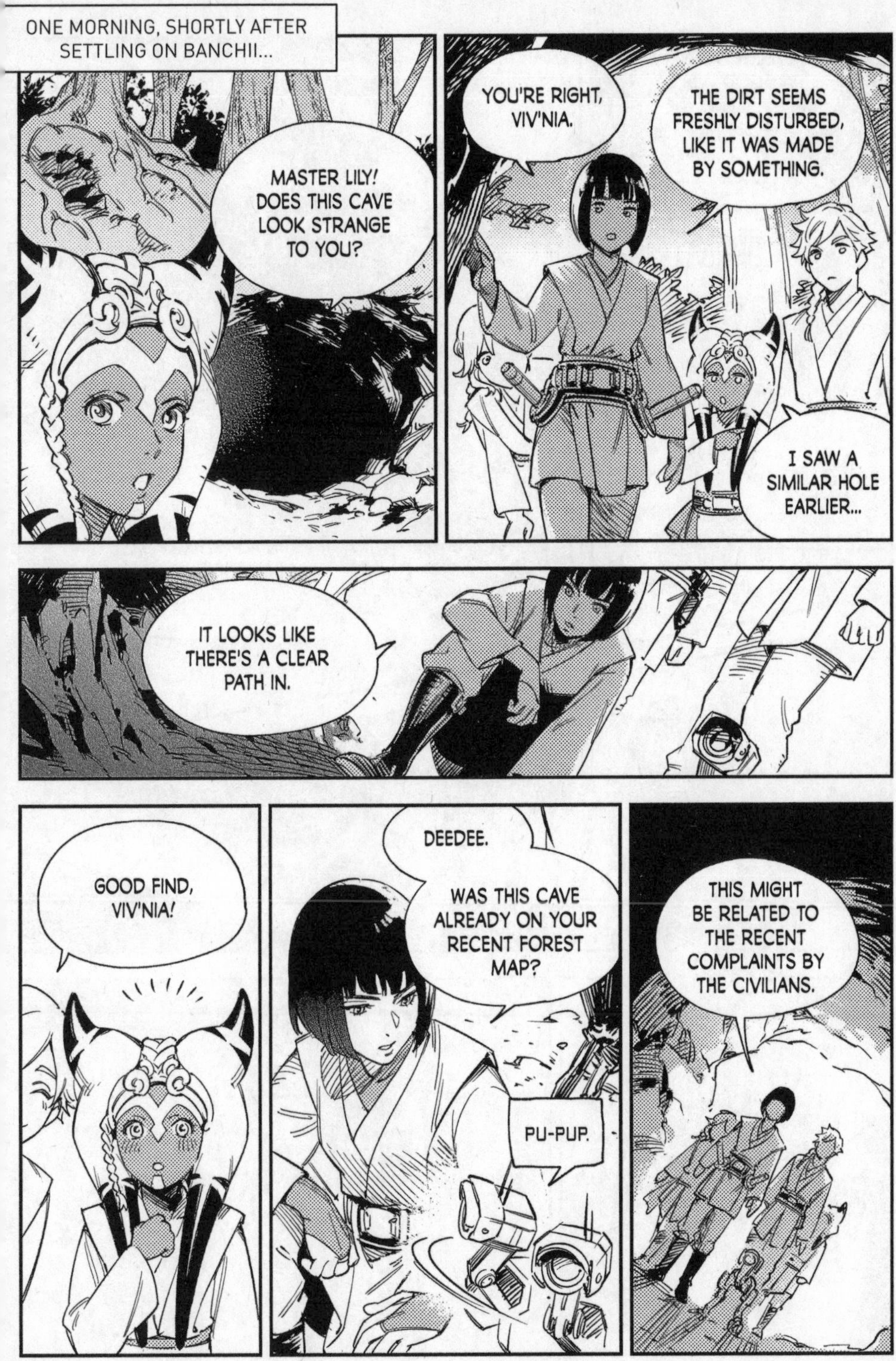
ONE MORNING, SHORTLY AFTER SETTLING ON BANCHII...
MASTER LILY! DOES THIS CAVE LOOK STRANGE TO YOU?
YOU'RE RIGHT, VIV'NIA.
THE DIRT SEEMS FRESHLY DISTURBED, LIKE IT WAS MADE BY SOMETHING.
I SAW A SIMILAR HOLE EARLIER...
IT LOOKS LIKE THERE'S A CLEAR PATH IN.
GOOD FIND, VIV'NIA!
DEEDEE.
WAS THIS CAVE ALREADY ON YOUR RECENT FOREST MAP?
PU-PUP.
THIS MIGHT BE RELATED TO THE RECENT COMPLAINTS BY THE CIVILIANS.

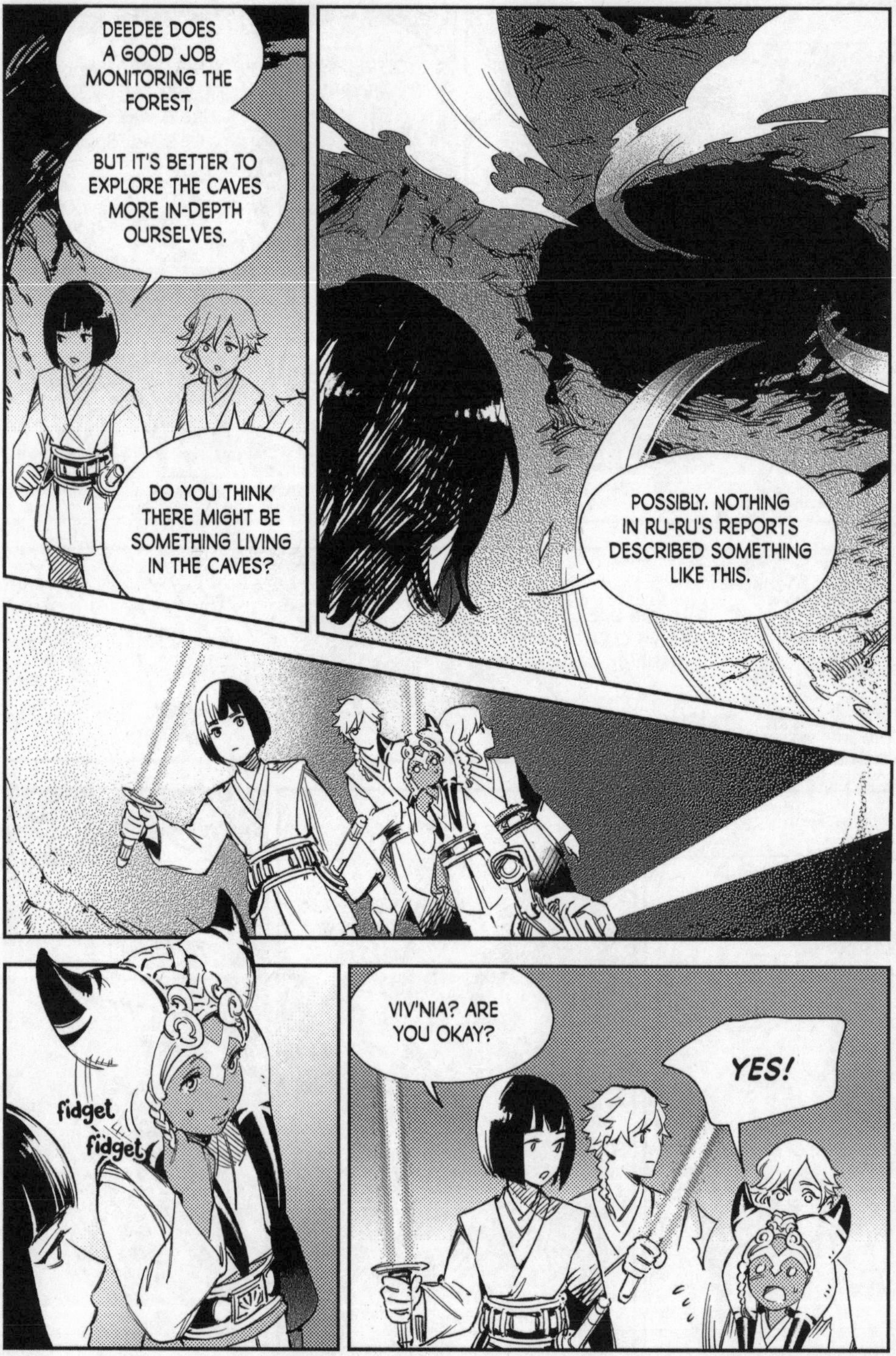
DEEDEE DOES A GOOD JOB MONITORING THE FOREST,
BUT IT'S BETTER TO EXPLORE THE CAVES MORE IN-DEPTH OURSELVES.
DO YOU THINK THERE MIGHT BE SOMETHING LIVING IN THE CAVES?
POSSIBLY. NOTHING IN RU-RU'S REPORTS DESCRIBED SOMETHING LIKE THIS.
fidget fidget
VIV'NIA? ARE YOU OKAY?
YES!

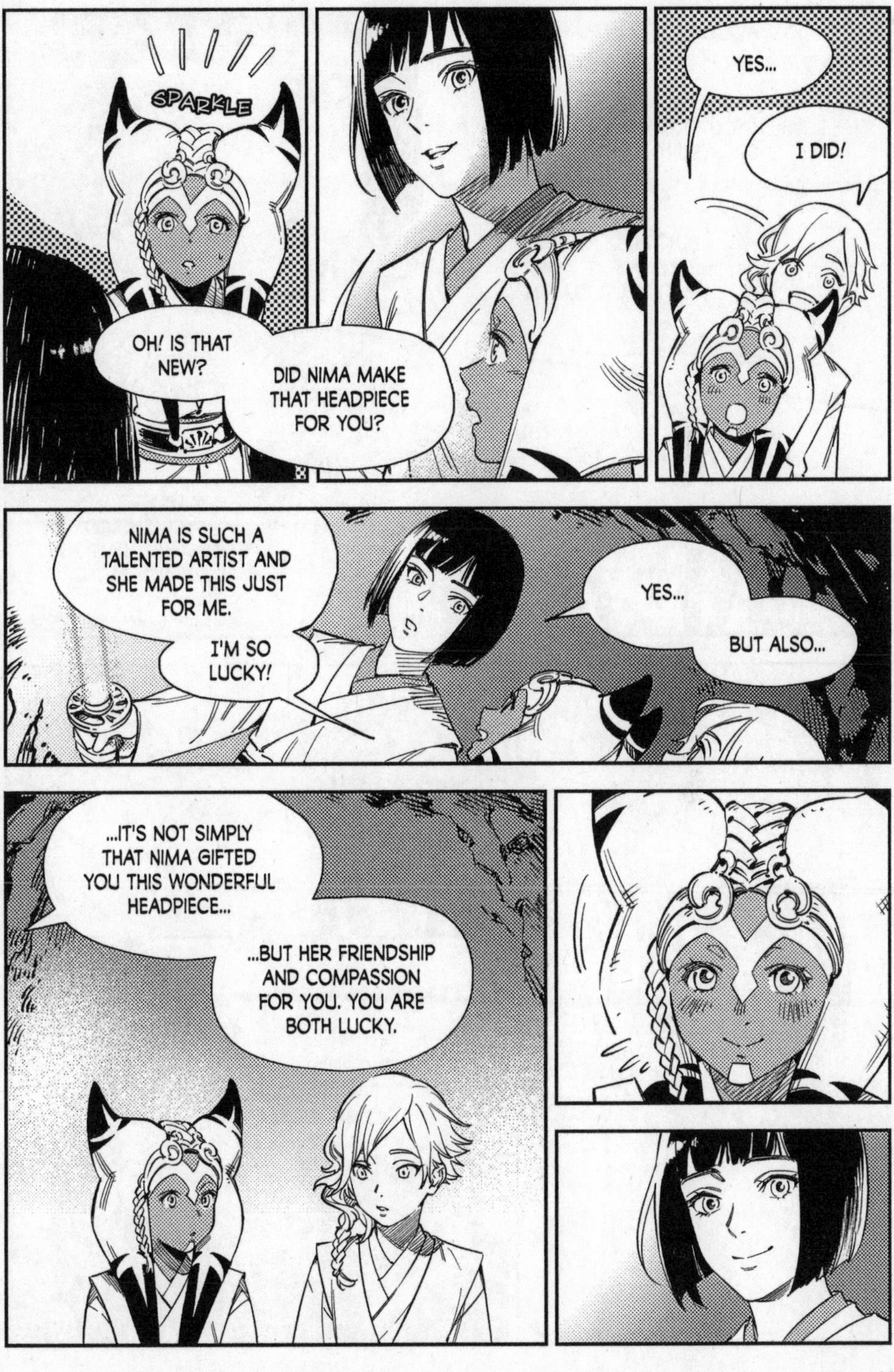
SPARKLE
OH! IS THAT NEW?
DID NIMA MAKE THAT HEADPIECE FOR YOU?
YES...
I DID!
NIMA IS SUCH A TALENTED ARTIST AND SHE MADE THIS JUST FOR ME.
I'M SO LUCKY!
YES...
BUT ALSO...
...IT'S NOT SIMPLY THAT NIMA GIFTED YOU THIS WONDERFUL HEADPIECE...
...BUT HER FRIENDSHIP AND COMPASSION FOR YOU. YOU ARE BOTH LUCKY.

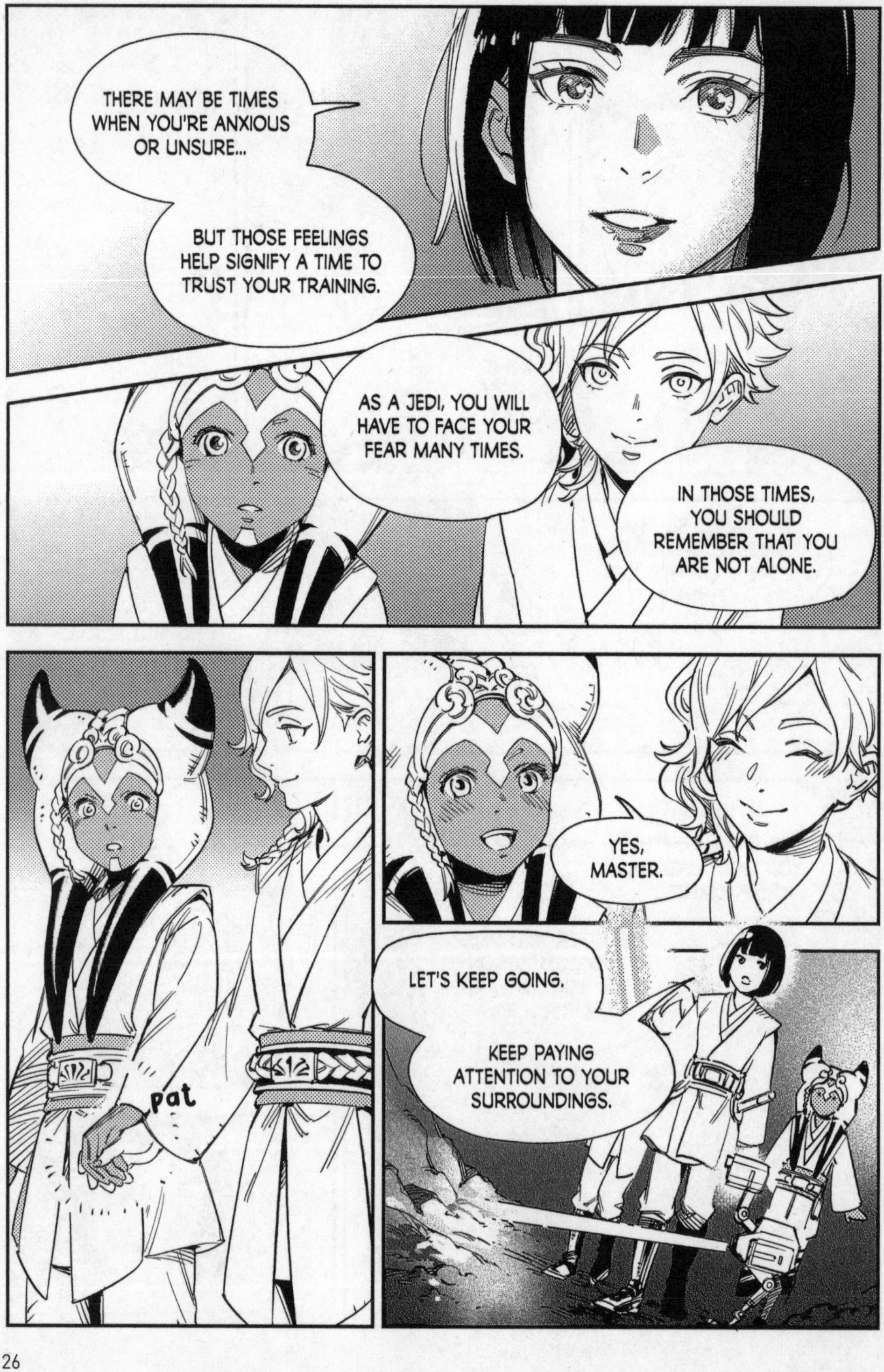
THERE MAY BE TIMES WHEN YOU'RE ANXIOUS OR UNSURE...
BUT THOSE FEELINGS HELP SIGNIFY A TIME TO TRUST YOUR TRAINING.
AS A JEDI, YOU WILL HAVE TO FACE YOUR FEAR MANY TIMES.
IN THOSE TIMES, YOU SHOULD REMEMBER THAT YOU ARE NOT ALONE.
pat
YES, MASTER.
LET'S KEEP GOING.
KEEP PAYING ATTENTION TO YOUR SURROUNDINGS.

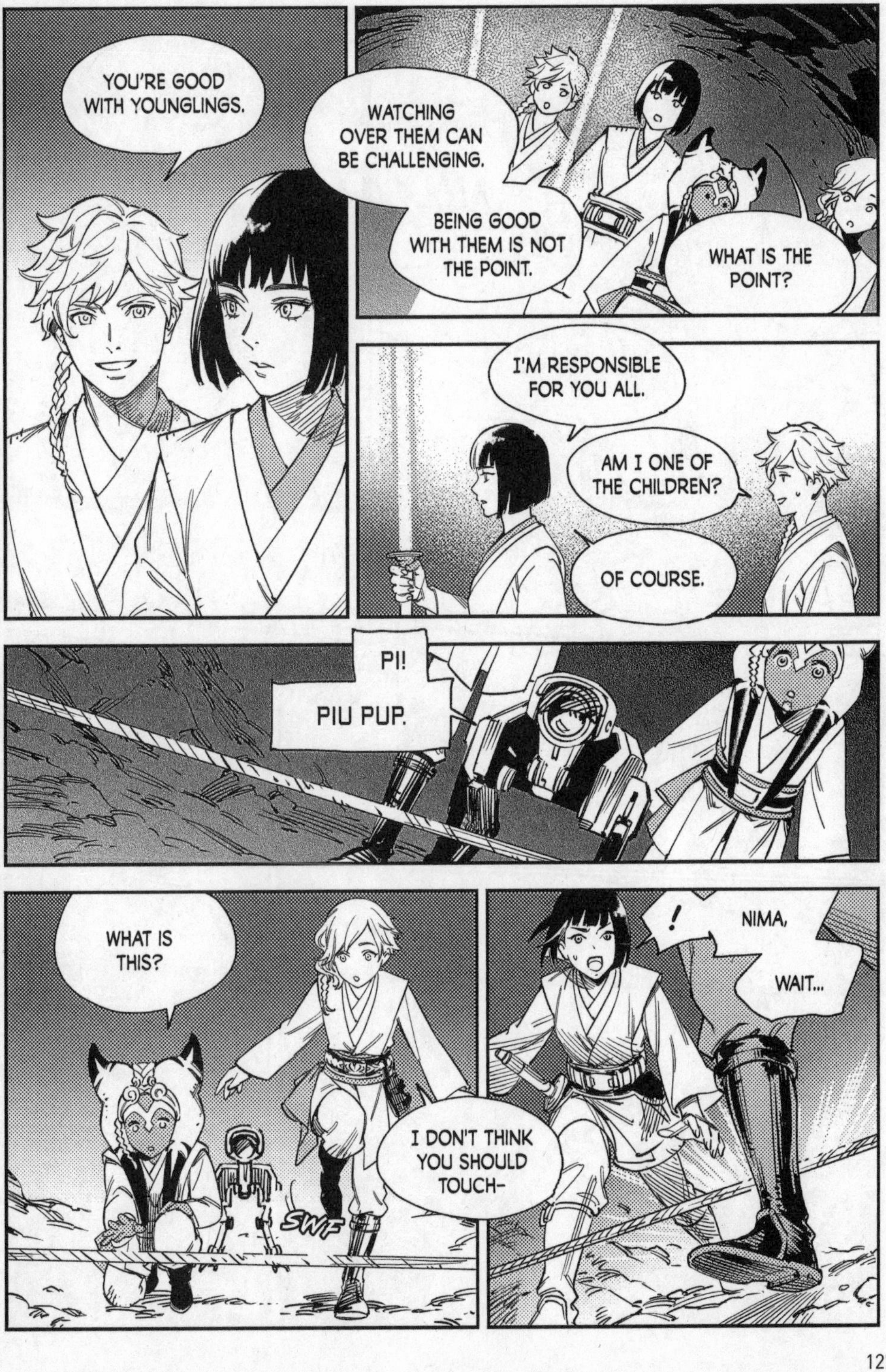
YOU'RE GOOD WITH YOUNGLINGS.
WATCHING OVER THEM CAN BE CHALLENGING.
BEING GOOD WITH THEM IS NOT THE POINT.
WHAT IS THE POINT?
I'M RESPONSIBLE FOR YOU ALL.
AM I ONE OF THE CHILDREN?
OF COURSE.
PI!
PIU PUP.
WHAT IS THIS?
SWF
I DON'T THINK YOU SHOULD TOUCH-
!
NIMA,
WAIT...

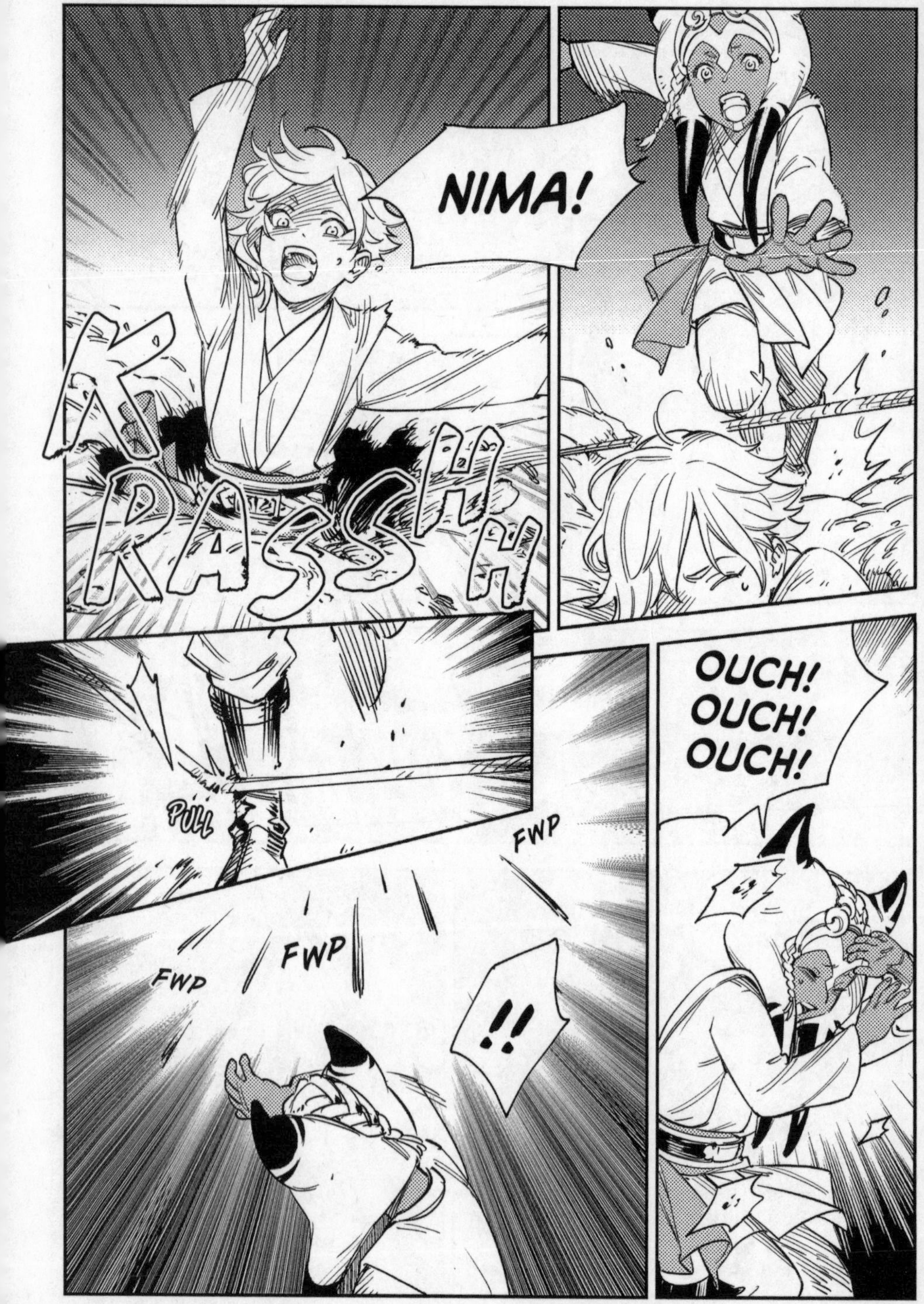
NIMA!
KRASSHHH
PULL
FWP
FWP
FWP
!!
OUCH! OUCH! OUCH!

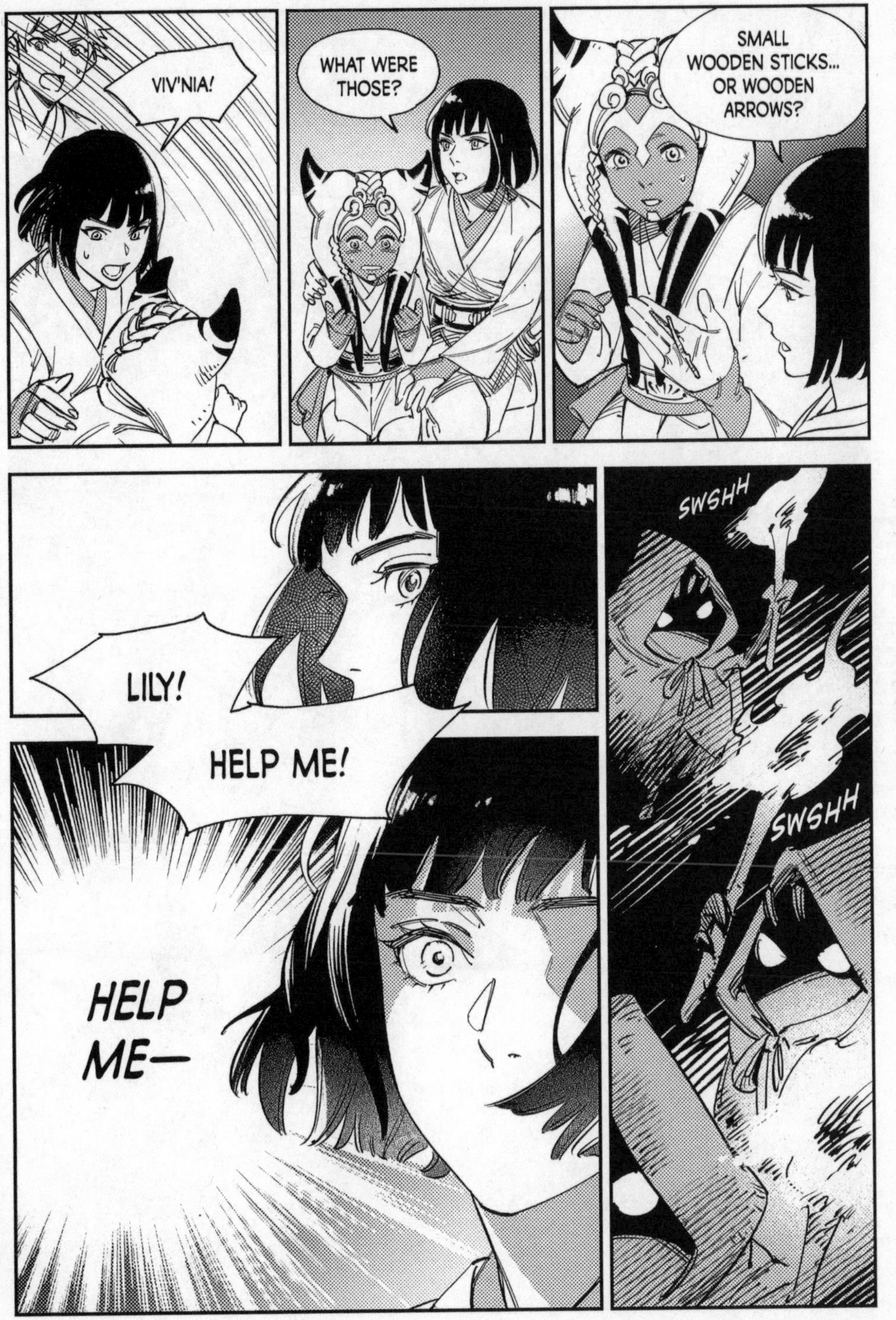
VIV'NIA!
WHAT WERE THOSE?
SMALL WOODEN STICKS... OR WOODEN ARROWS?
LILY!
HELP ME!
HELP ME—
SWSHH
SWSHH

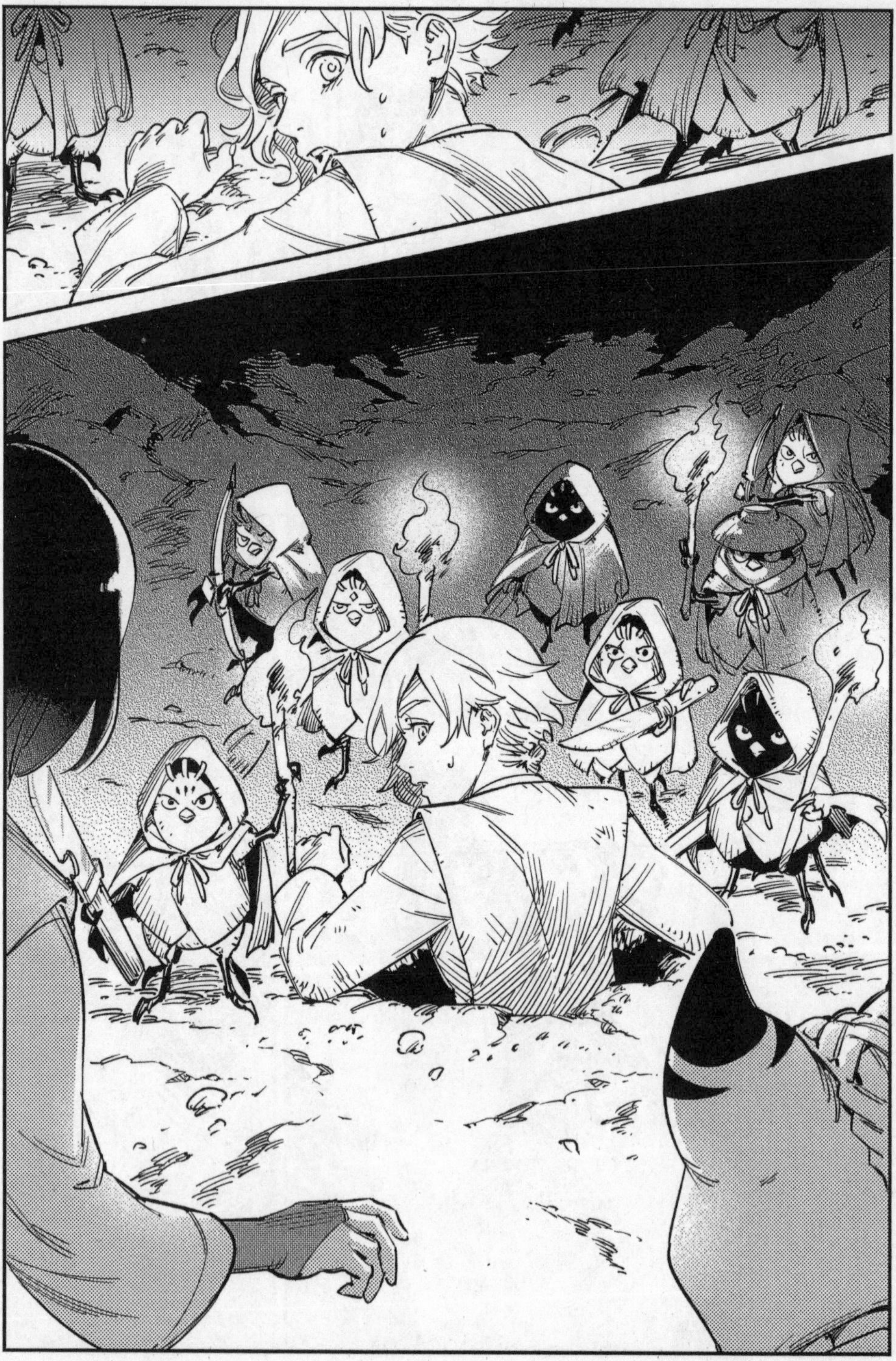

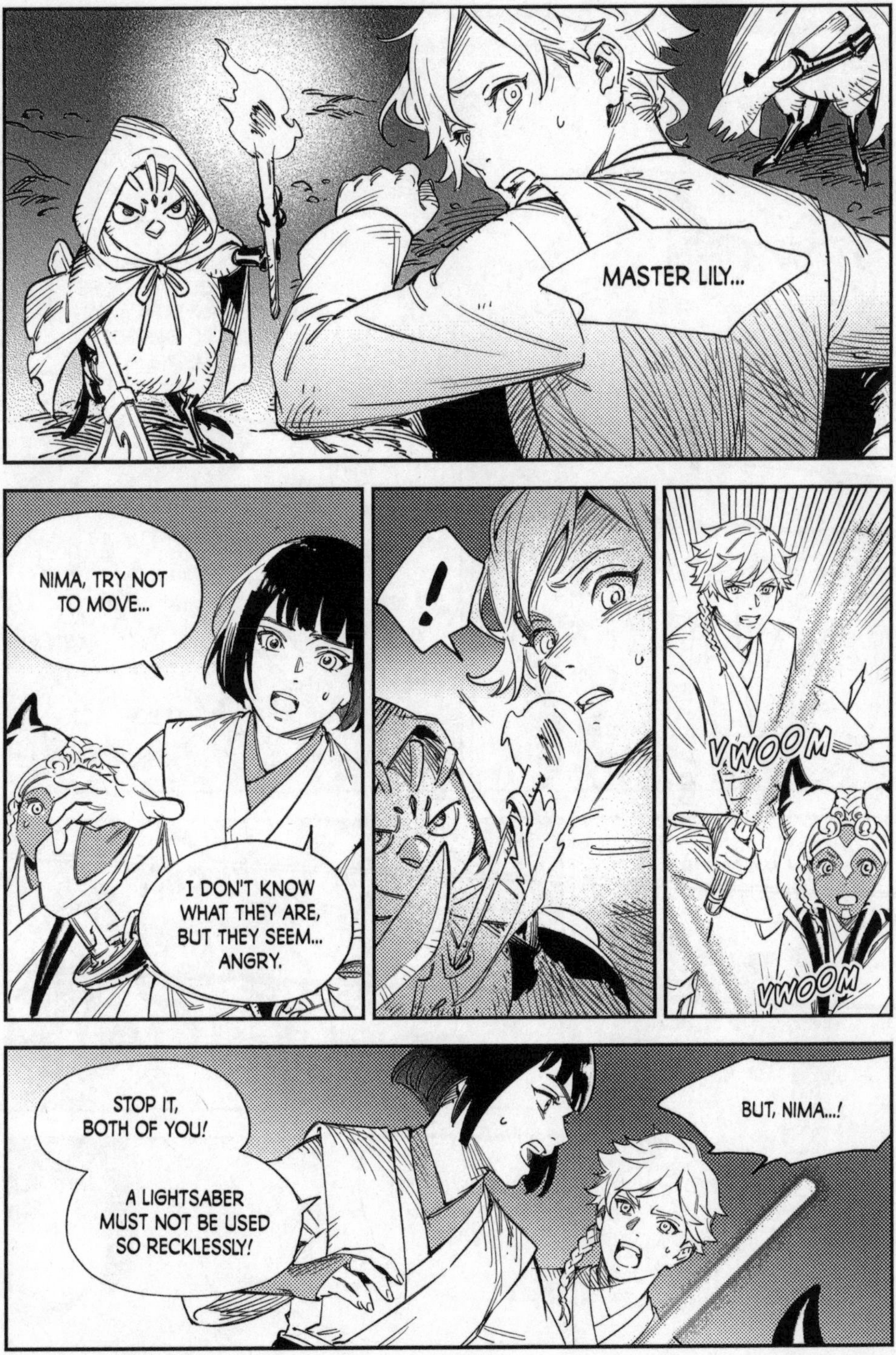
MASTER LILY...
NIMA, TRY NOT TO MOVE...
I DON'T KNOW WHAT THEY ARE, BUT THEY SEEM... ANGRY.
!
VWOOM
VWOOM
STOP IT, BOTH OF YOU!
A LIGHTSABER MUST NOT BE USED SO RECKLESSLY!
BUT, NIMA...!

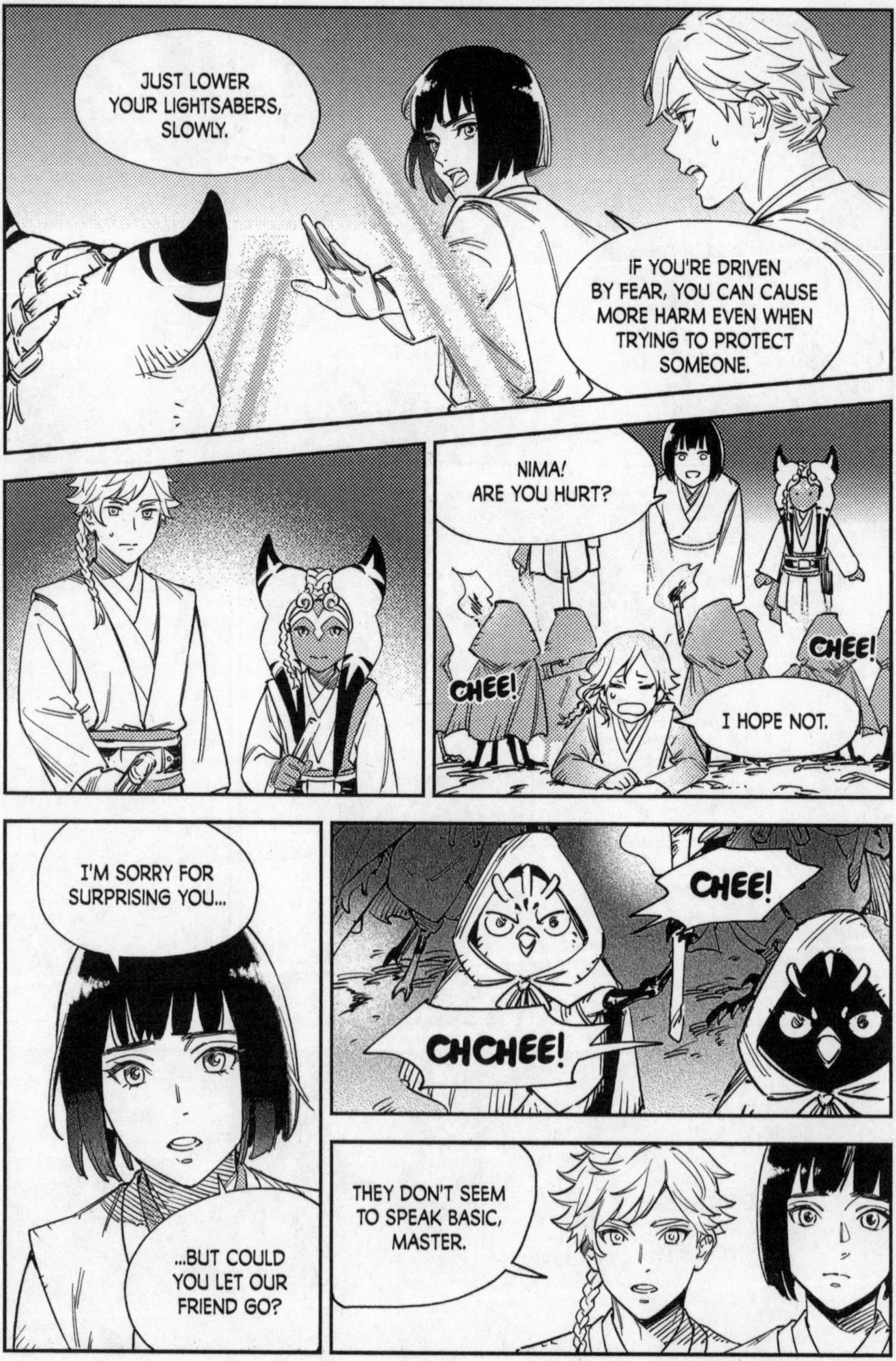
JUST LOWER YOUR LIGHTSABERS, SLOWLY.
IF YOU'RE DRIVEN BY FEAR, YOU CAN CAUSE MORE HARM EVEN WHEN TRYING TO PROTECT SOMEONE.
NIMA! ARE YOU HURT?
CHEE!
CHEE!
I HOPE NOT.
I'M SORRY FOR SURPRISING YOU...
...BUT COULD YOU LET OUR FRIEND GO?
CHEE!
CHCHEE!
THEY DON'T SEEM TO SPEAK BASIC, MASTER.

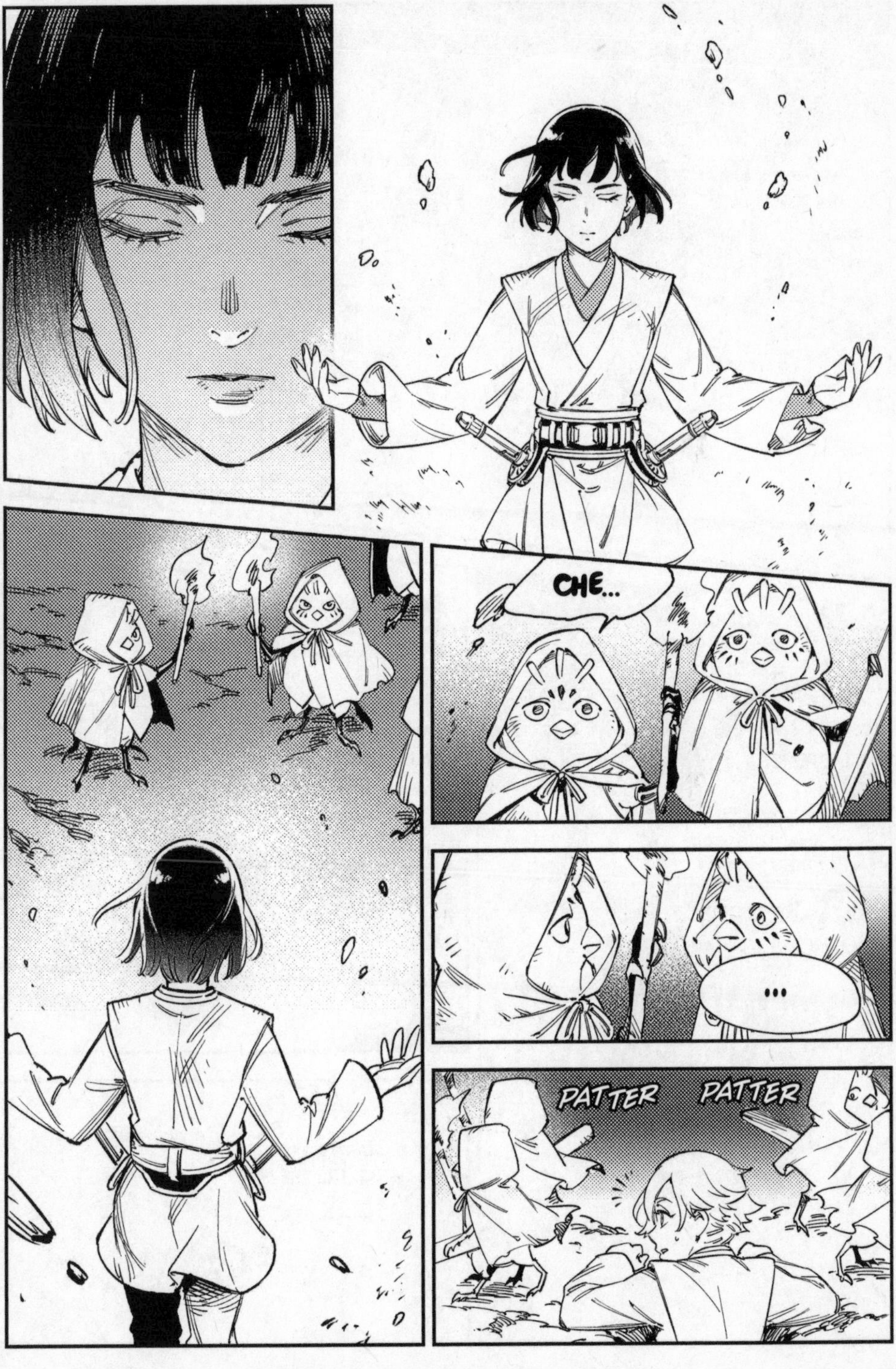
CHE...
...
PATTER PATTER

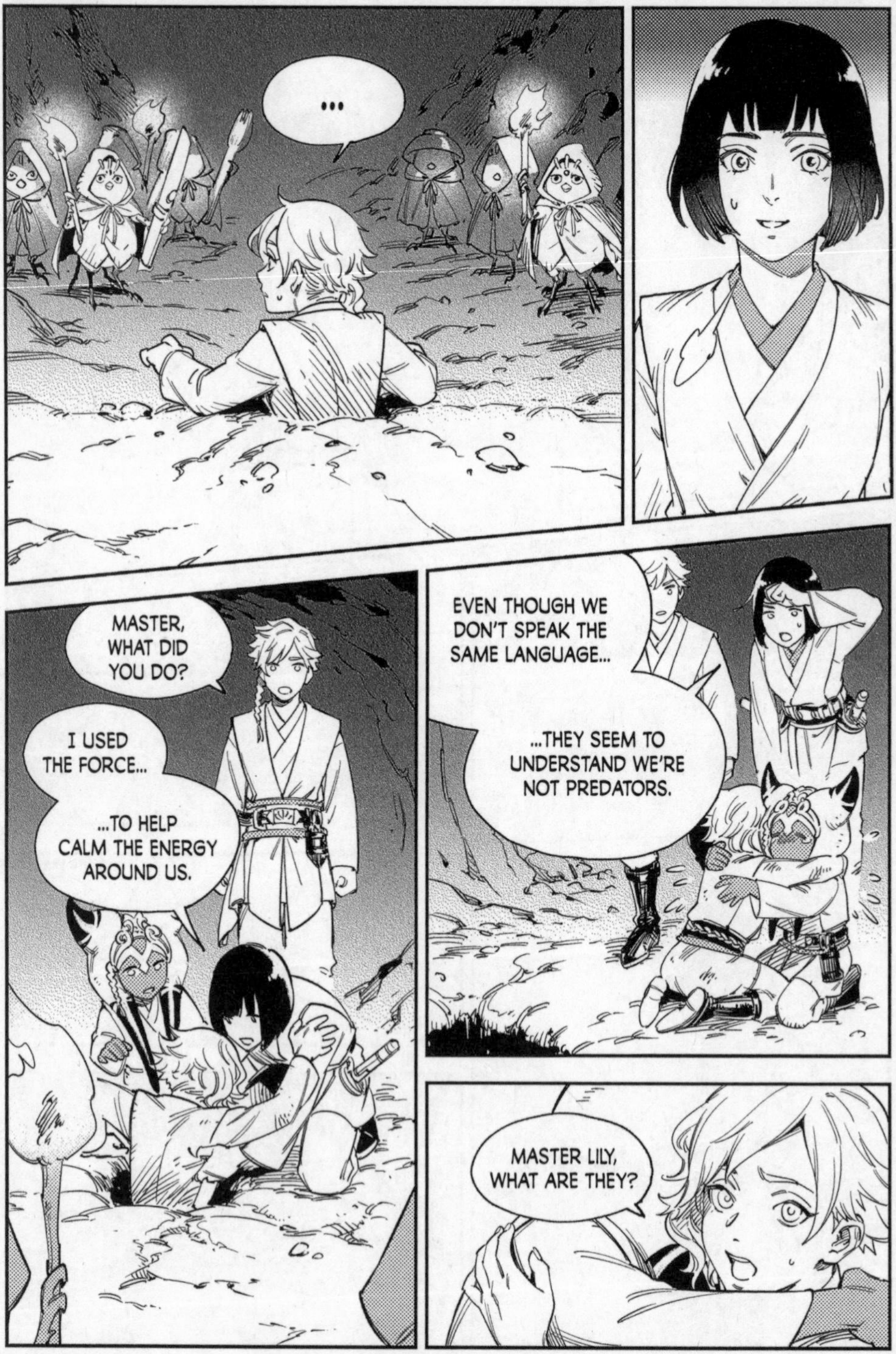
...
MASTER, WHAT DID YOU DO?
I USED THE FORCE...
...TO HELP CALM THE ENERGY AROUND US.
EVEN THOUGH WE DON'T SPEAK THE SAME LANGUAGE...
...THEY SEEM TO UNDERSTAND WE'RE NOT PREDATORS.
MASTER LILY, WHAT ARE THEY?

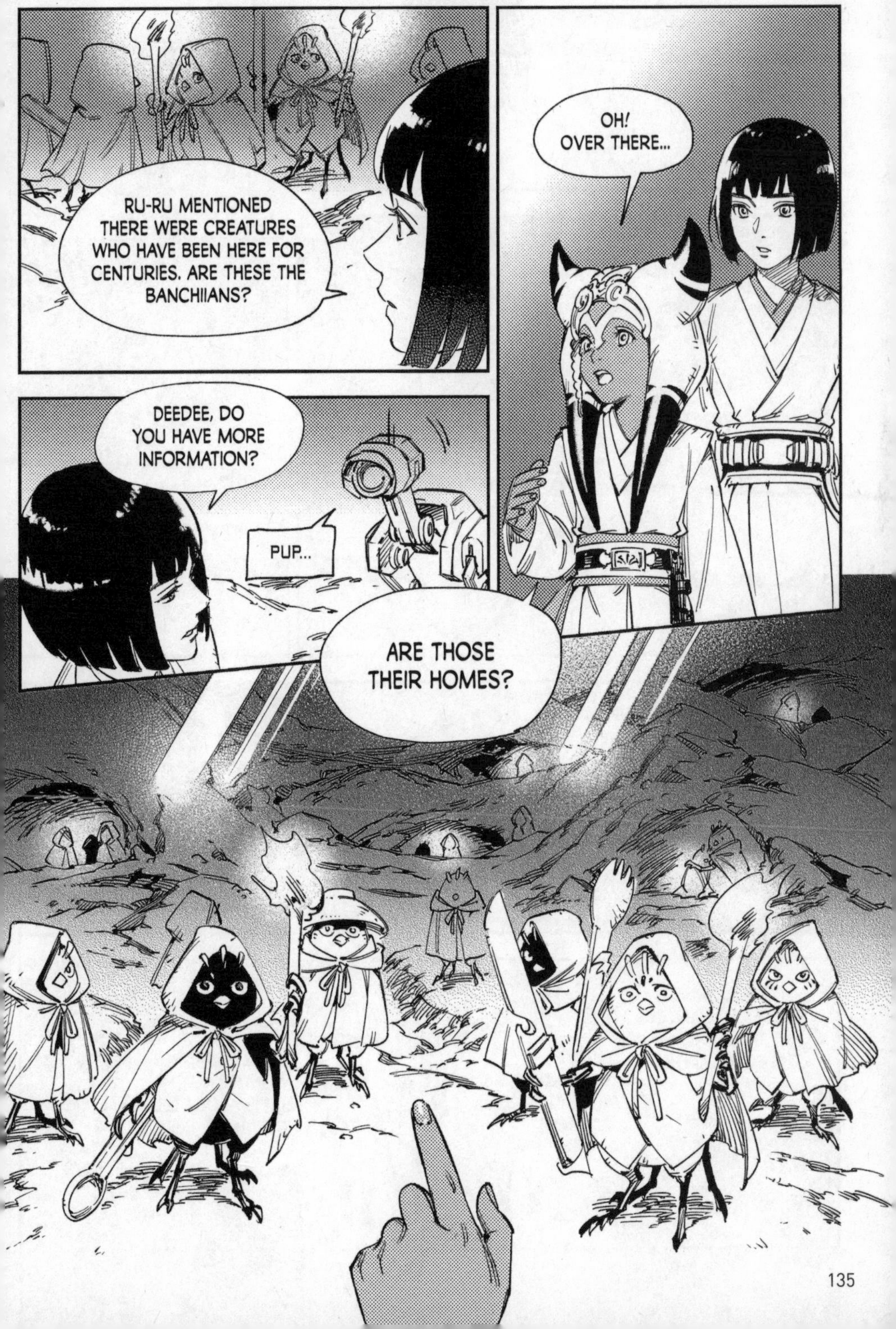
RU-RU MENTIONED THERE WERE CREATURES WHO HAVE BEEN HERE FOR CENTURIES. ARE THESE THE BANCHIIANS?
OH! OVER THERE...
DEEDEE, DO YOU HAVE MORE INFORMATION?
PUP...
ARE THOSE THEIR HOMES?

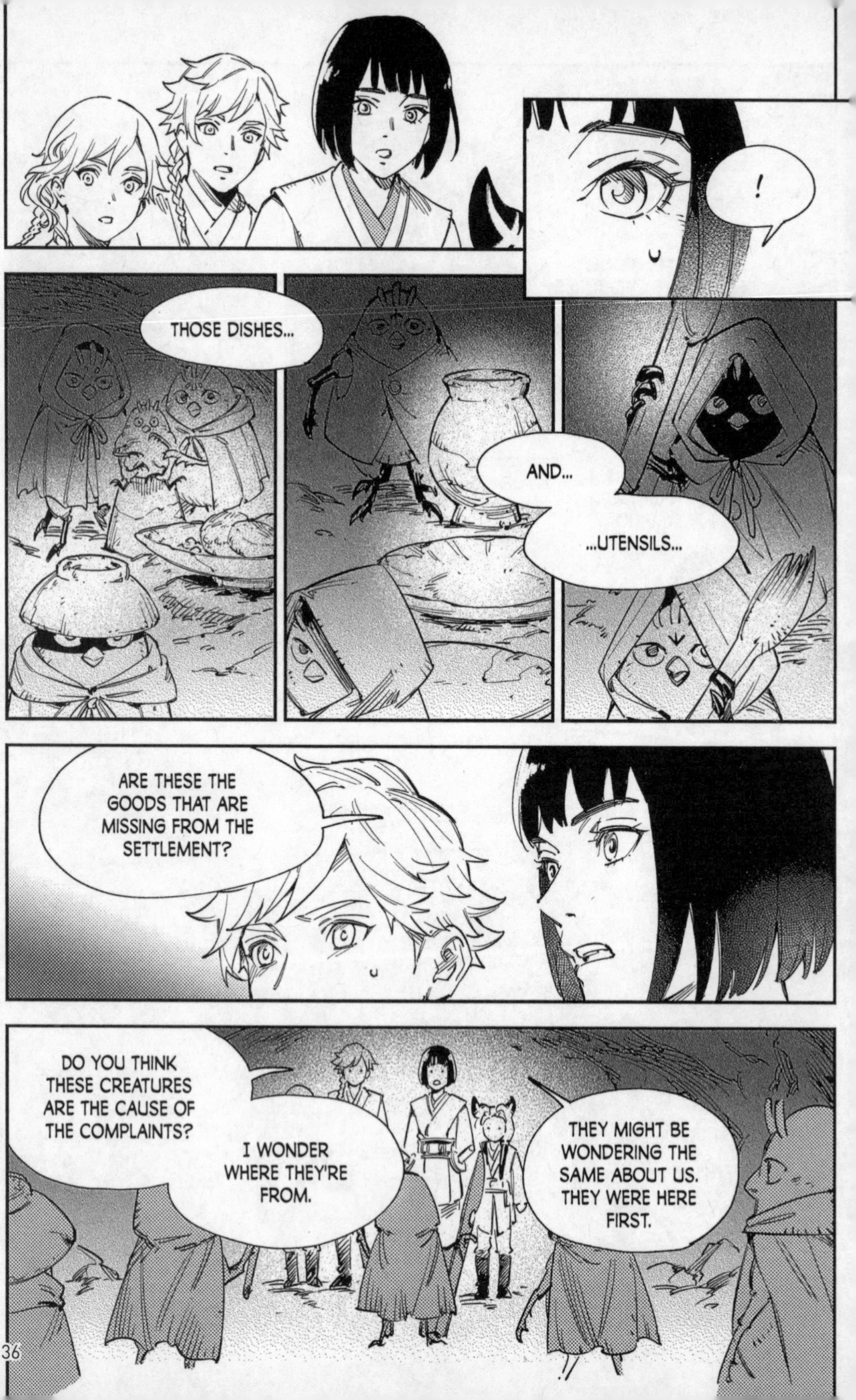
!
THOSE DISHES...
AND...
...UTENSILS...
ARE THESE THE GOODS THAT ARE MISSING FROM THE SETTLEMENT?
DO YOU THINK THESE CREATURES ARE THE CAUSE OF THE COMPLAINTS?
I WONDER WHERE THEY'RE FROM.
THEY MIGHT BE WONDERING THE SAME ABOUT US. THEY WERE HERE FIRST.

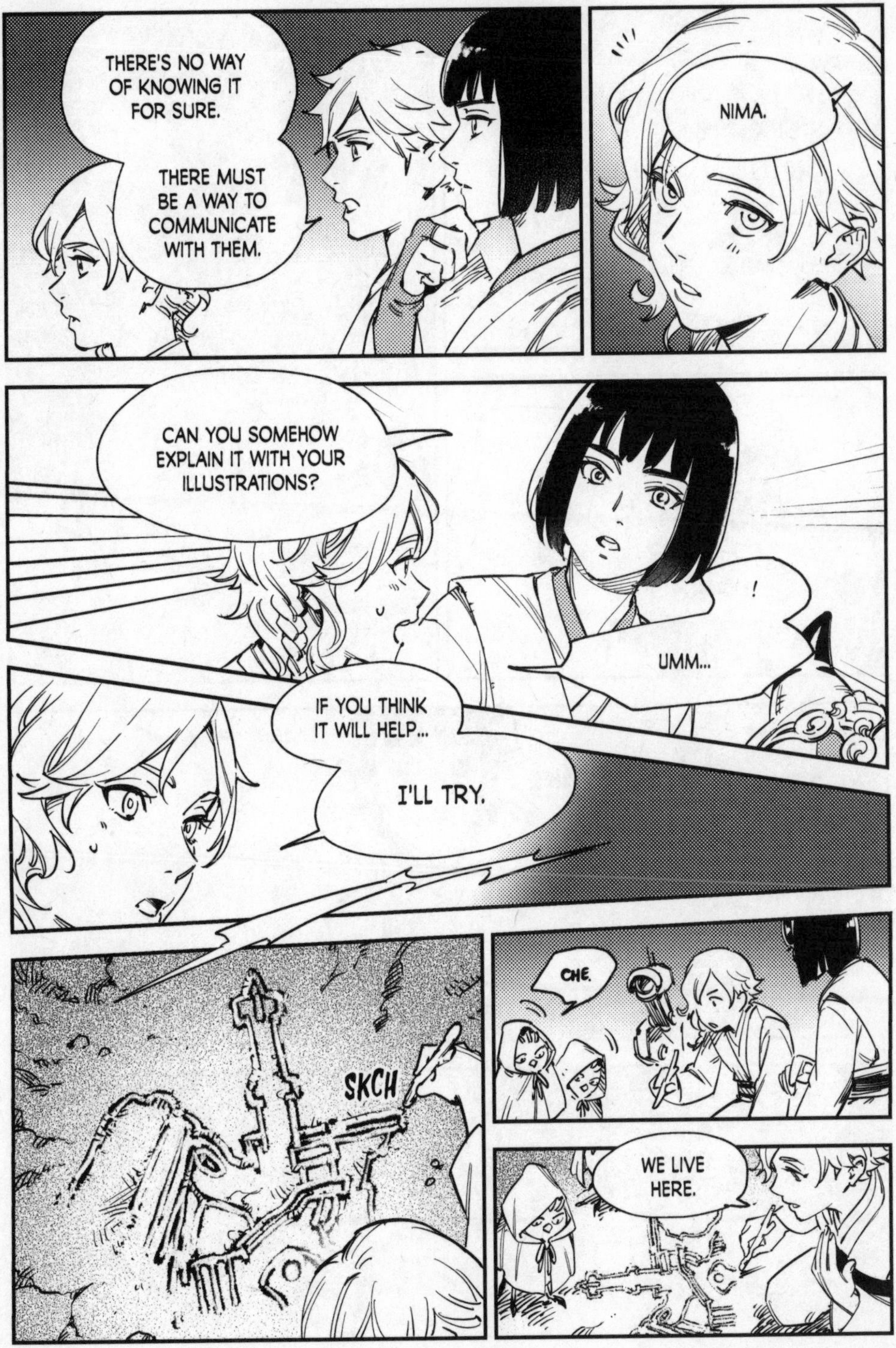
THERE'S NO WAY OF KNOWING IT FOR SURE.
THERE MUST BE A WAY TO COMMUNICATE WITH THEM.
NIMA.
CAN YOU SOMEHOW EXPLAIN IT WITH YOUR ILLUSTRATIONS?
!
UMM...
IF YOU THINK IT WILL HELP...
I'LL TRY.
SKCH
CHE.
WE LIVE HERE.

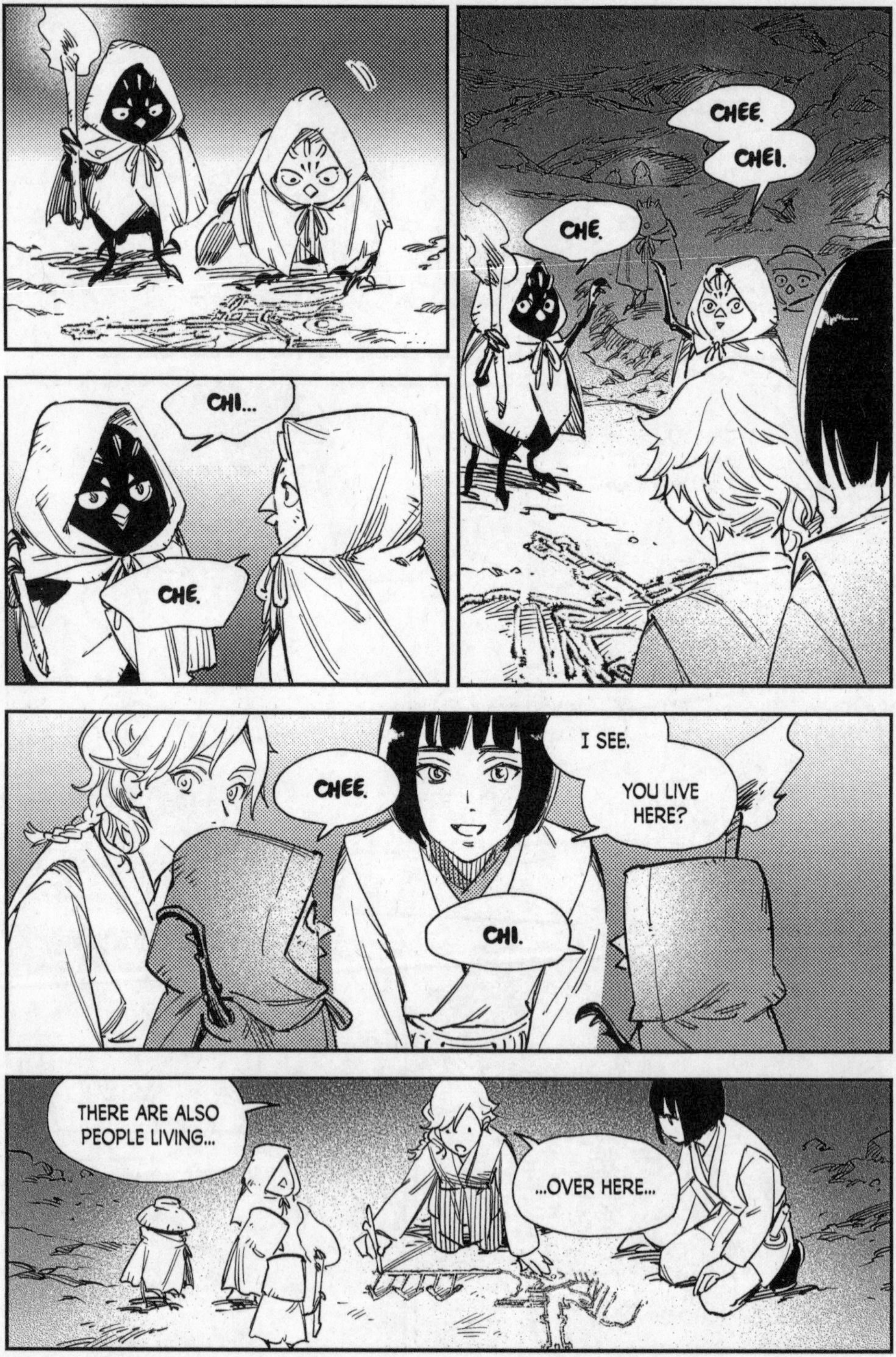
CHEE.
CHEI.
CHE.
CHI...
CHE.
CHEE.
I SEE.
YOU LIVE HERE?
CHI.
THERE ARE ALSO PEOPLE LIVING...
...OVER HERE...

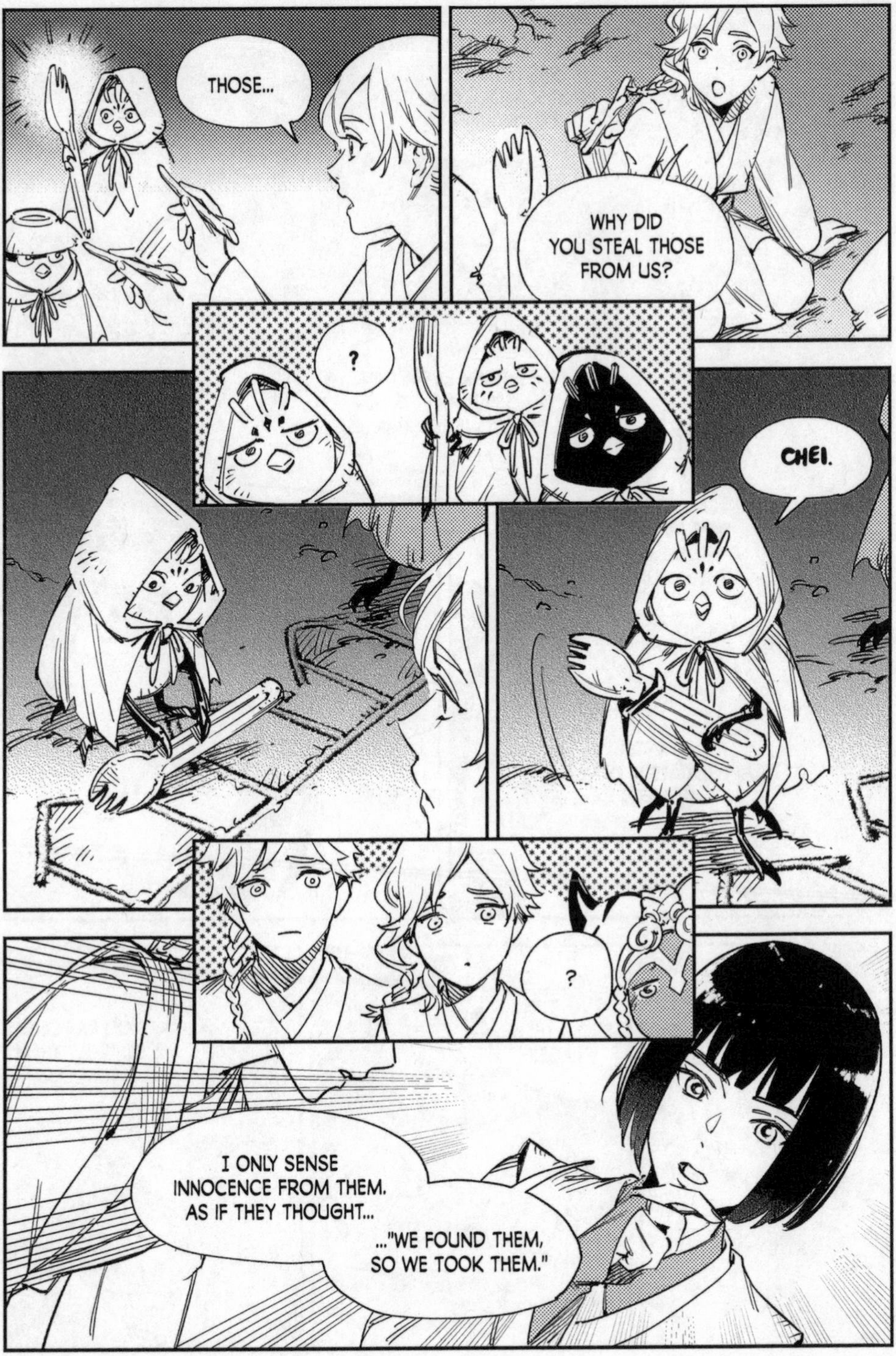
THOSE...
WHY DID YOU STEAL THOSE FROM US?
?
CHEI.
?
I ONLY SENSE INNOCENCE FROM THEM. AS IF THEY THOUGHT...
..."WE FOUND THEM, SO WE TOOK THEM."

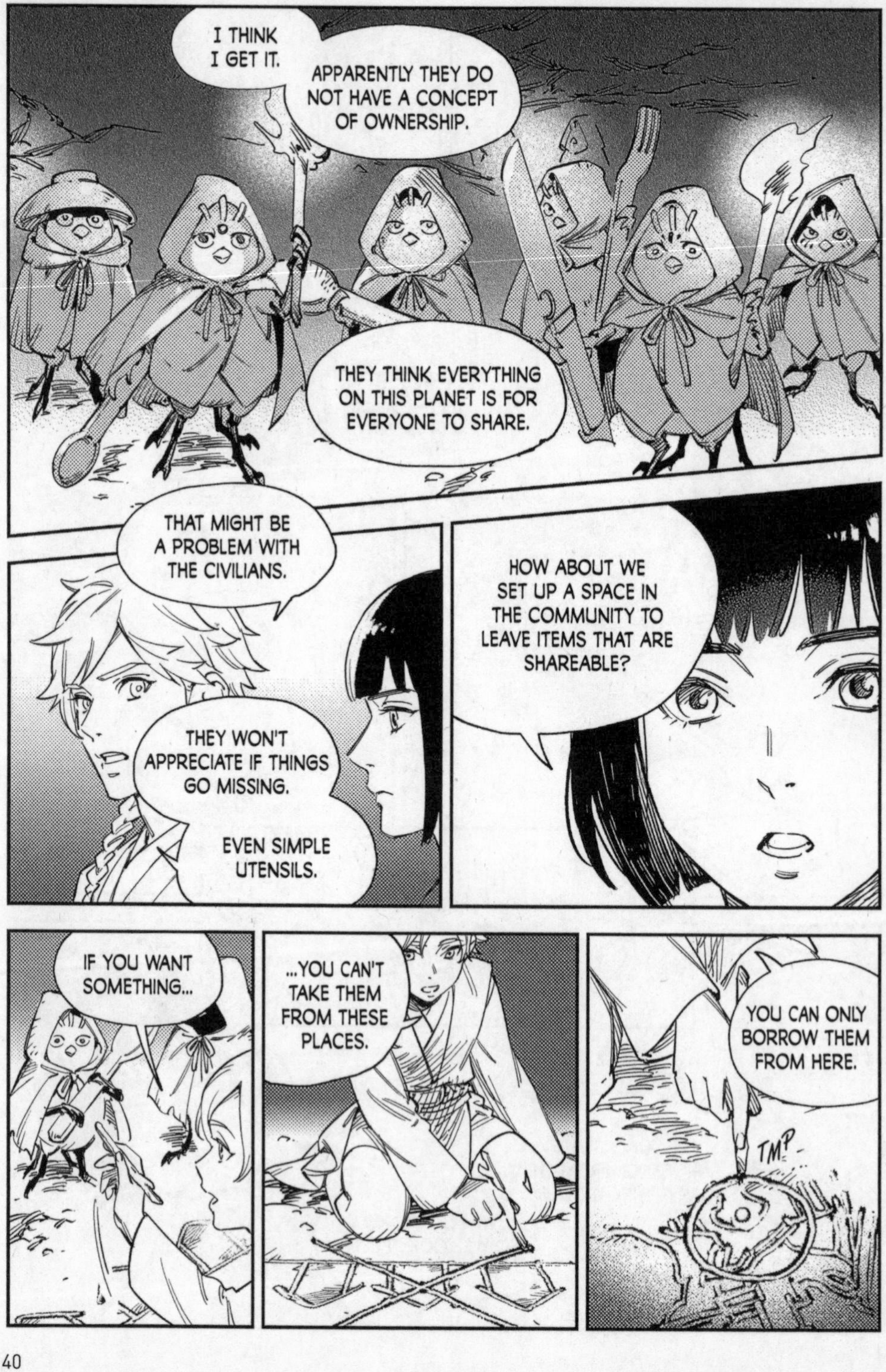
I THINK I GET IT.
APPARENTLY THEY DO NOT HAVE A CONCEPT OF OWNERSHIP.
THEY THINK EVERYTHING ON THIS PLANET IS FOR EVERYONE TO SHARE.
THAT MIGHT BE A PROBLEM WITH THE CIVILIANS.
THEY WON'T APPRECIATE IF THINGS GO MISSING.
EVEN SIMPLE UTENSILS.
HOW ABOUT WE SET UP A SPACE IN THE COMMUNITY TO LEAVE ITEMS THAT ARE SHAREABLE?
IF YOU WANT SOMETHING...
...YOU CAN'T TAKE THEM FROM THESE PLACES.
YOU CAN ONLY BORROW THEM FROM HERE.
TMP

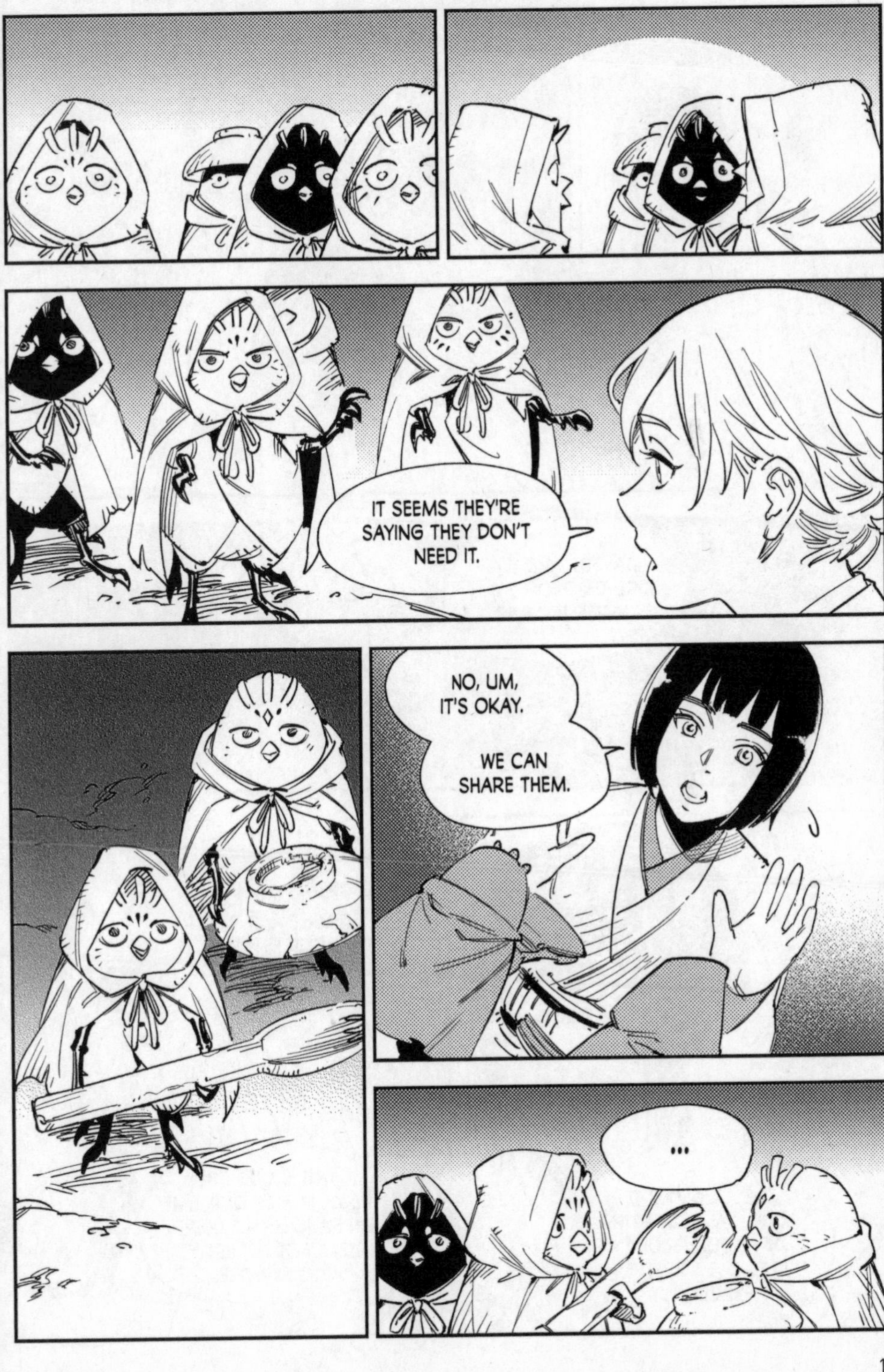
IT SEEMS THEY'RE SAYING THEY DON'T NEED IT.
NO, UM, IT'S OKAY.
WE CAN SHARE THEM.
...

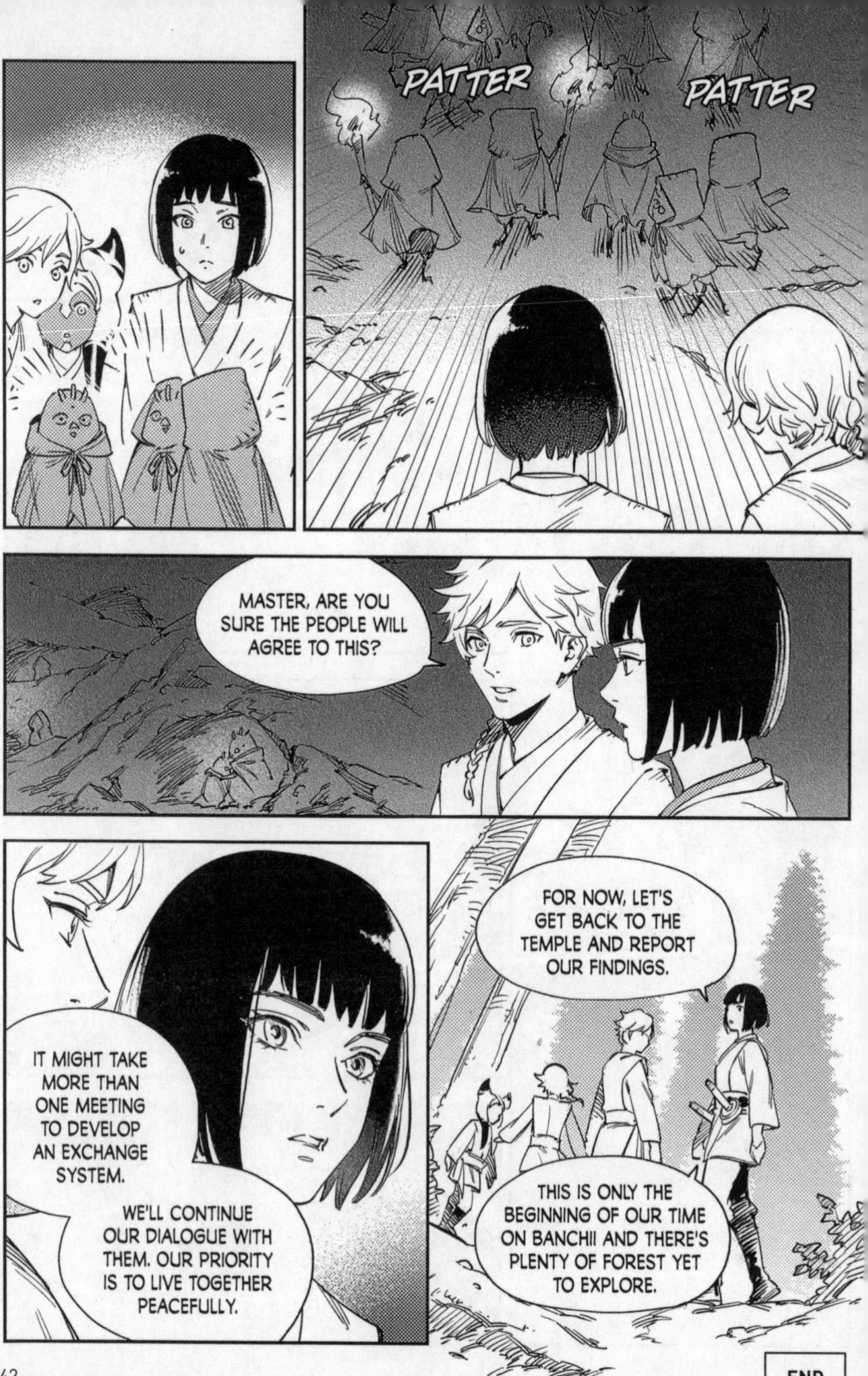
PATTER
PATTER
MASTER, ARE YOU SURE THE PEOPLE WILL AGREE TO THIS?
IT MIGHT TAKE MORE THAN ONE MEETING TO DEVELOP AN EXCHANGE SYSTEM.
WE'LL CONTINUE OUR DIALOGUE WITH THEM. OUR PRIORITY IS TO LIVE TOGETHER PEACEFULLY.
FOR NOW, LET'S GET BACK TO THE TEMPLE AND REPORT OUR FINDINGS.
THIS IS ONLY THE BEGINNING OF OUR TIME ON BANCHII AND THERE'S PLENTY OF FOREST YET TO EXPLORE.
END

STAR WARS
THE HIGH REPUBLIC

Centuries before the Skywalker saga, a new adventure begins....

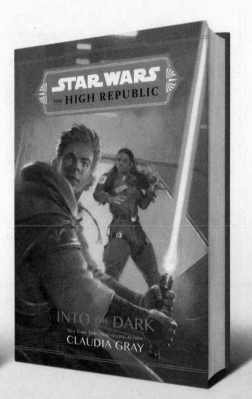

9781368057301 $14.99

9781368057288 $17.99

STAR WARS
THE HIGH REPUBLIC

THE EDGE OF BALANCE
VOLUME ONE

VIZ MEDIA EDITION

Story by SHIMA SHINYA, JUSTINA IRELAND
Character Designs by MIZUKI SAKAKIBARA
Art by MIZUKI SAKAKIBARA (*The Edge of Balance*),
NEZU USUGUMO (*The Banchiians*).

Special thanks to EUGENE PARASZCZUK,
KEVIN PEARL, CHRISTOPHER G. TROISE

Translation and Communications MAYUKO HIRAO
Cover Design JIMMY PRESLER
Copy Editor JUSTIN HOEGER
Editors MAYUKO HIRAO, FAWN LAU

For Lucasfilm
Senior Editor ROBERT SIMPSON
Creative Director MICHAEL SIGLAIN
Art Director TROY ALDERS
Lucasfilm Story Group MATT MARTIN, PABLO HIDALGO,
EMILY SHKOUKANI & JASON D. STEIN
Lucasfilm Art Department PHIL SZOSTAK

Published by VIZ Media, LLC
P.O. Box 77010
San Francisco, CA 94107

10 9 8 7 6 5 4 3 2 1
First printing, September 2021

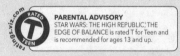

VIZ MEDIA
viz.com

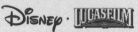

Disney · LUCASFILM

starwars.com